Lori Hayes

Coffee Break

A Crystal Coast Novel

This book is a work of fiction. Names, characters, and incidents either are the product of the author's imagination or are used fictitiously. Any resemblance to actual persons, living or dead, or events is entirely coincidental.

Published in the United States by Seaquine Publishing

ISBN-10: 1539182398
ISBN-13: 978-1539182399

DEDICATION

I want to thank Marilyn Acker for moving to the coast and for introducing me to the most amazing place on earth, including the wild horses of Shackleford Banks. With her support and encouragement, I became a writer.

BOOKS BY LORI HAYES

HIGH TIDE-A CRYSTAL COAST SERIES-BOOK ONE
COFFEE BREAK-A CRYSTAL COAST SERIES-BOOK TWO

ALSO WRITING AS LISA MORGAN—KIDS' HORSE BOOKS-*FOR FUN ADULTS TOO*

THE CHRISTMAS HORSE-THE HORSE CLUB BOOK ONE
TROUBLED HEARTS-THE HORSE CLUB BOOK TWO
MYSTERY HORSE-THE HORSE CLUB BOOK THREE
RUNNING WILD—SHACKLEFORD BANKS SERIES BOOK ONE

ACKNOWLEDGMENTS

I have many people to thank while figuring out the details of this book to provide as much accuracy as possible, but I can only list a couple of them unfortunately. I'm not a sailor, in fact sailing makes me seasick—insert humor—but I endured a couple of joyful trips on a sailboat, similar to the one in this book, to help me visualize what one of my favorites scenes in the book might feel like. I owe a lot of thanks to Captain Tom Hurley for answering my questions and reading my sailing scenes.

Also, I'm only a runner in my dreams. I have the utmost respect for runners. I salute you. I owe great thanks to Missy Foy, great athlete extraordinaire, for answering all of my questions.

And to Joe Sardone at 4J's Café and Bake Shop for letting me learn about the coffee business and for allowing me to pretend I own an awesome coffee shop such as yours. Also, I owe the vice president of a large bank in North Carolina a great thanks for taking time to have a lunch meeting with me so I could pick his brain.

I hope you enjoy reading Coffee Break as much as I enjoyed writing it. As always, thank you for being such a loyal reader.

CHAPTER ONE

Jenni Stallings had less than ten seconds before it turned bitter.

She poured steamed milk, heated to exactly 160 degrees, into the shot of organic espresso and chocolate syrup. Another perfect mocha. She handed the cup across the counter to one of her favorite customers.

"Thanks, darlin'." Mr. Davis waved a rolled-up newspaper in her direction, and then shuffled toward the door.

"Enjoy your morning," she called out. Days like today made her appreciate owning the coffee shop even more. Jimmy Buffett's Caribbean-style music played in the background, enhancing her good mood. A mental image of Bermuda shorts and Carolina marshlands sprang to mind and brought another smile to her face.

"With your coffee and smile, that's a given." Mr. Davis winked and reached for the door, where a man in his early thirties entered the shop. Sunshine poured in along with the sound of a wind chime from the vacant apartment above.

A glance at the stranger intrigued her. He looked familiar, despite the expensive business clothes that screamed he didn't live here. He stood tall, rigid. Locals weren't uptight like this man. Beach living had a way of smoothing out your soul.

He crossed the wide planks of the heart pine floor in long, even steps. When he stopped in front of her, he averted his eyes to analyze the handwritten menu behind the counter. She couldn't help but stare. His hair reminded her of the delicious chocolate brownies she served, and the rich hue of his eyes matched the Hershey kisses that sat on top.

Who was he?

He dropped his gaze to the pastries in the display case. "I'd like a cranberry scone and a tall mocha, two shots of espresso, please." What a smooth but commanding voice. She bet he spent hours in front of a mirror practicing business presentations.

"Absolutely. Help yourself to a scone." Despite his alluring stare, she reached above the espresso machine and grabbed a paper cup.

He continued to watch her. "Jenni Stallings. You look … almost the same as you did in high school." He locked eyes with her, a distant warmth in them. "Your hair isn't as red as I remember and you have fewer freckles, but you haven't changed much."

A delectable man from the past recognized her, and all she could do was gape at him. He looked like Dan Botticelli, a guy she'd dated in school, but the resemblance was only slight.

Dan Botticelli's brother? "Scott?" An image of the fatal boating accident flooded into her mind. It was his father's boat, therefore Scott's responsibility.

He reached across the counter to shake her hand and the inner turmoil returned. She'd dated one brother and adored the other. That was *before* the accident. That day changed everyone's lives. She set the cup on the counter, wiped her palms on her apron, embroidered with "Coffee Break," and hesitantly extended her hand in greeting.

"What brings you home?" She heard her own voice but barely recognized the high pitch.

The touch of his hand was brief. She fought to resist the pulsating warmth, the magnetic pull of attraction, and as always, she struggled to win the battle to resist him. Being near him caused too many conflicting emotions.

"I'm filling in temporarily as vice president for Coastal Carolina Bank in Morrisboro," he said, his gaze never wavering.

"Vice president? Impressive."

He shrugged off the compliment. "Vice presidents in our bank are abundant. I was nearby and thought I'd stop in to set up a meeting with you." His voice lowered and deepened considerably. "I'm evaluating your loan application."

"Oh?" Her eyes widened at his comment. If his tone held any hint, he didn't have good news to share. It was awkward, to say the least, to have a high school crush review her loan application and decide the future of her business. "Is there a problem?"

If she wanted her business to survive, she needed more money. Soon.

"Why don't we make an appointment, so we can sit down and talk," he suggested.

The thought of sitting in his sterile bank office, across from a cold, institutional desk, sounded intolerable. It was best to hear what he had to say today, on her turf. She motioned with her hand to include the coffee shop. "No one's in here. Let's discuss it now."

He cleared his throat. "My assistant, Cassie, filled me in on the specifics of your situation. She's rather concerned about your ability to pay back our money if we approve your loan. Quite frankly, I agree with her." He tugged at his red power tie even though it was already in perfect alignment.

She stood perfectly still, without saying a word, barely breathing. For a moment she almost felt her soul being pulled from her body. Had she heard him correctly?

Scott's avoidance of direct eye contact, combined with his fixed jaw, set her on edge. Tension squeezed her abdomen to the point she wanted to vomit.

"Layne said … the loan should be easy to obtain. What's the issue?" Even though she asked the question, Jenni wasn't ready to hear his answer yet. Rude or not, she managed to walk to the espresso machine and grind the almost-forgotten beans instead of giving him the chance to respond. When she finished, she said, “Layne told me to apply when I was ready. She said not to be concerned.” Well, Jenni was concerned now. She had invested most of her savings in Coffee Break, and without a loan she'd lose her beloved shop.

He set his jaw. “Layne Montgomery went on maternity leave for three months. I’m her temporary replacement.”

Maybe if she waited out the three months, he’d be gone and Layne would return. But then she’d be in the heart of winter and knee deep in the slowest time of the year. She’d be out of money. Waiting wouldn’t work.

"Besides, Mrs. Montgomery has nothing to do with it. The bank is taking a harder look at the loans we finance. Even if she were here, the outcome would be the same. It doesn't help that you misjudged your income this summer."

"Misjudged? Who told you that?" When he didn't answer, she knew he'd heard it from his assistant Cassie.

Cassie Forthright.

He lowered his voice again and handed her a credit card. “I’m sorry, but your business is a risk that the bank is concerned about taking. Restaurants have a high failure rate.”

Jenni cringed. “This isn’t a restaurant, it’s a coffee shop.” She didn’t mean to sound defensive but a sharp edge crept into her voice. “And I didn’t miscalculate my money. There was a sinkhole in front of my shop. The road construction crew unexpectedly closed off this part of the street to car traffic during peak season, which about killed my business. Cassie should know that.”

He shrugged. “Sorry. My job is to look at the numbers and to make a decision based on that.”

Jenni’s heart plummeted.

Regardless of her own dilemma, his decision affected other people. If he forced her to close the doors, where would the elderly men meet their friends over a cup of coffee? She loved to hear their personal stories of how life used to be. And what about the pregnant mothers who sat in the back of the room on the comfortable couches, knitting for their unborn babies? Then there was her father. What about the promise she'd made to him?

Jenni's tightened shoulders started to ache. If her shop failed, she couldn't bear to lose her sister yet again.

"It would help if you could personally guarantee the loan," he said.

She exhaled loudly. "I don't own a house, and I rent this place."

"That's a problem. Maybe someone else would guarantee it for you?" He raised his eyebrows as if to imply he knew someone who might be willing to help her.

Her gut twisted into a large knot. "Are you suggesting I ask my parents to help me? I can't do that."

"Of course not."

"If I could have more time," Jenni said, trying to keep her voice from betraying her. "My long-term goal is to open a chain along the North Carolina coast, and maybe farther." His unyielding expression, despite the fact he reached out and lightly touched her arm, filled her with disappointment.

Breathe. Don't let his bad news derail the vision in my mind's eye. "Give me a chance and I'll prove to be successful," she said. "I won't stop until I am." With his silence, her determination grew. The coffee shop was hers, and hers alone. She never wanted to apply for a loan in the first place. "I'm not a quitter."

When he remained quiet, she forged ahead, as though running uphill against the strong wind of a Nor'easter. "And Cassie? You wouldn't take sides and let her resentment toward me sway your opinion, would you?" Zeroing in on her kill was probably a bad idea. But she refused to allow him to intimidate her.

His angular face visibly stiffened, and the trace of warmth in his eyes disappeared.

She glanced at his left hand. No ring. She was surprised he never married Cassie.

"I'd never deny a loan based on personal reasons. I'm sorry about your sister and the boating accident. Cassie didn't plan to ... It was my fault, not hers."

"She was the one steering the boat." Jenni shot a pointed look at him.

He shifted his weight. "Can you make my scone to-go? I need to get back to the office."

It was just as well. Silently she pointed to the paper bags on an adjacent table against a wall. Because her business wasn't a restaurant, as he'd suggested earlier, and she didn't have a license to handle food, the pastries were self-serve only. She snapped a lid onto the cup and pushed it toward him.

He straightened his red tie again. "Have a great day." He said the words as though he actually meant them.

How was she to have a good day now? She watched her possible future slip out the door with him.

Jenni slumped against the counter, trying to drag in one slow breath after another to ease the lightheaded feeling that overcame her. She imagined the disapproval on her father's face, that knowing look that said he never believed she had what it took to own a business. Brittany had always been the smart one. She owed her deceased sister success; she owed her dad success. To make matters worse, Jenni suspected her father was hanging on until he knew she was financially secure, so when he died too, he could rest in peace. *Rest in peace*. What finality those words threatened.

The bell above the door tinkled again. Claire Rhoades, Big Cat's photographer and the newest addition to their seaside town, walked in. Through her camera lens, she used her tálent to capture the untamed beauty of the wild horses on Pony Island. Claire was an inspiration to Jenni. After all, she had encouraged Jenni to open the coffee shop, to follow her heart's desire.

"Why the long face?" Claire set a manila folder on the counter and pulled out a stool to sit on.

"Mr. Botticelli from my bank just paid me a visit." Jenni couldn't bring herself to say his first name. A mixture of fear and anger churned in her belly, and she wanted to hide the unwanted emotion in her voice from her perceptive friend.

"Was that the good looking man I just passed on the sidewalk?"

Jenni nodded. "It doesn't look like he's going to extend the financing I need to stay open."

"I thought you applied at my bank?"

"I did. Layne's on maternity leave." Trying to keep her composure, Jenni poured hot water into a handmade pottery mug, one of the little details she used to enhance the ambiance of her shop. She dropped the usual decaf tea bag into the liquid and passed it to her friend.

Claire's frown creased her flawless face. She slipped a strand of black hair behind her ear. "You can't lose this shop. It's more than a business. It's the only connection you have left to your sister."

"And to my father." She swallowed hard. "There's more. Scott is Dan Botticelli's brother."

Claire's eyes widened. "The man who was on the boat with you? The experienced boater who was supposed to be in control?"

Jenni blinked for a second too long. Maybe if she kept her eyes closed everything would disappear. "That's him." She could barely say the words.

"I'm sorry." Claire reached forward and squeezed Jenni's hand. "What are you going to do about the loan?"

"I don't know." Jenni leaned against the wooden countertop for support and wished she'd made herself a tea. She could use a hot mug to thaw out her ice-cold hands; she felt numb from the inside out.

"Can your parents help you financially?"

Jenni shook her head. "No. My mom's dealing with Dad's cancer and that's not going well. She's going to need the security of what's left of his money if he dies." Jenni's stomach twisted at the thought. "And I don't want my dad to know the shop might fail. He expects more of me than that. When I opened the place, I promised him I knew what I was doing. I want to succeed on my own, without my parents' financial support."

Claire stared into her mug as though deep in thought. After a moment she glanced up, her eyebrows furrowed. "Don't let pride stand in your way. If you need your parents' assistance, even advice, ask for it."

"I can't." After twelve years you'd think she'd stop trying to earn her father's forgiveness. "Are you feeling okay?" Jenni hadn't noticed before how pale Claire looked.

"No. I've been sick all week. I can't seem to shake it."

Jenni studied her friend closer. She had dark circles under her eyes and her skin looked pasty. "Let me know if I can do anything to help."

"I will." Claire pushed the manila folder toward Jenni. "Here are the flyers for the marathon."

Jenni flinched at the reminder. "I need to train harder if I want to beat Cassie this year." She'd win, even if Cassie was a retired professional.

"I see her practicing every morning," Claire said. "People are already making verbal bets about who will win."

Jenni tried to hide a surge of competiveness and shrugged. "Gran would scold me. She'd say that *Run for the Horses* is about more than beating Cassie. It's about earning money for the wild horses." At least she'd made an effort to repeat her grandmother's wise words, even if she didn't fully believe them. "My training schedule is okay for now, but before long I'll have to push harder. Coffee Break takes a lot of my time, but failing isn't an option."

"You'll persevere," Claire said, setting her mug on the countertop with a clank." Mr. Botticelli has no idea who he's up against."

No wonder Claire was her best friend. "Scott Botticelli likes getting his way," Jenni said, "but he never has with me."

Claire titled her head slightly. "Do you have feelings for him?"

Jenni took a deep breath. How to answer her friend's pointed question?

"The truth," Claire demanded.

"Okay. I used to fantasize about running away with him. White gown and the whole picket fence thing. But after my sister died, he left town."

"Why?"

"He went off to college, but he also said he couldn't stand the guilt. I understand that emotion well."

Claire let out a whoosh of air. "But if he wasn't steering the boat, why would he feel guilty?"

Jenni stared at her. "He feels bad because he was in charge and he failed."

Claire started to tap the countertop, each nerve-racking beat haunting Jenni. The drumming stopped. "It has to be more than that. I want to know why."

CHAPTER TWO

Scott Botticelli clicked the lock on his shiny black BMW and walked into the bank. Meeting Jenni again was harder than he'd expected. He thought he'd breeze into the coffee shop, schedule a meeting to discuss his apprehension about the loan, and walk out. That was pretty much what he did, but he hadn't expected the raw pain from the boating accident to return full force, hadn't expected the vulnerability in Jenni's eyes to touch him in places he kept locked away.

Usually he met his potential clients face-to-face to judge their integrity as well as the numbers. But Jenni set off emotional warning bells, and it scared him. He had to admit, it was a lot easier to say "No" to people he didn't know. It didn't help that his boss had rented a furnished apartment for him above Coffee Break.

As Scott approached his assistant's desk, Cassie straightened in her chair. She twirled a long piece of blond hair between her fingers and asked, "How did it go?"

"Fine." He hesitated a moment too long.

"Then that explains your frown," she quipped. "What really happened?"

Normally his assistants didn't talk to him with such familiarity. Annoying as it was, he supposed three years of dating Cassie during high school did that. Scott ignored her question and looked through Cassie, barely seeing the woman sitting there. Instead, he saw Jenni's shocked expression, despite her obvious battle to avoid revealing her feelings.

"Scott?" Cassie leaned forward and slid her hand on top of his. "What happened at the coffee shop? Are you going to tell me?"

He snapped his attention back to her, pulling his hand away. "Jenni has big plans to expand her business. She acted as if I were singlehandedly destroying those. Maybe I am." Normally he made a decision after a slow analytical process, and then he felt nothing, no guilt, no remorse. That's what made him so successful. He hadn't reached a conclusion yet about her loan, but he was leaning toward denying it. He'd have an answer by this afternoon.

"We have to protect the bank's investments," Cassie said, then crossed her arms.

He looked up from studying a neat stack of papers on her desk. "That's just it. The loan is a risk. Maybe I'm being sentimental about being home again. I'll get over it."

Cassie smiled, showing off her straight white teeth. "How about going to lunch today? The Shrimp Shack will ease your woes. Your brother and Rachel have done a wonderful job with it. When Jenni's dad owned it, it was nothing but a greasy spoon."

His throat constricted. Dan co-owned the Shrimp Shack with their father, who was a silent partner now, coming up on five years. Scott hadn't stepped foot inside the restaurant, nor had he been home to visit for that matter. At some point he needed to suck it up and see his brother.

She touched his hand once again. "Let's go have lunch. You'll feel better."

He wasn't sure if Cassie was being friendly or if she wanted to resume their old relationship, but he decided it was likely the first scenario. He usually didn't mix business with pleasure and fraternize with employees, but today he'd bend his own rule and dine with her. A distraction from Jenni, and her loan, he'd welcome. Besides, he loved shrimp. The thought of seafood reminded him of being home, thankfully only a temporary situation. He couldn't wait to escape to Raleigh again and the professional network he'd built.

"Yoo-hoo. Someone's lost in thought," Cassie commented.

He jerked his head upward. "Sure, that sounds fine—shrimp, that is." He needed to snap out of this funk and regain his equilibrium before people started speculating about his strange behavior. Gossip ran rampant in Big Cat and in the neighboring town of Morrisboro. He couldn't afford for people to start the rumor mill. It was bad enough that he agreed to dine with Cassie.

"How about lunch at one?" he asked. "I have a few things I need to accomplish first."

"That's fine. I have something I want to finish too." Cassie pulled her Rolodex closer and began to thumb through the thick files.

The look on her face made him wonder what she was up to.

***

One o'clock came faster than Scott had time for. He reluctantly closed out the computer program he'd been using when Cassie appeared in his office doorway.

"Are you ready?" A fresh scent of newly applied perfume wafted into the room and made him sneeze.

"As ready as I'll ever be. I have tons of work."

"It's always hard stepping into someone else's shoes," she empathized. "Let's go enjoy our lunch."

Cassie was a hard worker but she loved to play more. That was one thing he remembered most about her. Back then he hadn't minded, but now her work ethic was slightly annoying. He had a job to do, one he took seriously. He tensed when she wrapped her hand suggestively around his elbow and encouraged him to follow her to the door.

"Listen," he said, reclaiming his arm. "In general, I'm uncomfortable with public displays of affection, especially in the office." Right now he'd rather avoid dealing with any leftover emotions she might have from high school. He was having a hard enough time being home after so many years away. He'd left this place for a reason.

She looked taken aback, almost hurt. "I understand, but you've changed. City life has made you uptight."

Uptight?

"How do you live with knowing that a teenager lost her life because of us? I should have been more responsible."

Cassie stared at him. "Don't should yourself in the foot or the guilt will eat away your soul. It was an accident."

"Don't you feel any remorse?"

"Sure, but I've learned to set it aside as much as possible," she explained. Her heels clicked on the asphalt as they made their way across the parking lot. "Don't forget, I returned home two years ago and had to deal with seeing Jenni and the Stallings again. You've avoided the place. Healing is a process."

He suspected she hadn't begun to heal.

Resigned to obeying his Southern upbringing, he opened the passenger door of his car for Cassie, then slid behind the wheel onto the sleek leather interior. He revved the engine and shot off toward the smaller town of Big Cat again, leaving Morrisboro and the confining bank behind. The longer he remained home, the more the town seemed to close in on him. As he drove through the outskirts of Big Cat now, he lamented the fact that many of the shops had closed their doors permanently. Boards covered broken windows and for sale signs screamed failure.

When they parked in front of the Shrimp Shack, an immaculate blue and white building, Cassie climbed from his car as if she owned it. She played the corporate role well, with her sleek business jacket, skirt, and heels. Her blond hair bounced as she walked but never managed to blow in the coastal breeze.

She must use a ton of hair spray—something he couldn't stand. When they reached the restaurant door, he reluctantly held it open for her and walked in.

An older woman with short, curly hair stood near the entrance. "My, if it isn't Scott Botticelli himself."

He almost didn't recognize his mother's best friend, disguised with wrinkles on her face and a talcum-powder dusting throughout her hair. "Marge." He bent down to kiss the woman on her pudgy cheek.

"A quarterback legend returns to his hometown. Maybe you'll stay this time." She reached forward and gave him a warm, affectionate hug.

After a quick moment, he pulled away and glanced around his brother's restaurant. Maybe he'd get lucky and miss Dan today, although it was inevitable he'd run into him eventually in this tiny town. "I wish I could stay but I'm only here for three months." *Thank goodness*. She probably knew exactly why he was here and for how long, but that didn't stop her from planting the seed for him to remain in Big Cat. There was no chance of that.

"Well, we're glad to have you." Marge studied Cassie for a moment and raised her eyebrows.

"You remember Cassie from high school. She's my assistant at the bank."

"Oh, I remember her all right." Marge flashed Scott a probing look. "Right this way. To celebrate your return, I'll give you the best seat in the house, with the finest view of the estuary in all of Big Cat."

In all of Big Cat. She had no idea how big cities could be, or the temporary freedom they provided, but he appreciated the gesture. Marge didn't realize she'd hit a sore spot.

Scott followed her and couldn't help but admire his brother's taste. With the tables covered in white linen and the small vases filled with fresh flowers on each, he had to ponder when Dan had acquired such elegance. Scott decided to give credit to Rachel instead. When Marge stopped in front of a table for two, he avoided assisting Cassie with her chair this time. Instead, he sat down and gazed out the window.

He'd forgotten how the sun's rays made the water look so green, as though diamonds glittered across the surface. If he were being honest with himself, he'd have to admit he missed the water.

"I'll be back," Marge said. At Scott's nod, she patted his shoulder and walked off.

He couldn't pull his attention away from the view. The Oak River, with its yellowing marsh that provided fresh seafood and feeding areas for wildlife, ran alongside the Intracoastal Waterway. Off in the distance, the water wrapped around little islands and eventually blended into bright blue sky and ocean. The farthest island was Pony Island, where over a hundred wild horses roamed the dunes. The view provided just the serenity he needed to help him try to relax.

Lost in memories, he turned his attention to a yacht tied up at the restaurant's dock, and almost yearned to hear the water lapping against its sides.

He used to sail. He hadn't been back on a boat since ...

The server surprised him when she touched his arm. He wasn't sure how many times she'd asked for his drink order but she seemed impatient.

"Sorry. I'd like a sweet tea, please."

The server nodded and hurried off, freeing Scott's line of vision. Marge was seating an attractive redhead with short stylish hair a few tables away. What was Jenni doing here?

He loathed small-town living. How was he supposed to deny a loan to a longtime friend, especially when he ran into her whenever he turned around? Undoubtedly he needed to separate their already strained friendship from work.

Jenni met his gaze. Then she glanced at Cassie and frowned. No doubt she assumed he was threatening to turn down her loan because she thought he was still attracted to Cassie. The poisonous idea compromised his work ethic.

A little stab of remorse jabbed at Scott as he watched Jenni chat easily with Marge. She was friendly and outgoing, hence the reason she likely opened a coffee shop. And he found her downright sexy, even in khaki pants and a white top. She smiled and looked much happier than earlier today, after their confrontational discussion.

He watched Marge exchange a quick, parting hug with Jenni before she walked off. Jenni sat there alone, looking content, swirling a tea bag around in a cup. If things had turned out differently, between her sister's accident and the fact she'd dated his doting brother, they might have ended up together.

Cassie followed Scott's gaze to the nearby table. "Look who's here."

He didn't bother to answer. His eyes took in the way Jenni picked up her cup, with her hands wrapped around it as though it was wintertime. He imagined the woman was tougher than her petite body revealed. An aura of confidence surrounded her. He had to admit, she was even more attractive than when he knew her in school.

"I wonder why she chose to eat here," Cassie scoffed. "Considering your brother owns the place. You'd think she'd want to avoid running into you—"

"She usually eats lunch here," Marge interrupted as she rejoined them. "At least three times a week." Marge pressed her hands on the edge of the table and leaned toward Cassie. "Don't tell me you're still jealous of her after all these years?"

Cassie gasped and thrust back her head. "I've never been jealous of her. How dare you suggest …" When Marge continued to encroach on Cassie's space, Cassie stood and tossed her napkin into a heap on the chair. "Excuse me for a minute." She made for the bathroom at the far end of the room, her hips swaying in an exaggerated way.

"Marge?" Scott asked, but her comment shouldn't have surprised him. She was usually direct and believed in calling things as she saw them. More than once she'd caught him playing hooky under the pier when he was a boy and, instead of telling his mother, she let him have it right there in front of his friends. Many a time she had embarrassed him by her pointed comments, especially the time she'd caught him smoking with her son and a handful of girls behind the locker room after a football game. But those rebellious teenaged years were long gone.

He looked at her now. She used to seem towering and scary. When had she shrunk and turned into a sweet grandmotherly type?

Marge touched his shoulder. "I'm sorry, but I find Cassie rude. Besides, I can't stand negative comments being made about someone sweet like Jenni."

Scott remained quiet, contemplating Marge's words.

"You aren't planning to date Cassie again, are you? Hasn't she caused you enough grief?"

He looked at Marge. People were already speculating he and Cassie were back together.

Marge flicked her hand as if to dismiss the subject. "You haven't asked about your brother yet. He's doing well."

"I was going to." He took a long breath to hide his reaction, a skill he excelled at. "Is Dan here?"

Marge nodded. "He's busy right now, but when he finishes I'll send him over."

Scott tensed at her words. He couldn't run from the past any longer. The first step was coming home, but that didn't make healing any easier.

***

Jenni spied Scott Botticelli from the corner of her eye. She should have known he'd eat at his brother's restaurant at some point, but the thought hadn't occurred to her until now. It was too late to leave; she already ordered and he already noticed her. She did a double take when she noticed Cassie with him, although the woman's manipulative ways shouldn't surprise her. Still, seeing them together was a disappointment. Cassie wanted to make trouble. If Layne were still the bank's active Vice President, then

Jenni's future as a business owner had a chance, but with Scott at the helm, her boat had sprung a leak.

Scott looked up and their gaze met. Was that a hint of guilt in his eyes? Good. If it came down to saving her beloved business, she'd play on whatever emotions he had. Proving to her dad that she possessed the intelligence and dedication to be successful was much more important than allowing Scott to take down her dreams. She'd prove to them both that she had what it took to survive, regardless of the odds stacked against her. She was an overachiever just as Brittany had been.

Scott glanced away and Jenni considered his response a triumph in her favor. When the server set a shrimp salad in front of her, she thanked her politely and then dove in. The salad tasted so good that it was almost easy to block out the tension radiating from a few tables over. But not quite. When Scott gazed her way again, her burning cheeks gave her away.

Cassie flashed Jenni a possessive smirk. Jenni wasn't about to catfight for a man but the future of her coffee shop was at stake.

She finished eating, pushed her empty salad plate aside, and stood. Before she talked herself out of the crazy idea, she crossed the short distance to their table.

Cassie set her water glass down. "It's great to see you, Jenni."

Yeah, right. Unable to return the response verbally, Jenni nodded at Cassie before turning toward Scott. "I've been thinking about my loan. Maybe it's a conflict of interest for you to handle it."

"Actually," Cassie said, "without collateral, no bank will touch your loan."

Jenni prayed that wasn't true. Was Scott her only chance at saving her business?

"My sister and I dreamed to one day open a coffee shop together. If I lose my shop, Brittany will die all over again." She swallowed what felt like a tumor in her throat.

“I said I was sorry about your sister.” Cassie crossed her arms into a pretzel. “When are you going to stop blaming me? It wasn’t my fault.”

No, it was Jenni’s fault. She was the one who'd let Brittany talk her into a sunset cruise even though her intuition screamed "Danger." And Cassie was correct. Jenni did blame her. The other woman refused to take any responsibility for losing focus while steering the boat.

"Why don't we set up a meeting for this afternoon." Scott's stoic expression hid his emotions well but a tiny tremor in his voice hinted at bad news. "I've had a chance to make a decision about your loan."

Jenni had to force herself to keep breathing.

People were watching them now. A man with a tray of food showed up and, relieved to end the conversation, Jenni gladly stepped back. She bumped into Dan, who'd walked up behind her.

“For the record, I’m not going to lose my coffee shop.” Tears threatened to escape her eyes. She needed to leave now before she made a spectacle of herself.

"Why would you lose your shop?" Dan asked.

The Friendly Four, who had always hung out together through most of high school and hadn't seen each other as a group since the funeral, didn’t seem so friendly now.

“She applied for a loan at my bank,” Scott explained.

Dan looked confused. “Then why would she lose her shop?”

Jenni watched Scott closely. He raised his eyebrows at her, most likely to ask for permission to breach confidentiality. She nodded, giving him consent to discuss the situation.

“I have to deny the loan.”

Jenni's heartbeat stopped cold for a split second.

Dan glared at him. "Unbelievable" The air between brothers felt thick, like trying to run a marathon on a hot and humid Southern day. The tension felt agonizingly familiar. She remembered the day Scott decided to drop by for an impromptu visit to see his brother at college. Dan had arrived late at a cafe near the campus and walked in on Scott kissing Jenni. Honestly, it started as a welcome hug but somehow led into a prolonged, tender kiss. Her usual guard was down, having just broken off the relationship with Dan, although that didn't justify their behavior.

She'd never forgotten that kiss.

Here she was coming between brothers again.

Scott nodded at his brother. "That's right. I can't approve the loan."

CHAPTER THREE

The rest of the day dragged by in a blur, and the earlier confrontation with the Friendly Four never left Jenni's mind for long. At last, she flipped the closed sign around in the coffee shop's bay window and started to walk the four blocks home. Dread filled her with every step. Richard Stallings always recognized her failures and never hesitated to point them out. Her father would be certain to detect her angst about the loan.

She fought to maintain the sense of independence she'd found during college, before he used her family loyalty as a wedge to get her to move back into his house. Playing on his illness and her mother's neediness, he claimed Jenni's emotional support was crucial. She didn't doubt the seriousness of his cancer, that wasn't the problem. It was the way he'd demanded her return, as if she never met his expectations.

Well, he'd won. She was back, and even though she secretly craved her hometown like an aching desire for imported chocolate, she'd never admit the truth to her father.

She slowed her walk even more. Usually she appreciated the quaint fudge shop, the cozy ice creamery and all the small specialty shops that brought back memories of a younger time.

This afternoon, however, the entire town looked faded under a now overcast sky, as if whitewashed with a thin layer of salt. The typical aqua color of the Waterway had turned a steel gray hue, and the lush green marsh surrounding the uninhabited islands seemed pale and drab.

In an attempt to uplift her spirit, she drew in the distinct fishy smell of salt water. The scent never failed to fill her soul.

She belonged here, just as Coffee Break belonged among these shops. She'd fight whatever battles necessary to ensure the doors of her business remained open.

Still not ready for the inevitable confrontation with her father, Jenni detoured, climbing the steps of Claire's yellow, two-story photography studio with its wrap-around porch. A fat tabby cat lay curled in a rocker. Jenni bent down to pet it, soaking up the cat's warmth.

"I'd like to join you," she said to the cat, who offered a purr in answer. Jenni slid her hand down its silky coat and couldn't help but imagine how simple life would be if she were a cat. "One more." She patted the tabby's head, then made her way toward the studio's large window. She wanted to peer in to gage how busy her friend was before she went inside to thank her for the creative flyers.

A group of chattering women walked out. Two of them carried large bags, undoubtedly containing fabulous prints of the wild horses. Until now, Jenni hadn't noticed all the foot traffic coming and going from the building. Claire's photography captured a lot of attention, from nationwide magazines to the many tourists who bought her prints.

Jenni pressed her face into the cool glass of the window. Small clusters of shoppers hovered over several assortments of prints hanging on the different walls. A faint stream of classical music filtered through the window and lent an elegant touch to the upscale studio. Fortunately for Claire, business was booming, but it was too busy for Jenni to stop by for a friendly chat and some moral support. She reluctantly turned around and headed home.

When she reached the white, two-story home of her childhood, she ran effortlessly up the steep steps. Once at the top, she paused to watch a sailboat off in the distance. Higher up, they had one of the best views in town.

Jenni inhaled a long breath before she strolled around back to the porch. She mentally counted to ten and opened the door. When she entered the kitchen, filled with the pleasant aroma of a pot roast simmering all day in the Crock-Pot, the screen door slapped closed behind her, trapping her inside the small room. Regardless of the undercurrent of tension in the house, her stomach rumbled. Too bad the homey atmosphere did nothing but increase her uneasiness.

"Mom, I'm home."

"In here," Dorothy Stallings called from her husband's makeshift bedroom. The home health specialists recommended her dad sleep in the den so he would no longer have to navigate steps.

She walked down the hallway and into the dimly lit room that she'd recently grown to despise. She hated that her dad reduced his life to the confines of a stale, smelly room. It took a few seconds for her eyes to adjust. "Dad, can I open the curtains and blinds? The daylight will make you feel better."

He jutted his jaw outward and pretended not to hear.

The man was so stubborn. Jenni sank onto the corner of the hospital bed. "Have you gotten up lately?" She eyed his walker, pushed off to the side and covered with clothes. He hadn't used it anytime lately.

He stared at the dark curtain over the window that shielded him from the real world. "What good is it to practice walking when I'm not going to be around to enjoy it for long?" His lip quivered the tiniest bit.

A wave of sorrow smothered her. She took his warm hand in hers and held onto it. His skin still held a healthy color, even though dark circles underlined his dull eyes. His muscles seemed more flaccid, and he'd lost a few more pounds this past week.

"You are your worst enemy, Dad. Don't give up. The fighter in you always wins." He continued to stare at the wall, which she took as a sign that he wanted to end the battle to live. "You'll beat the cancer. And you made it through chemo and radiation with flying colors." The silence was nerve-racking. "Come on, you have to do your part and fight."

"Tell me about the shop." His voice sounded raspy. "How are the numbers looking?"

She slowed her breathing until it was almost undetectable. The question she'd dreaded. Never one to lie, she decided to level with him. "Not so good. The road construction hurt business more than I expected and we have a new vice president at the bank. Layne is on maternity leave."

Wait until he found out who was Layne's replacement.

"So the bottom line is they won't loan you money?"

She thought she saw a hint of concern on his face, but in a flash it disappeared. "No. I'll have to find another way."

He pulled his hand from hers and let out a succession of coughs. "Let me loan you the money; I'm not going to need it much longer."

She shook her head. Why did he always have to refer to death? "I appreciate your offer, but if something happens, Mom will need the money. Besides, I want to do this on my own. You of all people should understand that." Nervous energy danced inside her belly. How to make him understand? "No one helped you with Stallings."

"Stubborn. I should've let you play with your friends instead of making you work for me at the restaurant. That's what I get."

"Dad, I enjoyed working with you. And Coffee Break isn't a punishment, it's a dream."

"You have to pay a high cost for that dream if you want to be successful. You're young. Find someone to marry and be happy raising children." The words might have sounded like concern had his voice not carried rich sarcasm.

"What an old fashioned comment to make." She fought back the hurt. "Why can't you encourage and support my decision?"

He crossed his arms over his chest. "Because you need help. Hire someone. If you want to run a thriving business, you can't do it alone."

"That takes money. If I work until I build my cash flow, I can hire someone then."

"No. If you increase the hours your business is open by hiring someone, the money you make will offset the amount you pay your employee. You need a day off."

She definitely saw concern in his eyes. "Answer this," he said. "How long can you continue to work at this rate?"

She winced.

"Hire some semi-retired person. They're responsible and have time on their hands."

"Thanks, but I don't know." She exhaled slowly. An idea popped into her head, one her father would despise, and one she immediately tried to resist. Gran. She pushed the thought aside for now. "I'd hate to let the person go if the income doesn't offset her wage."

He huffed and turned his head, clearly dismissing her.

"Can I do anything to please you?" The hurt from his rejection burned deep. She sat still, waiting, but he refused to look at her.

"Like I said before," he growled, "find a husband and have kids. It's a shame Brittany isn't here to guide you. She was always a natural at business."

And Jenni wasn't. His words felt like a knife, carving out a hollow from deep inside her. She rose from the bed in deliberate motion, determined to hide her frustration and pain, even though she wanted to race from the room like a child. Why did he always have to compare her to Brittany?

"When are you going to forgive me for the accident?" she asked.

"Who said I blame you?"

Jenni hesitated until she got the nerve to ask him point-blank. "Do you think her death is my fault?" The silence was more than Jenni could stand. She needed to get out of his house, away from him, and wouldn't feel better until she felt the hard pavement under her running shoes. Jenni retreated upstairs to her bedroom and quickly changed into her running gear.

Once outside, she tried to force the hurtful conversation with her father from her mind as she started down her parents' street. Even though she preferred to run along the deserted beaches of Pony Island as she did most days, she'd gotten a late start today. Daylight always ended too soon in the fall. Unfortunately, she only made it to the corner of the street before thoughts of her dad returned. She tried to focus on the fresh scent of mowed grass, the pleasant chirping of birds. When that failed, she turned her concentration to the upcoming marathon.

Truth be told, running against her archrival was a bonus. She wasn't sure why Cassie bothered with the smaller race, especially since she used to run professionally. She'd quit competing because of type-one diabetes. Dealing with insulin shots while running had to be difficult.

The thought of Cassie only agitated her further. She continued to run several miles through the quiet streets of downtown, her mind continuously returning to the frustrating conversation with her father.

You'd think he'd be happy she'd embraced the "restaurant business" as he had. What did it take to please him? She ran harder. When she won the 26.2-mile race, her father would have to recognize her determination and deem her successful. Yes, she'd win the marathon.

Slow down, girl, pacing is important. She forced her body to obey.

Her anguish about her father had just begun to subside when she turned the corner. Across the street was the old cemetery, bordered by a low stone wall and filled with the graves of

Revolutionary and Civil War soldiers. A familiar man jogged past the arched entrance. Her day just got worse.

Scott looked both ways and then crossed the street to join her. He met her pace easily. Despite her earlier reminder to maintain a slower rhythm, she lengthened her stride, not wanting to run with Mr. Vice President.

He matched her speed again. When he didn't get the hint to leave her alone, she plucked the pink ear buds from her ears.

"What are you listening to?" he asked. "The same head-slamming music you listened to in school?"

Funny, but she'd only listened to those hard rock groups because he had. "Beethoven. It helps me relax."

A surprised-sounding laugh escaped his mouth. "Beethoven? You've got to be kidding?"

She frowned. "Do I look like I'm joking?" She increased her speed and he appeared to struggle to keep up.

"You're quite fast. I never knew you ran."

"There's a lot you don't know about me."

"Like what?"

"Like how I don't appreciate you threatening my livelihood."

"You've done that yourself." His breathing increased.

Jenni decided not to defend herself again. "Can't you keep up with me?" She didn't bother to disguise the personal satisfaction in her voice.

He raked in a breath. "I haven't run … in years. I've just rediscovered the pleasure." He shot a boyish grin her way and winked.

What did that look mean?

By the time she turned the next corner, he'd fallen behind. "Glad you've found the sport again," she called back. "I hope you enjoy it." At the next street, she turned right and kept the same pace. When she glanced back, Scott was nowhere around.

What had gotten into her? It wasn't like her to behave like that.

Jenni finished the last lap around downtown and began her cool down. It was starting to get late and soon she'd run out of daylight. Although she was in good shape, if she wanted to take the marathon seriously, she needed to increase the distance she ran as the race grew closer. She longed for the day she could afford to hire someone to help at the coffee shop, even a few hours a day or a weekend as her father suggested. Maybe he was right, she needed to hire someone.

Jenni crossed over to Front Street and saw Scott walking by Coffee Break. When she reached him she broke to a walk. "So how many years has it been since you ran?"

His dark-chocolate eyes tantalized her. "Too many. I used to run in college, but after I graduated and started working full time, I started skipping days, then weeks. Before long it turned into months, then years."

Jenni shook her head in disbelief. He was a workaholic. She could almost picture herself in the same position as him in years to come if she wasn't careful.

What cost *was* she willing to pay?

She wanted success all right, but not at the expense of family. Unfortunately Scott reminded her too much of her father. She knew what it was like to grow up in a house with a dad who was married to his work. As far as she knew, Scott never married, but when he did, she'd feel sorry for his wife and children. No thanks. The man Jenni wanted to be with would put her first.

His voice snapped her back to the conversation. "I live on a lake with this great running trail around it," he said. "When I bought the place, I imagined getting a dog and exercising with him every day."

"What happened?"

"I don't have time for a dog. I work a lot of hours, and it's not fair to keep him penned up in a house all day. He'd get lonely." Scott shrugged, as if to push aside the idea of a dog. "What about you? Do you run a lot?"

"Every chance I get," she said. "I plan to enter the local full marathon three months from now. Since I opened the coffee shop, though, my time is scarce. But I still squeeze in a run at least five days a week."

Jenni watched the sun dip behind a row of historic homes and the temperature cooled almost immediately as a fine mist began to fall. She untied a nylon jacket from around her waist and slid it on to prevent a chill.

Too bad he didn't have an outer layer to wear. If he wanted to take running seriously, he needed to dress smarter.

"I'm sorry about today." He wiped away a row of sweat from above his brow and rubbed his arms, most likely to stay warm. "It's not personal, you know."

"I understand. You have to make the best decisions for the bank. You think I'm a risk, and right now risks are not what a bank wants to take. But that's where you're wrong. I'm a survivor. I need to get through the winter, and once tourist season begins, I'll be fine."

He remained silent.

At her parents' street, she looked up the hill and saw her house with the lights glowing in the dusk. Jenni stopped before she crossed the road. "I *will* prove it; that's a promise."

His brow furrowed and he didn't respond.

She pushed away his doubt and waved. "Keep running and don't give up. I never will."

***

Don't give up. Those powerful words lingered in Scott's mind most of the night. Jenni intrigued him to say the least.

The doorbell to his apartment rang and when he answered, there stood Cassie with her arms full, carrying a paper bag. Cartons of Chinese food peeked out the top. He didn't want to hurt Cassie's feelings, but he didn't appreciate her showing up uninvited.

"Listen, Cassie. It's nice you brought food but—"

"We're working. I have the fax you've been waiting for." She pushed her way inside the door and brushed against him. Reluctantly, he followed her into the living room. She set down a file, pulled out the food cartons, and lined them up on the coffee table. "Do you have plates and silverware?"

"Of course. Listen; people will get the wrong idea if they see us together outside the office."

Cassie made a face. "It's just takeout food. Give me a break." She turned away and walked into the kitchen.

He could hear drawers and cabinets bang closed. Instead of following her, he sat down on the couch to avoid the close quarters of the compact kitchen. Moments later she returned to the living room.

She handed him a plate and a fork, then stuck a spoon in each container. She helped herself to a large portion. "I love sweet and sour chicken. Don't you?"

"Sure." He dipped into the fried rice instead and scooped out a heaping spoonful. He had to admit, her impromptu visit was kind of fun, even though he wished she was a certain redhead.

At some point he'd have to deal with his guilt about Brittany, but not now. Facing the truth seemed unbearable.

CHAPTER FOUR

Jenni could always plead temporary insanity. She must have lost her mind when she agreed to live with her parents again. Sure, her father had every right to be angry about dying, and her mother had every reason to be clingy and overprotective, but right now the tension was too much. Later that evening, Jenni practically ran to the back door to escape when her mom's high-pitched voice sang out, "Don't forget your curfew!"

Curfew? She was twenty-eight years old for God's sake. Her tense shoulders felt like a rock. Without answering, Jenni clicked the door shut behind her, then picked her way through the darkness to her car.

She'd get away and help Gran feed the Islander Ponies awaiting adoption on her farm. In order to protect the horses from starvation, the members of the Wild Horse Foundation caught a select few and brought them to the mainland. Gran fostered a handful of horses until she found good homes.

No matter what Jenni's mood, being around the Islander Ponies always relaxed her. Tonight they'd be a blessing.

She drove her paid-off but well-running Sentra down Gran's rutted driveway. The car's tires crunched on the sparse gravel and then bounced in a deep puddle. She flipped on her wipers to clear a light spray of mud off her windshield.

She loved Gran's little farm. Her grandmother owned maybe ten acres in which she made good use of the land. She had a barn with a few sectioned-off paddocks for the horses, and two larger grassy areas for the animals to graze. Gran even had a coup with chickens running around, so she could enjoy fresh organic eggs each morning for breakfast.

Jenni pulled up outside the cottage and tooted the Sentra's horn to announce her arrival. Within seconds Gran poked her head out the porch door and a dim floodlight popped on. The top of her gray hair frizzed wildly above a loose silver braid, which almost touched the small of her back. In the faded light, she looked to be in her fifties instead of her seventies.

"Well, I'll be," Gran called out. "I haven't seen you in at least a week. You must be wantin' to escape the claws of your parents." She laughed with a low grumble.

"You know me well, Gran. My parents are driving me mad." Jenni treaded carefully along the stone path. Even in the dim light she noticed the porch's chipping paint. Once she reached the rickety steps, she held onto the railing and carefully began to climb them, barely able to see.

Gran needed help keeping up the place. It was too much for one person to maintain alone. If Jenni offered to help paint, maybe her brother Keith could replace some of the boards on the steps, if he wasn't too busy with the day-to-day operations of owning the small passenger ferry that ran back and forth to Pony Island.

Jenni reached the top of the steps and leaned down to kiss her vibrant grandma on the cheek before following her into the house. Once inside, Jenni glanced around the living room, in disarray as usual. Despite its unkempt state, the room had a homey feeling and drew her in.

"I was just fixin' to feed the horses. You're timing is perfect, as always." Gran patted Jenni on the shoulder. "Be right back. I need to grab some carrots before we go out to the barn." Gran loved to pamper the horses with a handful of goodies at each feeding. She bounced from the room and disappeared into the kitchen.

While Jenni waited, she perched on the arm of the couch and eyed her grandmother's newest project. When Gran returned minutes later, Jenni pointed to the pile of knitting.

"What are you making?"

"That's a sweater for you. Go on, take a look." Gran beamed with pride.

Jenni held up the project. The sweater was a variety of bright pinks and white, undoubtedly pure wool. "Gran, this is gorgeous. Thanks."

"You can wear it when you finally go sledding. Maybe you'll have time to visit the mountains this winter."

Jenni didn't want to disappoint her grandmother, but she didn't foresee a vacation anytime soon.

As if Gran read her mind, she said, "You have to balance work with pleasure. The horses bring peace to my life. I don't know why you don't adopt one of them." She yanked a jacket off a hook by the door.

"I barely have enough time to work and run, let alone take care of a horse." Jenni didn't have money to support a horse, either.

Gran walked out onto the porch again and reached down to slip on a pair of muck boots. "I tried for years to convince your father to get one for you when you were young, but he refused. You know, he's always resented me and the horses."

"That's not true." What was Gran talking about? Intrigued, Jenni closed the door behind them and watched her grandmother closely.

"It's probably best if you don't adopt one, anyway." Gran's face looked so disappointed that Jenni reached out and touched her shoulder.

"I'll own one someday. But what you said about Dad … what did you mean?" Jenni knew her grandmother and father didn't get along well but never understood why.

Gran pushed the frayed ends of her blue jeans into the tops of her muck boots, and then stood tall. "He expected me to work more at Stallings, back when Grandpop owned it, instead of playing with my horses. When the restaurant went through financial trouble, your father blamed my lack of dedication. He stepped in and saved the business."

The *family* business.

Jenni had always thought she'd eventually inherit Stallings from her father, so it came as a surprise when she learned he'd sold it to Dan Botticelli and his father, Alberto, to help pay medical bills for a disease nobody bothered to tell Jenni about the first go around, five years ago. Heartbroken about his prognosis, and crushed about losing Stallings, those feelings didn't begin to describe the betrayal she felt about his secrecy. If the cancer hadn't returned, she'd have never known.

She could reason now that perhaps the sale of the restaurant was for the best. Truth be told, she wanted to be free from her dad's tight control.

And here she was, back in his house.

Subtle things started to add up in Jenni's memory. "Is that why he never let me have a pony, because he wanted me to be dedicated to the restaurant?"

"Yes. He thinks you're too much like me."

Jenni didn't think they were that much alike, except they both valued their independence. "Why haven't you mentioned this before?"

Gran scowled, then stepped down from the porch. She headed around the corner of the house with Jenni hurrying to keep up. A stream of bright light from a corner floodlight clicked on. "It's time you know the truth. Even though Stallings didn't go under, my heart hurts to think he'll die blaming me."

Die.

A deep fear stirred in Jenni, the numbing kind a little kid felt when she first realized she was lost in a crowd. The family stability Jenni had, as dysfunctional as it was, seemed to evaporate like fog lifting off the estuary in the early morning.

Her daddy was dying.

On an intellectual level Jenni understand her father's prognosis, but on an emotional level she wasn't ready to let go yet. Even though he frustrated her, she found herself longing for a better relationship with him. What would she do without him?

Jenni swallowed hard and reached out to take hold of Gran's arm to stop her. "You need to talk with him, explain your side of things. I know he loves you."

Gran seemed to repel the words and shrugged. "I hear you went running with the Botticelli boy."

Jenni's chin dropped open; news traveled too fast in Big Cat. And Gran's habit of changing the subject meant Jenni had touched on a sensitive topic, Richard Stallings.

"What's his name again, the Botticelli boy?" Gran asked.

"Scott." She hoped Gran wouldn't notice the lilt in her voice from the mere mention of his name.

The wise woman winked at her. "Good for you. He's a keeper."

"It wasn't a planned thing. I passed him on the road and we exchanged a few words."

An expressive grin lit up Gran's face. "That's a start."

"What about Brittany?"

"What about her?" Gran asked. She reached out and held Jenni by the shoulders. "Don't you think it's time to forgive him?"

Jenni stared at her grandmother's shadowed face. "Maybe, but I don't know if I can."

"Trust me, you can. It helps to forgive yourself first, though. You were only sixteen, too young to assume responsibility for your sister. She was old enough to take care of herself, anyway." Gran pulled her into a hug. "That boy is suffering from a bad case of guilt. Help him and you'll learn to love again."

Jenni absorbed the warmth of Gran's hug for a moment, then pulled back. "He's my banker, not to mention he declined my loan. That doesn't make a good start to a relationship of any kind."

Gran kept a goofy smile on her face. "Look past his stuffy suit. A little time in Big Cat will make him unwind eventually."

Scott needed a lot more than "a little time" on the coast to relax him.

"And some wild sex," Gran continued to say. "It's obvious he's been lacking in that department for a while.

Jenni's breath cut off for a sharp moment. She didn't want to think about Scott and the word "sex," not in the same sentence. "I can't believe you just said that."

"Don't let him get away again. By the way, are you going with the foundation at the end of the month to bring me two more horses?" Gran dropped her hands to her side but made no move in the direction of the barn.

Relieved by yet another change in subject, Jenni shook her head. "I work seven days a week. Dad's on me about hiring someone to help." Maybe he was right about the additional revenue from the extended hours more than offsetting the new employee's wages. Jenni didn't want to end up like Scott, uptight and too busy to enjoy life.

How to ask Gran if she wanted a part-time job? The idea had popped into Jenni's mind when her father had suggested she hire someone semi-retired. The downfall to the plan? Gran was always so busy, and Jenni's father would be livid.

Gran scowled in the yellow glow of the floodlight. "He's right, you know. You can't keep working long hours."

"I know. But my shop needs to be open more if I want to succeed."

"Tell you what," Gran said and started toward the barn again. "Since the ghost walks are only on the weekends now, and I only work on Fridays this time of year, I'll help you out."

"Oh, Gran. What about all the other things you're involved with?" Jenni wanted to make sure her grandmother didn't take on too much, although she'd love to hire her.

Gran shook her head. "Really. My schedule just lightened. Besides, I'd enjoy chatting with all the folk who come into your shop. It'd give me something to do." She splashed through a mud puddle in a low-lying area without appearing to give the water much thought.

Muck boots were good for that. Jenni wore regular sneakers, however, so she dodged the large puddle and followed Gran into the barn. The fresh scent of hay enveloped her, a familiar smell she loved. Gran flipped the light on and three of the Islander Ponies nickered. They poked their heads over the stall doors, begging Jenni to pat them.

She ran her hand down Frankie's nose, a chestnut mare with a white blaze. "Really? I mean, you'd enjoy working for me?" Jenni asked, glancing back at Gran.

"Yes, sweetheart. Why don't I come by a couple of times this week so you can train me."

"Can you work Saturdays? I'd love to have one day off on the weekends."

"Sure, as long as you promise to help out the foundation. They can use all the help they can get."

An ocean of relief and gratitude filled her. "Gran, you're the best. Thanks."

She'd deal with her father later. He might not be happy about whom she hired, but at least she'd followed his advice.

***

The next day, after the morning rush of customers slowed at the coffee shop, Jenni sat on a loveseat at a corner table to brainstorm. From her calculations, Coffee Break had less than ninety days to remain open. She needed to find a way to increase business fast.

She'd called several other banks to ask about a loan, but no one seemed remotely interested. As Cassie had so bluntly pointed out, without collateral, Jenni's loan was a risk. She and her family had a history at Coastal Carolina Bank, but evidently that wasn't enough. Scott took his job seriously, and that didn't help Jenni one bit.

She picked up the phone to call Sunshine Bakery. Susie was a local and one of those instant friends, even though she was four years younger than Jenni.

"Susie, do you have time to meet with me today? I'm interested in expanding my pastry order." Perhaps if she could increase the amount of revenue per customer, that would provide some immediate financial relief.

"I can be there in twenty minutes." Susie's voice always sounded so upbeat. "How's that for service?"

"Perfect." True to her word, twenty minutes later she breezed into the coffee shop, smiling as if she owned the world.

"I love coming in here to get my coffee fix," Susie commented. "I don't need to drink anything to taste it; the smell is so divine and rich."

Jenni grinned. She flagged for Susie to join her at the table and pushed aside her laptop. "Speaking of coffee, what can I get you to drink?"

"Anything is fine. Something low-fat if you don't mind." Susie set a binder on the table with a light thud and slid into the booth. She grabbed one of the overstuffed pillows and hugged it to her chest. "I love all these comfy pillows you have on the loveseats. It makes me want to curl up and read a book."

"Exactly the thought I want," Jenni said, matching her friend's enthusiasm.

After a half hour Jenni had selected several delicious-looking baked goods. She'd practically drooled over the photographs of cupcakes topped with butter cream, slices of carrot cake layered with cream cheese, and wedges of dark chocolate cake frosted with thick, rich icing.

She'd also made a decision, thanks to Susie's suggestions, to organize several book clubs to meet at Coffee Break. Jenni didn't make a lot of money off book clubs, mostly because they usually ordered one drink and then took up space for a couple of hours, but if they felt welcome, they'd return and bring friends. If anything, she'd keep people sitting in here through the dead of winter so the coffee shop appeared busy.

"Did the construction hurt business much?" Susie asked after she thumped the binder closed and pushed it aside.

Jenni nodded. "That's why I need a loan."

Susie shook her head. "That's too bad. Speaking of loans, I heard Cassie Forthright was already making the moves on Scott Botticelli, just like she did in high school." Susie rolled her eyes, then slurped the last remaining drops of a light frappe before she continued talking. "Someone spotted Cassie heading upstairs last night with a bag of what looked like Chinese takeout."

"Upstairs?"

"You didn't know? He's the new tenant that lives above you."

Why hadn't he told her? Anger jabbed at Jenni. It was bad enough that he lived above her coffee shop, but to invite Cassie for dinner above Jenni's domain made it worse. She felt Scott's presence pressing down on her as she imagined them getting cozy on the couch above her head. The old dynamics between him and Cassie were falling right back into place. Jenni's attraction to him made no sense, anyway.

He was a ruthless banker with whom she had bad personal history, not least because he practically screeched the plans for her coffee shop to a sudden halt. As she'd tried to tell Gran, a relationship with him didn't stand a chance.

Susie didn't miss a beat. "I thought you let your crush go a long time ago?"

Jenni thought she'd hidden her annoying admiration for Scott better than that. "You know about my feelings for him? I never told anyone." She leaned back against the couch and wrapped her hands around a warm paper cup. The comfort drink was a favorite of hers: a light mocha made with low-fat milk, sugar-free chocolate syrup, and a hint of whipped cream. She'd work off the calories running this evening.

"Are you kidding? I think everyone in school knew how you felt about him, including Cassie."

Jenni shook her head. "Impossible. Dan and I used to double date with them."

"That's why Cassie avoids you to this day. You were a threat then, and you're more so now."

"Why's that?"

Susie lowered her voice as if someone might overhear the conversation, although the place was empty. "With Scott home Cassie has to face her involvement with your sister's accident. She's jealous of you. She's always known your feelings for Scott. In her own confused mind, I bet that's why she refuses to accept any responsibility for the accident. If she did, she'd be admitting defeat to you."

Jenni inhaled slowly. All this was too much to deal with on top of her father's struggle with cancer and trying to save her coffee shop. "Maybe that's why she warned Scott against approving my loan."

"Bingo." Susie narrowed her eyebrows. "She'd jump at a chance to make you fail."

"I can't believe she's that vindictive." Jenni finished off the last bit of mocha and stood to toss the cup into the trash. "Cassie can't know about my crush. I didn't even realize the extent of my feelings until he walked in here yesterday."

"I wouldn't call her vindictive." Susie paused a moment. "I'm not sure she's aware of what she's doing. She just knows she resents you. And If you think back, you'll realize how strong your crush was. You just wanted to avoid breaking his brother's heart."

Susie hit the truth dead-on. "That may be, but I'm angry at Scott. He hasn't contacted me over the last twelve years. He's never truly apologized for my sister's death other than a meager 'I'm sorry.' Who does he think he is to waltz back into town and pick up the reins again? I don't work that way."

"You have every right to be angry, but for your own sake, you need to work through it. Now that he's back in town and you are reliving Brittany's death, the timing is perfect."

Susie was right, but letting go of the anger would strip away her defense mechanism, would make her feel the raw pain all over again. "By the way, there's still something missing from my order." Jenni realized she'd changed the subject just as abruptly as Gran usually did. "What about a selection of sandwiches or English muffins, maybe with eggs, cheese, and bacon on it?"

"Great idea, but you'll have to contact a restaurant for that. My recommendation would be the Shrimp Shack. I know they cater."

Jenni sighed. "That means asking Dan for help."

Susie flashed a wicked grin. "That could get interesting. But if you want to sell sandwiches, Dan's your best choice."

The bell above the door tinkled and in walked Scott.

"I'll place your order and have Tony deliver it tomorrow along with the usual," Susie said. "If you need anything else, just call." At that, she scooped up her binder and threw her empty cup into the trash. "Enjoy," she said to Scott as she floated past him. Right before she opened the door, she winked at Jenni.

"Scott," Jenni said. "I'm glad to see you." Of course, she was glad for business reasons only. She wanted to fill him in on her sales strategy, not that her plan to increase business would change his mind about the loan. She respected his business sense when she wasn't busy resenting his interference as an insensitive banker. She refused to give up on her dream, to give up on her sister. If she lost her business, her landlady would have to pry Jenni away from her beloved shop.

When Scott stopped in front of her, his expensive yet refreshing scent distracted her. She fought the desire to close her eyes and inhale a long whiff, fought the desire to imagine what his arms might feel like wrapped around her, under different circumstances. Her mind knew better than to indulge herself in a self-defeating fantasy.

Then she remembered how he'd conveniently forgotten to mention that he lived above her shop. She despised secrets.

"I'm not normally welcomed by people I've declined money to," he said. He wore another one of his power ties, but today he'd tied it noticeably looser. "I came in to buy breakfast." He leaned a little too close. He stared into her eyes, their gaze locking. "Again, I'm sorry about the loan. I usually don't have to turn down friends."

Friends. The way he said the word, with a sexy lighthearted drawl, stirred her insides against her will. He seemed more relaxed today, perhaps thankful he'd made a decision about the loan even though it was to her detriment.

He reached out, almost touching her arm, but stopped. "Jenni, I'll do whatever I can personally to help save your shop. I know how much it means to you."

She shook her head. She'd grown up working hard without complaining or asking for help. "Thanks. You've done enough." She realized too late how piercing her words sounded.

"Ouch." He scowled and pulled back. "Like I said, it wasn't personal. I get paid to do the best job I can do."

"I understand. I'd hate to have a job where money had to be the ruling force." He'd probably decline a loan to his own father if he thought necessary. Maybe Susie was right, and Jenni needed to release some of the resentment she hoarded. Her financial situation wasn't his fault, not entirely. "What can I get you to drink?"

He moved in front of the cash register, no longer making eye contact with her. Instead he stared at the overhead menu. "The usual. A tall mocha, two shots of espresso, and another scone. Those are delicious."

She took silent pleasure in his compliment and walked behind the counter, relieved to put more space between them. "Wait until tomorrow. You'll have your choice of goodies."

His eyes widened ever so slightly. "Goodies, huh? I like the thought of that." He leaned on the counter, toward her again, his eyes softening a degree.

Oh, too bad he smelled so good. If she had a shred of sense, she'd keep their relationship strictly professional. She backed away, thrilled to busy her hands. She made the mocha, pressed a lid on top, and pointed at the display case. "Help yourself."

"That's the best offer I've gotten all morning." He flashed her a lopsided half smile, then pulled a scone from the display case and slid it into a bag.

How dare he flirt? If he hadn't been flirting with her the evening of the accident, he wouldn't have distracted Cassie while she was steering the sailboat. A jealous Cassie whipped around to glare at them, inadvertently giving the wheel a sharp jerk. When Jenni looked back at her sister, who'd been horsing around on the bow of the boat, she was gone. It was dark and they couldn't see or hear Brittany. By the time they turned the sailboat around in the Intracoastal Waterway, there was no chance of saving her.

He touched her arm. "Are you okay?"

"I'm fine." She tried to shove the memory away, back into the far corner of her mind where she stored it. "So I hear there is a new tenant living above me."

He frowned as though confused.

Clearly, she needed to be more direct. "I hear you live above my coffee shop. Thanks for the warning."

"Warning?"

She rolled her eyes. "Don't tell me you're one of those secretive guys."

She swore he lost the olive tone to his skin.

How interesting. "Never mind, I don't want to know. Since you're here, I'd like to share my plan with you to increase sales." She'd start by mentioning the desserts, then the idea to extend the shop's hours with Gran's help. When her efforts proved profitable, she'd hire someone besides Gran to cover additional hours. She envisioned evenings filled with poetry and book readings, Friday and Saturday nights jazzed up with music. Whatever it took to attract patrons into her coffee shop.

If her ideas were successful, Coffee Break might survive the winter if no other major financial hits happened in the meantime.

“Jenni—”

“Please, hear me out.” He nodded, so she filled him in on her plan while she rang up his order.

He handed her his credit card and said, “You’re on the right track; good for you. But it’s going to take more than that. Your ideas will take time to work.”

Despite the uneasy feeling in her belly, she smiled. “As you said, it’s a start.”

"By the way, are you planning to run tonight?”

She chewed on her lower lip to keep from answering him.

“Forget it,” he said. “I shouldn’t have asked.”

If she were eighteen, she would jump up and down at the opportunity. But things were more complicated now.

“What about Cassie?” The words slipped out of her mouth before she could stop them.

His facial expression hardened and his mouth curved downward. He turned and strode toward the door. “Have a nice afternoon.”

“I’m going to run on Pony Island after I close," she said in almost a whisper, but he still heard. "My brother Keith owns the Sea Horse Ferry. I can meet you at the dock.”

What was she thinking? She’d just encouraged him to run alone with her on an uninhabited island. Not that he physically scared her, but emotionally he terrified her.

CHAPTER FIVE

"I'll do that. Thanks."

He looked at his watch. "We need to keep moving." Jeff stood and offered his hand to help her. He had to admit that occasionally, being too polite to women got him into trouble. Women often took advantage of him. He couldn't help it, though. His daddy and granddaddy had pounded it into his brain as a child to treat women with respect. One time he'd made the mistake of asking, "What if the woman doesn't deserve it?" He'd gotten a whipping he'd never forget.

She looked away from him and appeared shy, but took his hand anyway until she stood. Then she dropped it "Where is the next herd?"

"Northwest of here." He pointed off into the distance. "Goliath's land is beyond that farthest dune. Each herd hangs out in certain areas of the island. The stallions have worked out whose territory is whose."

She snapped her pack into place and brushed a thin layer of sand off her jeans. "Oka Scott stood next to a brightly painted yellow bench to wait for Jenni. He looked at his watch for the umpteenth time, even though he'd arrived early. She would show up.

He tried to relax by looking out across the wide channel, with its choppy, greenish blue water hitting the creamy shores of the scattered islands. A pelican caught his attention when it landed on a nearby piling. He had to admit, he loved the scenery and the wildlife on the coast, but he longed for the city more. Anything to escape his memories.

An old familiar script played in his mind again. If he could only go back and change that one evening, he'd do it in a heartbeat.

Coming to Big Cat was a bad idea. He should have put up more of an argument when his boss insisted he return. Let someone else cut back on the risky loans Layne wanted to accept. It was also a mistake to have enticed Jenni to run with him today. He told himself that exercising with her, getting to know her better was all part of the job. She was, after all, a customer of the bank. But that wasn't the only reason he wanted to spend time with her. He liked her, too much in fact. He needed to compartmentalize their relationship into a small box in his mind labeled work, then he might be able to ward off his increasing attraction to her.

"You look like you've been waiting awhile." Jenni stood there in black running shorts and a tight, neon pink running shirt. The fabric repelled sweat all right, and he had no right to be interested in how her shirt accentuated her athletic body. But her curves attracted attention, his attention. He'd always found her attractive. She seemed to have a vibrant energy about her. So much for compartmentalizing.

"I've been here about twenty minutes. In general, I'm notoriously early."

She chuckled. "And I'm notoriously on time, to the minute actually." She sat down on the bench to wait for the ferry while he remained standing. A handful of other passengers sat on benches closer to the dock. "If I show up early, I stress about what I could accomplish instead of waiting," she continued. "I fit as much into one day as I can, including my run, time for my dad, and a bit of pleasure."

“You sound as obsessed as me, except I forget to have downtime."

"I'm learning that balance is important. I have to remind myself of that often." She looked away at the estuary and breathed deeply several times, as if to draw strength from the water. When she turned back she asked, "What were you thinking about when I first walked up? You seemed sad."

"Nothing."

"You know, sometimes it helps to talk about it."

He drew in a long breath as she had done. He looked off in the distance while he talked. "I remember a mess of red curls. She was looking back at me on the boat, smiling. She waved at me. Then when I looked back, she was gone, overboard."

"Brittany. She had a crush on you." Her voice sounded raspy now.

"I ... know." He looked down at the sparse grass attempting to grow through the sandy soil. "I was intoxicated that evening. I asked Cassie to drive the boat." He shook his head. "Drinking at age eighteen. I haven't touched a drop of alcohol since." He swallowed hard. “She was always so happy. Why did she have to die?”

Jenni barely touched his hand. "It's okay to remember."

When he looked into her eyes he saw guarded compassion instead of hatred. "Thanks, Jenni." The subject was too painful to talk about in much detail. He needed to change the subject. "How’s your father? I heard he has cancer.”

“I think he’s depressed more than anything." Jenni slid her hand away so gently, Scott wondered if she'd ever touched him at all. Again she looked out at the water, appearing to absorb strength from its natural ability to heal. "He has lung cancer and wants to give up. If I could motivate him to get out of bed, I think his quality of life would improve.”

“Probably, but it’s not your responsibility to make him want to live.”

She stared at him. The sad look on her face made him want to scoop her into his arms. Thankfully he had good self-control. Wanting to help, he said, "I have an idea of how to get him out of the house. Your dad won't be able to resist. He'll practically leap out of bed."

Her face brightened and for an instant she looked like a teenager again. "If you can do that, I'll owe you one. A big one."

What a pleasing thought. "Anything I want?"

She looked scared to agree but shrugged. "Sure. How bad can it be?" she asked.

"You obviously don't know me well." Or at least the person he used to be. He wanted to find the rebel inside him again, before he forgot what emotional freedom felt like.

His cell phone rang, disrupting the moment. Cassie's name flashed across the display screen and he groaned. This better be important.

"What's up, Cassie?"

"I can't find the McDowell file. Do you have it?"

"No. I'm getting ready to run. I don't have any paperwork with me."

"Is it in your office?"

He always left his desk immaculate, and never tucked anything away in a drawer. In the short time they'd worked together, Cassie should know that. He doubted her call had anything to do with work, but more with wanting to verify whom he was running with. She had some irritating intuition that alerted her to whenever he was in Jenni's presence.

"I don't have the file. Look in the filing cabinet under "M."

A rustling noise sounded over the earpiece. "Oh, here it is. Sorry to bother you." She didn't sound apologetic in the least. "By the way, what are you doing tonight? I can bring by any faxes and messages you've missed. We can work over pizza."

He closed his eyes and rubbed them. "We've discussed this before. I don't want to—"

"Mix business with pleasure," she interrupted. "You might want to question your relationship with your running partner then. Aren't you defying your own rule?"

He resented his employee correcting him, but she was right. He was well aware that Jenni conducted business with Coastal Carolina Bank, but somehow the situation seemed different. She was a friend.

The small passenger ferry tooted its horn off in the distance.

"I need to go, Cassie. Try to handle things while I'm gone." He clicked off the phone. Jenni stood and they headed toward the dock, joining a group of awaiting passengers.

Jenni's brother, Keith, guided the skiff into the boat slip and waved at the two of them. A handful of returning passengers climbed from the boat, and after he helped the last one out, he called out playfully, "All aboard!" Scott swore he saw Keith wink at Jenni.

Keith offered his hand to help each person onto the boat. A middle-aged couple dressed as tourists, with cameras strung around their necks, chose to sit near the stern; a group of three women, perhaps friends who decided to rent a condominium for the week, huddled together on the starboard side. Scott and Jenni sat in the back, close to Keith.

Scott marveled at how obvious the resemblance was between sister and brother. They both had the same red hair, a spray of freckles across their cheeks, and an unnerving air of confidence that intrigued him.

"How long have you owned the ferry service?" Scott asked. What little he knew about Keith, who was five years younger, Scott never imagined him as the entrepreneur, business type. He'd pegged him as a creative artist, or maybe a passionate musician. He was clearly comfortable at the helm, though, in his element out here on the water.

"I've owned the ferry since springtime. Jenni helped me organize the books and taught me how to run a company. Then she opened her coffee shop and left me to fend for myself." Keith winked at his sister and Scott noticed the unmistakable respect in the man's eyes. "She's always been good with numbers. I don't know what I would've done without her help. I'm glad she has Coffee Break; she deserves it."

A slight twinge of guilt poked at Scott. He wondered if Jenni had mentioned the loan to her brother. "Has business been good?" Scott asked in attempt to redirect his thoughts away from the emotional aspect of Jenni's financial endeavors.

Keith nodded and reversed the boat's engine to glide out of the slip. He motored though the estuary and Scott could feel his tension slowly loosen a few notches. The cool wind on his face felt refreshing. He loved boats, loved the sea.

"My business suffered when the construction crew closed the street in front of her coffee shop," Keith said as he casually guided the ferry around a channel marker, "but I can't complain. Most of the tourists are set on seeing the wild horses, and since I own the only passenger ferry in town, they usually detour to find me."

"Keith's customers kept my coffee shop afloat," Jenni commented. "The construction hurt a few businesses at our end of the street. We rallied together and pressured them to speed up the construction process, although I'm not sure it helped. But the point is, around here people stick together and help one another."

Scott felt the sharp barb puncture a small hole in his banker's armor. The intimate moment they shared earlier about Brittany seemed to evaporate.

He knew Big Cat's unwritten code of honor: Thou shall watch out for thy neighbor. But he wasn't able to approve her loan, friends or not.

"Listen," Scott said. "Times are tough for everyone right now, including the banking industry. I only approve the strongest loans; the ones that I'm sure will be paid back. It's risky for banks to gamble on one-person businesses."

If her brother didn't know about the loan before, he certainly knew about it now.

Jenni leaned away, as if she wanted to climb from the moving boat. Thankfully she had nowhere to go and had to hear his viewpoint.

"As I said before, I understand." The way she scowled, however, proved she didn't readily accept the news.

The scent of her fruity-smelling sunblock caught in the wind and sidetracked him. More pleasant memories circled in his mind of the relaxed days of his youth when his father used to take him and Dan out on the sailboat. The good old days. Before the accident.

He wanted her to understand his decision wasn't personal. "I need to be choosy about the loans I approve for the bank's sake."

"I know what it's like to be worried about your livelihood," she said with a trace of fear in her eyes. She looked like a vulnerable baby rabbit caught in a farmer's trap.

A surprising urge to protect her made him reach forward and tuck a highlighted strand of red hair behind her ear. "I'm sorry, Jenni." He wanted to apologize about Brittany too, but couldn't.

She didn't move away from him, but the slant of her eyes declared the discussion over. It was a shame he couldn't have helped her with the loan. Sometimes he hated his job, as in this case, but mostly he thrived on the power to make a difference.

To reestablish his equilibrium, Scott gazed at the large expanse of green marsh starting to yellow, a sure sign of fall. "I don't remember the estuary being so breathtaking," he said. The water sparkled in the afternoon sun, and as they passed another small island, he imagined he was on a much-needed vacation in the Caribbean. Extending his legs out, he leaned back against the hard bench. The sun's rays almost penetrated the thick layer of city life. He fought the temptation to close his eyes and enjoy the warmth on his face and neck.

The shrill ring of his cell phone broke the tranquil ambience. "Cassie, I can't talk right now," he snapped. He wanted to leave work behind for the afternoon, which was a foreign concept.

"Your boss in Raleigh called. He said it was urgent."

Scott let out a whoosh of air. "Thanks. I'll give him a quick call."

Why now? Scott had already talked to him twice this afternoon before he left work. Reluctantly he dialed the number. From the moment Brant Calloway's stuffy assistant answered until the man picked up the line, Scott never stopped watching Jenni.

She leaned back, nestled her athletic body into a comfortable position, and closed her eyes. Exactly what he'd wanted to do. Unfortunately, she didn't seem bothered in the least that he took a business call instead of engaging her in small talk.

His boss didn't sound happy. "There you are, Scott. I've been waiting for you to call me back." Brant Calloway gave a new definition to the word "uptight."

Scott's shoulders tensed.

"We need to discuss layoffs," Brant said. "It looks inevitable."

Scott didn't want to discuss layoffs in front of Jenni; he wanted to run on Pony Island with her. Thankfully Brant's conversations were quick, though they usually packed a powerful blow.

Scott kept his gaze on Jenni, who looked to be dozing. In all honesty, he liked her on a personal level, something that pushed beyond the professional barrier he tried to create. He needed to find a way to earn her forgiveness. She deserved that. His thoughts jolted to a halt when the boat bumped into the only dock on the nine-mile-long, and just under two-mile-wide barrier island. Jenni sprang to life and launched from the boat.

Scott wanted to end the call and follow her, but couldn't.

"I want your input about who we can let go," Brant said.

"I need to think about it. I can call you later tonight, or first thing in the morning." Scott was having trouble focusing on the conversation. He hadn't been in slow-paced Big Cat for long, but already his intense boss was hard to listen to.

"Call me tonight, as soon as you have an answer."

Scott gritted his teeth from the added pressure. “Will do.” He clicked off the phone and climbed from the boat. He looked forward to running off the tension he’d just absorbed in the last few minutes.

Keith called out, “I’ll be here by six o’clock. It’s starting to get dark earlier, so make sure you’re here.”

“We’ll be exactly on time,” Jenni said.

Scott preferred to be early but decided to let it go, to enjoy being in the moment for a change.

Keith motored off and left the two of them alone on the deserted sandy beach; the other passengers had taken off in the opposite direction toward the ocean.

She shot him a challenging look. “I bet you can’t beat me to that dune,” she said and pointed at a twenty-foot sand dune not too far away. “Last one’s a rotten fish egg.”

Her competitive spirit surprised him. Before he had time to respond, she shot off and sprinted toward the mound of sand. She was fast but not fast enough. Short distances he ran well.

Scott saw her glance back. He had to smile at the shocked expression on her face when she realized he was almost close enough to touch her. She ran harder but he easily caught up. Right before they approached the dune, he lengthened his stride and passed her in time to reach the dune first.

Her astonished look said she wasn’t used to losing. “I thought you were out of shape?” she asked.

“I am. Just wait until I build my endurance. I’ll give you some competition then.” To soften the defeat, he wrapped his arm around her midsection and swung her in a circle, enjoying her sweet laughter. The faint scent of rosemary mixed with the pleasant aroma of coffee tickled his nose. The urge to kiss her was overwhelming. He reluctantly set her down, her warm body pressing against his. When she lifted her chin, their eyes met briefly. Somehow he managed to let go and turn away.

He had to be crazy to want to start something with her, especially since he was leaving in three months. He loved his life in Raleigh. Again, she deserved better than what he had to offer.

"We'll see about you being my competition," she said. She took off again, this time toward the beach. Without thinking, he chased her. The rare pleasure of playing evoked a sense of joy he'd long forgotten.

When they reached the water's edge, they ran at a slower pace and stopped only briefly so he could tie his shoe. The seagulls circled overhead, crying out an old tune while they scavenged for remnants of food. Salt from the air dotted his lips, which tasted so familiar a pang of nostalgia caused his soul to ache.

Eventually he asked, "What brought you back to Big Cat? Last I heard, you lived in Durham." On the few occasions he talked to Dan, he'd asked about her.

She frowned. "I moved home because of my dad. My parents aren't dealing well with his illness."

"I can understand that." Scott's focus was on his career, though, so he couldn't imagine walking away from his job for any reason. "I don't mean to sound insensitive, but how did you give up the life you created in Durham to return to Big Cat?"

"It was hard at first." She slowed her pace, most likely for his sake, so he could carry on a conversation while running. "I didn't make a lot of money, but I was next in line for a promotion. The job promised to be a large increase in salary. I was already doing a portion of the work, and they planned to expand my duties and create a new position."

"You left that behind?" he asked.

She glanced at him. "Some things are more important than a job."

"I'm sorry; I didn't mean—"

"It's okay." She looked away for a moment. "Let's talk about you, about your life in Raleigh."

"Okay. What do you want to know?" He couldn't imagine she'd find his life more interesting than hers.

"Why didn't you get married?"

He exhaled a long breath. "I did. My wife claimed I worked too hard and I neglected her, so she cheated on me. I was clueless until after the fact. Maybe she was right; I was too busy to notice she was having an affair. The divorce broke my heart."

"I'm sorry."

He stared down at the wet sand and his pace decreased. "I'm not very good at relationships, marriage."

"So you isolate yourself by working long hours." She slowed to match his pace again.

He looked up and tried to hide the pain. "Yeah, something like that." The truth behind his long work hours included more than his failed marriage and poor relationship skills, it included the underlying guilt about her sister, which he carried around with him like an overstuffed suitcase.

They ran in silence for a while before she pointed off in the distance. "Look, one of the wild herds."

Scott glanced at a dark brown stallion that stood at the base of a small dune. A few mares grazed nearby and a foal watched them curiously.

"I love the Islander Ponies," she said. "They represent freedom. My friend Claire Rhoades adopted one of the babies after an accident. Someone let his dog off the leash and it ran after the herd. The baby was only a week old and too young to keep up with his mother. He almost died."

"Is he okay now?"

"Yes. My theory is when you do good deeds it comes back to you in the end."

"You think so?" He wasn't so sure he believed in her philosophy. Breathing heavily, he broke to a walk. "What good deeds have you done lately?"

She slowed beside him. "I help with the rescue missions out here. When some of the horses turn two, we capture them and bring them to the mainland. Jeff and my grandmother board them until we find good homes."

"We didn't have the foundation when I was here last. Volunteering speaks highly of your integrity."

She looked at him. "What have you done to help society?"

He paused. "Lately, nothing." That thought disturbed him.

She frowned. "Should we head back? You're breathing hard."

"No, go on," he insisted. "Run as long as you want. I'll walk another mile and then turn around. At some point you'll catch back up with me."

She flashed him a questioning glance, and he waved her on.

"Okay," she said. "I'll be back in plenty of time to catch the ferry." Jenni picked up her pace again and he watched her for a long while, until she eventually disappeared around a bend off in the horizon.

He enjoyed her company and that confused him. His logical mind reminded him to be professional, not to let his personal feelings get in the way.

When he finally reached the dock again, he sat on the graying wooden planks and waited for the ferry, waited for Jenni's return. After a long hour, the minute hand on his watch seemed to move in reverse, one slow click after another. He focused his gaze on the farthest bend he could see, willing her to run around the point any second. When she didn't, and after another fifteen minutes dragged along, a familiar, childhood urge to protect Jenni stirred within him. Where was she?

Something was wrong.

CHAPTER SIX

Oh, Jenni loved to run. The weight of Coffee Break's financial problems, along with the burden of her father's unfortunate illness, always washed away within minutes of hearing her shoes crunch on the sand.

Without losing her footing, Jenni dug out her cell phone from the top of her sports bra and glanced at the display screen. It was later than she'd anticipated and no cell phone service. She executed a perfect half circle and headed in the direction of the dock. Scott was probably concerned about her, but Keith knew all too well how she lost track of time when she ran.

The only request her brother made was that she carry a cell phone for safety while running out here. Most often the phone had spotty service at best, but she went along with his request anyway.

After all, what could happen on an uninhabited island?

When she rounded the last bend, the ferry dock came into view. Keith had tied the boat to the far end of the bobbing platform and both men stood on the shore. From the way Scott flagged his hands back and forth, they seemed to be having an intense discussion.

When Scott turned, his arm stopped midair. Without a doubt he noticed her, and from the rigid way he stood, he wasn't happy. Scott started toward her with Keith right behind him. She wasn't sure if she should be thrilled because Scott cared, or alarmed.

They met halfway. Without hesitation, and to her surprise, he scooped her into his arms.

"I'm glad you're okay." He squeezed her closer and rubbed his large hand across her back.

She tried to ignore the heat of his touch. After dreaming about being in his arms for years, now that he held her tight she didn't know how to react. She'd like to stand still and enjoy his embrace, so strong and comforting, but then reality resurfaced.

"Sorry I'm late." Jenni pulled away from him and ignored her brother's curious stare.

"Like I tried to tell you before," Keith said to Scott, "she eventually shows up. She gets deep into her head when she runs."

Her brother was right. Life was simpler when she tuned out her problems by running. Unfortunately, Scott was one of the problems she tried to outrun.

Within the half hour, Jenni slipped through the kitchen door of her house. Her mother, dressed in the usual knit pants and turtleneck shirt, with a large cross hanging around her neck, conveyed ultimate conservatism. To some people the predictability would offer security; to Jenni it represented her parents' stifling control over her life. They expected her to live up to a high standard, one that seemed unachievable.

"You're late dear." Dorothy Stallings set a dish of meatloaf onto the old wooden table, which dated back to Jenni's early childhood memories. With only a glance at Jenni, her mother walked over to the stove and carried a small bowl of mashed potatoes to the sturdy table. Its fragile chairs, however, had been handmade by Jenni's uncle, who'd been a self-taught carpenter. Her mother refused to dispose of them, even though they were wobbly now. She resisted change, no matter how small.

Jenni fought the urge to gasp for breath. She wasn't suffocating; her mother just wanted dinner served exactly on the hour to please her husband. Jenni knew all about the impossible task of trying to please him.

Her mom lived to serve him. What would she do when he died?

"Remember last night, Mom? I mentioned wanting to run after work today," Jenni explained. "Sorry if I kept you waiting."

She missed living on her own, but then a shot of remorse darted through her. Her parents claimed to need her emotional support. The only way she'd live by herself anytime soon meant a nursing home for her father, much dreaded by the family, especially him, or the end of her father's life. Jenni much preferred her father's health and independence to her own selfish desires. She gasped for another breath.

That's when she saw the water on the counter, in Jenni's favorite glass. Her mother knew where she'd been all along. She picked up the glass and drank the cool liquid, feeling the surprising comfort of her mother's love. "Thanks, Mom."

"You're welcome, sweetheart." She gave Jenni a half hug and made her way back to the stove for a pot of steamed vegetables.

"Dorothy?" Richard Stallings called from the other room.

"I'll see what he needs." Jenni walked down the hall and into the dark den. She had to squint to make out her father lying in bed. It broke her heart to see how much he'd declined over the past couple of months. "Hi, Dad."

"I need to use the bathroom."

A perfect excuse to get him out of bed. "I can help you. When you're finished, dinner is ready. We'd love for you to eat at the table." In case he needed more enticement, she added, "Mom made one of your favorite meals."

He rolled onto his side and used his arms to push himself into a sitting position, just the way the physical therapist taught him. His arms visibly shook from the effort but he managed on his own.

"You can do it, Dad."

A grunt slipped from his throat. "You never give up, always wanting me to do more." He frowned at her, although she took his words as a subtle compliment. He was right, she wasn't one to quit easily.

"You're a fighter too," Jenni said. She respected his grit to get out of bed on his own and held the walker steady as he stood. He glanced at her, and for a fleeting instant his eyes softened. She swore she saw a hint of fatherly pride glisten in them.

Jenni basked in the brief sense of approval before it whisked away.

Oddly fulfilled, she realized she'd seen a glimpse of the kind of relationship they could have, if he lived long enough. Determined to encourage him, she said, "It will do you good to leave this dreary room. Food tastes much better when you eat it at the dinner table."

"See what I mean?" He waved a shaky finger at her and headed toward the bathroom with Jenni next to him. "If you dealt with that stubborn banker like you do me, you'd get your loan."

"I don't think he's stubborn so much as he's a good business man."

He scowled. "How can you defend someone who's out to destroy your business?"

"He's doing his job. His decision has nothing to do with me personally." Or did it? And why did she feel the need to defend Scott?

"As much business as I've done with Coastal Carolina Bank, you'd think they'd approve your loan based on that."

Expectations got you nowhere in life. She'd learned that lesson years ago, after dealing with her father's unfair demands about Stallings. Gran's words haunted her. He resented his own mother because she didn't share the same passion as him. Although to be fair, he had a generous, caring side too—when he wasn't battling for his life.

"I'll figure out something else," she said. "There has to be another answer besides Scott."

“Scott?” He raised his eyebrows. “You call your banker by his first name?”

“I went to high school with him. Why wouldn’t I?” She tried to hide the softness in her voice. The attraction was there no matter how hard she tried to deny it.

He stopped in the middle of the hallway. "Wait a minute. Are you talking about Scott Botticelli?"

Prepared for battle, she nodded. She had deliberately avoided telling him who'd replaced Layne at the bank.

"What's he doing in Big Cat? He hasn't been back home since the funeral."

Her dad couldn't even say Brittany's name. "Like I said before, he's here temporarily." Disguising the lilt in her voice was nearly impossible.

If you ask me,” he said, scooting the walker again, “I’d say you have personal feelings for your banker. Watch out.” The slightest hint of a smile touched his eyes.

“Believe me; I have no feelings for him other than professional.”

That wasn’t quite the truth, but her father didn’t need to know more. Then she remembered Scott’s promise and fought to hide her own smile. What brilliant plan had he thought of to encourage her father out of the house? If her dad stepped from the safety of these walls, if he breathed the outside air occasionally, maybe his will to live would increase.

He parked the walker in front of the tiny bathroom. “Wait out here for me. I don’t need you to watch me urinate.”

She smiled. Yes, the independent dad she knew so well was back, at least for now.

When he finished his private duties, they inched back down the hall. When they passed by the gloomy den, he hesitated, as if to decide whether to return to bed or to eat in the kitchen. He turned up his nose and sniffed. A small smile stretched at the corners of his normally taut mouth.

"Jenni, my bride made me meatloaf." He said it with such tenderness.

"Yes she did. She loves you, like we all do." That was as close as she allowed herself to say the endearment.

Love was a word never spoken in their house. She remembered the one time he'd said it to her; she was a teenager. She'd sat him down as if to conduct an important meeting—the only way to pull his attention away from Stallings.

He thought she wanted a raise for working afternoons and weekends at the restaurant. Instead, she'd said, "Dad, I have to tell you something important. I mean, *really* important. Are you listening?" When he said, "Yes," she yelled, "I love you" louder than intended. She ran from the room, but before she'd made it through the doorway, she heard him mumble those precious words back.

He had no idea how she ached to hear those words again.

"Don't just stand there, come and get it," her mother called to them. She carried a sturdy chair, borrowed from the dining room set, into the kitchen so he could sit without risk of the chair collapsing. Her mom refused to keep the chair in the kitchen permanently because it didn't match the others, but the reason most likely had to do with the fact that her husband was ill. She didn't want the reminder.

They followed her into the kitchen. Jenni's mom placed the chair at his favorite spot at the table, across from the little television on the countertop. He pushed his walker close to the chair, turned around, and sat with a thud. He jutted his nose into the air and whiffed again.

"Dorothy, you know how to make a man happy."

For Jenni, she knew it took more than cooking meatloaf. If she wanted his approval, that meant profits and good numbers. She planned to achieve financial success before he passed away. But the survival of her coffee shop was bittersweet. She suspected he was only hanging on until she achieved financial security. When she reached her goal, he would die. If she failed, he might live longer, but she'd lose his respect for sure.

He scooped a large helping of potatoes, a hefty amount of meatloaf, and a spoonful of green beans onto his plate. Moments later, after having eaten only a few bites of each, he pushed the dish away. "I'm full. I'm sick of this disease."

"Honey, don't talk like that in front of Jenni."

"Mom, I'm an adult." Jenni tightened her fingers around the frame of her chair. That was the problem with moving home; your parents insisted that you remained a child no matter your age. "He can say anything he wants. I completely understand why he's tired."

Her father cleared his throat. "I'm right here. Now help me back to bed … please."

At least he attempted to be polite. Jenni stood and followed her father back to the den. While he struggled to climb back into bed, he groaned.

"Are you in pain?" She could deal with most things, but not seeing her father suffer. If he didn't fight the cancer, he'd be gone soon. The thought unsettled her to the point her hands began to tremble.

***

The next day felt like Christmas. The deliveryman wheeled in trays of delightful deserts and danishes into Coffee Break. Jenni set each individually wrapped plate into the display case and eyed a piece of carrot cake. Her stomach rumbled. She held a slice off to the side to eat during one of her rare breaks. She'd been in such a hurry to leave home this morning to avoid her overbearing mother, who always got up before the sun rose, that she'd forfeited breakfast.

Her mom was driving her batty. She'd called first thing to demand Jenni's detailed agenda for the day, including the exact time she'd be home. Jenni understood her mom's concern about the promptness of dinner, but she drew the line when her mom lectured about how Jenni shouldn't run after a long day's work.

Coffee Break was her respite. After she finished organizing the display case with the array of baked goods, the bell above the door tinkled. She looked up to see Scott, with a hint of a smile, as he strode to the counter. The fresh scent of the sea drifted in with him. He wore charcoal gray dress pants and a white shirt, the top button undone, and no tie. He appeared to be making some progress in the relaxation department.

"Don't those look good." He stared into the case like a little boy drooling over a selection of candies. His shoulder lightly brushed hers, but if he noticed, he showed no reaction.

"What can I get you today? A tall mocha and a scone? Or would you like to try one of those desserts?"

"You're a good saleswoman. How dare you tempt my pallet like that?" He chuckled, even though it sounded rusty from lack of use. "A mocha for sure. I'll also take a dozen donuts to work and a slice of that carrot cake to snack on in my office later. I can't resist."

"That's the point," she said, brushing a piece of lint from the top of the display case. "My mission is to increase sales. If it works on the banker, it'll work on the customers."

He stuck out his lip and pretended the comment wounded him. "Hey, I'm a regular customer. Is that all you think of me as, the banker? That hurts."

"You don't want me to answer that," Jenni quipped. When his cell phone rang, she made her way behind the counter.

He clicked on the phone. "Dan." He hesitated for a moment. "I haven't been avoiding you." Scott glanced at her, then frowned. "I'll be there in ten minutes."

Instead of making the mocha, she set the cup on the countertop. "Is everything okay?"

He shrugged. "Not sure. My dad's at the Shrimp Shack and Dan needs help with him, whatever that means."

She was fairly sure he hadn't seen Dan since he'd bumped into him at the Shrimp Shack the day Scott announced he was rejecting her loan. She also didn't think he'd visited his parents since he'd been back in Big Cat.

"Are you going to run today?" he asked as he removed a clear plastic box of glazed donuts and a plastic clamshell of carrot cake from the display case.

"I always run. It's my passion."

"Do you mind if I tag along?" When she shrugged with exaggerated indifference, he smiled. "You can pretend you don't like me, but I detect something else." He leaned closer, energy radiating between them. "Besides, you're kind of cute when you play hard to get."

"Whatever." She furrowed her brows. He was right; it was becoming harder to feign disinterest in him. She wanted to back away but didn't dare. He ran his finger along her jaw line. She swallowed hard and forced herself to breath evenly. When he dropped his finger, she pulled away to make the mocha. She pressed the button that usually obeyed by spitting out two shots of dark, flavorful espresso. Nothing. She tried again, a clank, then silence. The most expensive piece of equipment in her coffee shop just broke.

CHAPTER SEVEN

Scott zipped into the Shrimp Shack's busy parking lot. He found a lone parking space at the far end, under a shady pin oak. Stepping from the BMW, he began to power walk toward the restaurant's front door. What could be so bad for Dan to request his help with their father? Furthermore, why was Alberto Botticelli hanging out at his son's restaurant on a warm, sunny day instead of playing golf with his high-powered friends?

Scott dreaded his father's overall negative attitude, and he could certainly do without seeing him for the first time in years under strained circumstances.

When he opened the door, Marge greeted him immediately with a grim look on her face.

"Your father's at the corner table. I have to warn you, though." She glanced in the direction of the dining room. "He's drunk."

"Intoxicated? In the middle of the day, in public?" Scott asked, mortified. His father owned a handful of fancy hotels sprinkled nearby along the coast. What was he doing, drunk where people could judge him?

Besides, alcohol was a bitter enemy. Drinking led to bad things, including one heck of a guilt-trip, painful secrets, and deep regret that tormented a person for life.

"This way." Marge avoided his numb gaze and led him into the dining room.

His father sat at a corner table laughing with one of his old friends, seemingly unaware of people staring. At first glance Scott wouldn't have recognized him. He'd gained a considerable amount of weight and his hair had turned shiny silver. He wore a tired expression on his face and seemed unhappy despite his overbearing laugh.

The Shrimp Shack patrons, including many longtime acquaintances along with a few new faces, silently pleaded for Scott to make his father behave. But no one ever told his father what to do; he answered only to himself. Scott found himself facing the uncomfortable reversal of roles, where the eldest son had to step up and confront his parent about inappropriate behavior.

"Wait a minute." Dan's voice sounded behind him. "Can I talk to you first?"

Scott turned to face his stocky, confident-looking brother, who was a far cry different from the gangly boy who'd wanted to fish or sail the day away. He'd done well for himself.

Tension radiated between them, even after twelve years. Following the accident, Dan had played the part of Jenni's protective boyfriend to the extreme. Understandably so, she'd felt responsible for the death of her sister. Dan, wanting to ease her pain, had turned on Scott, blaming him for being irresponsible. Dan had hit on the truth more than Scott wanted to admit, but his brother's animosity still stung. They'd always been close, until the fatal accident killed their brotherly bond. Apologies could never replace brutal words, and forgiveness seemed impossible.

"Sure." He'd hear what Dan had to say. Scott followed him to a vacant spot between a potted tree and the busy kitchen.

"Dad's making a spectacle of himself," Dan stated. "As partner in my restaurant, he says he isn't leaving."

Scott heard desperation in Dan's voice. "Has this happened before?"

"A few times. Usually he drinks at the Salty Mug. Sometimes the bartender calls me to come get him, or a friend will bring him home. Sometimes he drives."

Scott's chest felt heavy. Driving while intoxicated was inexcusable. He'd known that even at age eighteen.

"What about Mom? What's going on at home to cause this?"

Dan's face hardened. "If you think they fought when you lived here, you should see them now. Actually, the fighting has progressed to long bouts of silence. That's almost worse."

"Why didn't you let me know?"

Dan glared at him. "You don't answer your phone when I call."

Guilty. "I answered today," Scott said defensively. "You could have left me voicemails. I had no idea all this was going on." He'd been too absorbed in his own self-pity to have a clue his family was falling apart.

"This is about Dad right now, not us. We'll deal with our issues later." Dan nodded in the direction of their father, who'd knocked over his drink. People rushed to clean up the mess. "I need your help. Please take him home."

Home. Since Scott's arrival to Big Cat, he'd avoided driving down their shady street, avoided seeing the expansive house, devoid of all warmth. Simply put, the house was a shell that held memories of yelling and slamming doors, long stretches of grueling stress, for days on end. If he drove his father home, that meant he'd have to see his accusatory mother again. After the accident, she blamed Scott for creating a scandal in their small town, which was apparently more important than supporting her son's emotional needs.

"You don't have a choice here." Dan's voice interrupted the stream of thoughts running through Scott's head.

"That's where you're wrong." Scott did have a choice, but the panic on his brother's face stopped him cold. "But Dad needs help, so count me in."

His brother visibly relaxed. "He won't let you admit him to rehab. I've tried that before."

"Maybe he needs a reality check, something to slap him between the eyes." Scott ignored his brother's questioning eyes.

With the help of Dan, and a few of his staff, they managed to convince the older man to climb into Scott's car. Father and son were going to take a little drive.

His father remained quiet during the ride until Scott turned right at the crossroads instead of left toward home. His dad's artificially jubilant mood from earlier had turned ugly.

"Where are we going?" his father demanded. "You think you can show up when you feel like it and drag me around town at your whim? Take me home."

Scott kept driving. Moments later he pulled into the graveyard he swore he'd never visit again. He slammed the car into park. His hands were shaking but he had to do this for his father. He climbed out, went to the passenger side, and opened the door. With determination, he pulled his father from the car.

***

Jenni had no choice but to call Dan Botticelli. With the espresso machine out of order, she needed to supplement her income immediately. She stared at the phone. If she made the call, especially with Scott back in town, the old dynamics between the Friendly Four would intensify. Finally, as if the phone beckoned her to place the call, she picked up the receiver and dialed.

"Jenni, it's a pleasure. What can I do for you?" Dan's voice sounded rich and deep, much like Scott's. He didn't engage in small talk, never had.

"I'd like to set up a meeting to discuss ordering sandwiches for the coffee shop. Are you able to meet with me early this week?"

“Hang on a second.” He made a rustling noise. “I can meet tomorrow at two. Does that work for you?”

He sounded tired, or stressed perhaps, and Jenni wondered what the emergency was that had involved his father. But of course she didn’t ask. “Perfect. I’ll see you then,” she said, hanging up seconds before a flood of people entered the shop. Several customers left, however, after they read the sign that the espresso machine was temporarily broken. Thank goodness a small book club took up residence in the far corner, claiming the couch and four overstuffed chairs. Jenni was delighted when they walked up to the counter, unfazed by the broken espresso machine.

“Oh, look at that carrot cake,” exclaimed a lady about the same age as Jenni’s mother.

“And that chocolate cake looks sinful,” another woman declared. “I’ll have to order that.”

Jenni’s plan to double sales would have succeeded had they'd been able to order an espresso drink to go along with their dessert. Thankfully she'd had the insight to expand the pastry selection. Without it, sales would be dismal.

The women carried their purchases back to their table, and Jenni bent down to set a carton of cream in the small refrigerator under the counter. She jumped when a gruff voice barked at her.

The woman said, “Excuse me.”

Jenni stood to face one of her most difficult customers, Mrs. Forthright, a gray-headed woman with a bun clinched behind her head. Jenni hadn’t heard the bell tinkle and hadn’t realized Cassie’s mother had entered the coffee shop. The woman stared over her wire-rimmed glasses and down her crooked nose.

Jenni had the sudden feeling of being sent to the principal’s office, although she’d never personally experienced such a traumatic event.

“I’m sorry, Mrs. Forthright. My espresso machine broke this morning.” Cassie's mother always ordered a tall mocha. Today was no different.

She wrinkled her nose. “How can a coffee shop not have espresso?”

“Sorry.” Jenni apologized again, although she felt more irritated now than apologetic. “Can I get you something else?”

“Give me a black coffee then,” she demanded. “When will your machine be fixed?”

“Soon, I hope.” Jenni would try again to call Kevin Crane, the man who she’d bought the used espresso machine from, as soon as Mrs. Forthright left the shop. It was best to finish her order first and send her on her way.

“I hear you’re competing again in the marathon.” Mrs. Forthright spoke politely enough despite the scornful look on her face.

“I am.” Jenni stood taller, so as not to reveal feeling reprimanded.

“And I hear you’re telling people that you’re going to beat my Cassie. No one has ever beaten her before in our little race, so I’m not sure why you think you can outrun a pro.”

Jenni stared directly into the woman’s eyes without blinking. Cassie wasn’t a professional runner anymore. Despite her insulin-dependent diabetes, she could have continued to run professionally, although Jenni suspected Cassie’s reasons for quitting were much deeper than the unfortunate diagnosis.

To Jenni’s delight, Mrs. Forthright averted her piercing eyes, but not for long.

“I don’t care how hard you practice; you’re wasting your time,” Mrs. Forthright said. “I don’t know why Cassie bothers to race against people at this low level.” Her nose scrunched up and she looked as if she’d bitten into an unripe persimmon.

Jenni set her jaw. The best way to ensure her success was for someone to say she couldn’t do something. Especially if Jenni disliked the person challenging her.

Cassie’s mother was as arrogant as her daughter was, possibly more so. Once at the Shrimp Shack, Cassie was dining with her mom. A local fan walked up and politely asked for

Cassie's autograph. Cassie reprimanded the poor woman for interrupting her dinner, and later the innocent fan had become the talk of the town, as if she'd committed some horrible crime.

The Forthrights held amazing power because they knew how to schmooze the right people, knew how to spread poisonous gossip about those who were a threat. Most people failed to see through their façade, but not Jenni.

She planned to beat Cassie, all right, and to give her a good reminder to be humble.

Gran saw through Jenni's resentment, though. "You allow Cassie to bother you too much. You haven't forgiven her yet about Brittany's death." Gran always shook her head when Jenni complained about her rival. "You and your friends were young and made a horrible choice, but your own anger is eating you alive, sweetheart. Running the marathon isn't a way to punish Cassie, or to prove she's a failure. Don't give her that much control over you."

Jenni shook off the thought as she stared at Mrs. Forthright. "May the best runner win." She couldn't wait to get the woman out of her shop, but she hadn't ordered yet. "So what can I get for you?"

Mrs. Forthright scoffed at Jenni. "A tall decaf coffee and a piece of carrot cake."

The last piece of carrot cake. Despite her desperation for sales, Jenni wished a better person had wanted the delicious dessert instead of the bitter old woman. Maybe the sweetness of the cake would rub off on her. When Mrs. Forthright finally walked out the door, Jenni couldn't help but feel tense and a bit inadequate.

She glanced around at her beloved coffee shop. The few random customers were taken care of for the moment, and the book club members were engaged in an animated discussion, so she sat down at the counter to dial Kevin Crane's number. After the forth ring, his answering machine picked up and she left another brief but frantic message. Not only did her business rely on the espresso machine, repairs were expensive and could drive her out of business practically overnight. A new espresso machine was out of the question.

It wasn't until late afternoon when he called her back. "Jenni, I called Raymond at Crystal Coast Repairs. We just sell the equipment, but Raymond is your man." Kevin gave her Raymond's phone number and offered an apology.

While she appreciated Kevin's help, he hadn't taken much responsibility for the used machine he'd sold her. Next time, when she opened a chain of coffee shops, she'd buy a second machine as a backup plan. It was cheaper to buy one machine with two different heads, but if something broke, the entire machine shut down. If she had two machines, she wouldn't be in this predicament.

Depending on the cost of the repair, she might have to use the last of what remained of her financial cushion. She wished she hadn't decided to hire Gran, whose first day of work at the coffee shop started tomorrow. She hoped her dad was right about an employee paying for itself. At some point Jenni would have to tell him whom she hired. She'd managed to hold off until this point.

The next call she made was to Raymond, who turned out to be the owner of the repair shop. He promised to drop by Coffee Break within the hour. She chose to take Raymond's open schedule as good luck instead of reading his availability as a sign that nobody wanted to use his company.

After several customers opted to walk out of her coffee shop without a drink in hand, Jenni was relieved when Raymond strolled in exactly on the hour. He was a clean-cut, older man, and his overalls showed no sign of oil or dirt. "Howdy, ma'am. I'm here to look at your machine."

"Right this way." Jenni led him behind the counter to the silent machine. She prayed he'd fix it soon. She'd lost enough money from customers who'd had their minds set on a favorite espresso drink and refused to try something else.

While Raymond studied the piece of equipment, a woman walked in and handed Jenni a coupon for a free drink.

"If you don't mind me asking," Jenni said, "where did you get this?"

"From the photography studio down the street. I bought one of the fabulous photographs and the woman, Claire, I think her name is, gave me the coupon."

Claire was sending Jenni business; they had briefly discussed the idea of the coupons. Undoubtedly her friend would reimburse her for the free drink. Trying to help, she must have created the coupon on her own. What a good friend.

"Her photography is stunning," the woman said. "I bought a picture of one of the wild horses, a stallion I think. Very majestic."

Jenni perked up. "Brown, with a black mane and tail?"

"Yes. He's looking out to sea, as if he owns it."

"That would be Magic, my idol," Jenni said. He led his harem through hurricanes, droughts, windstorms, and he never gave up because of disaster. He persevered, just as Jenni would. She glanced at Raymond, who chewed on his bottom lip, as though unhappy about whatever was wrong with the machine.

"What kind of drink can I get you?" Jenni asked the woman, hoping she didn't want espresso. She took the coupon and secretly thanked Claire for trying to help.

"A mocha sounds good."

Raymond groaned and looked up. "It's going to take at least thirty days to get this machine up and running. I need to order a part."

Thirty days! Her business wouldn't survive that long without the espresso machine.

"I'm sorry, my espresso machine decided to quit on me," Jenni said to the woman, trying to inject some good humor in the situation even though she felt like curling up into a ball and hiding. "Can I get you something else?"

The woman studied the menu again. "A smoothie will be fine, strawberry please."

The rest of the day blurred together as customers came and went. News about the desserts travelled fast in Big Cat and people showed up to sample the goods. Unfortunately, news about the espresso machine also made its way around town. Business wasn't looking good.

***

No sooner had Scott walked into the bank, after returning from his father's drinking debacle, than the staff bombarded him with questions. When he strode past Cassie's desk, she handed him a stack of pink phone messages. "Mr. Stallings called you three times while you were out. I promised him you'd call back as soon as you returned."

"Thanks." Scott thumbed through the messages and walked into his office. What did Jenni's father want? He pulled out his chair and reached for the phone.

"Mr. Stallings, Scott here. How can I help you?"

"I'm glad you called back." Richard let out a succession of coughs before he continued to talk. "I wanted to find out about guaranteeing my daughter's loan."

"Have you discussed this with her?" Scott leaned back in his chair. He guessed that Jenni would resist her father's good intentions no matter how desperate she became, broken espresso machine or not. She was the type of person that valued independence. She'd also be concerned about her father's finances. After all, he sold Stallings to pay for his medical bills.

"Not exactly. Money is a difficult topic to discuss with her. Can you accept her loan without her knowing why?" Richard's voice faltered.

"Mr. Stallings, I have the utmost respect for you, sir. But please don't ask me to do that." Scott drummed his fingers on his polished desk.

"I wouldn't under normal circumstances, but there is nothing normal about dying. She won't accept my fate or my help. I need to know she is taken care of before I … can move on."

Scott grew silent, still drumming his fingers. Today started out rough when he got the call about his drunk father, and now the day was rapidly growing worse.

"Can you stop by my house so we can discuss this further?"

Scott glanced at the antique clock hanging on the wall. "Sure, I can do that." He had a mountain of work to do but could justify seeing Mr. Stallings. With the pending layoffs, involving people Scott cared about, and the daily calls from his boss in Raleigh, the tension was increasing. He had less than three months here. Once he returned to Raleigh, his job would be more secure. The saying "out of sight, out of mind" popped into his head. He wasn't quite out of his boss's mind, but he was certainly out of sight. He couldn't wait to return to the city.

Scott closed down his program, then grabbed his suit jacket. Old habits were hard to break, even if no one else in the small town wore a suit. He didn't belong, which he almost considered a good thing.

Cassie glared at him on his way out. "Do not, I repeat, do not leave this office wearing that coat," she said. "It's bad enough you wear a tie. Like I said before, you've changed. You're stuffy now."

"Thanks a lot. I didn't realize I had to check with you first about my wardrobe." He put her in place, or so he thought, until she huffed. Some battles weren't worth the argument. While he could fire her, he expected Layne would be upset if he started letting her employees go. Refusing to cave in to Cassie's demands, he folded the jacket neatly over his arm, as though that had been his original plan. He strode out the door.

Scott longed to see Mr. Stallings, who'd mentored him one summer while working at his restaurant. Jenni's father had played an important role when deciding what college to attend and what degree to earn. Scott idolized the vibrant man. But when he entered Mr. Stallings' makeshift bedroom, he had to squelch a gasp. A thin layer of fuzz sprouted from his mentor's head and he looked so vulnerable it made Scott's heart literally ache.

Mr. Stallings pointed to a worn chair in the corner of the room. Scott pulled it out and sat cattycorner to his bed.

"You know, Scott, I've always liked you." Mr. Stallings paused and appeared to be listening to see if Mrs. Stallings was eavesdropping nearby. Apparently satisfied that she wasn't, he continued the discussion. "There's something I want to ask you."

Scott scooted the worn chair closer to the bed and waited patiently for Mr. Stallings to state what was on his mind. The older man pushed a button on the remote to turn off the television. The conversation must be serious.

In a hushed tone, the older man said, "I'm concerned about Jenni. I want to make sure she's okay when I'm gone." He let out a few rapid coughs, and Scott noticed how his arm shook slightly when he covered his mouth.

"Jenni's strong. She'll be fine." Scott wanted to reassure him, but then again he wanted to avoid becoming too involved in the Stallings' family dynamics. He had enough drama of his own. Until recently, he'd preferred his strategy of avoiding his issues, and even though he needed to make amends with the past, that didn't make the task easier.

"I don't know if Jenni's coffee shop will make it," Mr. Stallings said, the distress on his face bothersome. "How am I supposed to die when she's not financially set?"

The man's concern made sense. He was holding on until he knew his daughter's future was more solid. Scott wished he could help. Actually, maybe he could. He had plenty money saved and could easily give her a personal loan to cover a new espresso machine, but if he knew Jenni as well as he thought, she'd refuse his assistance. An idea popped into his mind.

"She has no man in her life," Mr. Stallings continued. "I saw the way the two of you looked at each other in high school. Marry her. Please."

Scott tried to hide his shock. "Sir, I can't do that." He wasn't about to delve into the many reasons why he couldn't marry Jenni, or any woman right now. *Ever*. "As far as her coffee shop is concerned," Scott explained, "she's good with numbers and money. It's an unfortunate shame that her espresso machine broke."

"She didn't tell me." Mr. Stallings closed his eyes a second too long. "Let me help her."

"Jenni needs a personal guarantee by someone who has collateral. It's a way for the bank to collect the money if she defaults." Jenni would be miffed if she heard their conversation right now.

"Can my wife and I do that for her?" He coughed several more times and wiped his nose with a tattered white handkerchief.

"Yes, sir. But she wants to make it on her own."

Mr. Stallings shook his head in exasperation. "Explain that to me? Is that another way to say she's stubborn?"

"It means she wants to be independent, to know she can be successful without her parents' help," Scott explained. "Instead of stubborn, I'd describe her as determined." Not to mention she'd most likely refuse the offer out of concern for her father's welfare, and her mother's if she became a widow.

"Determined? Hmm."

Then Scott remembered his promise to Jenni, to encourage her father out of the house. "You know, I've been thinking. I bet Dan could use your expertise down at the Shrimp Shack. Even though he's changed the restaurant quite a bit, some things remain the same. For instance, your kitchen was known for its organization. Maybe you could offer some tips about how to better arrange the place." Scott hadn't run his idea by Dan yet, but he was sure his generous brother would agree to help Mr. Stallings. It seemed Jenni's father needed to feel important again.

Scott saw a twinkle in the man's eyes. Not only was he doing this for Mr. Stallings, but for Jenni too. She thought it was imperative he see the outside world again.

"How would I get there?"

"I'll drive. When you're ready to come home, no problem."

Mr. Stallings smiled and looked a few years younger in a matter of seconds. "I heard you own a fancy BMW." When Scott nodded, Mr. Stallings said, "Do I get to ride in that?"

"Yes, sir."

Then he shook his mostly bald head and his eyes took on a faraway look. "I can't. I haven't been out of this house in a long while, except to go to the doctor."

Exactly the problem.

"I understand. No pressure." If Mr. Stallings declined the invitation, Scott would have to challenge his creative mind and come up with something else. As he told Jenni before, it wasn't their place to convince Mr. Stallings to live, but she was right about one thing. It would do her father good to leave the house, even for a short period. The makeshift bedroom in which he spent most of his time was downright depressing.

"I do have one wish before I die."

"What's that?"

"I want to go fishing. It won't be easy, but I want to catch one more king mackerel before I retire my rods." Mr. Stallings' eyes glistened.

Was he afraid to die? Scott shoved the disturbing thought aside. Jenni's family issues weren't his business. He fought to keep a safe distance from the emotional pain.

But Scott cared, too much in fact.

He usually worked on the weekends, especially with the added stress of layoffs, but getting Mr. Stallings out of the house seemed more urgent.

He'd see to it that the man went fishing, at least once more. Besides, Scott hadn't fished since he was a kid. He could take Mr. Stallings across the causeway to a little spot on Tuckers Island where he used to fish at the pier with his brother. He might be able to borrow Dan's truck, with the handy rod and cooler holder mounted on the front. That way he wouldn't have to load fishing gear into his tight BMW. But he promised to take Mr. Stallings in his car.

"Why don't we go Saturday morning?"

Richard perked up. "Really? I'll get to ride in that flashy car of yours?"

Scott preferred to drive a truck again, but he hid his disappointment. "Sure, we can take my car."

"I don't know if this is a good idea," Mr. Stallings said, clearly concerned about what he'd agreed to. "What if I can't handle it?"

"You'll be fine. I'll make sure of it."

"What time on Saturday?" Mr. Stallings asked, smiling again. "We used to get up no later than four, but I don't think I can handle that now."

"Four? You must have been a serious fisherman." Scott considered himself an early riser, but not that early. "I usually started fishing around nine."

"You missed all the good ones. They bite early." Mr. Stallings exuberance was a drastic change from earlier. "But under the circumstances, I could be ready to go by eight." Mr. Stallings' tired voice carried a jubilant undertone.

"Eight, then. I'll come up to the house to get you."

"Yeah, I might need a little help." Mr. Stallings reached out to pat his walker, which was on the opposite side of the bed than Scott. "Guess I'll have to bring my aluminum buddy."

Scott's heart ached. He hated seeing the older man beaten down by cancer.

"Let's get back to discussing my daughter's finances. When can I sign the papers?"

Footsteps sounded on the hardwood floor in the hallway.

Scott glanced at his watch, shocked at how late it had gotten. Was Jenni home already? Bottom line, he didn't want her to overhear their private conversation. He was certain she wouldn't appreciate them discussing her finances, was certain Mr. Stallings shouldn't sign any such paperwork. "Who do you think will win the ballgame this weekend?" Scott attempted to change the subject as smoothly as the Stallings seemed to do, but he wasn't as skilled.

"My bet is on Carolina, of course," Mr. Stallings said. "They're the best basketball team."

Scott restrained a knowing smile. Avid Carolina fans would despise their kid attending Duke for college, and that's exactly where Jenni had gone. "That's a matter of opinion," Scott said as Jenni entered the room.

Her eyes narrowed when she saw him. "What are you doing here?" she asked.

"Thanks for an enjoyable discussion, Scott," Mr. Stallings interjected. "Anytime you want to keep a dying man company, please stop by."

"Dad, you aren't going to die."

His heavy-lidded blue eyes studied his daughter. "I am, sweetie. You need to accept that reality."

CHAPTER EIGHT

Scott showed up at the Shrimp Shack right before Dan left for the day. He'd miss running with Jenni as planned, but asking his brother for help was more important. This was his chance to absolve some of his guilt, to make an attempt to compensate for his part in Brittany's death. Nothing could change the outcome, which was caused by his stupidity, but he had a chance to help Jenni when she needed assistance. He'd see to it personally that she didn't lose her beloved coffee shop, but first he had to get his brother to agree to his scheme.

Dan pointed at a small table for two crammed against a wall in the bar area. "I'll join you in a minute. Have a drink if you want."

Scott flicked his hand to say, "Will do," and made his way toward the designated table with no intentions of having a drink. The mention of alcohol revived the recent memory of his father's disturbing escapade. Thank goodness his mother hadn't been home when he'd left his drunken father in the hands of their housekeeper. He didn't want to be around for that argument.

Dan pulled out a chair and joined him. "Thanks for helping with Dad. His drinking is getting out of control."

Scott nodded, leaning back against his chair. "I drove him to the graveyard to remind him of what drinking can do. It seemed to shake him."

Dan frowned and shook his head. "I wouldn't count on it. It's doubtful he'll remember."

Scott shrugged. Maybe his brother was wrong.

"I'm having a dinner party on Saturday night to celebrate the Shrimp Shack's fifth anniversary. Interested in coming?"

Slowly they were reestablishing their relationship, although they had yet to address the underlying issues. Maybe they didn't need to.

"Feel free to bring someone," Dan continued.

Whom would he invite? He hadn't kept in contact with anybody since he'd left town. Jenni popped in his mind but he quickly dismissed the thought. Inviting her seemed too much like a date. Then he thought about Cassie but didn't want to give her the wrong impression. Maybe he should go alone.

"Invite Jenni," Dan suggested.

"Wouldn't that be awkward as heck? Brothers don't date ex-girlfriends." There it was, one of the issues between them.

Dan scowled. "I'm happily married, bro. I'd love to see you with her."

How could that be? Scott remembered numerous emails from Dan during college, stating how he planned to marry Jenni someday, how they were a perfect fit. There were boundaries a loyal brother didn't cross.

"I'd like you to come," Dan said.

If Scott wanted to begin restoring their bond, he needed to go to the dinner party. "Count me in, but I'll probably come alone."

"Suit yourself, but if you change your mind, feel free to bring her along."

It wasn't like Dan to push so hard. "Listen," Scott said, "I need a favor." Not that Scott deserved any favors but his intentions were in the right place. "You can't tell anyone, except Rachel, of course. Jenni can't find out."

***

Jenni expected Dan to walk into Coffee Break any minute. Her nerves tensed, and the old memories of dating Scott's emotionally safe brother brought her right back to high school.

Gran had just finished with a customer who placed a large order of donuts for a meeting tomorrow when Dan walked through the door. He resembled Scott in so many ways, but Scott radiated a charismatic flair she couldn't explain. It was that magnetism she found difficult to resist.

Jenni pointed to a nearby table. "Go ahead and have a seat. What would you like to drink?" She'd ask Gran to pour it. Her training was going well, especially since she didn't have to make espresso drinks yet.

"A decaf coffee sounds great," he said as he walked past the counter, waving at Gran. He set a binder and a brown bag on the table, then slid into the booth.

"Got it," Gran said, overhearing the conversation. She poured the coffee while Jenni joined him. A moment later, Gran set a steaming mug on the table along with cream and sugar, then hurried behind the counter to wait on another customer.

He dumped sugar into his mug and pushed it aside. "I hear your espresso machine is broken."

News traveled way too fast in Big Cat. "Unfortunately, you heard right. I'm looking at it being down for at least a month."

He handed her the paper bag. "Maybe this will cheer you up. It's a sample of one of our easy-to-serve sandwiches. It's a whole-wheat bagel with an egg white, two pieces of turkey bacon, and a thin slice of low-calorie cheddar cheese."

She opened the bag to peek at her late afternoon snack. The delicious smell of turkey bacon wafted from the bag, causing her stomach to growl. "Thanks, Dan." She'd have to split the snack with Gran, but if the sandwich tasted as good as the aroma promised, then sharing was worth it. "That will be perfect for my customers who need a light, healthy breakfast on the way to work.

In order to comply with state law, though, I need the sandwiches sealed in plastic with an ingredient list labeled on the package. Can you do that for me?"

"Absolutely. Just place your orders ahead of time."

Perfect. "What other sandwiches do you offer?" They wouldn't completely compensate for the lack of espresso sales, but every bit helped.

He went over the different choices of meats, cheeses, and breads. What a delight to order such a wide variety. When he finished, he tipped his mug back and drained it, then pushed it aside. "By the way, I have a proposition for you."

"Oh?"

"Rachel and I would like to extend you a personal loan to buy a used espresso machine."

She widened her eyes and gasped at his generous offer. Never did she expect her ex-boyfriend and his wife, her old college roommate, to help her financially. "I don't know what to say, other than thanks." She couldn't take the money, even though she needed it. Her predicament wasn't her friends' problem to solve.

"Then say 'yes.'"

She met his gaze directly, resisting the urge to turn away. What kind of person let her friends bail her out? "I appreciate the offer, but I can't accept. It's never a good idea to borrow money from friends." The idea had to be Rachel's. She was always helping others.

"I thought you'd decline, so I drew up a contract to make it more official. You can pay it back monthly over two years, so you can afford the payments. But I also factored interest in so you wouldn't feel indebted to us personally."

Tempting, but she'd never put her friends in such an awkward position. Sure, she'd find a way to pay them back, even if her business failed, but she didn't want to strain her valuable friendship with Rachel.

"Please think about it. Thirty days is a long time to wait for your machine to be fixed. People want espresso drinks. If they don't get them from you, they'll go to the coffee shop two towns over. It's not that far away."

He made a good point, one she'd thought about before, but if she accepted his offer she'd feel like a failure. "I appreciate your generosity but I can't take the money. Thanks, though." She gave him a quick hug. His physique reminded her of his brother's, except Scott exuded an untamed, masculine quality that she never felt with Dan.

As soon as he left, Gran turned on her. "Why did you turn down his offer?"

She felt backed into a corner but owed her grandmother an explanation. "I know of an acquaintance in college who'd done just that, borrowed from friends to support his business endeavor. The business failed and, because he was without a job, it took too long for him to pay back the debt. He eventually paid it off, but in the meantime he lost two of his best friends. It would tear me apart to lose Rachel. And since Dan is Scott's brother, that adds another layer to a potentially bad situation. I appreciate my friends trying to help me, but I'm on my own."

"I disagree," Gran said. "You need to learn how to let people help you. You aren't in this big world alone, left to fend for yourself."

Jenni tried to push aside the sensitive nerve Gran had pinched. "You rarely allow people to help you, either. You value your independence as much as I do."

"That might be true, but I don't push away help when I need it." Gran started to wipe the counter even though it was pristine. "You inherited that trait from your father."

Jenni gasped. She was nothing like her father, was she?

The door opened and in walked Claire. Today was one of those days the coffee shop felt like a soap opera.

Claire had scooped her straight black hair into a youthful ponytail, and she had a noticeable spring to her step in spite of her pallid face. In her arms she carried a rather large framed photo. "I brought the pictures you said I could sell in here on consignment. The rest are in my car."

The small percentage Jenni would make selling the photographs would help bring in more money. "Great. I have a hand truck in the back room. I can't wait to see the pictures."

"They're of the wild horses." She set the frame on the floor and leaned it against the wall, then disappeared into the backroom. Within a minute she returned with the dolly. "My favorite picture is of Dante nursing in the marsh pond. I brought a copy to sell here."

"I love that one too," Jenni said. "I can understand why it's popular. By the way, do you know the name of the brown stallion that hangs around a couple miles north of the ferry dock?"

"That's probably Magic. They have designated territories, and that's his farthest point. He's a beauty, isn't he?" She turned the framed picture around. "Is this him?"

Jenni's breath caught. "Yes! Look at the way he stands, the way he naturally commands leadership. It might sound crazy but I think of him as my non-human mentor. He represents freedom and success. He has … presence." The stallion stood on a dune, his neck arched with pride.

"That's not crazy; I understand why you chose him. He's the highest ranked stallion on the island."

Magic not only survived in the roughest conditions, he thrived, just as she planned to do with her failing business. "I'd like to buy this picture. I'll put it in my bedroom at my mom's house. It'll give me a fresh perspective when I wake up and a gentle reminder before I sleep at night. It also has the added benefit of updating my childhood room from pink walls and white lace to business owner and entrepreneur."

Claire set it against the wall, the photograph facing outward. "Great idea. I'll give you a ten percent discount. Sorry I can't do more."

Jenni asked about the cost and inwardly flinched, but wrote a check anyway. To her, the picture was worth the expensive price.

Gran always said, "Surround yourself with things that make you feel happy, and joy will be inevitable."

"Thanks," Jenni said. "Can I get you a drink?"

"The usual sounds perfect." Claire's voice seemed to dance even more than normal. She placed her credit card on the counter. "While you make my tea, I'll bring in the rest of the photos." She turned and pushed the dolly out the door.

Jenni glanced at the picture once more, completely in awe, then made her friend a decaf green tea and set it on the counter. When Claire bounced back into the shop, pushing the dolly loaded with framed photographs, Jenni couldn't help but notice her cheerful step.

"You look vibrant today," Jenni said. "What's up?"

"I found out some great news." Never one to ramble, Claire bluntly said, "I'm pregnant!" A smile spread across her petite face.

Jenni scooted around the counter and pulled her friend into a tight hug. "Congratulations. I had a hunch you'd get pregnant before the end of the year. Is Jeff excited?"

"Ecstatic. He can't wait to be a father." Then a look of concern flashed across her face.

"Is something wrong?"

She shrugged her shoulders. "Not really. It's kind of silly but I had a bad dream that something happened to the baby."

Jenni inhaled sharply. Between Claire's mom dying of ovarian cancer, and all Claire went through trying to find her long-lost father, she'd experienced enough pain. Jenni hoped the dream was wrong. "Imagine a healthy newborn in your hands. The baby will be fine."

"I hope so." Claire didn't look convinced.

After she left, the last hour dragged by with hardly a customer. Gran wasn't working extended hours yet while she was in training, so shortly after her grandmother left for the day, Jenni turned the closed sign around in the window. She quickly changed into her running clothes and headed down the street. Halfway through her run she turned the corner and noticed a BMW waiting at the curb in front of her coffee shop. As she neared the car, Scott climbed out, dressed in running gear.

"What are you doing here?" she asked.

"Thanks to you, I'm in the habit of running. I can't run as far as you yet, so I decided to work longer and join you near the end of your run. Soon, though, I'll be in shape enough to run the entire route with you."

She didn't say anything as he fell into step next to her. She had to admit, on some level she enjoyed his company. Her mind screamed for her to be careful, however, to stay away from him.

After awhile he asked, "How did the meeting go with Dan?"

"He has an amazing selection of sandwiches. Unfortunately, even if the sandwiches take off, total sales will still be down with the espresso machine broken." They turned the corner and passed the arched entryway to the graveyard. Overgrown trees covered the crumbling wall surrounding the cemetery and the unmistakable ambiance filled her soul with pride. She loved this small town. Somehow Jenni needed to find a way to make her coffee shop successful, so she could make a living here. She never wanted to leave.

"Speaking of Dan, he invited me to his house for dinner Saturday night to celebrate the Shrimp Shack's fifth anniversary. Would you be interested in going with me?"

She must have looked confused because he explained the question.

"He said to bring someone."

Was he asking her out on a date? The thought of Brittany flashed in her mind, the anger fresh again. How was she supposed to stop seeing images of her sister whenever she was around him?

She opened her mouth to speak but no sound escaped.

"That's the morning I'm taking your father fishing," he reminded her.

His kindness toward her father meant a lot, but what about Brittany? Scott had played a significant part in her death.

"Why aren't you taking Cassie?" She almost preferred he ask his ex-girlfriend, his employee, otherwise the invitation felt too personal.

"Why ask her?"

"I don't know. I figured she'd convince you to take her." With her manipulative way, Jenni wanted to add. If Cassie heard about the party, she'd find a way to attend.

"Is that jealousy I detect?"

"Absolutely not." She made a point to roll her eyes dramatically. "I can't have a romantic interest in my banker. That's almost as wrong as dating an employee." She tried to soften the barb with a smile, but to her dismay he didn't seem to notice the insult to begin with. Leftover bitterness was ugly. Once again, Gran's wise words popped into her mind. "Forgive him, Jenni. Don't you think it's about time?" She was right, but anger was an old friend.

"I'm not really your banker, at least not for long." His breathing sounded steady even though they talked while they ran. "I'll be leaving in less than three months."

She raised her eyebrows at him, warning bells clanging loudly. He'd leave just as everyone else in her life did. Her mind screamed for her to be smart and not get involved with him. He planned to return to Raleigh; she intended to stay here. No future between them.

Jenni managed to put off making a decision until they rounded the last turn and reached his car. "Want a ride home," he asked.

"Sure." A simple ride home was safe, or so she thought.

When he opened the car door for her, a thought danced through her mind. If she accepted his dinner invitation as a networking opportunity, the idea would be easier to absorb than if she considered it a date. If she wanted to associate with other proprietors in the area, Dan's party was a good place to start.

"About Saturday night," she said after he climbed in the car. "I'll go with you."

The moment his car jolted to a stop in front of her house, she launched from it, wanting to escape the fact she'd just accepted a so-called date. To her surprise he followed her. At the top of the first flight of steps, she detoured to the front porch for privacy, instead of heading to the back door where her mother would be in the kitchen making dinner.

"I'll see you tomorrow," he said, leaning closer. He wrapped his arm around her waist and she swore she stopped breathing.

"Thanks for the company tonight." Her voice sounded no louder than a whisper.

He bent down, his lips just a breath away from hers.

Instead of kissing her full on the mouth, he tilted his head and brushed the side of her cheek with a warm, wet kiss. Tempting as it was to turn her head toward him, she couldn't move.

"Goodbye," he mumbled. He ran a finger slowly down the outside of her arm. Even though it was sultry outside despite being September, a chill made her tremble. Just like that, he was gone, his car purring to life. Enjoying the afterglow, she opened the creaky front door, only to face her father's curious stare.

CHAPTER NINE

Jenni's face grew warm. "Hey, Dad. I'm glad to see you in the living room." It surprised her to see him camped out on the couch instead of withdrawn in his gloomy den. She couldn't help but wonder if he'd seen the almost kiss through the large picture window, covered only by translucent sheers.

He squelched a knowing smile. "Surprise."

"You're home early, sweetheart," her mother interjected as she rushed into the living room, wiping her hands on the tattered apron she always wore. "Why did you come in the front door?"

Jenni's plan had been to avoid her mother's eagle eye, but much to her chagrin, her father had spotted her anyway. "It was a change of pace, Mom."

Jenni's father winked at her.

She flashed him a devious grin. "How did you get Dad to agree to the living room?"

Her father coughed. "Your mother threatened to make her dreaded sauerkraut and Polish sausage for dinner if I didn't leave my bed."

Her mom, now standing by the couch, squeezed his shoulder. "That's the only threat that seems to get you up and moving around. The physical therapist said that mobility will help keep you strong. I want you to live a long happy life."

He shook his head. "My time here is almost finished. Why can't people understand that?"

Someday he'd be gone from Jenni's life. A pang in her chest drove home that sad fact. "If you give up, Dad, it's all over." Jenni perched on the arm of her father's favorite recliner. "Why aren't you fighting harder?"

Her mother scurried from the room, as if she couldn't bear to hear the truth. Her reaction bothered Jenni.

"I am fighting," he said. "Otherwise I'd be gone by now." He pulled a two-tone blue afghan her mother had crocheted up to his shoulders. With a shaky finger, he pointed from underneath the blanket at a bookshelf that contained a wooden stable his deceased father had made for him. "I want to give that to you."

Jenni's breath caught. Grandpop's stable meant so much to him. "That's generous, but don't give your stuff away. Fight harder."

"Your model horses would fit perfectly in the stalls."

She swallowed hard. If it made him happy, she'd accept the precious gift, but she didn't want to think about what his gesture meant. "I'll treasure it always." He tried to hide his frown underneath the blanket. He wasn't ready to part with the stable yet. "I have an idea," she said. "Why don't we put it in your room for now? You can look at it when you need to feel better."

He nodded. "Tell me about the coffee shop. How do the numbers look?"

Conversations with him always turned to the uncomfortable topic of the coffee shop's financial situation. "The desserts are taking off, and I've ordered a selection of sandwiches to help sales."

Something in her demeanor must have given away her concern. "But it's not enough." He formed the question into a statement.

She shook her head. “No. I need to do something more.” Much more. "My espresso machine broke."

“I’ll give you the money. When your restaurant is more profitable, you can pay your mom back.”

She let the restaurant reference slide because the idea of paying back only her mom bothered her more. He’d live; the doctor felt certain he’d removed all the cancer. "I appreciate your offer but you have medical bills to pay." Otherwise, he wouldn't have sold his precious Stallings, the restaurant he'd promised her. “You taught me to be successful in everything I do. That includes my coffee shop.”

“I didn’t teach you to ignore common sense, but suit yourself.” His voice sounded gruff. She tried not to be wounded by his harsh words but failed.

“Like I said before, a business can’t operate successfully with one person. It’ll drive you into the ground. Get your espresso machine fixed, then expand your hours. With the changes you're making, it's only a matter of time before your employee starts to pay for herself.”

“I’m glad you brought up the subject.” She braced herself for his wrath. “I hired Gran.”

“You did what?”

“Hired Gran.”

“She’s almost seventy. What were you thinking?”

Jenni set her jaw. “That she’s semi-retired and responsible, the kind of person you suggested I hire. You were right, I can’t work seven days a week.” If the espresso machine wasn’t fixed faster than thirty days, Jenni wouldn't be working at all.

When he remained silent, she continued to defend her position. “I need someone for the afternoons if I’m going to increase the hours the coffee shop stays open. It’s a start.” When would she stop seeking his approval?

"I said to fix the espresso machine first, before you increase your hours."

She had to fight back tears from his obvious rejection. She never did anything right. "I hired her first, before the machine broke. But she agreed to train for free, so she's not costing me anything right now."

"There you go. How long will your machine be down?"

"Thirty days." Before he jumped on her for the long delay in getting the new part, she decided to ask for his advice, something she never did. "Dad, what can I do in the meantime? I need my espresso machine, or a way to get the replacement part faster."

He rubbed his fuzzy head, a habit he'd developed long before he'd lost his hair. It helped him think.

"Find an auction and buy another used espresso machine," he suggested. "That way you'll have a backup plan in case this ever happens again. A coffee shop can't be without its main piece of equipment."

He was right, but how was she suppose to buy another used machine? She wasn't about to broach the subject of money again with him, but he did have a point. Maybe she should reconsider Dan's offer.

***

"What do you mean she turned down the personal loan?" Scott asked his brother over dinner at the Shrimp Shack. "She needs the money to save her business."

"She politely said 'No.'"

"Can Rachel talk some sense in her?"

"Maybe, but I haven't told Rachel yet." Dan pushed his empty plate away. "I figured why mention the loan unless Jenni accepted."

"Man, you need to be honest with Rachel. If she finds out you withheld that information, she's going to be miffed." If he caused a problem between Dan and Rachel, he'd never forgive himself.

"And *Jenni* won't be mad?" Dan asked. "You're deliberately hiding the fact that the money is coming from you." Dan took a gulp of water, and then another. "Besides, Rachel's likely to tell her it's from you."

Scott jabbed the last ocean-caught oyster on his plate with a fork. He pointed it at Dan. "Don't keep secrets in your marriage, especially on my behalf." He stuffed the oyster in his mouth and chewed. "I don't want to be responsible for your divorce."

"Not everyone gets a divorce. I'm sorry that happened to you, bro."

Rachel walked up and slid her arm around Dan. "What you are two discussing with such intensity?"

Neither man answered.

Plan B was already formulating in Scott's mind. When Scott returned home, he made the most important phone call he'd made in a long while.

***

Between the stress of layoffs and the numerous phone calls this past week with his boss, Scott needed to get away from the office. He finally agreed to an early lunch with Cassie, rationalizing that if the vice president was operating on all cylinders, his team would hum more efficiently.

Twenty minutes later they walked through the front door of his brother's restaurant. Immediately he noticed a dash of red hair from the corner of his eye. Sure enough, Jenni turned around and stared at him and Cassie. She frowned and returned to sipping her soup, clearly dismissing him.

When Marge suggested they follow her, he shook his head. "I'll catch up with you in a minute," he said to Cassie. He headed toward Jenni's table and felt Cassie's glare attempting to burn a hole into the back of his pressed shirt.

"Hi there," he said. When Jenni's answer was barely audible, he tried again. "Would you care to join us?"

She looked up. "No thanks. I'm sure you and Cassie have important issues to discuss."

"No. We're just taking a break." By the look on her face, he guessed he'd said the wrong thing.

"I'd hate to interrupt ... business."

That felt like a slam. "I'd enjoy your company, but if you'd rather be alone, then I'll leave you to enjoy your lunch."

To his surprise, she pointed to the empty seats at her table. "Why don't you sit here, since I'm already settled?"

He waved to Cassie before she sat at a corner table for two. Had Cassie asked for the cozy spot? He sincerely hoped not.

Hesitantly, Cassie released her grasp from the back of a chair. Her frown, lasting only a fraction of a second, didn't go unnoticed. He wondered if her response had to do with wanting to avoid making conversation with Jenni, or wanting to dine with him alone. Either way, her attitude was becoming a problem.

***

Jenni watched as the woman reluctantly closed the distance between them. When Cassie reached the table, Scott slid out the chair opposite Jenni and helped Cassie maneuver it. What a gentleman. Jenni didn't recall his manners being so refined during high school, but then again, a lot could change over a decade.

"Are you planning to run tonight?" Scott asked Jenni, clearly oblivious about the personal competition between the two women.

Jenni nodded. "Of course. Nothing could keep me from training, except maybe a disaster."

"That would be a shame," Cassie said innocently enough, picking up a glass of water. Jenni knew exactly what she'd meant.

A new server named Alex interrupted their discussion to ask for Scott and Cassie's order. She'd taken Jenni's order previously. When Alex had finished and headed off to the kitchen, Cassie scoffed at the girl. "I can't imagine having black spiked hair with pink highlights. Hideous."

"I like her creativity," Jenni said, irritated by Cassie's snobbery.

Cassie rolled her eyes. “Are you entering the marathon, Scott?” Her eyes glossed over when she looked at him.

He cleared his throat, apparently uncomfortable with the direction the conversation had turned. “When is it again?”

“Between Thanksgiving and Christmas,” Jenni said, “before the cold weather hits.”

He chuckled. “You don’t know what cold weather is. I went to a business conference in Minnesota one time during the dead of winter. Now that’s cold. And I’ll never forget the year when Raleigh got hit with a foot of snow. Thankfully, that’s only happened once in ten years. You're lucky you rarely get snow here. We lost electricity for five days.”

We lost electricity? He must be referring to his ex-wife, and the thought, wrong as it was, bothered Jenni. She decided not to ask and instead allowed herself to fantasize about fresh snow and sledding. One day she’d make sure to experience the thrill, but the likelihood of taking a vacation in the near future seemed improbable.

The conversation paused until Cassie narrowed her eyes at Jenni. “Will you be ready to run the marathon?”

“Yes.” Barely, Jenni thought. She then realized Scott had conveniently changed the subject. Cassie had asked if he planned to enter the marathon and he hadn’t answered. Interesting.

A man approached with plates of food lined along his arm and a saucer and bowl in hand. He set the simple bowl of tomato soup by Cassie, placed the large club sandwich in front of Jenni, and positioned the plateful of seafood linguini with a white wine sauce next to Scott.

“Is that all your going to have?” Scott asked Cassie.

Cassie glanced at the meat on Jenni’s sandwich. “Some of us believe in watching what we eat.”

“And some of us are fit and believe in having protein in our diet,” Jenni countered in a pleasant voice. Two could play her annoying little game.

Fortunately, Dan walked up and offered a distraction. “It’s good to have the group together again.” He thumped Scott on the back, perhaps a little harder than he should have.

“The four of us together, just like old times.” Cassie set her spoon on the saucer holding her soup bowl. “We make a great foursome—you and Jenni, me and Scott.” She fluttered her eyelashes at Scott and poked her lip out in what she likely thought of as a sexy, pouty lip. One of Gran’s favorite comments popped into Jenni’s mind. She always encouraged kids to go ahead and stick their lower lip out, like a perch for a bird. If Cassie weren’t careful, a feathered friend just might leave a dropping.

Dan stared at Cassie. “Make that a fivesome. My wife Rachel is included.” He looked at Jenni curiously. “Well, we’re getting busy. Scott, I hope to see you for dinner Saturday night.”

Cassie sat straighter in her chair, her face practically bright enough to replace the lit candle on the table. If she didn't know about the party yet, she'd make it her mission to find out.

“I’ll be there.” Scott appeared to ignore Cassie’s behavior. Dan raised his hand and backed away. Once he left, Scott wiggled his eyebrows at Jenni.

She wasn’t about to discuss Saturday night in front of Cassie. No doubt, the woman would show up and try to claim him.

The first possible chance she got, Jenni excused herself from lunch and returned to the coffee shop. She had work to do.

Now, sitting at her favorite table, the one by the large window overlooking Front Street, she punched numbers into her laptop. The packaged sandwiches were already helping to offset some of the decline in sales, but the income wasn't enough. Even more desperate now, Dan's loan was sounding better by the moment.

“Jenni?” Gran interrupted. She led a burly man dressed in brown over to the table. “He needs your signature.”

She didn’t recall ordering anything. “What are you delivering?”

“An espresso machine.”

Jenni's mouth went dry. It was a solid minute before she could respond. “I don’t understand. Who sent it?”

He looked over the paperwork. “Dan Botticelli.”

Jenni gasped, and Gran yelped with joy. Why would Dan send her a machine after she'd declined his offer for money?

She needed to make a quick phone call before she signed off on the piece of equipment. Gran must have read her mind, because she scooted behind the counter and then met Jenni halfway with the phone. Four rings later, the call went into Dan's voice mail. Obviously he didn’t want to talk to her. She left a brief message and quickly hung up before he heard the vulnerability in her voice. Since she wasn't in a position to decline Dan's generosity, she signed her name.

“Thank you,” she said to the man.

Before he walked away, he said, “Ma’am? I have a note here that someone will install the machine tomorrow.”

“I appreciate it.” She didn’t know what else to say. She had to resist the temptation to send the espresso machine back, out of principle, but her dad's words flooded into her mind. *I didn't raise you to ignore common sense.* If she had to allow someone to help her, this seemed a good time to start.

When the man left, Gran shot her a quizzical look. "It's one thing for Dan to offer a personal loan,” Gran said, “but why is he sending this? Is Scott’s presence rekindling Dan's affection for you? Does Rachel know about the purchase?"

Good questions, ones Jenni didn't have answers to. "I know he loves his wife. I'm not sure why he's helping me."

Gran crossed her arms. "If he still has feelings for you, how are you going to handle that?"

Jenni hoped she didn't have to. "You're jumping to conclusions. I'm sure Rachel knows, and together they're trying to help a friend in need. That's all."

Gran looked doubtful. "I hope you're right. Why don't you call Rachel and ask?"

Jenni shook her head. "Not now. I want to give Dan a chance to call back first. If he doesn't, I'll ask Rachel at their party. Don't worry, Gran. He loves her, not me."

"I hope you're right, otherwise you're in a messy situation."

Her life seemed full of messy situations lately. She had to admit, though, that as the day slid by, the knot in her stomach eased. She had been worried about the espresso machine more than she cared to admit. Thank goodness for Dan's generosity, but something didn't add up. She couldn't figure out what his motivation was for helping her, and he hadn't said anything about the espresso machine earlier at lunch. Then again, they hadn't been alone.

She left Gran to cover the late afternoon shift and went for a run through the streets of downtown. Scott had started accompanying her for the entire run now, but today he wasn't waiting for her outside the coffee shop as he normally did. She rather missed his company. Each side street Jenni passed, she glanced down to see if Scott was passing by. When she finished her cool down and there was still no sign of him, she went home feeling unexpectedly testy.

She couldn't help but question if he'd show up tomorrow morning to take her father fishing. If he disappointed her dad, she'd never forgive him.

With her guard down, Jenni had allowed her mother to corner her in the kitchen. A glass of water waited on the counter and she'd slowed long enough to take a drink. Mistake.

"I heard you're running with Scott Botticelli," her mother said. "You know how I feel about him."

"Mom, your resentment surprises me. You are religious, yet you allow your anger toward him to tear you apart. I don't get it."

"He's dangerous," her mother said while she wringed her hands, a nervous habit Jenni remembered from as far back as the first grade, when Jenni had announced she wanted to sleep over at a friend's house. "Running with him isn't a wise choice. Nothing good can come from it."

Jenni refilled the glass with more filtered water from a container sitting on the counter next to the refrigerator. “We’re friends, Mom. Nothing more.” That’s what she tried to tell herself often, but lately the words didn’t ring as true as they once had.

"Dorothy?"

“Coming, dear.”

Jenni followed her mother into the living room and sat on the edge of the soft recliner. During their discussion in the kitchen, she never realized her father was sitting unsupported on the couch, without relying on the stack of pillows behind him. To her relief, he had a little more color to his face today.

"You're out of bed again,” Jenni said, “and from the sight of the Crock Pot, Mom didn’t make Polish sausage and sauerkraut. Good for you." Maybe he was getting better, despite his claims. She could only hope.

He looked up and flashed his wife an adoring smile that made her mother turn mushy eyed. "She threatened me with a beet sandwich and a side of pickled onions."

Jenni puckered her nose and chuckled. "Disgusting. That would do it." She was glad to see a trace of her father's old humor showing through. His strength didn’t last for long, though. He leaned back against the pillows and pulled the afghan over him.

“Well, look there,” her mother said, glancing out the window. “Scott Botticelli is jogging past our house. He doesn’t give up, does he?”

Jenni twisted in the chair to look out the window, more to keep her parents from seeing the excitement on her face than to ogle Scott. “Good, I’m glad he’s running. He needs to build his endurance.” Jenni hoped her voice sounded nonchalant, unlike her emotions.

Why hadn’t he exercised with her earlier? It was interesting how he had an entire town to run through, not counting the beaches of Pony Island, and he chose her street.

“What’s he increasing his endurance for?” her mom asked. “Is he going to compete in the marathon too?”

Jenni froze. First Cassie had asked that question, and now her mother. Oh, please don't force her to compete against him. Through the sheers hanging on the window, she watched him run past her house, never once bothering to look her way. What nerve.

By the third lap, when she saw him turn the far corner onto her street, she climbed from the chair to wait for him on the front porch. Why did he have to taunt her by running where she could see him? When he neared, she walked down the steps of the porch, so he couldn't miss her.

She tried not to stare at his muscled legs each time they sprang from the ground. No man should be that sexy, especially not him.

"Excuse me?" she called out when he didn't appear to notice her. He glanced up, then she saw a dingy brown dog following him from a distance. How odd. He didn't own a pet.

"Why do you keep running by here?" she asked, trying to disguise her high-pitched voice.

He broke to a walk. "This route makes sense. Routine." When he was directly in front of her house, he stopped.

She wasn't about to ask why he didn't show up earlier to run with her, although the question was driving her batty. "If you want routine, why don't you take the ferry to Pony Island?" They'd only run this stretch once before, that first day.

"It doesn't seem right to go over to the island without you."

She relaxed a bit. "Whose dog is that?" She pointed to the animal as it stood off in the distance. When she looked closer, she swore she saw the dog's ribs under his matted mess of a coat.

"I don't know. He's been following me the last two laps."

She' hadn't even noticed. "Do you think he's a stray?"

"Possibly. I planned to call his owner, but he doesn't have a collar." Scott turned and looked back at the waiting dog, which lifted his ears in response. "He's a friendly guy, but kind of shy."

"Are you going to keep him?" He'd mentioned before that he eventually wanted a dog. A pet would be good for him. It might help him think about something other than work.

"No way," he said.

She hesitated briefly. "My mom's making stew. Do you want to eat with us tonight?" Her mother wouldn't appreciate his company, especially since she'd just lectured Jenni about not getting involved with him. Perhaps out of a state of rebellion, Jenni wanted to invite him. Growing up, they spontaneously asked their friends to dinner often. Her mom always made enough food so they'd have leftovers the next two days for lunch, so quantity wasn't an issue.

The friendly smile on his face revealed his eagerness. "Sure. Let me finish another lap, and then I'll be all yours for the evening."

Her heart fluttered; her mind screamed, "Danger, stay away." Too late. He'd already accepted her invitation.

"Take your time," Jenni managed to say calmly. She waved goodbye and walked back into the house, feeling her father's knowing eyes on her.

CHAPTER TEN

Scott reached out to knock on Jenni's front door but stopped midair. The hammering in his chest concerned him. Maybe he'd pushed too hard running. It was possible his pounding heart had to do with seeing her father again, after the uncomfortable conversation about guaranteeing the loan without Jenni's knowledge. Somebody had to confess to her; she had a right to know. When Jenni answered the door, his pulse sped up even more, betraying the truth. This woman was the reason for his unnerving reaction.

Her face lit up at the sight of him, but despite her response, he sensed an undercurrent of apprehension. She seemed just as cautious about their growing attraction to each other as he did.

"I see your canine friend is still with you."

Scott glanced at the road. "Yeah. The more I think about it, the more I believe he's a stray."

"Poor guy. Do you want to put him on the back porch during dinner?" she asked.

"No. It's best if he finds someone else to follow."

Scott wasn't sure why, but he feared growing attached to the dog. His life was too unsettled to take in a pet. But in his experience, animals had a way of finding their new owners and adopting them, not the other way around, regardless of your current living situation.

"Well, I hope he finds a good home," she said. The look on her face suggested she didn't approve of his lackadaisical attitude to let the dog fend for himself. She shoved her hands in her jean pockets and stood there, watching the dog in silence.

"Is everything okay? If you'd rather I not eat dinner here, I understand."

She stared into his eyes for a long moment before she spoke. "No. Sorry. Please come in." She barely moved aside, and when he squeezed through the small opening in the door, he brushed against her. The touch sent a wave of excitement through him, but it was short lived. He soon understood her reluctance.

Mr. Stallings watched them carefully from the couch, propped against several pillows with an afghan pulled up to his chin. His face looked pale, his body fragile. From his current condition, Scott wondered if he'd be able to fish tomorrow.

"Mr. Stallings, sir."

"Scott." He pinched his lips together, possibly to avoid a smile, and pointed to a nearby chair.

Scott headed toward the antique piece of furniture. He had to fold his large body into the tiny seat made for a dainty woman at best. The confined quarters, including the compact living room, was anything but comfortable. The air smelled stale, like pending death, regardless of the delicious smells wafting from the homey kitchen.

"It's nice to see you out here on the couch, Mr. Stallings." The conversation sounded stilted even to his own ears, but what else was he supposed to say?

"Please, call me Richard. I prefer my bed, but I don't want sauerkraut and Polish sausage, or beet sandwiches for the next few meals."

Scott wrinkled his brow, trying to figure out what Richard meant.

“My mom threatened to make his least favorite meals for dinner if he didn’t spend a couple of hours on the couch,” Jenni explained, avoiding eye contact with either man.

Was she upset because he almost kissed her once? He actually understood why a relationship with him was a horrible idea; heck, he even agreed.

“Have you given any thought to our discussion?” Richard asked, his words shoving Scott against an invisible wall. Even though Jenni deserved to know the truth, Scott preferred the topic stay between father and daughter unless it progressed to the stage where it included him.

“What discussion?” Jenni asked, raising her eyebrows into an arch. She glanced at her father, then Scott. Neither man answered. “What am I missing?”

Scott glanced at Richard for help. When the man didn’t say anything, Scott realized he was on his own.

“Are you talking about the other day when I walked in on you two talking? I knew something was up.” She frowned.

Scott cleared his throat. “Your father offered to guarantee your loan.”

“What?” She glared at her father. “You did that without asking me? I appreciate your help, but I want to prove I can run a profitable business on my own, just like you did.”

Richard remained quiet.

“I can do it.” She crossed her arms into a tight knot.

Scott appreciated her determination. “Jenni, no one said you couldn’t be successful. He was trying to make it easier for you.”

“Men always stick together,” Jenni said.

Dorothy chose that moment to walk into the room. “Dinner’s ready.” She looked at Scott, obviously surprised to see him sitting in her living room. He got the distinct impression she resented his presence, but then she smiled. He needed to make things right with her too. He’d bet she still blamed him for Brittany’s death. Why wouldn’t she? He'd only seen Mrs. Stallings once since the funeral, and that was the other day when he'd stopped by to talk with

Richard. Respecting her feelings, he'd bow out of dinner and leave.

"I invited him to eat," Jenni said, setting her jaw in the stubborn Stallings way. "Sorry I didn't let you know earlier, but I got distracted." Jenni glared again at her father.

"I appreciate the offer but I should go home," Scott said. "I have work to do anyway." He ignored Jenni's raised eyebrows. She'd probably accuse him of working too hard again, but as she'd pointed out before, that was his defense to avoid issues. He added Mrs. Stallings to the growing list of people he needed to right the wrongs he caused.

"Please stay," Mrs. Stallings said. "Let's eat before it gets cold." She wiped her hands on her worn apron, most likely out of nervous habit more than anything.

Richard pulled himself into a sitting position and struggled to stand when he pushed off from the low couch. Again, Scott wondered how he'd get Richard to the pier to fish tomorrow.

He jumped up. "Can I help you to the kitchen?"

Richard nodded. "Thanks. If you don't mind holding onto my belt, that would give me a sense of security. It's nice having another man around here. Jenni needs a man in her life."

"Dad!"

"Men are good for a lot of things, Jenni." Richard lifted the walker and took a step toward the kitchen. "For one thing, a man, this man in fact, can give you a loan with my assistance." Richard stopped just outside the living room archway.

Jenni's mouth dropped open, her face turning crimson. "A man can give me a headache. And a man doesn't understand the importance of supporting a woman's business endeavor, instead of bailing her out." She dodged around them and headed toward the kitchen after her mother.

"She just doesn't understand," Richard mumbled. He stood still with his walker planted in front of him. "I want to know she's financially well off. How can I die when she's not settled?"

"So you're concerned because you love her?"

Richard clicked his teeth repeatedly before he answered. "Yeah, something like that."

"Does that mean you've never told her those words?"

"She knows how I feel. And, no, I've never told her except for once." Richard leaned on his walker, taking an exaggerated breath.

Scott tensed and grabbed a tighter hold of the man's belt. "Are you okay?"

"No. I'm not okay. That's what I keep telling people, but they ignore the truth." Richard stood taller and started to walk again. "That girl is what keeps me alive. I'm concerned about her."

How to reply to a statement like that? If Scott argued the point, the man might die right there. Then Scott would be responsible for destroying another member of Jenni's family.

When they strolled into the kitchen, the smell of homemade stew greeted him. His gaze met Jenni's, and he saw a raw tenderness there, a sense of vulnerability. When she took in her father's unsteady gait, the wounded expression turned to concern.

Jenni pulled out a mismatched chair at the head of the table for Richard, and then pointed to one of two chairs tucked in along the side. "Guests usually sit there." Without waiting, she took the wobbly seat next to his.

At different intervals during dinner, Mrs. Stallings hopped up to fetch her husband a glass of water, to replenish the butter for the potatoes, to set a home-baked apple pie on the table. He wished his own mother had this softer side.

"How do your brother and Rachel like the restaurant business?" Mrs. Stallings asked as she sliced the apple pie into generous proportions.

Scott took a moment to inhale the warm scent of cinnamon. He could almost imagine a similar life with Jenni, not that he could fathom settling in Big Cat with a family. No, he wanted to return to Raleigh as soon as Layne returned from maternity leave. Small-town living meant more than home-cooked meals and family, it meant boredom. And Jenni had her coffee shop here and a dream of opening more. There was no way a relationship would work with her, on many different levels.

"They love owning the Shrimp Shack," he said as he held out a dessert plate for Mrs. Stallings to slide a large piece of pie onto.

Richard dropped his fork onto his plate, the loud clank causing everyone to startle.

"Is something the matter, honey?" Mrs. Stallings asked.

"The Shrimp Shack. What was wrong with the name Stallings? I worked hard to build the respect that name carried."

"It still does, sir," Scott said. "Dan's restaurant is a different place than Stallings was. Stallings was a fine establishment, as is the Shrimp Shack."

Richard growled. "You young folks come in and take over, inspired by all your ideas and dreams. Owning a restaurant is hard work. It requires long hours with a trustworthy team. And it takes money."

There it was. His rant was about Jenni.

Jenni sat taller, more rigid. "Dad, you were young when you took over Stallings. Youthfulness is a good thing. You followed your dreams with Stallings, and then you sold it for quite a profit. I'm going to follow your example."

Richard snorted. "You have to make money first before you can expand and sell out."

Scott grew quiet and the family tension was gnawing at his patience. He shifted in his seat, hard despite the homey little flowered cushion on the chair. Instead of being immersed in their private family conversation, he could be home working.

But he wasn't home, so he continued to eat his dessert, savoring every bite. "Mrs. Stallings, this pie is the best I've tasted. Even my brother's restaurant doesn't have desserts this tasty." He wasn't about to call it the Shrimp Shack again.

"Good way to avoid an unpleasant discussion," Richard said. "I imagine years of working at the bank have taught you to redirect conflict. I admire that."

Jenni scowled at Scott. “You suck-up. All my life he’s hardly given me an ounce of praise, and you get his approval just like that. You weren’t even trying.”

“Now kids, don’t fight.” Mrs. Stallings stood to collect the dessert plates. “Life’s too short.”

“Exactly what I’ve been trying to tell everyone,” Richard said.

***

Jenni worried about her father fishing tomorrow. His coloring was pale and he’d required Scott’s help to get him back to bed.

Her mother walked over to the sink. “Let me finish the dishes.”

“I’ve got it,” Jenni said.

“Jenni,” her mother whispered, “go talk to Scott. Ask him to be careful tomorrow.”

She touched her mom on the shoulder. “Dad’s in good hands.” At least she hoped so, but to be sure, she'd talk to him about her father's health.

Jenni motioned to Scott and they retreated to the privacy of the back porch. When she sat on the porch swing, she tapped the vacant spot next to her. He hesitated, then joined her.

“You’re lucky,” he said. The porch light accented the dark, five-o’clock shadows on his face. She yearned to touch the light stubble.

“How so?”

“Your family is so close.”

“You’ve got to be kidding,” she said.

He leaned back against the wooden swing and slowly pushed with his feet on the porch floor. The swing moved in a slow rhythm. “Other than my brother, who I haven’t talked to much over the years, I’d say I barely have a relationship with them. Family is important to me, yet I take a lot of the blame for our distance. I was too busy to come home to visit, even for the holidays. The only reason I went to Dan's wedding is because Rachel's from Raleigh, so they had it there."

Jenni missed Rachel's wedding because she knew Scott would be there.

"Why?" She thought she knew the reason Scott avoided coming home but wanted to hear him admit the truth.

He stared at her. "I don't know. My parents have always fought, but before I left home for college, the arguing got worse. My mom accused my dad of having an affair but I know better. He loved her so much. They just didn't know how to get along."

She felt his pain seep through her. She'd expected him to talk about Brittany, not his family. "If you don't want to discuss it …"

"No, it's okay. I want to tell you." He looked away, most likely to regroup. "My mother condemned me when my own marriage failed. She said I hadn't tried hard enough. I gave it my all in the beginning, but eventually I buried myself in work to dull the pain. My mom was right, though, I should have tried harder. But you know what? My parents are together still, but they aren't happy. I didn't want a marriage like that."

"I don't blame you. I wouldn't, either." Jenni had never met his parents, and now she realized why his brother most likely never introduced her to them. He didn't want to drag her into a house full of fighting and tension. "Don't forget, it takes more than one person for a relationship to fall apart. Each person has his or her own journey. You're only responsible for your own."

"My own journey," he repeated.

"That's right. You might share your life with someone, but you aren't accountable for other people's insecurities and fears. They have to overcome those alone. You can guide them, while you work on your own issues, but if they aren't willing to grow, to learn, then you can fast outgrow them."

"How did you become so wise?"

"My grandmother. Over the years, she's taught me how to cope with my problems in a constructive way. The only one she hasn't been successful resolving, probably because she hasn't achieved it herself, is dealing with my father."

"What's wrong with your relationship with your father? You both seem close." He glanced at the back door.

"That's where you're wrong." She watched him closely; it was imperative that he understand the dynamics between her and her father. That way he'd understand why it was so important that her business succeed without the help of her parents. She didn't want him to encourage her father to use the house as collateral. Her mother needed her home, free and clear of all debt.

"In comparison to my family, yours seems almost perfect." He leaned forward and rested his elbows on his bare knees. He had to be cold. The night air was chilly and he only wore his running clothes.

"You're mistaken. My mother hovers, and my father always finds fault with my decisions."

He shrugged. "Don't most parents do that? I get the same thing about my divorce."

She looked at him. "Maybe. But he scoffs at me whenever I follow my dreams."

"What is your dream?" He studied her as if he didn't want to miss a single word she said.

"I want to be successful in my business endeavors. Like I said before, I want to open a chain of coffee shops along the coast and then sell them for a large profit."

"And that's where you differ from your father."

"How so?"

"He inherited his father's business, made it profitable just in time for retirement. You are a trailblazer."

She found his analysis interesting.

"Did he want to pass Stallings on to you?"

She swallowed hard. "Yes."

"What happened?"

"He wanted me to go college and learn about business first. Unfortunately, before I graduated he had to sell the restaurant to pay off medical bills." She looked down at her stocking feet, now growing cold from the cool air. Outside the screened porch, she could hear rustling leaves blowing in the stiff breeze.

"And my brother bought your inheritance."

Jenni shrugged. "Things happen for a reason. No one plans cancer." She turned away, so he couldn't see a tear streak down her cheek. "I worked at Stallings since I was a kid. It was educational in its own way, but once I got to college, I saw the importance of going to school. I wanted to learn how business really worked. Maybe it's best that he sold Stallings. It would've limited me to Big Cat, and to one restaurant. I want the flexibility to live where I want."

"I thought you loved being here?"

"I do. But I want it to be my choice, not his. That's the beauty of following my dream with the coffee shop. I can expand and live wherever I wish. But honestly, I don't see myself moving from Big Cat."

"So you want independence, along with his acceptance."

And forgiveness, but she didn't admit that. Eventually she answered, "Yes. That pretty much sums it up, except my dad is angry and blames me."

"Ah, but as you said, that's his journey."

"True. Are you glad you're back home?"

He cringed. "To be honest, no. I can't wait to get back to Raleigh. The faster the better."

She felt the sting of disappointment. "Why are you in such a hurry to leave?"

"Because I love the city, even if it's a small one. I miss my house on the lake and the trail around it, not that I've walked on it much lately. I also miss taking clients to upscale restaurants. What's in Big Cat?"

She got defensive. "I used to feel that way until I moved back. Don't forget about the salty air, the fresh seafood from the shrimp boats, the wild horses, all the amazing water and marsh.

The next time you drive over the causeway, take a good look at the scenery."

"I'll do that."

"Are you avoiding your family here, their criticism?" she asked. "Is that why you stayed away so long?" Or was it because of the accident, which they had yet to discuss in any depth.

"Maybe. Is that your reason for staying away so long?" He raised his eyebrows at her.

She sucked in her breath. "I don't know."

"Why didn't your brother buy Stallings instead of purchasing the ferry service?" He'd conveniently changed the subject, for which she was thankful.

"Keith had always hated the restaurant," she explained. "He's an outdoor person and had always despised working in the kitchen. The ferry fits him perfectly. It's too bad I couldn't have bought Stallings, to keep it in the family."

"Let the blame go, Jenni."

She slumped against the back of the swing. "It's important for me to make amends with my father. I want him to die with a peaceful mind. He's worried about my future, and I think that's why he's hanging on. The selfish part of me is glad he hasn't given up yet."

"That's understandable."

"Your plan to take him fishing tomorrow is making a sick man very happy. I'm grateful to you."

"No problem." He visibly shrugged off the compliment.

"You don't understand. When he talks about it, he lights up. I haven't heard him this excited about anything since before his doctor diagnosed him with cancer." She leaned toward Scott, wrapped her arm around his back, and squeezed him into a quick hug before she pulled away.

Her awkward display of affection hung in the air.

"Honestly, I can't help but worry about tomorrow," she admitted. "I need to warn you, so you know what you're getting into."

He looked at her.

"Dad gets tired sometimes when he walks from his room to the bathroom or kitchen. You saw a hint of that tonight, but that was Dad on one of his good days. It gets worse. When he isn't feeling well, he'll try to sit down, even if there isn't a chair behind him."

"Trust me, Jenni. He doesn't weigh that much, so I can easily keep him from falling."

Why was he so eager to help her father? "My mother will be sick with concern. Please call me if you need me."

"I will." He leaned closer. She thought he might kiss her, but he rubbed his thumb across her chin instead. "You can count on me."

She could count on him to help with her father, but not to apologize for the bad decisions he made the day her sister died.

Scott tipped his head and the warmth of his mouth touched hers lightly. She held her breath, hardly able to comprehend that she was kissing him back.

CHAPTER ELEVEN

Saturday morning came fast. Scott had tons of work to do, and he hadn't taken an entire day off since his boss had promoted him to vice president of the bank. But he'd offered to take Richard Stallings fishing, and that was exactly what he planned to do.

Big Cat was a different lifestyle, one he wasn't sure he wanted to get used to again. He could barely remember his childhood, where his only concern was girls, football, fishing, and hanging out with the guys on the pier.

At five minutes to eight, he pulled up outside the Stallings' home and looked up at the house. It might be a challenge to help Mr. Stallings down all those steps. Even if they went out the back way, they'd still have to navigate the steepest section. He told Jenni he'd take excellent care of her dad, and he intended to make good on his promise.

Scott climbed the steps and rapped on the back door. Before he knocked again, Jenni pulled the door open.

"Hi there. He's all ready." Jenni, her hair wet and curling from her morning shower, smelled of fresh rosemary. An array of freckles splattered across her untouched cheeks. Last night's kiss popped into his mind. He'd never felt that kind of attraction to anyone.

Mr. Stallings appeared behind her, dressed in an old fishing hat with a lure stuck in the side. He practically swam in a baggy denim jacket that made his body look even more tiny and frail. A pair of suspenders held up his faded pair of jeans, which he'd tucked into tall rubber boots.

"Let me help you." Scott reached out to hold onto Richard's belt as the older man thumped the walker past the open screen door.

"I'll walk you both down to the car." Jenni hovered close by but let Scott take the lead. It felt good that she trusted him with her father.

Richard whistled when he saw the shiny car. "I see you brought the BMW." He grinned like a boy.

"It's kind of cramped. The fishing rods take up most of the room."

"It's worth it." The pleasure in the older man's voice was unmistakable.

The journey down the steps proved easier than Scott expected. Getting back up them, however, might be a different story. He would worry about that later. For now, he'd enjoy the moment.

He opened the passenger door and a brown dog poked his head from between the seats.

Jenni screeched with delight and leaned in to pet him. "Is that the dog that was following you?"

"Yep. He waited for me until I left your house. I tried to ignore him, but he tagged along behind my car all the way down the street. I had to stop."

"Are you going to keep him?"

"No. I can't," Scott said. "I don't have time for a dog." The dog whined in protest. "I'll foster him until I find a home."

"What if no one wants him?" She patted the dog's head once more and backed out of the car. "What are you going to call him?"

Scott frowned. He didn't dare admit how much comfort the dog had already offered him, especially in an apartment that didn't feel like home. "I named him Pirate." He'd almost hate to see the dog go.

"He's too sweet to be called Pirate."

"It's either that or Black Beard."

She shrugged. "If those are the only two choices, I guess Pirate."

"Let's go fishing," Richard complained. "We can argue about the dog later.

Scott kept a tight hold on Richard's belt, although Jenni's father was doing so well he could probably lighten his grasp. "Go ahead and climb in, Mr. Stallings. Pirate will stay in the backseat."

Richard reached out and grabbed hold of the doorframe, leaving the walker bravely behind. Once settled, he fiddled with his seatbelt but had trouble clicking it into place.

"I'll help you with that," Scott said. He squeezed his large body between the glove compartment and Richard to fasten the seat belt.

A light touch on his back surprised him. He glanced back and stared into Jenni's eyes. She mouthed the word "Thanks." Scott's heart warmed to almost feverish. He nodded and quickly backed out of the doorway.

"Have fun, Dad." Jenni leaned in and kissed him on the cheek. The second after Scott closed the door, her expression grew somber.

"He'll be fine. I know most of the men down at the pier. If I need help, I can ask them."

"Okay." Her grim expression still revealed concern. "I know I keep saying this, but thanks. I appreciate what you're doing for my dad."

He swallowed hard. "And for you."

Her father tapped on the window with his knuckles.

When Scott opened the door, Richard fixed his eyes on his only daughter. "Will you come with us?"

She swallowed hard. "You want me to go fishing?" Her voice was barely audible.

"Yes," Richard said. "And Pirate wants you to join us. Didn't you hear him whining as soon as the door closed?"

Scott would bet that Pirate had done no such thing. Richard wanted his daughter along but was uncomfortable admitting the truth.

She glanced up at Scott. "Do you mind?"

"Of course not. Besides, it's your father's special day at the pier. If he wants his daughter along, I'm all right with that."

Richard coughed, a fit that lasted at least half a minute, and reminded Scott just how sick he was. The trip to the pier was likely his last fishing adventure.

"At least you're off this morning," Richard said to Jenni. "I can't say I agree with who you hired, but listening to me is improvement."

The jab was unfair but Jenni didn't seem to react. "I need to run into the house and get a few things," she said. "I'll be right back."

She darted up the flight of stairs with ease. Scott marveled at her vibrancy.

While he waited for her return, he folded Richard's walker and stuffed it into the trunk of his car on top of a briefcase and a manual. Again, he pondered how he'd get the man back up the steps.

***

At the end of the long pier, Jenni watched the smile grow bigger on her dad's face as he cast the first lines of the day. His hands trembled slightly, and the tip of the fishing pole oscillated. Even though he tried to hold it steady against the pull of the strong incoming tide, he reached forward with one hand and caressed the pole with the affection of a long-ago angler.

Her father's lips puckered and his chin quivered ever so slightly.

She set a hand on his shoulder in an attempt to comfort him. He allowed the touch for a second but then shrugged it off. At first she felt rejected, but then sadness for the emotional pain he was obviously experiencing overcame her. How devastating it must feel to know you'd never hold a fishing rod again. He was saying goodbye to his favorite passion in life.

Jenni backed away to give him privacy, although she found it difficult not to be right there next to him. She slid into a folding chair next to Scott, who held his own pole with Pirate lying at his feet. The morning was turning out to be sunny. A hint of warmth penetrated through the early morning chill, with a promise that the day would be perfect for fishing. She leaned back and propped her feet on the wooden railing in front of her, beside her father's walker. As tough as it was, she had to allow her dad to work through his emotions.

She glanced at Scott, a man she owed an ocean of gratitude. He had given a gift to her father, to her family. Today he'd made a miserable man's dreams come true. If they were lucky, the outing might jump-start her father's desire to live longer. She wasn't ready to let him go yet.

Scott looked up and met her gaze. His baseball cap shadowed his forehead, but she made out those large chocolate eyes anyway. Right then she felt a wave of adoration for him.

"Oh! He's running!" Her father held the rod high and jerked it three times to set the hook. "Fish on!" The reel started to sing.

In one deliberate motion, Scott jumped up and handed his pole to Jenni, then darted over to her father. "Let me know if you need help."

"I got it, Scott. The kings are in. Come on, baby." The action was starting to get intense, his reel screaming. He kept his pole high while the fish took up the slack in the line.

When the king eventually started to tire, Jenni's father reeled the fish in a bit at a time. A bearded angler helped him gaff up the king to avoid snapping the line. When they landed the fish, the angler whistled. "That's a nice-sized king."

Jenni was so proud she didn't attempt to talk, for fear her voice would fail. Her father beamed as the other man gave him a congratulatory thump on the back. Pirate growled. "It's okay, boy," her father said to the dog. Then he grinned at the man. "Call it Stallings' luck. It runs in the family." He struggled to dump the fish into a cooler.

"Stallings' luck, huh?" Scott glanced at Jenni.

"That's right," she said. "I'm lucky to be here today with the both of you."

"You're also lucky because you're going to make your business the most unique coffee shop along the barrier islands. That's Stallings' luck, too." Scott studied her too closely. "I admire your determination."

She didn't know what to say. "I appreciate that." Uncomfortable with Scott's stare, she watched her father slip live bait onto another hook before he cast it back into the blue water. He seemed tired. Maybe they should leave while he still had energy, but she hated to end his fun.

"You know, Dan sent me a used espresso machine," she said to Scott, mostly for shock value. "It surprised me."

Scott rubbed his unshaven face with his hands. "That was generous."

"Thought you should know," she said. That's all he had to say about the unexpected delivery? "Dan probably saved my business. I'm not sure why he wanted to help, but I'm thankful." Jenni would ask Dan about it tonight at the dinner party. She'd also make a point to make sure Rachel was comfortable with the situation.

Scott pushed his hands into his jean pockets. He was the only man she knew who wore pressed jeans, a button down shirt, and loafers to fish.

Her father appeared to ignore their discussion. He'd settled against the back of his chair and pretended to focus solely on his line. Jenni could tell, though, that he'd heard every word.

"Do you want to take out the sailboat with me tomorrow?" Scott asked.

He wanted to sail on his father's boat, the one Brittany had fallen off? Her immediate response was to say no, but then Gran's words flooded her mind. *Take Scott's return as an opportunity to heal from Brittany's death.* Gran was right.

"Okay." She wondered if he'd been on a sailboat since the accident. She doubted he had. The trip would be good rehab for him as well.

Just then her father caught another king mackerel. Jenni glanced around the pier. No one else seemed to be catching much of anything.

Because of her father's fatigue, Scott helped him land the king eventually. After the excitement was over, her father announced he had to make an emergency trip to the bathroom. With Scott's help, he managed to stand.

"Go. We have to hurry," her dad said.

Scott's eyes grew wide.

Her father made it halfway to the bathroom before his legs gave out.

Scott held him up even though her dad tried to sit down right there. "Jenni, ask someone to help me. Quickly."

She hurried over to a group of men she didn't know, except for the bearded angler named Paul, who'd assisted them earlier. "Can you help with my father? Please?" She'd never seen her father so vulnerable, so scared.

Immediately Paul hopped up and went to Scott's side. One of his buddies followed. The three men hoisted her father, still in a sitting position, into the air.

"Bathroom," Scott called out. Two more men opened the door to the small store at the mouth of the pier, then opened the men's bathroom door. Pirate whined and followed, with his leash dragging along the old wooden planks. Jenni stopped outside the men's bathroom, stunned by the experience. He would be okay. Her father was in capable hands.

It seemed to take forever for the men to carry her father out of the restroom. "Let's head to my car," Scott instructed. He looked at Jenni. "I'll come back to get our equipment later. Let's get your father home."

She agreed and grabbed hold of Pirate's leash to walk him out of the store and across the crowded parking lot. She'd felt grateful to Scott before, but words didn't begin to describe her gratitude now. He was truly a special man.

The circumstances required two men to maneuver the car door and to situate her father safely in the vehicle. When Scott shut the door, he said, "We forgot his walker."

"I'll run back and get it," Paul said. The husky man jogged back into the store.

"How are we going to get him up the steps and into my house?" Jenni asked, perplexed. Her mom wasn't going to be happy.

Scott wrapped his arm around her and pulled her close. "He's okay. It was a long morning and he got tired. That's all."

She looked into his gentle eyes.

"He had a good day, Jenni. It meant a lot to him."

She nodded. "You're right." Her dad was probably observing their display of affection from his front-row seat in the car.

"The guys offered to follow us to your house. One way or another, we'll get him inside. Trust me."

She did trust him, even though she didn't want to admit the uncomfortable truth. People watched and Jenni grew increasingly uneasy. Before long, the entire town would know Scott Botticelli held her in his arms.

Jenni pulled away from him and climbed into the back of the BMW with a whining Pirate. "Dad's all right," she whispered to the dog. "Good boy." Pirate pulled against Jenni's hold on his collar and jutted his nose into her father's elbow. Her dad was leaning against the passenger door, his head resting against the window.

He managed to glance back at her, his eyelids heavy but his expression filled with excitement. “What an ordeal. But at least I caught two king mackerels.”

“That you did, Dad.”

The return trip home was slow going, thanks to Scott’s cautious driving. A convoy of trucks followed them across the causeway and through the streets of downtown Big Cat.

When they pulled in front of the Stallings’ home, her mother ran outside. After Jenni climbed from the BMW, her mom’s eyes darted from her to the line of trucks now parked along the street.

“What took so long?” Jenni’s mom called down to them. “You’ve been gone for hours.”

“Dad’s fine.” She chose first to reassure her mother before she mentioned what happened. “He had a blast fishing.”

She pointed to the fishermen who walked together as they approached Scott’s car. “Who are they?”

“Friends.”

Her mother looked questionably at them. Jenni knew she wondered about the contrast between Scott and the men. He was a businessman, dressed in crisp clean clothes, and they were local fishermen, dressed in torn jeans and faded t-shirts. What her mother didn’t understand was the men cared and were there to help her husband.

Even though Scott usually appeared uptight and rather arrogant, Jenni liked the fact that he’d once hung out with the locals on the pier. Underneath his tense exterior, he possessed a down-to-earth, likeable nature. Today he had focused on something other than work. He'd reconnected with real people.

Jenni’s mom hurried down the steps. She needed to know the truth, with as little detail as possible, or she’d panic. “Dad got tired,” Jenni said. “Scott and these generous men are going to bring him inside.”

Her mother made an unidentifiable noise from the back of her throat.

"He'll be fine," Jenni said, not only to ease her mother's mind, but to also calm herself.

Scott opened the passenger door, and with Paul's assistance, they lifted her father out of the car. Jenni knew all too well that her dad, despite the weight he'd lost, was still heavy. A third man helped carry him toward the steps.

Jenni and her mother stepped aside so they could pass by, and then followed closely behind. The men carried him up the first five steps and rested a moment, before continuing up another set of steeper stairs, which led to a sidewalk. They walked around front, and when they reached the porch steps, they were breathing heavily and sweating. Jenni yanked open the squeaky door so they could carry him into the house.

Jenni's mom, panting from the sprint up the steps, pointed down the hallway. "Please, put him in his den. That way I won't have to move him later."

The men did as she asked. When they finished, and Scott had tucked him under the covers, Jenni's mother broke down and started to cry. Scott held her in his arms. "He's okay, Mrs. Stallings."

She plucked a tissue from a box on the nightstand and wiped her eyes. Jenni had a hunch that whatever complex issues her mother had with Scott prior to today, she'd pushed aside, at least for the time being.

Jenni stared at her father, who was already sleeping.

"He had the best day fishing," Scott said, rubbing her mother's back. "I bet if you ask him later, he'd say it was worth it."

Touched by Scott's tenderness, Jenni's mood lifted. It was good for her mother to see this side of him. "He's right, Mom. Wait until you see the two mackerel he caught."

Paul, who stood in the doorway, said, “Ma’am, he even caught the biggest king in the history of the pier. That’s something.”

Jenni glanced down at her father again. Despite his exhaustion, he wore a small smile on his pale face. If anything happened to him, she’d be lost He needed to live.

CHAPTER TWELVE

Jenni waited on the front porch for Scott to pick her up for dinner. She was looking forward to going somewhere on a Saturday night instead of sitting home with her mom while her dad slept.

Scott's car shot into a parking spot beside her house. Making her way through the lit path from the streetlamp, she held onto the stair railing with one hand and clutched a small paper bag with the other. She made her way down the steps. When she reached the bottom, he got out of his car and opened the door for her. Their gaze met in a narrow strip of light.

"How's your dad doing?"

"Today was long for him, but in between naps, he was telling fishing stories to anyone who'd listen. He retold the highlights to my brother while they ate baked fish tonight at dinner." She thrust the bag toward him. "Leftovers from my mom and a bottle of wine."

He stiffened. "That was thoughtful of her."

"Oh, I forgot you don't drink alcohol. I can take the wine back in the house."

He shrugged. "That's okay. It's a nice gesture and other people will drink it."

His aversion to alcohol reminded her that at some point they needed to have a long conversation about Brittany.

As though he read her mind, he changed the subject back to her father. "The expression on your dad's face, when he caught that first mackerel, was priceless." He grinned. "I can understand why he's tired. I am too."

Their eyes met again, and she thought he might kiss her, but he quickly turned away. He walked around the back of his car to stow her bag of goodies behind the driver's seat.

Disappointed but relieved, Jenni climbed into the car. Pirate appeared from the backseat and licked her cheek. "Hey, boy. What are you doing here?"

"He wanted to come with me," Scott said as he climbed in. "He started to whine when I tried to leave him behind."

"Maybe he's afraid you won't come back." She rubbed the dog's head. Pirate looked as though he wanted to melt right there.

"Probably. That's going to be a problem when I go to work." He slammed his door, started his car, and sped off.

Why couldn't he see how much the dog needed him, and how much he needed Pirate?

Within minutes they pulled in front of a newer brick house with a pitched roof. Scott held her elbow gently as they walked up the sidewalk, illuminated by little lights. Someday she'd have a house with cute little lights.

Scott reached out and rang the doorbell, Pirate close to his side.

When Rachel answered the door, dressed in a classy black dress and heels, Jenni immediately regretted her choice in clothes. She wore her only pair of dress jeans and a brown cashmere sweater bought on impulse before she'd moved home.

Rachel hugged her. "You look smashing, Jenni."

What reassurance. Silently she thanked Rachel for the compliment and hugged her. Warmth radiated between the two women. Rachel was one of those truly nice people. She also had a smart business sense about her, a certain confidence that came from success, which Jenni hoped to accomplish in the near future.

"You look wonderful too." Jenni pulled back and handed her the bottle of wine. She felt Scott's light touch on her lower back as he stood behind her, still in the doorway. Intimate. He touched her as if they were a couple.

Rachel looked down. "I see you brought Pirate. Butch will enjoy a companion."

"I'm glad you don't mind that I brought him," Scott said. "I should have asked first."

"He's always welcome." Rachel ushered them inside. "Please, mingle until dinner is ready, which will be in about ten minutes. Jenni, help yourself to a drink at the bar." Rachel scurried away, leaving Jenni to follow Scott's gaze to a familiar woman who stood in front of the bar.

Cassie's eyes locked with hers.

Why was she here? She didn't work for the Shrimp Shack, as most of the other dinner guests.

Decked out in a low-cut red dress and revealing a healthy amount of cleavage, Cassie sashayed across the room and wrapped her arm around Scott. She gave him a light kiss on the corner of his mouth.

Pirate growled and leaned into Scott's leg.

Did Cassie normally kiss her boss? A wave of jealousy passed through Jenni. She'd thought of tonight as a date. Confused, she watched the interaction between the two of them.

Scott smiled, a tight-faced and uncomfortable grin. Perhaps he felt unnerved by Cassie's display of affection. Was there a one-sided office romance going on, one that Cassie initiated despite the possible ramifications of hitting on her boss?

Never mind that Scott showed up with Jenni. The woman showed no respect of others.

"I'm glad you're here," Cassie said to Scott. "I was starting to wonder if you were still coming tonight."

"I stopped to pick up Jenni first." He shifted his eyes from Cassie to Jenni.

Jenni feigned a smile when Cassie glanced at her.

"How nice of you. You're such a gentleman." Cassie shot a disapproving glance up and down Jenni's full length.

Oh, come on. She wore cashmere for goodness sake. It's not as if she showed up in a t-shirt. At least her dark jeans were classy and stylish, and she wore brown dress shoes to match her sweater. So what if she wasn't a person who liked to wear dresses.

Jenni reminded herself that she didn't need this woman's approval.

This was a test of some sort, that's all. If she wanted people to think of her as a business owner, it started here. No one could see inside Jenni's mind. If she projected confidence, that was what others would notice.

She stood tall and smiled with true kindness. Cassie frowned again, but it didn't matter. Other guests seemed attracted to Jenni's friendly demeanor, walking up to her and introducing themselves. Alex, the young server from the Shrimp Shack, the one with the spiked hair, held out her hand to greet Jenni. Despite her youthful, funky hairstyle, she was actually a few years older than Jenni had estimated originally.

"I'll get us something to drink," Scott said to Jenni. When he walked away, Pirate ran off with Butch, a large German shepherd. A man opened the back door and the dogs ran into the backyard. Cassie took Pirate's place, following Scott. They appeared to get into an argument before they reached the wet bar.

A soft but confident voice interrupted Jenni's thoughts. "I've wanted to apply at your coffee shop for a while now," Alex said. "I need different hours than the restaurant can give me."

Jenni felt a little awkward discussing possible employment with Dan's server, especially after he'd sent her the espresso machine. "What hours do you want from Dan?" She tried to stick to the safer topic.

"Late afternoons and early evenings. I want to go to Crystal County Community College in the mornings."

Perfect, except she worked for Dan.

"In case you didn't know," Alex continued, "I sometimes help your grandmother feed the horses when she needs help. I recently joined the *Wild Horse Foundation*. Anyway, your grandma mentioned that you wanted to expand your coffee shop's hours."

True. Gran was always trying to help. "That's right; I'm hiring," Jenni said. "To be honest, though, I feel uncomfortable stealing Dan's server from him."

"It wouldn't be stealing if I go willingly. I'd give notice."

From across the room, Scott flashed a crooked half smile at Jenni and winked. He was chatting with Marge, the hostess at the Shrimp Shack. If he only knew what she and Alex were talking about, he wouldn't look so happy.

Jenni swallowed a lump of guilt. Business was business. Scott believed that to his core. "I'll let you know when I'm ready to hire," Jenni said, still looking at Scott.

Dan and Rachel chose that uncomfortable moment to walk up. "Jenni, I'm glad you came tonight," Dan said, nodding at her. He looked at Alex, then back at Jenni. "I see you two have met."

Oh, boy.

Alex saved the evening. "We have, but I was just excusing myself to get another Pepsi. Can I get anyone a drink?"

Dan and Rachel shook their heads and Alex excused herself. "Alex is a wonderful employee," he said. "She's one of the best servers I have, even though she's fairly new."

Was that a warning to stay away from her? Alex sounded like the answer to Jenni's hiring dilemma. At some point she needed to expand the coffee shop's hours even more. She'd have a difficult choice to make soon, and would have to find the right way to handle the situation.

"Thank you for the espresso machine," Jenni said, jumping at the opportunity to change the subject. "It couldn't have arrived at a better time."

She swore Dan looked confused.

"Sure thing," he said. "I'm glad it showed up." He seemed to scan the room for someone, perhaps Scott.

"An espresso machine?" Rachel asked.

"Mine broke and a used one showed up with Dan's name on the paperwork." From Rachel's glare at Dan, it was obvious she didn't know about the purchase.

"You bought an expensive machine without talking to me first?" Rachel asked her husband.

Scott returned to Jenni's side, this time without Cassie attached to him. He cleared his throat and said, "That was a nice of you both, buying the espresso machine." Scott raised his eyebrows to the couple as if to convince them.

Dan looked at Rachel. "We'll talk about it later."

"You can count on it." Rachel politely excused herself and left the room.

Dan punched his brother in the arm. "Thanks a lot, bro."

Before Jenni or Scott could respond, Rachel announced dinner, cooked by the chef of the Shrimp Shack. A waiter dressed in black served filet mignon, Caribbean-style shrimp sautéed in butter with vanilla beans and unsweetened coconut, long green beans sautéed in olive oil with thin rings of Vandalia onions, and garlic mashed potatoes topped with rich brown gravy.

Before the waiter served dessert, a flourless chocolate cake, Dan raised his glass and toasted his star employee of the month, Alex. Jenni avoided looking at her.

***

You can do this. Just take one step onto the boat and the rest will get easier. Scott commanded his feet to obey his mind. He tried not to look at the bow pulpit where Brittany stood that dreaded evening just before she fell overboard. It was twelve years ago but felt like yesterday.

He reached out and placed one foot onto his father's twenty-eight-foot sailboat, *The Great Escape*. He had to scoff at the name now. Once he got past this milestone, he'd enjoy sailing again. Actually, he missed it.

"Bro, you just have to do it."

Scott whirled around to see Dan and Rachel standing on the dock, their arms full of towels, a swim bag, a cooler, and paper grocery bags. Scott was glad he had the foresight to ask his brother to come along. Dan hopped onboard and reached out to his wife. "It's that easy. Just make your mind up and go for it."

Go for it. Scott stood there, one foot on the deck of the boat and the other planted firmly on the dock. It wasn't too late to turn back and cancel the sailing trip. He'd simply call Jenni and tell her he changed his mind. She most likely didn't want to step onto this boat anymore than he wanted to.

Pirate nudged his leg.

Dan reached out and offered his hand to him. *Take it*, Scott thought. He grabbed hold of his brother's hand as if it were a lifeline. Dan pulled him onboard and thumped him on the back.

"You did it. That was the hardest part."

The hardest part. Scott refused to look at the bow, refused to picture Brittany standing there pretending to be different statues, trying to be funny. Why hadn't they made her listen when they told her to stop goofing off? Why had he been drinking, allowing alcohol to cloud his judgment? If he had been at the helm as planned, he wouldn't have been flirting with Jenni. The accident wouldn't have happened. *Stop*! He felt like he was going crazy with the memories.

"Scott, you'll be fine." Dan pushed him toward the helm. "Touch the wheel. Remember what it feels like to stand there with the wind blowing in your face. Smell the brine. Taste the salt on your lips."

Scott nodded, reaching out to touch the cold metal. Yes, the wheel felt good between his hands. He ran his open palm around it. He allowed himself to remember years of pleasant sailing trips with his brother and father. This setback was only a rough storm, one he'd eventually survive. He'd made the first big step already just by standing in the cockpit. Each minute he stood there, he felt years of tension melt away from his shoulders.

"Let's make her ready to sail," Dan said.

"Not so fast." Rachel slid between them. "You both owe me an explanation about Jenni and the espresso machine. I got part of the story last night from Dan, but it didn't make a bit of sense."

Scott shrugged. What could he say? The plan made perfect sense to him.

"I understand you offered Dan money, so he could loan it to Jenni?" Rachel asked. Her eyes drilled into Scott's. "When Jenni said no, you bought her an espresso machine instead, in our name, without consulting us? Why didn't you loan Jenni the money yourself?"

Scott shook his head. Was she a crazy woman? "Jenni would never let me help her financially."

Rachel leaned closer, inches from his face. "Of course she would. And if she didn't, then you need to respect her by not telling her, you're being dishonest."

That never occurred to him. "I want to help her however I can. This is a perfect way for me to absolve my guilt about her sister's death." He willed his eyes not to look at the bow again but they disregarded his plea.

"You're missing the point. You need to discuss the accident with Jenni."

Rachel was getting on his nerves. "I've lived with guilt for twelve years. I don't want to talk about it." But it was eating him alive. "Helping Jenni makes me feel a tiny bit better. She deserves to succeed; she's lost enough in her life." His voice was getting louder and he had to fight to lower it. Rachel was only trying to help. "Please don't tell Jenni the espresso machine is from me."

***

Jenni arrived exactly on time Sunday morning and parked at the marina. She'd been to the boat slip before, back when she'd dated Dan, and of course, when they'd gone out on the dreadful sunset cruise. The memories flooded her mind full force. She tried to push them back into the safe corner of her mind, but they refused to stay there for long.

As a distraction, she forced herself to remember other sailing trips, ones with positive memories. One time they'd gone sailing with Scott and Cassie. Jenni had spent the day avoiding Scott's shirtless and tanned body. Today, however, she just might indulge and look all she wanted. After all, it would be just the two of them, on a boat in the middle of the ocean, miles from the coast.

She climbed out of the Sentra and walked around the back. From the trunk she pulled out a day bag stuffed with personal items and a small cooler filled with food. She'd packed a stack of turkey sandwiches, each with a slice of cheddar cheese, a few huge oranges, and a large bag of red grapes. She also packed a block of Gouda cheese and crackers, but no wine to accompany the picnic. This time she brought plastic wine glasses and sparkling water.

As she approached the boat slip, she slowed her pace to watch Scott. He stood on the boat's deck, an intense expression on his face as he busied himself with lines. Although his posture revealed tension, his casual attire made him appear relaxed. Instead of the usual suit and tie, he wore a pair of sexy, faded jeans, and a nautical blue and white t-shirt. She loved the white ball cap that he wore backward on his head. The man was in his element.

Then she noticed movement from below. Dan stood at the helm. What was he doing here? How naïve she'd been to think the trip was a date, an excursion for two. Then Jenni noticed a woman sitting on one of the benches—Rachel. Disappointment turned into annoyance. She'd looked forward to being alone with Scott. Why hadn't he mentioned inviting the others?

Scott glanced up and waved to her. The smile on his face immediately dissolved any anger she felt, but the disappointment returned. She saw their romantic lunch slip away. She'd packed enough food to feed all four of them, but that wasn't the point.

When she reached the boat, Scott held out his hand and helped her aboard. He touched her back lightly with his other hand and guided her toward Dan and Rachel. The heat from his fingers sent goose bumps across her flesh in the most sensual way, despite the already warm morning.

"We'll be ready to go in a few minutes," he said with a smile, reaching for the cooler on the dock.

She lowered herself into the cockpit, and before she had a chance to say hi to Dan and Rachel, Pirate bounced up to her, wagging his tail.

"Hey there, boy." She rubbed the dog behind the ears, thrilled Scott had brought him along. Rachel waved to her, and Dan grunted.

"Wait for me!" A woman's shrill voice broke the peaceful ambience of the hot sun and calm water.

"Who invited her?" Scott asked. Apologetically, his eyes met Jenni's. He shrugged, as if he didn't understand how Cassie had caught wind of the trip. His silent apology offered her some reassurance, though she'd rather get a cavity filled than spend an afternoon on a boat with Cassie.

"I invited her," Rachel admitted. "I didn't think anyone would mind."

Mind? Had Rachel not thought about the dynamics involved with inviting the same crew out on the same boat as the evening Brittany had lost her life? Jenni stared at the bow and willed the memories away.

She redirected her attention to Cassie when the woman grabbed Scott's outstretched hand and bounced onto the deck. She enfolded her body into his and kissed him on the cheek. At first they looked like a couple, but then Jenni noticed that Scott didn't return the intimacy. He didn't keep hold of Cassie's hand, and he didn't touch Cassie's back lightly as he had hers.

Cassie climbed into the cockpit and sat on the far side of Rachel, as far away from Jenni as possible. Jenni preferred that too. Scott and Dan worked together to unfasten lines and then, with Scott at the helm and Pirate at his feet, he put the engine in reverse and eased the boat out of the slip. Dan walked over and scooted between Jenni and his wife on the port side.

"I'm sorry I didn't get a chance to talk with you much last night," Rachel said to Jenni. Dan squeezed his wife's hand, something apparently bothering him.

"I understand. It's hard to talk to everyone when you're entertaining," Jenni said. She noticed the warning look on Dan's face, aimed at his wife. Was Rachel withholding something from her? She knew her former roommate well, and if Rachel kept a secret from her, Jenni would know about it sooner or later.

From the corner of her eye, Jenni glanced at Cassie, who seemed quieter than normal. Was she bothered by being on *The Great Escape* again with the Friendly Four? Impossible. Cassie didn't seem to have an ounce of remorse over the accident. Or did she?

Once they left the Big Cat Inlet Channel and entered the open waters of the ocean, Scott pulled on the halyard to raise the white, flapping mainsail. The boat heeled twenty degrees as it picked up speed. Jenni ducked under the boom to the starboard side, so she could sit closer to Scott. Pirate scooted over and curled up at her feet. She wondered if Scott had a commitment to keep him yet, or if she needed to find a good home for the dog. What better way to make Scott realize how much he already cared for Pirate.

He glanced at her and smiled. Yes, a true smile. He motioned for her to stand by him.

She grabbed hold of his hand and let him pull her closer. The wind blowing through her short hair felt liberating. She tried to block out the thought of the others watching them, tried to enjoy the moment. Jenni did notice, however, that Dan and Scott exchanged a look she couldn't read.

"Do you want to steer?" Scott asked.

She shook her head. "I don't think so." Her childhood hadn't been all about boats, as his had been. She'd spent her summers at Stallings.

"It's not that hard. Come closer." He gently pulled her between his arms and stood behind her. He leaned down and his breath tickled her ear. "Just hold your hands here on the wheel. Align the bow of the boat with the lighthouse out there. That will keep you going straight."

She didn't want to look at the bow. *Don't think about Brittany. Focus on him instead.*

His cologne smelled fresh, clean, like a spray of ocean water.

She fought the urge to close her eyes and conjure up delicious thoughts about him. The front of his body pressed into the back of her. How was she supposed to concentrate on steering the boat? She told herself he just wanted to steady her, that's all. Or maybe this was his way of making up for the other passengers joining them.

She leaned against him so he could hear her more easily. "What do I do? A wave runner is coming right at us."

"Nothing. Sailboats have the right of way. Most boat owners know that, but you can never be sure about people who operate wave runners." He shook his head. "A lot of people rent them and have no understanding of the rules. There isn't much you can do except stay on course. We're a lot bigger than they are. If they're stupid enough to get too close, that's their problem."

She clenched the wheel. Perhaps another death was imminent, since the Friendly Four were back on the sailboat together. "He's behind us now, playing in our wake." What non-existent wake a sailboat had. Why didn't the annoying teenager find another boat to play behind?

"It's okay. Just keep straight. Be aware of him but don't lose your focus. If they get closer, I'll take care of it."

Jenni wasn't used to trusting someone. It was out of her comfort zone on many different levels.

The wave runner sped up, riding close behind them now.

"Crazy kid! I'll be right back," Scott barked.

"No, don't leave me."

"You'll be fine. Just keep steering straight ahead." He pulled his body away from Jenni, and out of the corner of her eye, she saw Scott lean over the back of the boat. He waved his hands. "Not so close!"

Evidently the kid ignored him because Scott yelled again. "No!"

The wave runner zipped alongside them. Jenni concentrated on aiming the boat toward the lighthouse. Please don't let her hit the kid. She couldn't handle another boating incident.

She heard Scott yell and then Dan.

"Stay on course," Scott said to Jenni. "I'm not risking my passengers for some idiot goofing around on a wave runner." Scott seemed to have learned a lesson on that front.

The kid zoomed in front of them. Jenni clenched her fingers tighter on the wheel. Please let the kid get out of the way.

A speedboat zipped by and the teenager turned and shot after them.

When Scott returned to the helm, Jenni was shaking. "It's okay." He wrapped his warm arms around her. "He's off aggravating someone else."

"When he went in front of us, I thought we were going to hit him. I thought we were going to kill …"

"We're fine. Everyone's safe."

She leaned her head back against his chest, even though she sensed the others watching them. She didn't care. They could stare all they wanted.

"One time I was on a powerboat with some friends from college," Scott said as he rubbed her cold arms. "A wave runner came up beside us, if you can imagine, and my friend didn't know he was there. We turned our boat to head back home, and we smacked right into the guy. He was lucky enough to live. I'd never been so scared in my life."

Jenni gasped. "I've heard Keith complain about wave runners, but I don't think he's had a problem. They mostly stay away from the ferry. Guess they don't go fast enough to make much of a wake."

"Neither do sailboats, but that doesn't stop them." Scott frowned.

She trembled and he held her close for another moment before pulling away again. "Turn the boat into the wind, like this." He turned the helm and the boat lost all power. "Just hold her steady. You're a pro, already." He winked at her. "Be right back."

Jenni did as he asked, wondering what he planned to do. Scott stepped up onto the deck and walked toward the mast. He pulled on a halyard, raised the jib to catch more wind, and secured the line. He returned to the cockpit and adjusted the jib sheet with a winch.

Then he reached around Jenni again and held onto the helm. "Okay, now we're going to close haul, which means we're going to ride as close to the wind as possible. The boat picked up speed immediately, heeling enough that Jenni held on for balance. A spray of water shot over the port side, and Cassie screamed. The water left the woman soaked from the waist up. Jenni grinned. Gentle paybacks were sweet.

Eventually they sailed around a sandy bight and into Lighthouse Bay, between Pony Island and Cannon Island. A small herd of horses waded in the water not far from the shore. "The horses must be heading to a grassy flat out in the water, which is only exposed during low tide," Jenni explained to Scott. Claire had taught her so much about the wild herds. They were on the southeast side of Pony Island, a beach she didn't get to see often. They'd traveled the ocean side, instead of the sound side as the ferry always did.

"Does anyone want to eat lunch on Cannon Island?" Scott asked. "Or keep sailing?"

If Jenni had her way, she'd spend all day on the sailboat. Having had enough excitement for one day, though, she'd retired from steering the boat and leaned back on the bench to relax. She kicked off her flip-flops and she stretched out across the seat, noticing Scott kept glancing at her legs. She rather enjoyed his attention.

"I'd love to get off this boat for a while," Cassie complained. She glared at Jenni, as if Jenni's presence bothered the woman.

Too bad, Jenni thought. Cassie shouldn't have come along on the excursion if she had a problem. "Either way is fine with me," Jenni said casually. She refused to let anything or anybody ruin her laidback mood right now.

Dan and Rachel looked at each other and nodded. Dan said, "Either way is fine with us, but since Cassie wants to get off the boat, that's fine."

"All right then." Scott guided the boat into the deeper part of the inlet, just across from Pony Island. "This is as close as I can get. Put the cooler and whatever else you want into the dinghy. It holds six people comfortably, but with Pirate and the supplies, it'll be tight. Two people can swim, or we can make two trips."

Cassie let out an exaggerated gasp. "That water's cold!"

"Not really," Scott said. He tossed his hat onto the bench then slid off his shirt, exposing his naturally tanned skin and muscled body.

Jenni wanted to run her hands across the dark hair on his chest. A slender dark line of hair trailed below his belly and disappeared into his swim shorts. Then she noticed Cassie's stare and felt a twinge of jealousy. She wished the other woman would back off. It was obvious he wasn't attracted to Cassie. Or was he?

CHAPTER THIRTEEN

Jenni stripped off the outer layer of her clothes. She was glad Claire had talked her into buying a new swimsuit at the end of summer on clearance. Her friend had convinced her that the blue and white striped bikini went well with Jenni's chestnut hair. She had to trust Claire on that one. Jenni felt a bit self-conscious in front of Scott, who was staring intently at her.

Not to be outdone, Cassie seductively removed her clothes, one piece at a time, exaggerating each movement. Scott glanced at her, maybe for a moment too long, but his eyes returned to Jenni. To capture his attention again, Cassie bent over and made a dramatic effort to push her clothes into an oversized bag. Scott still didn't look.

"Who wants to ride in the dinghy?" Dan asked, breaking the tension in the air.

"I definitely want a ride," Cassie said, slowly rubbing a layer of suntan lotion over her crossed legs. "I have no interest in stepping foot into that cold water." She smoothed the lotion around her foot and rubbed each toe seductively.

Obvious women like Cassie always stunned Jenni.

Rachel flicked her hand. "Me, either. The water's a bit too cool for me this time of year."

Everyone looked at Jenni. She shook her head at the thought of riding in the dinghy in close quarters with Cassie. She'd swum in much colder water than this. In fact, some of her best memories were of swimming on Pony Island's shores in the offseason with her friends. She didn't like the crowded beaches with all the tourists, so she did most of her swimming in the colder months.

Without hesitation, Jenni climbed onto the side of the boat and hopped off. When the cold water about sucked the breath out of her, she had to restrain a gasp. It was colder than she'd imagined, but under no circumstances would she allow the others to know how she wished she'd taken the dinghy. Scott jumped in after her, either unaware or uncaring of just how cold the water was. Dan apparently made the better choice and decided to stay behind to help his wife and Cassie load the picnic supplies into the dinghy.

Pirate barked at them and looked like he wanted to jump in after them. Rachel held onto his collar and encouraged him to stay behind.

"Race you to shore," Jenni challenged, glad to get away from the others.

"You got it. Let's go!" he said. In a fraction of a second, they created a spray of splashing water. She struggled to beat him but soon realized she'd made a mistake. The deeper water was too cold.

She slowed and the race ended before it really got started. Unaware she'd quit swimming, he continued to power toward the shore. She supposed she could make it back to the boat; it was much closer than the island. Or maybe she could hitch a ride in the dinghy when Dan passed by.

Scott must have glanced back because he stopped swimming. She could see him bobbing in the water looking for her. She waved her arm to attract his attention.

"Are you okay?"

"The water...," Through chattering teeth she tried to yell loudly enough for him to understand. It had been foolish to initiate the race to begin with.

Scott swam toward Jenni. When he reached her, he turned around so his back was facing her and treaded water. "Hop on my back. I'll help you to the shore."

He wanted her to climb onto his back? Her mouth went dry. How could she touch him like that, all the way to the shore, without giving into temptation?

"Come on, Jenni. The longer you tread water, the more energy you're going to use."

She climbed onto his warm back and wrapped her bare legs around his slippery, muscular waist. For a man who stayed inside all the time, he sure had some muscle. Maybe he had workout equipment in a room at his house in Raleigh.

Scott didn't move at first. Was he enjoying the intimate moment as much as she was?

He rubbed his hand up and down her leg, and then said, "Hold on tight." He took off like a motorboat and she had to wrap her arms and legs tighter around him so she didn't slip off.

She loved the way his muscles worked hard underneath her body, loved the way she rode him bareback like a horse. Every thrust forward heightened her awareness. He was strong; he was sexy.

Jenni snuggled into his neck and closed her eyes. To her surprise, her lips rested on the side of his neck but he didn't seem to mind. And she didn't move away. The brine that ran off his face and onto her lips tasted divine. She resisted the urge to run her tongue along the ridge of his cheekbone to taste more salt. *Oh, please hurry and get to shore before I ravish you right here.*

The hum of the dinghy interrupted her fantasy. Dan had horrible timing. Part of her wanted to pull away from Scott as fast as possible, and the other part of her wanted to seduce him. It was bad enough that she was clinging to Scott's back the way she did. What would the others think? Did she really care?

The boat slowed beside them. “Is everything okay?” Dan asked. He stared at them with what seemed to be a combination of concern and confusion.

Rachel grinned as if she knew something that Jenni and Scott barely realized. Pirate strained against Rachel’s hold on his collar, wanting to jump in after Scott. Cassie, of course, glared at Jenni as if she wished she’d drown.

“Jenni got too cold,” Scott explained. “We’re fine, though. We’re almost there.”

“Okay. Let us know if you need help.” Dan motored off, once again leaving them alone.

Just before they reached the shore, Scott stopped swimming. He slid Jenni around the front of him and held her bottom. She wrapped her legs around him. “I can reach,” he said, “but I doubt you can.”

Despite the cold water, she felt his arousal between her thighs. “Thanks for the free ride,” she mumbled, barely able to speak.

“It was my pleasure, more than you know.” He kissed her softly on the lips, licking the water droplets off her mouth.

She wanted to make love to him right there, regardless of what her common sense commanded. It was too bad the others waited on the beach.

“We’ll continue this later, I promise,” he whispered and kissed her again with a little more urgency. “You’re driving me mad, girl.” He pulled away from her mouth and scooped her into his arms. “I’ll carry you until you can reach the bottom.”

She was perfectly capable of swimming that short distance, but she wasn’t ready to release him yet.

About fifteen feet from the shore he finally let her go. "All good things come to an end. We can take a walk later, just the two of us." His voice was rough and masculine. He’d been just as turned on as she had been.

She held onto the promise that they’d continue their intimate moment later.

They climbed from the water, where a loyal Pirate patiently waited for them, and Jenni wished she had her towel. Goosebumps rose on her arms. By the time they approached the group, Dan had the emptied the dinghy and stood there watching them, raising his eyebrows. She blushed. Thankfully, he tossed them each a thick, warm towel. Rachel and Cassie were busy organizing lunch on a blanket, involved in a conversation.

Jenni couldn't help but notice that even though Cassie appeared poised right now, she seemed to barely control a rage boiling just under the surface. Jenni needed to watch her back.

Scott joined his brother, who'd taken a short stroll down the beach. Jenni walked over to the other women to help with lunch. Rachel was more than appreciative and Cassie ignored her all together. Jenni dipped into the cooler she'd brought and pulled out the sandwiches and grapes.

"Looks like someone planned a romantic trip for two," Rachel observed when she noticed the two plastic wine glasses for the sparkling water. "Sorry if we intruded."

Jenni looked up. "No problem. It's turning out fine." She tried to hide her disappointment from Rachel.

Cassie got up and walked to the dinghy to grab another blanket, leaving Jenni and Rachel to talk. Then Cassie joined the men, no doubt hitting on Scott now that Jenni wasn't there to distract him.

"You know, Cassie doesn't mean to be so rude."

"Really?" Jenni found that hard to believe.

"She wants to make up, to put the past behind her. She just doesn't know how."

Jenni fought the urge to laugh. "Oh, come on, Rachel. You don't really believe that, do you?"

Rachel shrugged. "That's what she told me. But she wants Scott back."

Of course she did. "Why? I mean, why does she chase after him to such an extreme?" Chilled, Jenni wrapped the towel tighter around her. Thank goodness for the warmth the terrycloth offered.

"Cassie believes she'd have married Scott had the accident not come between them."

Although Jenni disagreed with Cassie's assumption, it explained a lot. "Cassie blames me then. If Scott hadn't been flirting with me, she wouldn't have over steered the boat. If that hadn't happened, Brittany wouldn't have died. Scott and Cassie wouldn't have broken up. She thinks their break up was my fault."

"That's right. And if the accident hadn't happened, she wouldn't have suffered with guilt the past twelve years."

"Guilt? I wasn't aware she knew the meaning of the word." Jenni's temper started to flair.

"Her mother believes the root cause of all diseases is stress."

"Are you saying Cassie blames me for her diabetes?" Jenni asked. "Doesn't she take responsibility for her own life?"

Rachel shrugged and glanced in Cassie's direction. "She quit running because of diabetes."

Jenni had heard enough. "There was a professional runner who competed for years with diabetes, successfully. Cassie didn't have to quit, she chose to."

"That's where you're wrong." Rachel quieted her voice. Cassie had finished chatting with the men and was heading their way. "She actually quit because she was pregnant and diabetic. It turns out Cassie also has an eating disorder. She lost the baby."

Pregnant. Fear took over and Jenni couldn't stop thinking about one nagging question. "Who was the father?"

"It wasn't Scott's, if that is what you're thinking. But Cassie also blames you for the loss of her child."

"What?" Jenni could hardly believe what she was hearing.

When Cassie approached, Jenni avoided looking at her. Gran's words comforted her. *Everyone has their own journey in life, Jenni.* Wasn't that the understatement of the decade?

"Dan agreed to come today because Scott hasn't sailed in a long while." Rachel changed to subject deftly. "Dan sails every chance he gets."

Suddenly, Jenni was sick of the abundant subject changing among her family and friends. People needed to start addressing some serious issues, including herself. As it was turning out, Scott's return home was offering a chance for the Friendly Four to heal old wounds.

She didn't know why, but she felt the need to defend Scott. "He seemed to sail just fine today without Dan's help." She couldn't help but wonder if Scott had asked Dan to come along for a different reason. Had he wanted his brother there when he finally stepped onboard his father's sailboat again?

Rachel smiled and touched Jenni's hand. "Scott did a great job, but weather conditions aren't exactly optimal. There's a chance of storms this afternoon. The weather can change fast. It's also a good opportunity for them to bond."

"And I've been preventing that," Jenni said as she looked over at the two brothers, who were now laughing next to the dinghy.

"No, we crashed your party for two. You are doing exactly what you should do. They have time to bond; look at them."

Cassie sat there quietly, listening for a change. What was up with her?

"Thanks, Rachel. I'm glad you're here," Jenni said. A silent look passed between them. Rachel seemed to understand the difficulty Jenni was having with Cassie being along on the trip.

Rachel flagged the men. "Let's eat!"

Scott ran toward them, pushing his brother away, and vice versa. They looked like two little, hungry kids running to reach the table first after a hard day playing football. Pirate ran beside them barking. Jenni giggled at Scott's enthusiasm. She hadn't seen this animated side of him since his return to Big Cat.

Once they finished eating lunch, Scott leaned back on the blanket. "Why don't we spend an hour or so here, swimming or shelling, and then we'll meet back at the dinghy?"

Dan grabbed his wife's hand gently and caressed it. "That works for us. Rachel wants to collect more shells for a project she's making."

Everyone looked at Cassie. "I can always walk to the lighthouse. I've wanted to go up in it again."

"Perfect," Scott said and winked at Jenni.

Instantly she knew what he wanted. He planned to continue what they'd started earlier. She tried to push the anticipation away but it refused to budge.

"We can take Pirate with us," Rachel offered. She was giving them a chance to be alone together.

As soon as they repacked everything and had it organized in the dinghy, Scott grabbed two towels and a blanket. "Come on. Let's go have fun." He grabbed her hand and encouraged her to run down the beach with him, not in training for a marathon, but for play.

"Let's go around the far bend," he suggested. "Everyone else went the other direction."

Before long they discovered a secluded cove with a narrow strip of sandy beach, an ideal swimming area for a couple who wanted privacy. A patch of trees near the edge of the beach made the area even more secluded. "How about over there?"

He jutted his chin toward a sandy alcove surrounded on three sides by small dunes. She nodded, unsure of what she was actually agreeing to. If the tingles running through her body held any indication, she was in for an adventure.

When they approached the cozy nook, he kneeled to spread the blanket on the sand. Then he picked her up and carried her out into the cool water. She wanted to protest but she was enjoying the royal treatment too much to deny herself. The water was only waist high until he kneeled, which made it up to their shoulders. Kissing her neck, he turned her around so she straddled him.

"The water isn't as cold in the cove as it was by the boat," he said, his lips just inches from hers.

“Thanks goodness,” Jenni whispered. She knew she shouldn’t kiss him, because once she did, she wouldn't be able to stop the inevitable. The light breeze blew away what little restraint she had. He leaned forward and lightly touched his lips to hers. They were warm and soft at first. He tasted of a pleasant tropical blend of sea salt and oranges. He deepened the kiss ever so slightly, making her feel the heat radiate from her wet mouth all the way to her toes.

The slight lapping of water added rhythm to their kissing. He pressed her into him more. The cool water felt like a hot tub, blazing warm on this Indian summer day.

His hand caressed her back while he kissed her with hunger. She’d waited half a lifetime for this kiss.

Opening her mouth wider, the heat of his tongue surprised her. The passion that poured from him made her instantly melt. His hardness pushed between her thighs and he groaned. “Jenni.”

“Don’t stop.”

“Are you sure? I mean, I don’t want to stop.”

“Me, either.”

She felt him slip his fingers against her bikini bottom. She’d never wanted anyone as much as she wanted him right now. He kissed her hard with desire.

“Not here,” he mumbled.

She kept her mouth pressed against his as he carried her out of the water and to the hidden blanket. He laid her down gently and hovered over her, running his tongue across her neck and leaving a hot trail of wetness. When he reached her mouth, he kissed her with urgency.

Every kiss, every touch felt like fire against her wet, cool skin. He pulled out a foil packet from his swim trunks and flashed it at her with a boyish grin. He’d thought of everything and she appreciated that he wanted to protect her.

He had her bikini off in a matter of seconds, and he tossed his suit to the side. He pushed his tongue deeper into her mouth as he slipped into her with. A burst of emotion filled her. She’d fantasized many times before about this moment, and couldn’t believe he was making love to her finally, out here on the beach. She barely heard the calls of the seagulls over their own groans of pleasure. Their release was sweet.

***

Scott collapsed next to her, lying halfway atop Jenni to block her from the breeze. He kissed her neck gently and breathed in her scent. Never in his life had it felt so good to be with a woman.

He'd been celibate since his divorce. That was a big deal in his book, but he resisted the urge to share the news with her. She might not understand what that meant to a man.

"Let's take another dip in the water before we leave," he suggested, fully content to stay right here forever if she said the word.

"Race you to the cove?" She wiggled out from underneath him and sat up, reaching for her bikini top.

He shook his head. "My, you are competitive." Thankful his arms were longer than hers were, he yanked the tiny garment off the ground and tossed it farther out of reach. "This swim is in the buff, sweetheart."

"What if somebody walks up?"

"They'll get an eyeful."

Her eyes widened. "If I didn't know you better, I'd say you enjoy living on the edge."

"I haven't heard that since high school." His life had changed drastically since that carefree time. "I've been told more than once that I'm uptight, but never thought I'd be accused of living on the edge again." He laughed and stood. "Let's skinny dip."

"Okay, but warning. You might turn me on again."

He held out his hand to help her up. "Then you won't complain when I ask you to spend the night at my apartment."

She covered her cheeks with her hands. "I can't. My mother will have a fit."

"Jenni, you aren't a teenager anymore. If it will help, I'll ask her." He laughed at her wide-eyed expression and scooped her into his arms.

"I'm not a baby, either. I'd appreciate it if you'd stop carrying me like one." She kicked her legs for emphasis. When he didn't set her down, she gave in and rested her face against his neck. "Okay, you win. I'll spend the night, but I need to go home to help with my father first."

"Deal." He waded out into the water, and submerged them underneath. When they came back up for air, they were both laughing and kissing. "Oops, I got your hair wet. Sorry."

She splashed him. "I'm sure it needed it after all that lovemaking. What would the others think if I came back with crazy-looking sex hair?"

"That we made wild love?"

She splashed him again. Their playfulness felt so natural he wondered why he allowed himself to stop having fun in life. The uptight corner that he'd been boxed into felt suddenly limiting, more so than living in a small town. That, he had to admit, was a surprise.

"Scott?" Dan's voice broke through the afternoon.

Jenni stilled "It's Dan!" She slipped behind him and sank under the water until it covered her shoulders.

"It's okay," Scott grumbled. "Dan!" He hollered to his brother before he could round the bend. "We'll meet you back at the dinghy. Give us five minutes."

"No problem," Dan yelled back. The cove was quiet once again.

Jenni started to swim toward the shore but Scott reached out and grabbed her slippery foot. He pulled her back to him and scooped her into his arms. He carried her back to shore, to the little nest they'd made in the alcove.

As soon as he set her down, he tossed her the bikini. She pulled it on quickly. "That was too close," she said.

"He didn't see anything. You were under the water. And if he did, we looked like two people kissing."

"Not just any two people, he saw us kissing. That doesn't bother you?"

"Why should it?"

She shrugged. "I don't know. I didn't think you wanted anyone to know … we are involved."

He leaned forward and kissed her again. "The whole world can know as far as I'm concerned." He tipped his head back and yelled. "I'm involved with Jenni Stallings. Did you hear that?"

No one answered.

"You've lost it," she said and laughed.

"Are you ready to leave?" He grabbed the blanket and shook out the sand.

"I guess." She wrapped herself in a towel, then handed him the other one.

He squeezed her close to him. "At least you've finally submitted to my charm, Jenni." Man, she made him happy.

She bit him lightly on the neck. "Jenni and the word submit don't belong in the same sentence."

"And you're spunky," he commented. "Race you back to the dinghy?" Before he'd barely said the last word, she shot off in the direction of the boat. He hated to share her with the others so soon. They reached the dinghy too quickly.

"How was your swim?" Cassie asked. Her question carried a spiteful but curious edge.

He let the inquiry pass without much thought. "Fine. How was the lighthouse?"

"It was quite a climb up there, but the view was most entertaining." Cassie flashed him a chiding smile.

He heard Jenni huff but refused to let Cassie get one up on him. "The view was even more fantastic from ground level."

"I bet it was," Cassie snorted. "I can't wait to share the news with all of Big Cat."

From the corner of his eye, he saw Jenni stiffen. Great. That was just what their relationship needed, to get caught in the wheels of the gossip mill. He didn't have time for this nonsense now. He studied the darkening sky.

"You breathe one word of this," he said to Cassie, "and you'll find yourself unemployed."

"You can't fire me for telling the truth."

"Try me." Concerned about the weather, he strode toward Dan.

"How can you have fun when your dad is at home dying?" Cassie fell in step with Jenni, and Scott barely heard the mean words.

"Grow up, Cassie." Jenni wasn't accepting Cassie's rude comments, either.

Scott reached back, took Jenni's hand, and led her toward the dinghy where the others waited. Jenni kept glancing back at Cassie. "Don't let her bother you, Jenni. You have a right to a life." He knew she was feeling guilty for playing on a sailboat, making love to a man she shouldn't be attracted to in the first place, while her father was at home dying. She was probably questioning her loyalty as a daughter. That was exactly the reaction Cassie wanted.

"Those clouds on the horizon are dark," Dan said, interrupting Scott's thoughts.

"We need to get back to the boat and listen to the weather," Scott commanded. "We'll have to make two trips with the dinghy."

"You and Jenni are already wet," Cassie scoffed. "It would make the most sense if you swam to the boat, so we can get there faster."

"For one thing," Scott explained, feigning patience, "no one should be in the water in case of lightning. We need to get out of here fast."

CHAPTER FOURTEEN

When everyone was back in the sailboat, Scott turned on the radio. Sure enough, they were in the direct path of a severe storm. "How long do you think we have before it hits?" Scott asked Dan.

"Maybe an hour or two. It doesn't seem to be moving real fast."

Scott looked off in the distance at the black sky. "I'd like to use the sails if possible."

"We'll move faster with them," Dan agreed.

Scott placed his good luck hat on his head. "If we run into trouble, we can always shorten sail." It felt good to collaborate with Dan. Scott missed the good ole days more than he admitted.

"I agree," Dan said. "By the way, you sound like Dad. He still refuses to use the motor unless he has to."

Scott laughed and it felt good. He swore a deep knot of tension released. "Dad used to sail all the way around Pony Island, adding at least two hours onto a trip, just so he could use the sails when the wind wasn't in his favor."

"He's a true sailor, just like you."

Scott didn't deserve such a compliment. "Let's hope we get back to the harbor before the storm hits. I don't want to be out here unless we have to."

They worked together in harmony, even though they hadn't sailed together in years. Before long they had the boat headed toward home and the storm.

Scott sensed something else besides the weather was bothering Dan. Was it Scott's intensifying relationship with Jenni? Was his brother secretly jealous? He decided to ask Dan the first chance he got.

That chance didn't come any time soon. The storm rolled in much faster than they'd predicted. The powerful wind caused them to pick up speed, but they were still only halfway back to the marina when they saw the first lightning bolt.

Rachel and Cassie darted into the below cabin for safety. Jenni, instead of running for dry cover, stayed on deck and offered to help.

"Go inside, Jenni!" Scott barked out the order harsher than he'd meant to, but he had a surprisingly strong urge to protect her.

She frowned. "Give me a task, otherwise I'll make my own."

Dang stubborn woman. He appreciated her offer but wanted to keep her safe. There was no chance of that. "If you insist. You can bring the swim bags below, and anything else we don't want to get wet." At least that would get her into the cabin and out of the open cockpit.

She busied herself by collecting the swim gear without complaint, even after the first large drops fell onto her backside.

The wind grew stronger and the boat heeled forty-five degrees. Pirate slid across the floor of the cockpit. "Let's get the sails down," Scott yelled so Dan heard him. "This storm's coming fast." He tried to recall everything his father had taught him.

"Jenni, can you grab life jackets and rain coats out of the cabin?" Scott asked with urgency. "They're under the settee, the one with the blue pillows on top. Hurry. And please take Pirate with you."

She made for the cabin, grabbing onto Pirate's collar and pulling him. The dog wouldn't budge. She slapped her leg with enthusiasm until he finally agreed to go below.

"The jib, we need to get it down," Dan reminded Scott.

"I'll go," Scott offered. The boat jerked and he held onto the wheel for support. Even though the situation required immediate attention, Scott wanted to apologize to Dan first. "Hey, sorry. You know, for not calling or keeping in touch over the years." Scott swallowed hard. His chest swelled with emotion. It didn't help when he saw the pain on his brother's face. "I'm also sorry about Jenni. I'll leave her alone if you want." He wasn't sure how he'd pull that off but a relationship with his brother was important.

"I told you, I'm over Jenni. She's just a friend now," Dan said. "The jib needs to come down. First you need to put on a life jacket."

Scott appreciated Dan's concern for his safety. He was glad his brother agreed to come along on the sailboat. He didn't want to think about handling the boat in a storm alone, especially since he hadn't sailed in years.

Jenni reappeared, carrying an armful of yellow slickers and three life jackets. She walked across the slippery fiberglass toward him and lost her footing when the boat rocked.

"I got you," Scott said. He pulled her closer and kissed her salty lips for a quick moment.

She looked back and forth between the two brothers, as if she knew they'd been talking about her. "Here, take these." Jenni shoved a slicker and a life vest at each of them, and pulled on her own. Her red hair, which looked even darker wet, stuck to her forehead. Beads of rain ran down her cheeks.

This woman was causing mayhem in his mind. Scott prayed Dan had told him the truth about not having feelings for her. It would about kill him to break off his budding relationship with her. She looked so vulnerable standing there, and was so noble for helping. He wanted to take her into his arms again but didn't. The jib needed to come down.

This was one of the rare times Scott wished his father had a newer boat. He needed to bring the sails down by hand. He pulled the slicker on and fastened the life jacket over the top. Then he turned the boat directly into the wind, relieving the pressure on the sails. They went slack and started flapping loudly. Dan centered the boom.

"Jenni, can you take over at the helm?" Scott yelled over the wind. If she helped, that would free Dan to assist with the sails. "I need to go on deck."

While Scott saw concern in Jenni's eyes, he didn't have time to reassure her. She took over the helm without reservation.

"Hold her steady for me. I'll be right back." He planted a quick kiss on her lips, then made his way toward the deck.

"Be careful up there!" Scott barely heard her words.

Dan tossed him a line. "Tie this around your waist."

Scott understood Dan's silent message. If he fell overboard, the moving boat would leave him in her wake to fight the waves alone. Just like Brittany. Scott shuddered but blamed it on the rain-drenched clothes he wore. He tied the line around his waist.

Before Scott stepped onto the deck, Dan grabbed his arm. "Be careful up there, bro. Give me your hat, so you don't lose it."

His good luck hat.

A large wave rocked the boat for emphasis.

"Sure thing." Scott yanked it off and handed his favorite hat to Dan, wishing he felt as confident as he'd sounded.

He ignored the butterflies dancing in his stomach and stepped onto the wet deck. With a shaky hand, he grabbed hold of a line to steady himself. He'd done this before, but that didn't lessen his anxiety or slow his pounding heart rate. Nothing this adventurous had crossed his path since high school. He was grateful he had a line tied to him, one that was made fast to the boat.

The waves crashed against the boat, momentarily rocking The Great Escape farther onto her side. Scott held on tight as he released the halyard from the mast. He concentrated on taking one cautious step after another, grabbing onto whatever he could, toward the dreaded bow. He tried to push aside the horrid memories of losing a young teenager over the bow pulpit.

Let the guilt go. A temporary surge of adrenaline shot through him and for a moment, he felt like the agile football player he'd once been. He maneuvered on the deck as he'd done many times before, when he'd sailed with his father and Dan through worse storms than this. But the memories made this storm more difficult. The boat rocked so much that he dropped to his knees, taking care to secure his hold as he crawled out to the jib. When he reached the bow, he remembered searching for a body in the dark water, remembered the loud silence of his own traumatic storm.

Focus. He had to concentrate on what he was doing. The others were counting on him.

The wind blew against his face, the cold rain stinging his cheeks. He tried to wrestle the sail down, but the wind whipped it around and tried to snap it from his hands. Unexpectedly, the mental lines that restrained the workaholic banker in him released a sense of freedom so strong he swore the raging storm decreased in intensity. He managed to flake the flapping sail onto the deck and secure it. The boat rocked hard again. Now he had to crawl back to the safety of the cockpit.

Thankfully the boat steadied a bit as he worked his way across the deck. Right before he reached his destination, as his hand grabbed for Dan's outstretched arm, another wave rocked the boat hard. Scott's knee slipped and he lost his hold. He slid across the deck in what seemed slow motion.

No! Grab hold of something, anything. His leg hit a stanchion with a painful thump, and the lifeline, wrapped around the edge of the boat, slowed his likely plunge into the water. His upper body slid across the sleek fiberglass deck, the one he'd spent so much time cleaning as a child, until his arm slammed into another stanchion. He reached out and clutched the cold metal between his swollen fingers. Don't go overboard. Jenni. Think of Jenni.

The rocking of the boat slowed enough that Scott regained his foothold. With shaking hands, he pulled himself across the deck toward the cockpit.

He had to beat the next set of waves. Pull harder!

His bloody hands burned as he held on tight. The cockpit was close, but it had been close once before. Don't lose sight of the goal.

Almost there. Just another three feet.

The cockpit was within reach. He grabbed onto the edge with one hand and Dan grabbed hold of the back of the life jacket, hurling him into the cockpit. Scott slammed onto the cockpit sole with a thud.

Dan whooped at Scott's success. It was a long-needed welcome home.

"Scott!" Jenni called out.

When he looked at her, she sent him a distraught grin and flashed a quick thumbs-up with both hands still on the wheel. If he hadn't won her heart before, he'd certainly won it now.

When Scott tried to stand, Dan reached out to help. His brother's slap on the back reminded him of earlier days when his father encouraged his sons to be the best sailors possible. Back then, his father was happier and wasn't a drinker. Scott longed for happiness, a connection to the people he loved. He wondered if it was possible to find peace among his fighting parents.

Dan mashed Scott's favorite ball cap back onto his head.

"The mainsail?" Dan's voice cut through the pain Scott felt in his hands and right leg.

Dan wanted his opinion? After he'd almost gone overboard and made a mess out of pulling down the jib? He hadn't met his own high standard, so the consult surprised him. Maybe Scott needed to lighten up.

"What do you think?" Dan asked. "Make the call, Captain."

Captain? The old nickname felt as familiar as his beloved baseball hat. Had his crazy stunt on the deck caused Dan to respect him again?

"It needs to come down," Scott said with authority. With the storm as bad as it was, they needed to use the motor.

A large wave knocked against the boat and caused the vessel to lean. Still weak from his earlier adventure, Scott fell onto the floor of the cockpit and gasped at the pain. Man, this storm was getting the better of him.

“Scott! Are you all right?” Jenni yelled.

Scott barely heard her with the wind in his ears. When the boat rocked hard again, he rolled in her direction. He smashed into the console with his shoulder and cursed, the first time in years. He hadn’t felt such throbbing pain since he’d fought an opposing team’s quarterback after Scott’s team lost an important game. Being on the sailboat today reminded him of all sorts of scattered and painful memories. He pulled himself to a standing position.

Scott leaned down, just inches from Jenni. “I’m fine. Want to do that again?” he quipped.

Another crashing wave tossed him into her.

“No thanks!”

“Scott, I need help with the main,” Dan hollered. He started the boat's motor to make sure it worked.

“Twenty bucks if you get us back to the harbor safely,” she said in a half-humorous tone.

“Let’s up the stakes," Scott said. "Agree to spend tonight at my apartment.”

“Deal.”

“Scott! Get over here now.”

Scott hurried to his brother. They worked together, and he missed the camaraderie he used to share with Dan and their dad.

“Ease the sail down!” Scott yelled.

Lowering the mainsail little by little, so the whole thing didn’t come down at once, would be the easy part. The difficult task would be to keep their balance enough to stand while they reefed the main.

The waves knocked the boat around while Scott tried to steady himself. He’d had enough trauma to his body for one day, and with Jenni spending tonight at his apartment, he needed to protect what wasn't yet bruised or injured. As he let the halyard up to lower the main, Dan flaked the drenched sail onto the boom as best he could.

"We'll be back at the harbor in twenty minutes," Scott said. "It's been nice sailing with you, brother." Battling the bad weather had given a sense of adventure back to his life.

"Anytime, Captain. This storm was practice for your upcoming encounter with Mom and Dad. You know, you have to reconcile with them at some point."

Scott groaned. He dreaded addressing the issues with his parents. "You're right. Why do you think I stayed away all these years?"

***

"Listen, maybe this isn't a good idea," Jenni said as they stood outside her parent's house. "Gran's here."

"Why would they care if you spend the night with me? You're an adult," Scott reasoned.

"The second I moved back into their house, they seemed to forget my age."

"Are you afraid of confronting your parents?"

"Of course not," she said a little too defensively. "I'm trying to save you from an uncomfortable moment. My dad and grandmother don't get along." That was a vast understatement. "And besides, my mom's going to preach about premarital sex. You've been warned."

"They can't be worse than my parents."

She disagreed. "Are you afraid to confront yours?" Without meaning to, she'd tossed his own words back at him.

"No." He stared at her for a long moment before he grinned. "Afraid wouldn't be the right word. Maybe apprehensive."

"Why would a self-assured man like yourself be apprehensive about facing your parents?"

"I feel responsible for their problems." He looked away. "They fought when I went away to college; my mom wanted me to stay, my dad wanted me to pursue my goals. When I got married and bought a house in Raleigh, they fought about that too. It seems no matter what I do, I cause disharmony in their marriage."

"Stop right there," she said. "They are responsible for their own happiness. Their fighting has nothing to do with you."

He turned back and stared at her, his eyes haunted. "You're probably right. If they're miserable, you would think they'd separate. But they despise divorce. I failed them again."

"You didn't fail at anything. Your divorce is your business, not theirs. You can't live your life to please your parents." Jenni stopped talking. She realized the weight of what she'd just said.

"Exactly. It seems we both have the same lesson to learn." He took her hand and led her up the flight of stairs. Before they reached the back door, he pressed a kiss to her lips. "There is nothing wrong with wanting to spend the night at my house. Just remember that."

Jenni pushed open the screen door with Scott at her heels. "I wonder where everybody is. Usually Mom's in here cooking dinner." Jenni's belly tightened into a perfect square knot. She walked quicker, down the hall toward the den where her father slept. She stopped so short in front of his doorway that Scott bumped into her.

"If you want to die, then go ahead," Gran declared. "You have a choice to make. Focus on what you want. Stop complaining and appreciate what you have. Take a look around you."

"I'll make a choice. I want you to leave me alone, Mom." Her son's deep voice echoed through the small room.

"If you have the strength to bark at me like that, then you have enough spunk to live. Get out of this bed."

Scott whistled under his breath. "And I thought my family fought," he whispered.

"You haven't seen anything yet," Jenni warned.

"Virginia Lynn? What are you doing hiding out in the hallway?" Gran asked.

"Uh, oh." Scott chuckled.

"I'm giving you space." Jenni stepped into the doorway and peered in at Gran first, then at her mother and father. No wonder Gran felt frustrated. Jenni's dad was unshaven, his hair mussed, and he still wore his pajamas even though it was dinnertime. He was most likely tired from fishing yesterday.

"Oh, hello Scott," Gran said, her tone layered in heavy syrup. She adored Scott, always had. Jenni suspected Gran knew how much she cared about the man and that was her way to show approval. Gran flagged him into the room.

"You two look like hell," her father barked. "Didn't you have sense enough to come in from the rain?"

"Oh, my," Gran said. "You were sailing in that storm, weren't you?"

"Yes, but thanks to Scott, we're home safe."

"You took my daughter sailing in that bad weather?" He actually sat up in bed. His arms shook from the exertion, or perhaps from anger.

Jenni knew exactly what her father was thinking. He'd already lost one daughter on that sailboat, and he wasn't about to lose another. She walked over and hesitantly rested her hand on his shoulder. For once he didn't tense from her touch. "Dad, I'm okay. Scott did a great job." Out of the corner of her eye, she swore Scott puffed out his chest with pride.

"What were you doing sailing in that storm?" He asked Scott again.

"It was sunny when we left, sir." Scott stepped forward. "We wanted to get out on the boat and enjoy the day, that's all. Squalls pop up out of nowhere."

Her father scowled at Jenni. She felt like a child again. "Why weren't you working at your coffee shop? If you want it to succeed, you need to be there instead of running off to play on a boat."

His words stung. She tried to push the hurt aside, to answer him without letting the emotion seep into her words. "I believe you were the one who suggested I hire someone because I needed a day off. I took your advice."

He almost growled. "You were off yesterday, when you took me fishing. Today makes two days in a row. And I didn't mean for you to hire your grandmother." He flicked a dismissive hand at Gran, who had agreed to cover for Jenni today. "She never bothered to help at Stallings, so why's she willing to help in your restaurant now?"

Let it go, Jenni thought. He'd call her coffee shop a restaurant until the day he died.

"Excuse me," Gran interjected. "I helped at Stallings a lot. Just because you expected me to work more is no reason to discount all my long hours. Despite your opinion, I did more than play with horses."

"I never said that's all you did."

"Maybe not with words. It's obvious in the way you talk to me, though, the blame you put on me after Stallings almost failed."

"I did no such thing." He whipped his head around to glare at Jenni and Scott. "You don't need to hear this conversation."

"Dinner is in the refrigerator," Jenni's mother added.

Jenni ignored the comment. "You seem to forget that I'm twenty-eight years old. I can handle an argument."

"I don't care how old you," he said. "You're staying in my house."

He gave her the perfect lead-in. "By the way, I'm sleeping over at Scott's tonight. Keith agreed to stay here in case you need help, but he won't be over until later." Scott's body pressed against her back, his warmth reassuring.

Her mother drew in a sharp breath. "Jenni, you know better."

The room swelled with tension, but Jenni refused to shrink under pressure. When Scott slipped his hand into hers, she experienced an unfamiliar emotional connection to him. The intensity scared her.

She tried to ignore her mother fingering the cross around her neck, tried to ignore her father's face turning red.

"You'll do no such thing." He pointed his finger at Jenni.

Oh, how Jenni despised that finger. He'd tormented her with the gesture all through her younger years, aiming it at her whenever he disapproved of something she did.

"Your daughter's an adult now," Gran said. "It's time you realize that."

"That doesn't give her reason to commit a sin," he said.

His accusatory words pushed Jenni to the edge of her tolerance. "My personal life has nothing to do with you," she said. "If I want to spend the night with Scott, I'll do it. I don't need your permission."

To her surprise, her dad leaned back against his pillow. Unsure if the argument had worn him out, or if he'd simply given up because she'd stood up to him, she didn't know. She felt somewhat guilty about talking to her parents that way, it defied how they raised her, but the sense of freedom was telling. Why hadn't she confronted him years ago? Feeling relief, she turned and left the room. She was going to spend the night with Scott. Period.

Scott followed Jenni to her room. "Your Dad can be intimidating."

"Tell me about it. I'm not one to back down easily, though."

He seemed to heed her warning. "I'll remember that." He walked over to an antique desk pushed into a corner of her bedroom. The wooden stable her father gave her sat on the desk and attracted his attention. He ran his finger along the individually cut shingles that made up the roof. "Did someone make this?"

"My grandfather. Before he died, he gave it to my father." She swallowed hard. "Now he's giving it to me." She'd meant to put the stable by his bed, so he could take comfort from it during those difficult times when he wanted to feel better.

"That picture of the stallion," he said, pointing to the framed photograph hanging above the desk. "He's the one we've seen on the island."

"That's right. His name is Magic," she said. "He's a natural leader, well respected by the herd."

He stared at the photograph.

"I want to have that kind of presence in the business world," she explained. "I want the community to take me seriously, to support my goals for expansion." She tore her gaze away from the photograph and looked at him. "I'm determined to be successful."

"Why are you pushing so hard? What are you trying to prove?"

How dare he question her motive? She squelched her annoyance before he noticed. A display of temper would only prove he hit a nerve, and she wanted to hide that fact. But why, she had to wonder, had his question threatened her to the point where she wanted to make him leave?

He understood too much. One thing was for sure; he wanted to test her, and she never backed down when challenged.

Jenni met his gaze directly. If he wanted to know what drove her hard, she'd tell him. "Because I'm a survivor." Jenni would endure her father's blame, would tolerate his disapproval. That's right. But she didn't know if she'd survive his death.

She strode to the closet and tugged an overnight bag from the shelf, determined not to let the exchange keep her from what she wanted. She'd waited too many years to be with Scott, just to let it slip away. She began shoving the bag full of clothes, barely paying attention to what she packed.

Deep down she'd always known what drove her, dysfunctional or not, but she'd never admitted the truth to anyone before, not even to herself. "I'm a lot like my father. I plan to be successful, as he was with Stallings. But he tries to discourage me from having a "restaurant," because he doesn't think I'm good enough."

Scott shook his head. "Wrong. I'd bet anything that he doesn't want his daughter to have to work so hard, that he wants to know you'll be financially secure."

He was right. Her dad had actually told her that, but until now, she hadn't absorbed what he'd really said. "That's why he's still alive," she said. "Why he hasn't let the cancer steal him away to his death yet."

The pain of hearing the words aloud caused a single tear to slide down her cheek.

Scott touched the wet streak. "He loves you, Jenni."

"Maybe."

In order to avoid a complete, emotional breakdown, she pulled away and continued to pack. When she lifted a pair of hot pink pajama pants and a white tank top, Scott stopped her. "You won't need those."

She felt her cheeks grow warm. His penetrating eyes only enhanced her desire and she dropped the pajamas onto the bed.

"That's better. Grab a toothbrush and let's get out of here." He picked up her bag and tossed it over his shoulder. "I want to spend every second of tonight tantalizing you in ways you've only dreamed about."

He had no idea of the fantasies she'd conjured up over the years.

CHAPTER FIFTEEN

"I never thought I'd appreciate a hot shower so much," Jenni said as she ran a washcloth over Scott's wounded shoulder.

"Ouch. Watch the soap, will you?" Despite his complaint, he bent down and kissed her softly on the lips.

"I'm just getting started." She glanced over his bruised body, covered with tiny scrapes from the adventure on the sailboat earlier. "And I promise you, the best is yet to come." From his smile, she knew her eyes flashed with excitement and revealed the wicked thoughts that danced in her mind.

"Promises, promises." He grinned and steered her hand lower. Before long, the water turned cold, causing her to shiver. He guided her out of the shower, grabbed two towels stacked neatly on the sink, and led her into the immaculate bedroom. Without bothering to use the towels, he yanked the sheets aside and lifted her onto his bed.

His warm lips and hot tongue pressed against her skin as he kissed every inch of her body. The man was even more sexy than her most erotic dream of him. She closed her eyes and savored the sweet sensation, all the while anticipating the precious moment of when she'd gladly return the favor.

The tension slowly built to the point she thought she'd explode. But he made her wait, even though patience wasn't her forte. She knew what she wanted, and she wanted him now.

He was in no hurry.

Finally, when he decided to reward her in a most pleasurable way, he entered her. The rush of emotions surprised her, and she had to fight back tears of joy. The man she'd dreamed about, pretended so often to make love to, was kissing her neck with more tenderness than she ever imagined. They made slow, passionate love, until eventually he rolled off Jenni and held her in his strong arms. Between the late evening growing cooler and the damp sheets chilling them, they snuggled under the down comforter to keep warm, not wanting to leave each other long enough to turn on the heater.

"You're something," he whispered as he stared at the ceiling. "After all those years pining after you in school, I never thought I'd actually have the pleasure of dating you, much less making love to you."

"What? You wanted to date me in high school?" She leaned on an elbow to look at him. When he turned his head toward her, she gazed into his dreamy eyes.

"I've wanted you for as long as I can remember. You didn't know that?"

"No. I thought you always wanted Cassie, even until recently. She was your high school sweetheart."

"No, you were my high school, sweetheart. But I couldn't have you because you dated my brother."

She relaxed into him and snuggled her cheek into his warm chest. Out of the few men she'd had serious relationships with, she'd always held back because of him. She adored this man since she could remember. "I gave up on you after you asked out Cassie. I agreed to date Dan because he's a nice guy, but I always wanted you. I had no idea the feeling was mutual. I guess it doesn't matter. We ended up together."

"That's right," he said. "I'd like to keep it that way."

***

The week flew by. Gran was working out well in the coffee shop, and business was beginning to offset her wages as Jenni's father had predicted. Now that she had another espresso machine, the sandwiches helped to increase sales. Coffee Break was starting to make a profit.

The bell above the door tinkled and in walked Claire. Jenni had been so busy lately she'd barely gotten a chance to talk much with her friend. To her disappointment, Claire's face was pale and she wore a frown. The baby.

"Claire, have a seat." Jenni scooted around the counter and pulled out a stool. "Is everything okay?"

Claire shook her head. "Not really. I started bleeding, so I went to the doctor. They said to take it easy but there isn't a thing they can do to help. If I miscarry, they say it's for the best." She looked so sad that Jenni's heart actually ached.

"Bleeding doesn't necessarily mean you're going to miscarry."

"True. But it doesn't mean I won't. The baby's heartbeat still sounds healthy, at least for now." Claire propped her head up with the palm of her hand. Dark circles underscored her eyes and she looked as though she hadn't slept much.

"Keep imagining holding your healthy baby in your arms," Jenni encouraged. "Everything will be okay."

"How do you know?" Claire looked as though she might break into tears. "I'd like to believe you."

"I can sense it." Jenni hoped she was right.

"Thanks. You're a good friend." Claire reached out and touched Jenni's arm. "How are things going with you? With Scott?"

"We're fine." That was the truth, except Jenni was having second thoughts about Scott.

"You seem on edge." Claire was always so perceptive. Even though she was worried about her pregnancy, she was inquiring about Jenni's confusing relationship. "Shouldn't you be beaming with happiness? You finally got the man."

"I'm scared," Jenni said.

"Of what?"

"Feeling vulnerable." Jenni never allowed herself to be in that position. Why start now? "He's leaving in a few weeks to go back to Raleigh."

"So what? Long distance relationships can work," Claire said. "Raleigh's not that far. Two and a half hours tops."

"I don't have time to be running up there. I have a business to run," Jenni said, waving a hand in the air. "Especially with my dad dying. I need to be here." She pointed at the floor for emphasis.

"Relax. Enjoy the journey. If he's the one for you, it will work out."

Jenni wasn't so sure.

No sooner had Claire left, than Scott walked in. He strolled to the counter and leaned in close, apparently oblivious to the room full of people drinking coffee and eating sandwiches. She wanted to back away from him but refused to let the watchful eyes of her gossiping customers bother her. Anything they witnessed was the truth, anyway.

"Hi, sugar." He planted a kiss on her lips and didn't seem concerned about who saw them.

For now, Jenni decided to tune out her nagging fears about him leaving. "If you're up for a run on Pony Island this afternoon, then meet me at the ferry," she challenged. "Today, though, you have to keep up with me or you lose."

He gasped, which gave her a small sense of triumph. She'd beat the banker at any game he wished to play.

"You're on. Twenty bucks says I can keep up." He leaned even closer.

"Then get ready to pay." She forced a grin.

He brushed his finger along her jaw line. "If you're so confident, why don't we up the ante?"

***

"Are you sure you can handle all this business alone, Gran?" Jenni asked.

"I got it. Go enjoy your run, and make sure you don't behave with that gorgeous man." Gran pointed toward the door.

Jenny decided to trust Gran. She needed to leave Coffee Break now, before she changed her mind. As soon as she stepped foot outside the door, a voice startled her.

"I thought I'd meet you here instead of the ferry." Scott flashed her a twenty. "I came prepared, just in case I lose the bet. But don't count on it." His smile appeared genuine today. "Or did you want to up the ante as we discussed before?" he asked.

"We discussed no such thing. Let's stick to twenty bucks."

"Chicken," he teased.

"Hardly. Don't worry; I'll win," she said, "although I'd hate to crush your ego." She tried to hide a smile but failed miserably. Jenni reached into a potted rosemary bush and dropped her key chain under a spindly branch to hide it. For good luck, she ran her hand along the branch. The pungent smell filled the air.

"Are your sandwiches still selling well?" He shoved his money into the small pocket of his shorts and led the way down the lightly populated street toward the ferry. He seemed eager to run today.

"I sold out during lunch," she said. "The egg white bagel went first, then the turkey sandwiches. Dan was thrilled when I placed a slightly larger order for tomorrow."

"Impressive. Maybe your coffee shop will survive."

"Maybe?" Her belly clenched and she walked faster. He sounded just like her disapproving father. "It's nice to know you believe in me."

"I didn't mean it like that. I was trying to compliment you." He increased his pace to keep up with her.

"Thanks, but keep your compliments to yourself from now on. I don't need that kind of support." She walked with vigor to release her irritation.

When they reached the ferry, Keith's boat was nowhere in sight. Jenni glanced at the cell phone in her hand, fifteen minutes until the next scheduled departure.

Scott reached out and touched her arm. "Listen, I didn't mean to insult you."

She turned her back to him. Normally she ran to clear her head from the day's stress, and with him along, if he was going to question her business skills, he'd add a component of frustration instead of peacefulness. She had enough emotional turmoil at home. Her family dynamics were anything but tranquil.

The ferry rounded a small island in the estuary and Keith tooted the horn. Jenni waved eagerly and walked down to the dock with Scott right behind her. She watched as Keith pulled into the boat slip. Her brother tossed a line to George, an older man he'd recently hired on a part-time basis.

"Are you ready for your run?" Keith looked from Jenni to Scott. Who knew what her brother was thinking? She never explained why she'd wanted him to spend the night at their parents' house, and he didn't ask. He was polite that way. She bet he'd heard the likely gossip circulating around town, though.

"We're ready." It felt like a huge step to say "We" and include Scott.

They stepped onto the ferry, this time the only passengers aboard. The boat pulled away from the dock and soon they were travelling through the marshlands. A Great Blue Heron stood still at the edge of a yellowing patch of tall grass and watched them, ready to take off in flight if needed. She could relate to the feeling.

Usually Jenni dated safe men, meaning guys who didn't upset her equilibrium—not that she was dating Scott exactly. She liked to manage her emotions as far as men were concerned. She glanced sideways at Scott. He was dangerous to spend time with and made her want to flee like the heron.

Before long, the boat glided easily into the boat slip on Pony Island. "Okay, you know the drill, sis. I'll pick you up at six o'clock. Try not to be late this time."

Scott jumped from the boat and offered his hand. Against her better judgment, she reached for him.

He grinned suspiciously when he helped her on the dock, and before she knew what he was up to, he took off running. The man had a head start in their race. She waved at Keith, who slowly motored away from the dock, then she took off after Scott. Surprisingly, he'd made decent headway in a short amount of time. When she caught up with him, she noticed he seemed slightly winded. With twenty bucks as the agreed upon bet, she didn't have to think hard about whether to pass him or not.

She slowly ran past him, keeping an even stride. Instead of acknowledging him, she concentrated on placing her feet on the wet sand in front of her. The footing wasn't great with the driftwood and the horses' fresh hoof prints, and required she pay extra attention.

She made sure to keep him within view by risking a fleeting look behind her occasionally. He surprisingly kept up, even though he remained at least fifty feet back. She'd hate to have to compete against him in a marathon.

Today he ran longer than he had so far. Jenni glanced back and noticed him slowing. She continued running, cleared a large bend, and enjoyed the sound of her shoes as they thumped on the wet sand. She was in her element, as he'd been on the sailboat.

Fully aware of where she placed her feet, Jenni darted another look behind her. Scott was nowhere around. He had most likely broken to a walk or turned back.

She glanced ahead of her again. The view of the cove always astounded her, the peacefulness of the white sand and aqua water. The maritime forest on her right competed for her attention. Jenni gazed at the woods and slowly inhaled the smell of decaying leaves mixed with the salty breeze. The island fed her soul. She especially appreciated the rugged driftwood that littered the beach in abundance.

By the time she looked down again, her shoe landed on a fallen branch. It rolled underneath her weight, and she gasped as she lost her balance and hit the ground hard. The wind sucked out of her and a cramp tightened under her ribs. She dragged in a slow breath, one after another, and tried to remain calm.

Her right ankle hurt. She didn't think it was anything serious, until she tried to stand. The intense pain warned her not to risk further injury. Marathon runners needed to protect their precious legs.

Had Scott turned back? Would he round the bend and find her lying on the ground? She pulled in enough breath to scream his name but all that escaped her mouth was a deflated yelp. Panic threatened when he didn't appear.

"Scott!" The breeze blew the opposite way. He wouldn't hear her pitiful cry for help, no matter how loud she managed to yell. Unfortunately, she had no choice but to keep calling. "Scott!"

He was probably long gone by now. If he grew concerned at some point, he might come looking for her. But after the last time they ran out here, he might think she was lost in her head again while running, as Keith like to say.

Unnerved, Jenni sensed something watching her. She looked up to see Magic scrutinizing her, most likely to assess if she endangered his herd. His black mane and tail blew in the breeze, his brown coat beginning to thicken into a wooly blanket for winter. He didn't feel threatening, and he seemed more curious than anything.

"Thanks, gorgeous one, for checking on me," she said. He cocked his head as if he wanted to answer but couldn't. Where was his harem? She scanned the area and sure enough, his mares grazed on the Spartina grass some distance behind him. She thought about her mission to run the marathon. "I'll run that race for you, Big Boy, and I'll donate my winnings when I beat Cassie Forthright. We'll generate money for you guys, I promise."

She swore the stallion nodded.

Jenni rubbed her ankle. It started to throb now that her adrenaline began to subside. She needed to be proactive, before Scott walked farther away, before the sun set.

"Scott!" Jenni called out again, with force this time instead of panic. Nobody answered. She dug into the top of her sports bra to retrieve her cell phone and thumbed through her contacts. She didn't have his cell number. She swallowed her pride and dialed her brother. He'd be happy she carried a cell phone finally.

No service. Now what was she supposed to do? She'd have to rely on Scott for help. Soon it would be dark and cold.

CHAPTER SIXTEEN

Scott cleared a wide peninsula and sensed Jenni nearby. He squinted against the peach-tinted sky and scanned the creamy white, sandy cove. He felt her presence but dismissed the feeling when he didn't see her anywhere.

He had to admit, running on the exotic island was one advantage over exercising around the rather crowded lake of his Raleigh home. It felt good to work out, and time spent with Jenni was always a bonus. He didn't mind forfeiting twenty bucks to convince her to run with him, especially out here.

He spied a fallen tree up ahead and decided that would be his turn-around point. With a destination in mind, he slowed to a rapid walk along the water's edge, pleased about the increase in his stamina.

Who knows, maybe he'd enter the race Jenni talked about, *Run for the Horses*. The idea had popped into his head when she'd first mentioned it.

If he put his mind to it, he could even win. A perfectionist, he always strove to win whatever he focused on, from banking to a marathon. The more he thought about it, the better he liked the idea. He needed something to drive hard toward besides work.

He'd keep quiet and surprise Jenni the morning of the race. After all, she might enjoy a little friendly competition between them.

When he reached the fallen tree, he glanced at his watch. Keith would be waiting for them soon. But where was Jenni? He expected her to pass him by now, on her way back. Even though he remembered her tardiness the last time, and the unnecessary concern she'd caused him, he narrowed his eyes against the darkening sky. He saw no trace of her other than a trail of footsteps in the sand. She'd eventually catch up, but it bothered him that she ran out here alone.

Maybe his natural instinct to protect a woman he loved was taking over, a feeling he thought would lie dormant a good while longer. Uncomfortable with the direction of his thoughts, he turned around to head back.

A muffled sound, perhaps from a hurt animal some distance away, circled around him in the breeze. He stopped and squinted again, scanning the area. It was hard to tell which direction the noise came from, if he'd actually heard something. It might have been the wind, or maybe one of the wild horses.

He heard the noise again, louder this time.

It sounded like a woman, a hurt woman. "Jenni?" His mind started to imagine all sorts of horrible scenarios. His heart began to pound double-time in his chest. If anything happened to her …

"Where are you?" he called louder. The contrasting shadows that danced across the shoreline made it difficult to make out anything other than basic outlines.

"Over here!"

He noticed a branch moving back and forth in the distance. A large stallion stood on a small sand dune, almost as if he guarded something.

Scott's heart pinched at the sight of a lump on the ground—Jenni.

He ran to her, dropped to his knees on the soft sand. The stallion protested, arching his neck, and for a moment Scott thought the steed might attack. Then, to Scott's relief, the stallion turned away and drove his herd down a dark path that led into the woods.

Jenni groaned next to him. He reached out but hesitated. If he touched her as gently as he wanted, he'd be admitting his true feelings for her. He wasn't ready to admit them to himself, let alone to her. Making love with Jenni had stirred feelings in him that opened serious wounds.

"Can you help me up? I twisted my ankle on a piece of driftwood." She pointed at a half-decayed branch lying on the beach. "I'm okay, but I can't walk."

Ignoring his inner turmoil, he whistled. "That's swollen." They'd need extra time to reach a place on the shore where Keith could see them from the boat. He glanced at the sky again. They had to get out of here now, before they'd have to navigate the driftwood and the tidal pools in the dark.

"Hang onto me," he said. Reluctantly, he wrapped his arms around her waist and lifted her off the ground with ease. She pressed so close to him, he felt her warm breath tickle his bare neck. When she stood, he held onto her athletic and sexy-as-hell body as she took a slow step.

"Ouch. I hope I didn't break my ankle." She winced with pain each time she put toe-touch pressure on her foot.

The marathon. It was imperative he convince her to stay off her foot.

"Let me carry you," he offered.

"Absolutely not."

"What about the race? Do what's best for your ankle."

She shook her head.

He resisted the urge to pick her up anyway and instead encouraged her to lean against him. She was so close, felt so soft that he briefly closed his eyes. A faint combination of ocean spray, coffee, and an earthy aroma of rosemary enveloped him. In an instant he visualized the potted rosemary bushes, along with lavender, thyme, and oregano growing in the small garden boxes pressed against the entrance of Coffee Break. Jenni smelled like the organic herbs she grew.

He never dated down-to-earth women and wondered why not. He loved the way he felt when he was around her.

Scott tried not to notice how her trim curves naturally molded into the contours of him, tried not to look at the woman he held, for fear he might make love to her right here. Time was of the essence. He cleared his throat. "We need to call your brother, so he knows why we aren't waiting for him at the dock." Anything to distract him, to take his mind off her.

Jenni slowly blinked and stared at him.

She surprised him by sticking her hand into the top of her sports bra. He turned his head away, commanding himself not to think about sex right now. What in the world was she doing? It was almost dark, and they needed to start walking.

To his relief, she pulled out a cell phone. She waved it at him casually. "I have phone service now." With pain etched in her voice, she explained the situation to her brother, her gaze never leaving Scott's. "It was an accident, Keith. No, I ran off ahead of him, but he found me." She hesitated. "Thanks. See you soon." She turned to Scott. "He's going to cruise along the shoreline until he finds us."

Keith would never see them in the cove. That meant they had to walk farther, one slow step after another, toward the sound.

Before long the sky grew black. It became difficult to navigate the beach and maintain even footing. "Come on, Jenni. We're almost there," he encouraged. They needed to reach the shore before they heard Keith's boat, so he wouldn't pass them by.

Finally, they barely approached the edge of the cove when he said, "Let's stop here. You don't need to walk any more on your foot."

"How will Keith know where we are?" She sounded concerned.

"He'll find us." He held Jenni tighter, partly to comfort her, partly to keep her warm. Her skin felt cool and goose bumps rose on her arms. He moved behind her and cradled her in an embrace while they waited. "Why don't you call him again? Let him know where we are."

She dialed but nothing happened. "I lost service."

"It'll be okay." He rubbed her arms and hoped her brother found them soon; the temperature was dropping rapidly. He could insist on carrying her, but that held no guarantee Keith would find them any sooner. Fifteen minutes passed before they finally heard the rumble of a boat's engine.

"He won't hear us yell," she said. "We're downwind."

"I heard you earlier," he said, mostly to reassure her. But Scott agreed. Over the boat's engine, Keith would have trouble hearing them. He cupped his hand over his mouth. "Keith!" His voice reverberated through the late evening. It was so dark now the likelihood that Keith would notice them seemed doubtful. "Keith," he hollered again, louder. If Keith passed them, they'd be in trouble.

Instead, the boat slowed and a floodlight searched the water's edge. Eventually the beam stopped on them.

"Hang on a minute," Keith yelled. He guided the skiff toward the shore and Scott heard the boat's engine reduce to an idle. "Sorry, it's low tide. I can't get closer because of the shoals. You'll have to wade out."

Scott stepped into the cold water first, and then swept Jenni into his arms. She squirmed against his hold and slipped.

"Stop moving," Scott commanded. "I don't want to drop you."

"I need help walking; I don't need to be carried."

"If you can barely walk on the sand, how are you going to tromp through muck and water?" Thankfully, she went still in his arms. When he reached the boat, he lifted her over the gunwale. Keith reached out and steadied her.

After Scott climbed aboard, Jenni huddled on a seat with a towel wrapped around her. That was just as well; her brother was watching. Besides, Scott had more than reached his tolerance for resisting her and figured it best to let the towel keep her warm instead of him. Concentrating on her ankle seemed a smarter choice.

"Keith, do you have a flotation cushion?"

Without answering, Keith turned around and yanked one from inside a bench, then reclosed the lid. With a frown, barely evident in the pale light of the rising moon, he tossed the cushion to Scott before turning the boat around and heading toward the mainland.

Scott wondered what was up with her brother but decided not to ponder the question for long. He redirected his attention to Jenni. He sat beside her and placed the cushion on his lap. "Let me have your foot. We need to get your shoe and sock off."

The pain had to be bad because she actually lifted her leg across his lap.

With delicate hands, Scott untied her shoe and managed to remove it. Her foot was more swollen than he preferred. Who knew when she'd be able to run again?

Jenni groaned.

"I'm sorry." He winced. "Almost done." As gently as possible, he worked the sock off her foot. As he slipped the fabric off her toes, he allowed his finger to caress the top of her foot lightly. She shivered from either the pain, or his touch. He wasn't sure which.

She tried to pull her leg away but he held onto it. "Don't," he said. "Keep it on my lap to elevate it."

She sighed. "Okay, you win. Actually, speaking of winning, I owe you twenty bucks."

"No, sweetheart." The endearment slipped from his lips and he stilled. He hoped her protective brother hadn't heard him, for her sake. "You would have won the bet if you hadn't fallen. Why don't we call it even, until next time?"

She nodded slightly and reached forward to assess the damage to her ankle. When her fingers accidentally brushed against his hand, she didn't pull away. Was she giving him permission to pursue their relationship further in front of Keith?

"Wow, the swelling's getting worse," she said, her voice sounding husky. "I don't have time to be laid up."

"If you sleep with your foot elevated on a pillow, it will decrease the inflammation. We'll put ice on it tonight."

"We?" she asked. "I can't spend the night at your house again."

Scott looked away, toward Keith, who appeared focused on driving through the blackened maze of marsh grass. There was something almost tranquil about being in the estuary at night, with the boat's red and green lights casting a dash of color on the calm water.

"I'm not going to dump you at home and leave," Scott said. "At least let me help you get set up first."

"My parents are still miffed."

"Right." He shifted her foot lower on his leg. The contact was driving him to thoughts he shouldn't be thinking right now.

He rubbed his fingers across the stubble on his face. What was he going to do? He cared about her, about the success of Coffee Break. He needed to tell her about his involvement with the espresso machine. Rachel had been on him to confess, and she was right. Even if Jenni never talked to him again.

Maybe if he admitted how he truly felt about her, she'd forgive him. But that wouldn't work. She'd take the truth as a personal betrayal.

The skiff bumped into the dock and interrupted his thoughts. Home at last. Funny how Big Cat was starting to grow on him again and felt welcoming. He never imagined that possible.

Scott climbed from the boat and helped secure the lines; George was most likely gone for the night. When they were finished, Keith picked up Jenni and handed her over the side to him. It was a good thing she was petite. Scott struggled to carry her across the rocking dock and uphill to the bench near the ferry's ticket booth and set her down.

"I'll run and get my car," he offered. "I parked in front of your coffee shop."

"Thanks."

Surprised by her cooperation, he hurried down the street to retrieve the BMW before she changed her mind. It would be just like her to start walking on her own. Within ten minutes, he pulled in front of the ferry booth and climbed from the car.

That's when he saw Keith, who stood in front of Jenni with his arms crossed. His frown was obvious in the stream of light radiating from the single street lamp next to her. What were they arguing about? Didn't Keith approve of his sister hanging around him?

When Jenni heard Scott's car door shut, she awkwardly tried to stand.

"Hang on a minute." He rushed toward her.

"Sis?" Keith questioned.

Clearly bent on ignoring her brother's warning, whatever that might be, she wrapped an arm around Scott.

"Lean on me," Scott suggested, although he suspected that leaning on anyone, physically or emotionally, defied her nature. Once again she did as he asked and looped an arm around him.

No sooner had they reached the car, than he heard her brother's footsteps crunching on the gravel footpath leading away from them. Scott didn't look, he had his hands full trying to open the car door and attempting to deposit her gently on the seat. Once he started the car, she began to shiver. He flipped a switch and the heater flooded the car with a wave of warmth. "That should help. Try to imagine one of your mother's wool afghans around you, or drinking one of her cups of hot cocoa."

Jenni snapped her head toward him. "Interesting how you view my mother as comforting." She laughed in a way that made him think she rolled her eyes when she'd said the comment.

"Why not? Compared to my family, yours is cozy." He hoped she didn't get a chance to get to know them anytime soon.

CHAPTER SEVENTEEN

Scott wondered how he was going to get Jenni up the flight of steps. He looked at her house, lit up and awaiting her. The fresh memory of trying to carry her father up the stairs popped into his mind. He groaned. Where were the fishermen when he needed them?

Unfortunately, Jenni didn't wait around long enough until he formulated a plan. She opened the door and began to climb from the BMW.

"Wait." He ran around the hood of his car to her side and jabbed his elbow toward her. The last thing she needed was to put full weight on her swollen foot. "Let me carry you up the steps."

"Absolutely not." She clamped onto his arm, her hand still cool despite the effort from the car's blasting heater to warm her on the way over. "I'll be fine, if you don't mind me holding onto you."

Mind? She had to be joking.

Even if he disagreed with her decision not to let him carry her, he respected her determination to push harder when certain events tried to knock her down.

Scott managed to assist her up the steps in slow motion, helping her hobble around to the kitchen. He liked the warm, friendly feeling of using the backdoor. His own family maintained a formal appearance to the world, even to each other, unless his parents were fighting. It was hard to maintain formality with angry words spewing from their mouths.

"Can I come in and see your dad?" He wanted to call a truce from the other night. He wasn't planning to apologize for encouraging Jenni to spend the night with him, but he did want to make peace with the man.

She hesitated. Not wanting to impose, he left Jenni at the door and stepped away. "Never mind. I can see him another time."

Jenni shook her head. "If Dad's awake, it'll be good for him. Come in." She pushed the screen door open, and he helped her into the neat and tidy kitchen.

The familiar smell of Pine Sol greeted him. The house always smelled fresh after Mrs. Stallings did her weekly cleaning. It reminded him of high school and the Friendly Four. He and Dan had often stopped by to pick up Jenni first, on the way to Cassie's.

"What are you grinning at?" She'd glanced his way in time to catch him reminiscing.

"Your house smells like cleaning solution today. It brings back memories."

She looked confused. "I don't smell it." She inhaled a long, slow breath through her nose. "Well, maybe I do, barely."

"No one ever smells their own house." He heard Mrs. Stallings' heels clicking on the hardwood floor in the hallway. When she approached, he greeted her politely. He got the impression she liked him even less than before. The warmth of the hug they'd shared after he took Mr. Stallings fishing had evaporated. He understood why. She didn't want him to lead her daughter down what she considered a sinful path.

"Hi, Mom. Scott wants to see Dad, if he's still awake."

She nodded without answering and led the way.

With Scott's assistance, they followed her down the hallway toward the den. When Mrs. Stallings glanced back, she stopped midstride. "What happened to your leg, Jenni? You're limping."

"It's nothing, Mom. I just twisted my ankle running."

"You need to sit down immediately and ice it," her mother commanded.

Jenni turned her head, but Scott saw her face turn a slight shade of pink first. He wondered why her mother's concern embarrassed her, and wished his own mother doted on him the way hers did.

"Promise me, when you're finished seeing your father, you'll take care of that foot."

"Okay," Jenni said under her breath.

They entered the room with Jenni's arm wrapped around Scott for support. Richard pressed the controller for the hospital bed and the back lifted him into a sitting position. "Other than disrespecting my wish the other night," Richard said, "I'm glad to see you two finally together. That makes me happy."

A gurgle escaped Jenni's throat. Her face turned an even brighter shade of pink than it had with her mother.

At least Richard wasn't mad anymore.

"I've been waiting for the day Jenni brought a man home," Richard continued to say, "although I must admit, I never thought you two would actually get together."

"Dad!" Jenni pulled away from Scott's hold. "He was helping me with my ankle. I sprained it."

Richard chuckled, a low, raspy sound. "You're still denying your attraction to each other?"

The room suddenly became hot and Scott glanced at the doorway. Freedom lay just beyond it. "Sir, I came by to drop Jenni off and wanted to see how you were doing after the fishing trip. If there's anything I can do for you, please let me know."

"There is something you can do, but we'll discuss it again later." Their eyes met briefly, and Richard shot a pointed look at

Jenni. "He's a gentleman, with obvious good breeding and manners. He's perfect. After I'm gone—"

"That's enough, Dad. Don't talk like that. By the way, did you get out of bed to eat dinner tonight?"

"You change the subject almost as well as Gran. But to answer your question, no. I wasn't hungry until now. Can someone help me to the table?"

The thought of Richard needing assistance into the kitchen saddened Scott.

Jenni stepped forward and flinched from obvious pain.

"Virginia Lynn Stallings, you go right into the living room and elevate that foot," Mrs. Stallings commanded, although Scott recognized her firm order as love. When you lacked something as basic as that in your own life, love was easy to recognize.

"I'll help him," Scott offered and moved toward the older man's bed. Richard held up his hand to stop Scott, and without complaint, he pushed aside a red and blue striped afghan. He moved around in the bed until he sat on the edge of the mattress and planted his stocking feet onto the floor.

Jenni bent down, appearing to bite back a groan from pain. She offered to slip on her father's shoes. "You need to wear these when you walk."

"That physical therapist filled your head with nonsense. I can walk in my stocking feet." Mr. Stallings reached out and rubbed his daughter on the shoulder, another sign of affection that Scott was fairly sure Jenni didn't recognize.

"Dad, socks are slippery."

Scott watched the dynamics between them. Jenni wanted to help her dad, but he resisted most everything she said. He was a difficult man on a good day, but there seemed to be something else going on here.

Mr. Stallings grumbled but let her don the shoes.

"Scott, can you follow him into the kitchen?" Jenni asked.

He nodded but wondered how she'd make it into the other room without his assistance. When her mother closed in to help her, Scott felt better. Jenni was in good hands. He followed Richard toward the kitchen, and halfway there, Mrs. Stallings steered her daughter into the living room.

Scott didn't know much about cancer or the course of the disease, but Jenni's father didn't seem to have much time left. In Scott's opinion, they should allow the man to stay in his bed and die in peace.

"Can you bring in my chair for me?" Richard asked, standing in the hallway as they passed the dining room. "It's in there."

Scott let go of him, hoping the man could stand long enough for him to retrieve the chair. It was odd that the sturdy piece of furniture didn't take up permanent residence in the kitchen, but he guessed Mrs. Stallings had her reasons for keeping it in the other room. He decided not to ask.

When they finally reached the kitchen, Scott placed the mismatched chair at the table for Richard. He didn't relax until the older man was firmly seated.

"Dinner is in the microwave. Can you warm it for me?"

"Of course." Scott went to the microwave, opened it to check on its contents, then pushed the buttons. While he waited, he tried not to think of the sad irony in serving the feeble man supper from a microwave when he used to cook all day for his patrons. When the microwave beeped, Scott set the plate on a hot pad in front of Richard, who thanked him and dove in.

When he finished eating, a small amount at best, he looked Scott square in the eyes. "You're a good guy. I appreciate you taking me fishing the other day."

"I enjoyed it too." Scott admired the man who sat before him. When he died, Scott was going to miss him.

***

The upcoming marathon lurked like a predator from a shadowed corner in Jenni's mind. If she wanted to race, her ankle needed to heal fast. Last night she'd spent an hour icing it for twenty minutes at a time without much success. Unfortunately, the swelling was still significant.

Thank goodness Gran agreed to work early. Until she showed up, Jenni would survive by taking ibuprofen and forcing herself to take breaks whenever possible.

When the morning rush quieted, Jenni plopped on a loveseat with a bag of ice. If the coldness brought down the inflammation and increased her chance of running soon, then it was worth the downtime.

Actually, downtime was a relative term. Just because she sat with her foot elevated didn't mean she would spend idle time being unproductive. Already this morning she'd gone over the monthly budget and projected expenditures. Business was increasing but not fast enough. She needed to implement her other ideas, but to do that she needed to hire someone to work evenings and afternoons when Gran was off. She'd have to talk to Dan about hiring Alex, who'd stopped by a few days ago to inquire again about the possible opening. Jenni had put her off, but now that she was hurt, she needed more help.

In the meantime, Jenni continued working on a flyer to hang next door in Stephanie's Book Shoppe. Late last night, long after Jenni's parents had gone to sleep, she'd sat atop her bed with a sketchbook and a set of charcoal pencils. She loved creating a detailed yet simplistic scene from a blank piece of paper. The result was a sketch of a small group of women drinking coffee together and chatting. They were nestled in comfortable-looking chairs, each smiling with a book in front of them. In bold print at the top of the flyer, Jenni invited book clubs to take a Coffee Break at her shop.

"By all means," Stephanie had said. "Please bring your flyer by. I don't know why I didn't think of it."

"I can hang yours in my shop as well. We can help each other," Jenni said. The plan was simple, and it promoted teamwork between the two neighboring shop owners.

Jenni looked over the flyer one last time, the drawing scanned on her computer now, and hit “print.” En route to the printer in the back room, she held onto whatever stable fixture along the way, depositing the bag of ice in the sink. Once there, she snatched the flyer from the tray. It looked even better printed out. Satisfied, she hobbled back to the main room and set it next to the cash register. Just as she picked up the phone to dial Stephanie, the bell tinkled and in walked Cassie.

She bounced toward the counter, her clicking heels jarring through Jenni’s body like a jackhammer. When Cassie reached her destination, she flashed an overrated smile.

What was she up to? She never stepped foot into Coffee Break. Was she here to taunt Jenni about the running accident?

Thankfully most of the equipment was within several feet, so Jenni could hide her limp.

Cassie leaned on the counter, revealing a large amount of cleavage from her low-cut blouse. “I need two decaf coffees, one for me and one for Scott.” Her smile grew larger when she said Scott’s name, as if her intention was to make Jenni jealous.

When was the woman going to give up on chasing Scott? Since when did he send his assistant to retrieve coffee? Was he too busy to drop by himself? She hoped he’d stop in to find out how she was holding up with her ankle. He seemed concerned last night. Maybe he was avoiding her for some reason, or maybe he felt vulnerable and it scared him as much as it did her. A thought sprang to mind. Scott always ordered a mocha, not a decaf coffee. If he’d truly sent Cassie, then she’d know his preference.

She decided to let Cassie figure out the mistake on her own. “Two decaf coffees coming right up.” Jenni turned to fill the order but Cassie reached out and grabbed hold of her arm.

“There’s something you need to know about Scott,” Cassie said.

“Is he all right?” If something happened to Scott, Jenni hoped she wouldn’t learn about it from Cassie.

"He's fine. It has to do with your relationship with him." Cassie chewed on her lower lip.

She was only trying to cause trouble. Beware.

"I know we've had issues in the past," Cassie said, looking away for a moment. "I need to be honest with you, though. We both know Scott's bothered by Brittany's death. But I wonder if he's trying to redeem himself to the town by making people think he's dating you."

What business was it of Cassie's? Was she acting out of jealousy, or was she really concerned?

"Think about it," Cassie continued. "If you accept him as a friend, people will forgive him. Then he can let his guilt go. Do you think he's using you?"

Jenni's belly tightened. "He wouldn't do that."

"Why not? He's only here for a short time, and then he leaves. He has nothing to lose."

Jenni blinked. Her logic actually made sense.

After Cassie left, Jenni tried to dismiss the disturbing conversation, but it continued to bother her. Not much later, Scott popped in for a brief visit.

Jenni hung up the phone, still unsuccessful with talking to Stephanie about the flyers, and hobbled to the espresso machine.

"I'm back for my daily mocha." He grinned with a dazzling smile. "By the way, I'm hooked on your carrot cake. I'll take another one."

Mocha, huh? She bet he never received the decaf coffee from Cassie. "Glad you like carrot cake," Jenni said. "It's the best I've tasted." Well, other than Gran's. She planned to mention Cassie's visit but he interrupted her thought.

"How's your ankle this morning?" He glanced at the melting bag of ice on the counter from her last "break."

"I wish I could say it felt better, but I'd be lying. It's swollen and it hurts." She plucked a cup from the stack. How best to address Cassie's suggestion?

He didn't act like a man who was using Jenni.

"Do you think you need an X-ray? I can drive if you need a ride."

"I appreciate it, but I'd like to wait. I'm pretty sure it's just sprained." She dumped the beans into the machine and turned it on. The loud sound of grinding filled the room for a moment.

As soon as she finished and limped back to the counter with the mocha in hand, Scott pulled out his credit card. "I guess you won't be running for a while."

Scott's warmth seemed so genuine. Cassie had to be mistaken.

"Doesn't look like it." Jenni frowned when she thought of the race. She'd have to work twice as hard at the gym on the elliptical machine, an exercise she could handle. It wasn't a great substitute, but it was better than nothing. "If you run tonight, take me along with you in spirit. And make sure to push yourself harder."

"Absolutely. This will give me a chance to get in better shape." He leaned so close to her she could almost taste his lips. When he spoke again, his voice sounded deep and sexy. "Then, when you're able to run again, I'll have no problem keeping up with you. Who knows, maybe I'll even outrun you."

She frowned at his competitive attitude and leaned away. "No fair. You can't challenge me like that while I'm laid up."

"Keep your twenty bucks warm in your pocket. It won't last there long."

The man was an irritant, like a relentless mosquito buzzing around. "Run all you want, sweetheart," she said. "I'll still beat you. I don't plan to be out of commission long."

"Sweetheart? I rather like that word." He leaned even closer and his warm breath danced on her cheek. He planted a wet, sizzling kiss on the corner of her mouth. Without pulling away, he said in a husky voice, "Get better soon. I don't want to hear you complain about being out of shape if you're laid up too long."

He backed away, his kiss leaving behind a hot imprint.

"What's this?" He pointed to the flyer on the counter.

"I need to bring that next door to Stephanie. I'm going to encourage customers to buy books from her bookstore, and she'll suggest they read the books at my coffee shop. It works for both of us."

"That's a good idea, to befriend a competitor."

"I wouldn't say she's actually my competition, but working together seems like good business practice."

"I agree. Do you want me to run that over? You shouldn't be walking around unless absolutely necessary."

Again, he didn't sound like a man who was using her. "Sure, if you don't mind." She decided not to mention what happened with Cassie.

"If I minded, I wouldn't have offered." He snapped up the flyer and waved. "See you soon. I need to get back to the office."

"Appreciate it," she called out as he opened the door. She didn't know how he justified stopping by Coffee Break, but she enjoyed his impromptu visits. Perhaps he told his staff he wanted to check on a customer. She guessed there was a certain truth to that.

Gran walked through the door ready to relieve Jenni. "Thanks, Gran. What would I do without you?"

"I don't know. My guess is you'd survive." Gran tossed her hand-knitted bag in a cabinet under the counter. "By the way, with your hurt ankle, will you still be able to drive the horse trailer this weekend for the rescue?"

Gran lived and breathed for the animals. Jenni shared her enthusiasm but not to the extent Gran did. But Jenni had promised to help the foundation.

"I'll be there," Jenni said. "No one else knows how to drive the trailer, except for Jeff, and he's already helping with the mission. That would be too much for him."

Gran looked concerned. "But are you able to drive?"

"My right foot is fine, so driving isn't an issue. Helping the foundation was the deal we made when you agreed to give me Saturdays off."

Gran sighed. “If you change your mind, let me know. We still need another volunteer, preferably a man to help with the lifting."

"I can ask Scott." He seemed almost bothered when he’d admitted to not doing anything to help society lately. Besides, time spent with him would reveal his true feelings for her. Cassie was likely trying to cause trouble.

Gran looked around for the first time since she'd walked in. "If business keeps up, you’re going to need to hire someone. What about that sweet girl, Alex?"

CHAPTER EIGHTEEN

Saturday morning, Scott waited at the Sea Horse Ferry for the rest of the rescue crew. As usual, he'd shown up twenty minutes early, and that was after he'd stopped by Coffee Break for his morning mocha. Gran, as everyone in town called her, had greeted him with a smile. She'd been full of appreciation because he'd agreed to help on the mission.

A grin escaped him. He was about to spend another day with Jenni.

"Do you always smile when you're alone?" Jenni asked, hobbling with a crutch to the yellow bench he leaned against. Keith was with her and waved as he hurried toward the dock to ready the boat.

"Actually, before I returned to Big Cat, I never smiled," Scott answered. "I never realized it before now."

"It's pleasing. When people smile it brightens their whole face. Sunshine and water will do that to a person." She smiled as if to prove her point.

The ambiance might be part of the reason for his uplifted spirit, but the other part stood in front of him. Lately he had trouble keeping his mind off her. He pointed to her ankle. "What's with the crutch?" he asked. He had hoped she'd heal fast so she could continue her training. He knew how important running the marathon meant to her.

"I borrowed crutches from Claire, but it was too hard to use two of them and carry coffee around the shop. I downsized to one." Despite the injury, she looked particularly vibrant today. She wore faded jeans that molded to her body in perfect proportion and a soft pink sweatshirt with a hint of a white t-shirt poking out from underneath. He had to resist the urge to touch the fuzzy fabric.

“Has the swelling gone down?”

She frowned and glanced at her ankle. “Some. It feels better this morning, but I need to be careful with the sand. Mostly, I plan to hang out by the boat in case I’m needed. I dropped the horse trailer off at the ranger dock and Keith drove me here. When we have the horses, I’ll drive the trailer to Gran’s farm. That’s my job in all this.”

Scott was a little confused but figured he'd learn the routine as they went. He didn’t know why he agreed to go today, when he had work to do at the office, but he supposed another weekend off would do him good. He wondered why no one else showed up to help on the mission but didn’t ask.

“Keith is waving at us. Let’s go.” Jenni stepped forward and, with Scott right next to her in case she lost her balance, they made their way down the hill to the dock. He wanted to help but she was getting along fine without him.

Keith watched them closely. Scott wasn’t sure, but he thought he saw protectiveness in her brother’s eyes, a warning for him to be careful where Jenni was concerned.

Once they were on the water and a good distance from shore, a patch of fog enveloped them. Fog wasn't uncommon on the water, even with clear visibility on the mainland. When Scott was little, one of his favorite games was to visit the pier on hazy mornings to play pirate on his dad’s boat with Dan. Occasionally some of the neighborhood kids, mainly Jeff Rhodes and his brother Tom, joined in and pretended to shoot cannons at them from their father's boat in the next slip. He tried to hide a smile as he remembered hanging out with Dan.

Jenni moved in her seat and bumped into Scott, snapping his mind to the present. The wind blew her hair in a sassy style around her face, and he inhaled a whiff of rosemary. He would never again be able to smell that herb without thinking of her. He wanted to bury his face into her hair, into the smooth flesh of her neck. To his horror, a muted groan escaped his lips.

She glanced back at him and smiled, those straight white teeth driving him crazy. And her mouth. He tried to resist staring at her tongue when she licked a droplet of water from her lips.

He turned away quickly and caught Keith's glance. The man seemed to read Scott's tainted thoughts easily. Jenni deserved better. She was worthy of knowing the truth about the espresso machine. She was worthy of being with someone who could offer marriage and kids, along with a cozy house in Big Cat. That wasn't him. He couldn't wait to return to the city, to his business meetings and busy schedule. He wanted a dynamic life, not a wife and kids. But he was fast losing control of his rational mind and balanced perspective that he was so noted for.

If he had to stay here, Big Cat would slowly kill him.

The dock on Pony Island appeared through the thinning fog. Another boat, he guessed Jeff's, waited in one of the four slips, and three people stood on the dock. He recognized Claire Rhoades; she was one of his clients at the bank. The other two were cousins, Jeff Rhoades and Paula Kraft, and even though he hadn't seen them since high school, Scott recognized them immediately. Jeff was a large man who looked to lift weights, and he was married to Claire. Paula was the area's large animal veterinarian, but no one dared to call her the dreaded word "vet." She preferred people to call her a veterinarian. From what Scott heard around town, she was one of the best.

Keith pulled into a slip next to them. He tossed a line to Jeff, who deftly secured it to the dock. Scott was the first one out of the boat and reached forward to help Jenni. He felt everyone's gaze on him when she grabbed hold of his hand and pulled herself onto the dock. Apparently her friends were unsure of his motives concerning her. Did their hesitance have to do with his decision to decline her loan, or with what happened to Brittany? He wasn't solely responsible for her sister's death. He realized that now.

Jenni seemed not to notice their protective instincts. When she joined Claire and Paula, she laughed and chatted with them easily, despite their occasional glances at him.

Scott stood by the ferry alone. Normally he didn't feel like an outcast; he was usually the one in charge. Today he joined someone else's mission as a volunteer. That word felt as strange as being among old friends again.

Jeff climbed from his boat. He walked toward Scott and thumped him playfully on the back. "Hey, man. Haven't seen you in a long time."

"Too long. Heard you got married." Scott glanced at Claire, who laughed and shot a look of longing toward her husband. Scott felt a pang of envy for the happiness they found. "I always knew Dan would be first to marry, then you."

"Tom was first. My brother has two kids."

Surprised by that, Scott chuckled. "I guess it has been a long time."

"Everyone's married except you."

"Actually, I was." The pain stung deep. "Guess I'm not cut out for it."

Jeff's eyes narrowed. "Then you better watch your step with Jenni. She has a lot of friends here, and some of them aren't happy that you're back. You've caused her enough grief."

Scott couldn't disagree with his point. "Certainly people understand that we all make mistakes. I've made my share of them."

"Jenni's struggling right now in more ways than one. People around here stick together, friend." Jeff thumped him again on the shoulder. "Think about it. And make sure you don't break her heart."

Keith hopped from the ferryboat and onto the dock. From the expression on his face, he heard the last part of Jeff's comment. "Jeff's right. Treat my sister right, or you'll have to deal with me." Normally Keith was a quiet man, so his threat hung heavy.

"Let's go," Paula called out to them. "Usually Magic's herd hangs out somewhere over there." She pointed to a cluster of foggy dunes just inland from the dock. "Dan had to cancel last minute, so we're one man short. I can help carry one of the horses, or we can make two trips. I'd rather do it in one, though, so we don't spook the herd. Jenni's going to stay by the boats to help when we return." Paula pointed to a bag and asked Scott to carry it. Then she asked Jeff and Keith to each carry a handmade gurney, made out of two poles and a tarp.

Paula led the group off the dock, and Scott, concerned about Jenni's safety, looked back at her. She gave him a thumbs-up. He didn't like leaving her behind, especially when she was hurt. She waved him away but the encouragement to walk on didn't help. He raised his eyebrows, pulling his cell phone from his pocket and holding it up. He asked the silent question. Did she have hers, in case she needed him? She dug her hand in her jeans pocket and retrieved the phone. She blew him a kiss. Promises.

Promises lead to heartbreak, most likely his.

***

Before his return to big cat, Scott hadn't explored Pony Island in years. During the time he spent working in Raleigh, thriving on the fast-paced environment he'd created, he never thought he'd yearn for the isolation the island offered. Even though he couldn't wait to return to the city, he gave himself permission to enjoy the nature that surrounded him.

"The herd is over there," Paula said as she pointed to Magic, the wild brown stallion that Jenni idolized. "Let's climb that dune. He knows we're here, but we don't want to alarm him." She seemed to be talking directly to Scott, most likely because the others were familiar with the routine.

Scott nodded. He plodded behind the others through the deeper sand at the base of the dune. He was glad to be in fairly decent shape.

Once they reached the top, Paula spoke softly. “Let’s sit down and act like we’re just hanging out.” The group did as she said; she was the leader, the knowledgeable veterinarian.

Scott admired Paula's take-charge attitude, which reminded him of Jenni somewhat. Jenni had a softer side, though, a vulnerability she tried to hide from the world. He needed to keep in mind the inevitable, to appreciate Keith and Jeff’s advice not to hurt her. He was moving back to the city when Layne returned from maternity leave.

“Scott, can you hand me that bag?” Paula asked. She wanted the pack he’d carried up to this point. When he passed it to her, she unzipped it leisurely and pulled out a rifle case. She opened it without a sound, revealing a tranquilizer gun.

His expression must have prompted an explanation because Jeff began to fill in the details. “We use a dart to medicate the horses, to make them sleepy, so we can safely carry them back to the boat. You and Keith can take one of the two-year-olds, and Paula and I will carry the other.”

He preferred to help someone other than Keith, but he wasn’t about to complain. He was here to offer his assistance. If volunteering to help the Islander Ponies meant a lot to Jenni, they’d be important to him too. This was another opportunity to redeem himself.

When the two chosen horses were dazed, Paula stood. “Let’s go, slowly. Watch the dominate stallion; he can be protective of his herd.” She led the way down the dune and took her time approaching the stallion’s harem. “Don’t get between him and one of his mares, or between a mare and her foal.”

Scott heeded Paula's warning. He watched the stallion as they neared. He didn't know much about horses, but he knew enough to understand that Magic viewed them as a possible threat.

"Magic's fine," Paula assured Scott. "As long as we don't mess with one of his mares, he won't bother us. The two-year-olds are at the age where Magic will kick them out of the harem anyway. They will wander the dunes and hook up with other bachelors until they become strong enough to acquire their own mares."

Scott found the information intriguing. All his life he'd swam off the shores of the island's beaches and never realized that the horses were anything more than something interesting to look at. He silently thanked Jenni for giving him the opportunity to help today. He resisted the urge to call her to make sure she was safe.

Keith pointed to the horse nearest him. He looked exactly like Magic, except he had a white star in the center of his forehead and a little white snip on his nose, almost a checkmark. "Let's carry this one."

"That's Ross," Jeff said. "His mama is the pregnant one over there." He pointed to a mare watching them intently.

When Scott and Keith made their way to Ross, Keith said, "You take the back end, but be careful when you lift him onto the gurney."

Scott flashed Keith a good-natured look. "Thanks a lot, man. If this horse poops on me, I owe you one." He heard Keith's low chuckle.

"I was talking about his back hoof kicking you. He isn't completely asleep."

Startled, Scott looked up; he hadn't thought about the possibility of Ross kicking him. He had a lot to learn about rescuing horses. If he wanted to keep seeing Jenni, the mission provided an opportunity to get to know her brother better.

"On the count of three, pick him up," Keith instructed. They positioned their hands on the bay horse, then lifted him onto the gurney gently. He was a cute thing, with big brown eyes and a fluffy black mane that looked as wild as the horse himself. Wait until Jenni saw this youngster. She'd fall in love for sure. To his surprise, the horse's vulnerability tugged at Scott's heartstrings. It was sad they had to remove him from his natural habitat, but for the survival of the herds, they had no choice.

Scott and Keith had to coordinate their steps as they carried the dazed horse on the gurney behind Paula and Jeff. Claire walked alongside her husband and petted the horse they carried, making sure he remained in place on the tarp. Most likely Jeff hadn't wanted his pregnant spouse to help carry the horse. Scott didn't blame him one bit. If he had a wife, a pregnant wife nonetheless, he'd want to protect her as well.

Within the hour the fog lifted, and Jenni and the boats came into view. Even though she was a tiny, blurred vision off in the distance, she was a pleasant sight that helped ease his stiff shoulders from carrying the gurney through the cumbersome sand. Thankfully, the horse didn't weigh all that much, and Scott and Keith worked well together as they maneuvered around scrubby bushes and tidewater pools. He'd forgotten how quiet mornings on the island were.

Scott glanced down at the sleepy Ross, whose eyes were open and staring off in the distance. No matter what reservations Scott might have had about volunteering, he secretly admitted that this little horse touched him in a way he hadn't thought possible. He hoped the foundation found a good home for the colt.

Jenni encouraged Scott to reconnect with his hometown and to get involved with the community. He wasn't sure, but it was possible she wanted him to see the vulnerable side of people again, something he'd forgotten about. That thought disturbed him.

Paula looked back at Scott. "You're a valuable volunteer. It's too bad you'll be leaving Big Cat early."

Scott's grip tightened around the handle of the gurney. "Early?"

"Layne's my sister-in-law. She's excited about her decision to return from maternity leave sooner. Like I said, too bad you'll be moving back to Raleigh, because the foundation needs more volunteers like you."

Layne never mentioned returning to the bank earlier than planned. He wasn't ready to leave Big Cat yet, or Jenni. Scott wanted a chance to reestablish the broken relationships that resulted from Brittany's death. He'd run away once before, and look at the wake he'd left behind. By being here, he had no choice but to rebuild the relationships.

CHAPTER NINETEEN

Jenni stared at the horizon, never allowing her eyes to roam from the shoreline for long. Off in the distance a cluster of movement caught her eye. The rescue group had walked around a dune and onto the beach. She barely made out Scott's muscular form while he carried what looked to be a gurney. Excitement from seeing him, as annoying as it was, pulsated through her traitorous body.

She didn't want to be attracted to him. He'd be leaving before the end of the year, and after Cassie's accusation about him using her, Jenni was cautious.

She watched as they neared and rather liked that Scott and Keith carried one of the gurneys together. On the ferryboat earlier, she'd sensed some tension between them. Perhaps by working together with the horses, they could resolve whatever issues lay between them.

When they grew even closer, she noticed Scott and Keith stopping often to reposition the foal on the gurney. Wanting to help, Jenni stepped off the dock. The tip of her crutch sank into the sand. She hobbled several feet, but unfortunately, the resistance of the sand was too much. The marathon was too important a race to jeopardize the healing of her ankle.

Scott's gaze met hers. When the rescue group approached, he grumbled, "What are you doing out here with your foot? I thought you were going to stay on the dock?"

What could she say? "I'll be fine." Curiosity got the better of her, and she stepped forward to assist.

The little horse stole her breath. He looked just like Magic.

"You're limping," Scott barked.

"Okay, Mom," she quipped. She reminded herself that his irritation was out of concern. He cared about her well-being. Or did he? Perhaps Cassie was right, and he was using her. His concern about her ankle would likely impress the others.

He leaned forward and whispered in her ear. "I want you to run the marathon. Take good care of yourself."

His breath, warm against her neck, made words difficult to articulate. "I … will," she said, barely audible.

"Jenni, pay attention," Keith scolded. "Make sure Ross doesn't fall."

Brothers were such a pain sometimes. She hobbled alongside them, and using her free hand, she pulled Ross's leg back onto the gurney. With the little white marking on his nose, he was the cutest horse she'd ever seen. A longing to adopt one of the Islander Ponies nagged at her. Maybe someday she'd have enough time and money to get one. She rubbed the fuzzy horse, whose fur was thickening in preparation for winter. Jenni watched them carefully load the sleepy horses onto the skiffs, one horse in each boat. She climbed in Keith's skiff and knelt beside Ross, tucking a blanket around him. Sensing someone watching her, she glanced up to meet Scott's gaze.

Cassie's words made sense, but Jenni felt confused. She thought back to the pier, when he'd taken her father fishing. The concern he'd shown that day couldn't have been artificial. Hadn't he gone to such heroic efforts because he cared for her too?

She comforted Ross until they reached the ranger's dock on the mainland. Carefully, the men unloaded the horses from the boat, and to Jenni's surprise, Dan showed up to help carry them into the awaiting horse trailer.

"Dan," Jenni said before she climbed into the driver's seat of the truck. "I need to talk to you later." She owed Dan the courtesy of discussing Alex's possible employment with Coffee Break. By purchasing the espresso machine and letting her pay him back slowly, he'd most likely saved her business. Honesty was essential in keeping their friendship. "It's important, but it can wait until after we're finished with the horses."

His eyes widened, as though she'd unearthed a disturbing secret.

***

Jenni went to Scott's that evening for an elaborate dinner. Using a Dutch oven, he'd simmered a hearty dish of diced chicken and chunks of sweet potatoes, smothered in a rich peanut sauce. He served the tasty meal over wild rice. She was glad he knew how to cook well, because if they ever ended up together, she'd have to rely on him to make dinner. Maybe it was a good thing she hadn't inherited Stallings, otherwise she'd have had to learn to cook. That used to be her father's job, while hers had been most everything else.

When they finished eating, he stood to clean off the table. Before she could offer to help, though, he stopped her by wrapping his arms around her waist. She wanted to remain in his embrace all night, but unfortunately, she couldn't stay long. Her parents were expecting her home early. There would be no other carefree nights spent in his bed. The one act of rebellion, while it had felt liberating, had caused endless arguments with her parents. They didn't need the added stress right now. She was starting to understand that time with her father was most likely short lived and should be appreciated, no matter how difficult he was. Pointless fighting needed to be limited.

Then, thanks to Cassie, there was another reason she wanted to avoid spending the night with Scott. She couldn't help but question his motivation for dating her. Jenni had evaluated what Cassie had said and planned to monitor the situation.

Just as they'd settled in to watch a movie, her cell phone rang. When Jenni didn't make a move to answer, Pirate barked at her. By the third ring, she got up and plucked the phone off the countertop. The call might be about her father.

It was her mother all right, but she didn't need help with Jenni's dad.

"Gran fell."

"What?" Jenni's heart practically stopped beating.

"She went out to feed the horses. The porch railing gave way and she tumbled down the steps."

Jenni berated herself for not asking Keith to fix the steps as she'd intended. "Is Gran okay? I mean, is she hurt?"

"She called 911 and an ambulance came. They took her to Crystal County Hospital." Her mother hesitated. "I know this is a lot to ask, sweetheart, but would you go over there and feed the horses?"

"Yes, but then I'm going to the emergency room," Jenni said. "Did she break anything?" Gran was strong and vibrant. How had this happened?

"It's too soon to know, but I suspect she broke her hip. And Jenni, she was insistent that the horses be fed before anyone showed up at the hospital. You're the only one in the family who knows what to do."

"No problem." She'd find a way to take care of the horses, even though she hobbled around with a crutch. "We'll meet you at the hospital in an hour." At first she hadn't realized she'd said "We" and included Scott.

"I can't leave your father."

Jenni glanced at the clock. "Does Dad want to see Gran?" She had an idea. "Where's Keith? I bet we could round up enough guys to carry him down the steps and get him into the car."

"No." Her mother sounded sad. "Keith's at the ferry. He's going to the hospital as soon as he can. And your Dad won't go. He says it serves Gran right."

"What a horrible thing to say, Mom." It was past time for the rift between her father and Gran to be resolved.

"I'm sure he didn't mean it. He's still upset about their argument. She pretty much told him to get out of bed or die." Her mother sounded as though she had to fight back tears. "He'll come around. Your father loves Gran, even if he's too stubborn to admit his feelings."

"Why can't he say the words to anyone?" Jenni asked. "His time is running out."

She grew quiet. "What do you mean?"

"Mom, he's dying; he's giving up."

"Don't sentence your father to death." She sounded angry. "He's not going anywhere for a long time."

"Oh, mom." Her mother had a bad case of denial. If Jenni had to guess, she'd bet her mom feared being alone. Jenni didn't blame her. Even she worried about what life would be like once her father passed. For one thing, there would no longer be unsolicited advice about how to run a restaurant. Actually, to be fair, he did offer good suggestions occasionally. She slowly smiled, although she felt sad.

A light sniffle sounded from the earpiece. Her mother's safe life was shattering in so many tiny pieces that she'd never be able to repair it completely. Silently Jenni promised to do the best job possible to ensure that her mother not only survived, but that she thrived. Keith would eventually step up and help too, once he dealt with his own denial.

"Hang on." Jenni covered the phone and tried to regain her composure enough to tell Scott what happened. He watched her closely, so she fought harder to hide the emotion swelling in her throat. Jenni wasn't used to confiding in anyone except her best friend Claire. Then again, Claire had experienced more pain in a lifetime, more pain than Jenni could imagine, so Claire was a safe friend.

"Is Gran okay?" he asked after Jenni briefed him.

"She had to call an ambulance." Jenni turned away and bit back tears that threatened to erupt. "She needs me to feed the horses before I go to the hospital. Mom can't leave my dad."

Scott frowned. "Why don't I help with the horses, so you'll finish faster, and then I'll stay with your father." He ran his finger along her arm. "Then you can drive your mom to the hospital."

His thoughtful offer touched her in a way she'd never expected. An outer layer of her protective wall stripped away and suddenly she felt vulnerable, a dangerous emotion since he'd be packing and leaving for Raleigh soon.

***

The BMW pulled up in front of Gran's barn shortly after the disturbing call from Jenni's mother. Gran was a constant in her life. If anything happened to her, Jenni didn't know how she'd function. She'd personally see to it that Gran's porch was repaired, even if she had to learn how to rebuild a railing herself.

She walked into the barn and flicked on the overhead light. The horses nickered and stuck their heads over the top of their stall doors to greet them. She bet they missed Gran. Jenni hobbled with her crutch from stall to stall and introduced Scott to each horse. Gran treated them like humans, so they'd come to expect the utmost respect.

They stopped in front of the dark brown colt's stall. "You already know Ross." Not only did he look similar to Magic, his mannerisms were alike as well. If she had the money, she'd love to adopt him.

Scott rubbed the colt's face and smoothed back the wild forelock from the horse's eyes. "You're a fine one, Ross." Pirate barked in protest. Scott reached down to reassure the dog. "You're a good boy, too."

"I hope Gran finds a good home for Ross."

Scott looked at her. "What does it cost to take care of the rescue horses?"

"A lot. Gran does most of the work, so that saves money. But she's getting older, and with her hip she'll have to hire someone to clean stalls and to feed." Jenni would help as much as her injured ankle and busy schedule allowed.

"There are veterinarian bills," she continued. "Paula donates her time, but we still have the expense of spring and fall shots, and any booster shots the babies need. We have a farrier who donates his time to trim the horses' feet, but if they need shoes, he charges the horse foundation. And feed. We have to introduce them slowly to feed and hay. Once their digestive system can handle the new diet, they'll eat more. All that costs money. And if we have a drought, we have to import hay from up north."

"I had no idea. Is the reason behind the marathon to raise money?"

"Yes." Jenni felt a pang of anxiety. In order for her to run in the race, her ankle needed to heal fast. Time was running out.

When they finished with the horses and drove to Jenni's house, her mother was watching out the back door for them. No sooner had Scott parked, Mrs. Stallings slammed the screen door and hurried down the steps. Scott gave Jenni a half hug and then climbed from the car.

"I appreciate your help, Scott," Jenni's mom said.

"Sure thing, Mrs. Stallings," he said, walking around the front of his car. "Please let me know if I can do anything else." Scott waved goodbye to Jenni and looked again at her mom. "And tell Gran I'll come by to see her soon." He handed the keys to the BMW over and darted up the stairs with ease. His stamina was increasing quickly.

Pushing aside the urge to run again, Jenni distracted herself by watching her mom dangle his keys in her hand. He trusted her enough to let her drive his luxurious car. They were making progress.

Within fifteen minutes, Jenni and her mother entered the emergency room of Crystal County Hospital, fully prepared to spend the next several hours waiting. To their surprise, they were ushered into the depths of the emergency department immediately.

"Gran, are you okay?" Jenni asked when she walked into the small cubicle and saw her grandmother lying in a hospital bed.

Gran smiled. "I couldn't be greater. Did you see that handsome doctor?"

Jenni had passed him in the hallway outside Gran's cubicle. "He's probably in his forties, if you haven't noticed." Gran seemed to forget she was in her early seventies. "Just promise me one thing, Gran. If you ever remarry, please make sure my grandfather isn't close to the same age as me."

"I'll do no such thing, darlin'. You'll have to accept whoever I end up with."

"Did you find out anything yet?" Jenni's mom asked.

Gran frowned. "I broke my hip all right. They need to put a pin in me and want to keep me locked up here for a couple of days. Afterward, they might send me to an old folks' home. No thanks."

"They won't keep you for long," Jenni said. "You'll go to a skilled nursing facility for rehab, probably the same place they sent Dad."

Jenni's mom slumped into the only chair in the room, her face pale.

"Mom, are you sick? Do you need a wet paper towel?" Her mother had needed many a cold compress when her husband was going through treatments. Jenni wondered how she ever made it through childbirth. Jenni's father must have been a saint.

"Please, sweetheart." Her mother pulled out a marathon brochure, one that Claire had designed, from her purse and fanned her face.

Jenni stared at the brochure. Every day she didn't run, the tension built. She wanted to win. No, needed to win.

"Maybe if you faint, that hot doctor will come back into the room," Gran said. "I want a fan too. It's warm in here."

"Gran, please get your libido under control," Jenni scolded. "Aren't you supposed to be in pain or something?"

"Doc said I have a high pain tolerance." Gran batted her eyes.

"Jenni? Wet paper towels please?" Her mother leaned her head against the puke green wall, badly in need of a coat of paint.

Jenni folded several paper towels together and ran the stack under cold water from the sink. "This is the best I can do." She passed her mother the wet paper.

Her mother dabbed her face dramatically. Jenni had to wonder if she put on this act for show, or if she really was sick. From her pale face, Jenni determined she was about to pass out. "Mom, put your head between your legs." Jenni shoved a small kidney-shaped basin at her.

A nurse dressed in blue scrubs walked in. "We're going to admit you to the hospital, Ms. Stallings." The woman looked from Gran to Jenni's mom, who was inhaling long breaths through her nose, and exhaling them through her mouth. "Are you okay, ma'am?"

"She wants all the attention," Gran said. "But I don't mind. Admit her instead, and I'll go home."

"My mom gets squeamish," Jenni explained. "She does this a lot. She'll be fine after she sits like that for a while."

"I'll bring her a ginger ale. Be right back." The woman left the room and returned moments later with a paper cup filled with chipped ice and a small can of soda. "Have her sip this when she can. It'll settle her stomach."

"Thanks," Jenni said. Again, she wondered about her mother's future after Jenni's dad died. Would she be able to function without her husband? Would Keith stop hiding and help keep things afloat, or would everything sit on Jenni's shoulders?

Think positive, she told herself. Gran always lived in the moment and things usually worked out for the best. But would the technique work for Jenni?

"I'll take some ginger ale now," her mother said. She reached a shaky hand toward Jenni.

"Let me help you." Jenni poured a small amount into the cup and helped her mother hold it while she sipped. "You'll be okay, mom."

Another hospital employee walked into the cubicle. "Ms. Stallings, we're ready to take you to your room."

Jenni was surprised Gran agreed, but what choice did she have? The real concern would be after her surgery. She was the type to check herself out, even when she needed help.

Gran settled in her new hospital room when a knock sounded at the door. Jenni looked at the doorway, surprised to see Scott standing there. Since Jenni and her mom had brought the BMW, he must have driven her parents' old Camry or Jenni's car.

He peeked into the room. "Anyone home?" he quipped. "I brought you a surprise."

Gran's face lit up. "I knew you were special the first time I met you."

That explained Gran's adoration of him. "Are you hitting on Scott too?" Jenni laughed. "I asked you to marry someone older than me."

"He's older than you by a couple of years." Gran grinned and waved him in.

"Hang on a second." Scott stepped back into the hallway. He reappeared, pushing a wheel chair carrying Jenni's father, who held a bouquet of yellow roses and ivy greens.

Scott was amazing. He'd somehow succeeded in convincing her father to leave the security of his house, to visit Gran, nonetheless.

"Surprise." Scott walked over and planted a kiss on Gran's wrinkled cheek.

She frowned at him. "I was expecting a teddy bear, not my son."

If Scott was offended, he didn't show it. "This is even better than a stuffed animal. I arranged someone to help carry him down the steps to the car, so he could come see you."

If Scott managed to end the rift between her father and Gran, he'd deserve a medal.

Jenni's dad sat there looking subdued. Scott reached over and plucked the flowers from his lap. "These are for you, Gran."

Warmth filled Jenni. The familiarity of Scott calling her grandmother "Gran" suggested he cared about her. He naturally fit into Jenni's family. Again, he didn't seem like a man who was using her to redeem himself. She chewed on her lower lip. It was possible, though.

"Thanks, sweetheart." Gran winked at Scott. "I love it when men bring me flowers, which isn't all that often."

"They're from Richard," Scott said. He didn't respond to the huff that escaped from Jenni's dad.

Jenni mentally took notes on how to handle her father as well as Scott did. He simply didn't engage in the negativity, and he somehow managed to maintain a positive attitude. When her father didn't lash out verbally, Jenni counted Scott's heroic efforts as yet another success. She'd try the technique, instead of allowing her father to frustrate her.

"So what's the verdict on your hip?" Scott asked. "You seem ready to jump out of bed and get out of here."

"The doctor insists that I broke it. They'll do surgery tomorrow. I plan on leaving as soon as I can."

"Why would you do that?" Scott asked in such a logical way that it made Gran stop to think about her answer.

"I have horses to take care of."

"I can stop by in the mornings to feed them," Scott offered.

Jenni stared at him. Did he just offer to feed Gran's Islander Ponies?

Scott apparently ignored everyone's shocked expressions. "Jenni showed me how to feed tonight. I enjoy being out there with the horses, and it shouldn't take long. I can do it before I go to work."

"I'll have to pay someone to muck out stalls. It's cheaper if I do it." Gran set her jaw. She wasn't used to letting people help her. "It's best if I get out of here quickly."

"Gran," Jenni reasoned, "you're in no shape to be shoveling horse poop. I love your independence, but your own health comes first."

Keith walked into the room and approached the foot of Gran's bed. He must have overheard the conversation from the doorway. "Gran, I can muck out the stalls during my slow time at the ferry. I've hired a part-time employee who can take over while I'm gone."

Jenni smiled slowly. Everyone was coming together with an offer to assist Gran. Jenni couldn't help but wonder if it would be this way when her dad died. She tried to redirect her thoughts back to Gran, but couldn't help glancing at him. Even though he looked tired, he seemed glad, almost relieved, that his family had pitched in to help Gran. He even appeared peaceful.

"I can feed in the evenings," Jenni offered.

"I know what you're trying to do," Gran said. She waved an accusatory finger at them. "I appreciate what you are doing, but I don't want to go into an old folks' home. I'm young, if you haven't noticed."

"It's not as bad as you think." Richard Stallings uncrossed his arms. "The place is actually uplifting and the staff is attentive."

Gran wouldn't know since she'd never visited her son in the rehab center. Jenni suspected, based on Gran's comments, he'd told her not to come. Undoubtedly, he'd hurt Gran's feelings.

"They have an entire section allocated for rehab patients," he continued to say. His voice shook with emotion, but he didn't let the most difficult time of his life stop him from encouraging Gran. "It's a new building, less than two years old, and fancy. They have these big chandeliers hanging in the entrance."

Jenni recognized the progress her father was making toward reconciling with his mother.

"Just think, Gran, you'll have the staff waiting on you." It was Jenni's turn to flip a potentially undesirable situation into a better one, as Gran had taught her. "I recall a couple of young, attractive men working there. I'm sure they'll be delighted to take care of you. Enjoy it." Gran was the hardest working woman Jenni knew, and she deserved a little pampering.

"Okay." Gran sighed. "I'll go to the rehab center, but only because I know you will take good care of my horses."

At least Gran hadn't called the skilled nursing facility an old folk's home again. She'd made a significant adjustment in her attitude.

Later, after Scott dropped Jenni's dad off at home, they were sitting in the BMW in front of Coffee Break and Scott's apartment. That was the first chance she'd gotten to ask him about the flowers. "How did you talk my dad into giving Gran a bouquet?"

Scott chuckled. "I didn't give him a choice. I made him wait in the car while I ran in to buy the flowers. I shoved them into his arms so I could push his wheelchair up to Gran's room."

"Amazing. He'd argue with me if I tried that."

"How do you know?"

"I guess I don't." She'd love to be able to stand up to her father like that.

"I ignore his crabbiness. Since I don't give him the reaction he wants, he gives up."

"I've been dealing with Dad all these years, half scared of him," she confessed. "You mean it's that simple?"

Scott shrugged. "Yeah, pretty much."

"And how did you get him to agree to visit Gran in the first place?"

"I told him I had a couple of fishing buddies coming over to help me carry him down the steps. He asked me 'Why,' and I told him we're going to see Gran."

Jenni's mouth gaped open. "I don't get this. He just went along with that?"

“The mention of fishing buddies might have helped, but yeah. I think you give him too much control. As I tried to convince your Gran earlier, he’s a teddy bear.”

Her father—a cuddly, stuffed animal? She tried to picture him from Scott’s point of view, but failed. “He’s been grumpy since Brittany’s death, and even worse since his diagnosis of cancer." She shook her head in disbelief. "Maybe he just likes you, or perhaps it’s because you aren’t related to him, so he believes he has to be polite.”

“No. He cursed at me a few times. I smiled and continued carrying him down the steps. He seemed to respect that.”

“Unbelievable.” If what Scott was saying was true, maybe there was a possibility of a truce between them before her father died.

CHAPTER TWENTY

Jenni meant to talk with Dan about Alex, but he'd practically run away from her once they finished the horse rescue. With Gran's accident, another opportunity hadn't been forthcoming. Alex showed up first thing Monday morning for an interview.

"Alex, please have a seat. What can I bring you to drink?"

"A decaf coffee, if you don't mind." Alex didn't meet her gaze and chewed on her lip instead. She headed toward the first booth.

Jenni remembered when she was that age. Her first job, outside of working at Stallings, was when she left for college. She applied at a coffee house similar to this one except it was near campus. Even though she had a lot of restaurant experience, at the time she knew next to nothing about coffee. She ended up with the job, which had taught her much of what she knew about coffee today.

Maybe she'd make a difference in Alex's life. Who knows, Alex might wind up with a master's degree in business too. She reminded Jenni of her younger self.

The interview went well, too well when she considered Dan's feelings. Would he mind losing such a great employee? Of course he would.

Once Alex had warmed up to Jenni, she came across as eager and willing to learn. With her enthusiasm and her connections to the younger generation, she'd be a great asset to Coffee Break.

Right before they finished the interview, the bell above the door tinkled and in walked Scott. He'd left his stuffy tie behind. He was finally relaxing a bit. One day maybe he'd lose the suit pants. He looked at Jenni then at Alex. A frown slowly spread across his face.

Not willing to share her private business with him, she jumped up. "Don't you look nice today? What can I get you?"

He studied Alex, but spoke to Jenni. "I want to feed my carrot cake and mocha addiction." He turned his watchful eye on Jenni. "What's up? It looks like you might be interviewing Dan's server."

Before Jenni could answer, he asked, "Does Dan know about this?"

Jenni debated whether to enlighten Scott or not, but decided that telling him was a fast track to disaster. He'd tell Dan before she got the chance.

"It was my idea," Alex chimed in. "I need different hours than Mr. Botticelli can give me. It wasn't Jenni's fault."

Jenni shook her head. "I meant to talk with Dan before the interview. The fault is mine."

Scott's stormy eyes revealed his anger. She couldn't blame him for protecting his brother.

"That's right," he said. "The professional thing would have been to discuss it with Dan in advance."

"Maybe," Jenni said. "But Alex has a right to privacy. Maybe she didn't want her boss to know she was interviewing." She felt the sudden urge to defend Alex.

Scott's eyebrows formed a single line across his forehead. "Hiding one's intent from Dan raises a red flag. That sounds like betrayal to me."

The betrayal was Jenni's. After all, she planned to hire one of Dan's best employees after he'd been so generous to her. Guilt did bad things to the mind. Then again, with Gran in the hospital and Jenni's ankle hurt, she was desperate for help.

"It's best to find another job first, before you tell your boss you're looking," Jenni reasoned. "Employees do it all the time."

Alex cleared her throat. "Excuse me. I don't want you two fighting over my decision to leave the Shrimp Shack."

Scott looked at Alex. "No one's fighting. We're having a discussion about principles here."

Jenni stiffened. "How dare you attack my professionalism. Help yourself to your carrot cake." She wasn't about to allow him to question her morals, especially in front of Alex.

"Never mind. I've lost my appetite." He turned and left the shop.

"I'm sorry about that. I didn't mean to cause trouble." Alex stood and looked ready to run out the door.

Jenni needed to do something fast. With Coffee Break's increasing business, Alex was the perfect answer to her dilemma.

"I'll take care of it," Jenni said. "In the meantime, carry on as normal. Remember, you have the right to look for another job. It's nobody else's business except Dan's."

"Thanks, Ms. Stallings."

"And please call me Jenni."

"Yes, ma'am. I really want this job." Alex waved goodbye and hurried out the door.

Jenni ignored the tension in her belly and picked up the phone to dial Dan. She had her mind made up; she wanted to hire Alex. But loyalty to Dan won out. If he didn't support her decision, she'd back off. Unfortunately, Dan was out of the restaurant for the next several hours. Instead of discussing the issue with Rachel, since she dealt with Dan directly when it came to business, Jenni left a message for him to return her call. She wanted to touch base with him before he found out about the interview from Scott.

As she hung up the phone, Claire strolled into the shop.

"Why the serious expression?" Claire asked, looking as if she felt much better today. She pulled out a stool and sat by the counter.

"I want to hire Alex, the server at the Shrimp Shack, to work late afternoons and evenings. I'm trying to get hold of Dan before I hire her."

Claire looked confused. "Why's that a problem?"

How to explain? "Scott walked in here toward the end of the interview and drew his own conclusions. He thinks I've betrayed his brother. Maybe I did. After all, he financed my espresso machine when I was desperate."

"That's between you and Dan. It's none of Scott's business." She rolled her eyes. "Ah, but Scott has feelings for you."

Jenni set a mug of hot tea in front of her friend. "Why should that matter?"

"Because that changes things. Since he's interested in you, and because he thinks you betrayed his brother, he assumes you're capable of betraying him too. He cares about you more than you think."

Jenni looked down to avoid Claire's gaze.

"Just curious, why didn't you date him in high school?"

Jenni swirled a tea bag in her own mug before she met Claire's stare. "He asked out Cassie, instead. Then when his brother asked me to the movies, I agreed. We ended up exclusively dating for two years. Don't get me wrong, I liked Dan. A lot actually."

"But Scott was different." Claire sharpened her stare. "What's the real reason?"

Jenni sucked in a breath. *Tell her the truth.* "Scott scared me. He was a senior and I was a sophomore. He played football; I sat in the stands and watched. He drank, I didn't." But there was more to the story. So much more.

"Have you forgiven him yet? About Brittany?"

Jenni hesitated. "No."

Claire shook her head. “What will it take? Brittany is gone. She’s never coming back.”

Jenni swallowed hard. Only Claire could get away with such a comment. “I don’t know.”

“Are you afraid to let your emotional wall down?” Claire asked. “If he returns to Raleigh without closure, he won’t come back. I know I said long distance relationships can work, but this situation is different. You need to talk to him about the past.”

The bell tinkled above the door.

“Excuse me,” Scott said, standing tall and looking more uptight than usual. He was back to wearing his power tie.

Claire turned around. “I'll take my tea to-go if you don't mind."

“I hate to interrupt your female bonding time,” he said, “but I owe you an apology, Jenni. I ran into Alex, and she explained what happened. I’m sorry I jumped to conclusions.”

He’d been judgmental toward her. How was Jenni supposed to trust him? “I called Dan," she said, "but he wasn’t in this afternoon.”

Scott frowned. “He isn’t going to be happy about losing his star employee. Dan prides himself on training the best staff. He had plans to eventually train her to be manager.”

If that was the case, Alex may well change her mind about working at Coffee Break.

"I forgot to ask,” he said. “How’s your ankle?" He glanced from Jenni to Claire, who still waited for her to-go cup.

“It’s improving. I plan to ditch this crutch by the weekend,” Jenni said. “I’m eager to start running again. The race is coming up fast.”

He remained silent. Upstairs Pirate started barking. “What am I going to do with him? He doesn’t like being alone all day. I need to find him a good home.”

Jenni was aghast. “Bring him down here. He can stay with me for the day.”

"I hear you found a stray," Claire asked.

"His name is Pirate. He comes with me everywhere I go except work. If he's going to bark when I'm gone, that's a problem."

"Finding someone to take him will be easy," Jenni said. The only way to make Scott see how much the dog meant to him was to threaten to take Pirate away. "I know someone who might want him if you decide you don't."

***

The phone rang first thing the next morning. Jenni hated to be a bearer of bad news, especially when Dan's upbeat voice vibrated on the other end of the line.

"Thanks for calling me back." She tried to match his enthusiasm, but she wasn't looking forward to the upcoming conversation. She reminded herself that this was part of owning a business. "I recently had a discussion with Alex, your server. She mentioned wanting to attend classes at the community college, but she needs to work afternoon hours and weekends to accommodate her schedule." Jenni inhaled slowly to keep her voice steady. She looked forward to the day that discussing topics like this would be easier. "Alex approached me about working at Coffee Break, but I wanted to discuss it with you first."

Silence.

"Dan?"

"I'm here. I have to admit, you took me by surprise. I thought Alex was happy here." He grew quiet for a moment. "I know she mentioned changing her hours, but I didn't realize she was willing to quit if we couldn't meet her request."

"I'm sorry. I didn't mean to imply she wasn't happy there; I'm sure she is. It's just that she heard I'm hiring, and my hours happen to fit with her schedule. Like I said, I wanted to discuss this with you before I made any move to hire her."

"I appreciate your honestly. I'm unhappy, though, about possibly losing one of my most valuable employees. I'm going to sit down and talk this over with her. I have to tell you, I'm going to fight to keep her."

Jenni had planned to back off, but she couldn't. Alex was exactly what Coffee Break needed.

***

The next morning, the sandwich delivery from the Shrimp Shack never showed up. Jenni gave Dan the benefit of the doubt; there must be a misunderstanding. Still, an underlying tension radiated just below the calm exterior she tried to project. She thought about Alex. Was he upset enough about Alex that he stopped Jenni's order? That didn't sound like Dan, but neither did a no-show delivery.

Jenni picked up the phone and dialed the Shrimp Shack. A young woman answered on the second ring.

"This is Jenni Stallings at Coffee Break. Is Dan available?"

"He's not here today. He went to Raleigh on business." The woman's voice was friendly but unfamiliar. "May I help you?"

She needed to speak to someone soon. "Is Rachel there?"

"She went with him. Tabatha's in charge while they're gone. Would you like to speak to her?"

"Please." Seconds turned into minutes before Tabatha finally answered.

"What can I help you with, Jenni?"

Jenni? They were on a first-name basis and they'd never met? The woman had an unfamiliar accent, which explained why Jenni didn't know her from school. "I didn't receive my morning delivery. I'm just wondering if there was some kind of mistake."

"Hold on a minute." A minute turned into five.

Jenni didn't have time for this. Several customers came in and she apologized as she filled their order with the phone pressed to her ear.

Finally the woman came back on the line. "We can deliver the sandwiches first thing in the morning."

“I don’t want them tomorrow; I need them today. As soon as possible.” Jenni fought to keep the agitation out of her voice.

“Sorry, but the person in charge of making the sandwiches is already gone. He comes in early and leaves when he’s finished.”

“Well, he obviously wasn’t finished. Can you please have someone complete my order and send it over before the lunch rush?”

“Like I said, I’m sorry, Jenni. I can’t do that.” The woman’s voice held no indication of concern whatsoever. “We can deliver your sandwiches first thing tomorrow morning.”

“For the record, I’d appreciate being called Miss Stallings. I can understand an oversight, but I find your carefree attitude unprofessional. It seems to me, since my order was overlooked, someone on your staff could help remedy the situation.”

“I’m sorry you feel that way, ma’am.” Tabatha placed emphasis on the word “ma’am.” “I understand your dilemma but there isn’t a thing I can do about it now. Had you called earlier, while Greg was still on the clock, I could have helped you out.”

Jenni clamped her teeth together to avoid an argument. “That’s fine. I’ll take the matter up with Dan when he returns.”

“Have a good day, ma’am.” A click replaced the woman's clipped voice.

Why had Dan hired such an incompetent worker? Was this his way of punishing her because Alex wanted to work at Coffee Break?

***

The next day it happened again. No sandwiches. Jenni picked up the phone and dialed the Shrimp Shack.

“Dan’s not here," a kinder woman said. "He won’t be back until tomorrow. Can I take a message?”

Not wanting to leave a message, or to talk to Tabatha again, she asked for Marge.

"How can I help you, sweetie." The older woman's voice sounded so friendly, welcoming.

"I haven't gotten my order the last two days. My customers are asking for sandwiches." Jenni bit back a derogatory comment about Tabatha. "I'd like to have them delivered right away, before the lunch rush."

"Let me transfer you to Tabatha. She takes care of that."

"No!" Jenni didn't mean to bark at Marge but she couldn't hide her irritation. "I mean, I tried talking with her yesterday and got nowhere. Is there somebody else I can talk with?"

"How about Greg? He's in charge of making the sandwiches."

"Perfect. And Marge, thanks for your help."

"I'm sure it's a simple mix-up. Let me transfer you."

Several minutes went by before someone answered again. "This is Tabatha. How can I help you?"

Jenni's shoulders tightened. "I'd like to speak with Greg, please."

"He's busy right now. Would you like to leave a message?"

"No. I'd like to talk with him." Jenni swallowed hard, trying to maintain her composure. "I'll only be a minute."

"Miss Stallings," Tabatha said. Even though she'd exaggerated the use of her name, at least she remembered not to call her Jenni. "Like I said, he's busy. Either you tell me what the problem is, or you can leave Gregg a message."

"I haven't received my sandwich order again. I'm not sure what the problem is, but I need it before the lunch rush. If someone could deliver this morning—"

"That's impossible," Tabatha interjected. "Greg's busy filling other orders. I'm sorry about the confusion—"

"What happened to customer satisfaction? Never mind. I'll talk to Dan when he returns tomorrow." Jenni hung up the phone, her body trembling. She'd resolve this with Dan. Then she remembered tomorrow was Saturday, his day off. She left a message on his cell phone.

Frustrated, Jenni picked up the phone again and dialed the Shrimp Shack. This time, when a man answered without identifying himself, she asked for Alex. When Alex picked up the phone, Jenni paused. The girl sounded so upbeat. Had something happened with the job situation to lighten her spirit?

"Miss Stallings, I mean Jenni. I'm so glad you called."

"You are?" The comment surprised Jenni. "Why's that?"

"First off, Dan offered me a large pay increase."

Jenni half expected that. After all, he said he'd fight to keep Alex. "Congratulations then."

Alex chuckled. "No, you misunderstood me. It's not about the money; it's about the hours. He can't help me with that. I want to work for you if you haven't hired anyone else."

Jenni felt relieved. "I'm still hiring. I'd be glad to have you as an employee. By the way, do you know why I haven't received my sandwich orders today or yesterday? I can't seem to get answers."

"You should have asked Greg. He answered the phone when you called."

Jenni's irritation increased. "Can I talk to him?"

"I can transfer you, but you'll probably get Tabatha."

"No thanks. I've already tried that." She needed the situation resolved quickly. Every day she didn't receive the sandwiches, she lost money.

"It's not like them to miss a delivery. Hang on a minute." Alex's voice grew muffled. "Cassie Forthright's in Tabatha's office right now with Greg. That's interesting."

Interesting indeed.

"Never mind. When would you like to start working here?"

"I want to give a two-week notice, but I can work in the meantime for you in the afternoons. My classes don't start until after the first of the year."

Jenni smiled at the thought of keeping her shop open longer each day. "Perfect, Alex. Why don't you come by Monday afternoon when you get off from the Shrimp Shack?"

"I'll be there."

CHAPTER TWENTY-ONE

Anxious to talk to Dan, Jenni decided to eat lunch at the Shrimp Shack on Sunday afternoon. He wouldn't miss the after-church lunch crowd, and the issue with the missing sandwiches was becoming urgent.

Marge seated her at a table for two pushed against the far wall. Unfortunately, Cassie sat at the next table over with her parents, apparently pretending not to notice Jenni's arrival. That was for the best; Jenni didn't know what she'd say to her, anyway.

Alex approached the small table. Uncomfortable as it was, she was Jenni's server. "Did you talk to Dan about the sandwiches?" Alex asked.

Jenni shook her head in frustration. "No. Every time I called, he wasn't available."

Alex glanced at Cassie and scowled, then looked back at Jenni. "I'll send him over to your table first chance he gets."

"Thanks." Jenni hoped she was doing the right thing by hiring Alex. Even though her ankle was healing nicely and she'd ditched the crutch, she was desperate for help.

Cassie laughed at something her mother said, and they both looked at Jenni. She almost felt sorry for them. They must be miserable people to behave like that. From the corner of her eye, Jenni watched as Cassie's father ordered for them. Pampering them was probably a huge part of the problem. Cassie was Daddy's spoiled little girl.

Moments later, Dan walked up. He was professional but not overly friendly. "Good afternoon, Jenni. How can I help you?" Usually he smiled and flashed a wave whenever he saw her, but not today.

It was important for him to know that Alex was the one who sought her out, not the other way around. He couldn't accommodate her schedule, so either way he was going to lose her. But on an intellectual level, she understood why he was hurt and angry.

Jenni noticed Cassie's outstretched neck, even though she tried to pretend disinterest. Jenni didn't want to discuss the sandwich issue with Cassie listening, because she suspected she had something to do with the missing orders. But what choice did she have? She needed to figure out the underlying cause, and if Cassie had meddled, the truth would surface soon.

"I realize you've been out of town," Jenni said, "so I understand that mix-ups can happen. The last few days I haven't gotten my sandwiches delivered. I'm not sure why, but when I called and talked to Tabatha, she told me that the order couldn't be delivered until the following day."

Dan's face slowly hardened.

"Anyway, the next day the order didn't come and Tabatha told me I'd have to wait another day. I have yet to receive my order. I'm sure there's a logical explanation, but I wanted to bring it to your attention."

"You sure it was Tabatha you talked to?"

"Yes."

Cassie turned away but not before Jenni noticed the smile on her face. Why would she interfere with Coffee Break? Would Cassie's jealousy extend to disrupting her business?

Dan frowned. "I gave Tabatha specific instructions to have Gregg make your sandwiches first, to have them delivered immediately. Your business opens earlier than our other customers."

At least Dan appeared to be on Jenni's side regardless of the tension radiating from him. Thankfully, he hadn't retaliated because she wanted to hire Alex.

"I'm sorry about the confusion," he said. "I'll see to it that you have your order first thing tomorrow morning. And I will talk to Tabatha."

True to his word, Monday morning a delivery truck pulled up outside Coffee Break. A man jumped out and, whistling a tune that sounded like Jimmy Buffet, he wheeled Jenni's sandwich order through the door. Thank goodness Dan had come across. She made a mental note to call and thank him for his attentiveness. Without the selection of sandwiches the past few days, profits had decreased significantly.

By noon, she'd sold all the sandwiches; the turkey and Swiss went first. Claire bought the last pimento and cheese out of the display case.

"How's your grandmother doing?" Claire asked. Her unsmiling face, a sharp contrast for Claire's usual sunny disposition, alarmed Jenni. Often she showed great discipline in not sharing what most bothered her, until just the right moment.

"Gran has a crush on another doctor, so she willingly complied with surgery and rehab." Jenni feigned ignorance about Claire's problem for the time being and rolled her eyes. Her friend would talk about what upset her soon enough. "Mom's with Gran now, thanks to Sally, Dad's certified nursing assistant." Her parents hired Sally to work weekdays, which freed Jenni's mom to run errands, and in this case, to spend the day with Gran. "She came through surgery without a problem."

"I'm glad someone's with her. The support is important."

Jenni worried about her independent-minded grandmother. "She's capable of handling most situations without help, but I agree, family support is crucial. It's also good for Gran to know we're watching her closely. It wouldn't be unlike her to get up in the middle of the night and leave the hospital."

"Maybe she'll settle down if she knows the community will step up and take good care of her horses. If you need help feeding them, we can rally people to help; they love the Islander Ponies almost as much as Gran does. I'm sure Jeff and I can help."

"I appreciate the offer. Right now we're covered. Scott's feeding in the mornings, Keith's mucking out stalls, and I'm on the evening shift."

"Scott's feeding? Obviously something's changed from the last time I've seen you." Claire chewed on her lip as if to ponder the change in Jenni's attitude. "Does he accept you hiring Alex now?"

"I'm not sure." Jenni pointed to the last little corner of the pimento sandwich. "Is your baby full?"

She smiled. "Yes. And the baby is doing great. Thankfully my bleeding stopped." She rubbed the tiny bulge under her shirt. "And my morning sickness is beginning to subside."

"What a relief." So the baby wasn't the reason for her friend's troubled expression.

Claire frowned and chewed her lip faster. "Listen. There's something you need to know."

"What's that?" Nothing could ruin Jenni's day. Dan came across for her, profits were already increasing because of it, Gran's surgery went well, and Claire's bleeding had stopped. What could she possibly need to know?

Claire hesitated. "There's a bit of gossip circulating around town. I can't prove who started it, but the rumor is that you're dating Scott just because you want him to reconsider your loan."

Claire might as well have punched her in the belly. The air gushed right out.

“Sorry. I thought you should know.”

Jenni struggled to breathe. “I know who spread that. What I don't understand is why she's causing trouble."

“I hope the gossip doesn’t impact your business.”

“It hasn’t so far," Jenni said. "We’ll see once the rumor circulates through town.” That shouldn't take long once tongues started flapping. “Do you think people will believe the gossip?” Jenni’s business had started to increase lately, before the sandwich mix-up, and she wasn’t sure she even needed a loan.

“Yes, I think it’s a possibility,” Claire said. “Unfortunately, people believe the worst, even if it's untrue.”

A group of pregnant women giggled from the corner of the room. Some of them had small children in strollers, and a few toddlers ran in circles around them. An adorable little redheaded boy held a half-eaten cookie in his hand and had chocolate smudged around his mouth.

Claire watched the playgroup with such longing, that Jenni pushed aside her own pain about the gossip circulating through the rumor mill to comfort her best friend. “Just think, that will be you soon.”

“I hope so.” She rubbed the tiny bulge again. “I’ve always wanted a family. Now’s my chance to have my own.” Claire's expression took on a peaceful gaze as she watched the young kids chase each other.

Seeing Claire happy filled Jenni with hope. Miracles can happen. Her miracle was Coffee Break, with its success, along with the dream of opening a chain. No matter what anyone believed, no matter the gossip that ran rampant, she planned to achieve her goal. Once Alex started working for her, Jenni could implement her other ideas to increase business. The money from her latest improvements needed to keep coming in steadily, and then she’d be well on her way.

“Tell me about Scott.” Claire shoved the last bite of sandwich into her mouth and washed it down with a large swallow of decaffeinated green tea. The baby must have changed its mind about being hungry.

“What do you want to know about him?” Despite Jenni's momentary surge of confidence, a nagging feeling warned her that she needed to pay attention to the circulating gossip. Her intuition was usually right, and from the knot tightening in her belly, the rumor promised to be harmful. Gran would scold her for thinking such negative thoughts, thus attracting more her way, but Jenni couldn’t help it.

"Anything and everything." Claire covered her mouth and muffled the next words out of her mouth. “It’s obvious you love him.”

Jenni about choked. “Love? What gave you that idea?”

“The look in your eyes when you talk about him. Like now.”

Jenni immediately wiped the dreamy feeling away. In the future, she had to be more careful with her emotions. If Claire noticed, then Scott definitely would. That’s when expectations started, when the man knew how much you cared about him. Then he left you behind, or died.

“Word of caution. If you pretend you don’t have feelings for him, you’ll lose him again.” Claire touched Jenni’s hand. “That happened once before.”

Jenni shrugged off the comment, not ready to examine her complicated feelings for Scott so closely yet.

One of the pregnant women, Lynn Shelly, walked up to the counter. “I’d like to buy a cookie for my son. His friend has one and I finally gave in.” She plucked a chocolate cookie from the display case. “I can’t blame him, they are delicious.” The woman dug out a five-dollar bill from her purse and set it on the counter.

“I confess. I eat at least one a day.” Jenni smiled and rang up the purchase.

“And yet you stay so fit.” Lynn shrugged. “While you’re at it, please add a strawberry smoothie to my order.”

"Yes, ma'am. I aim to please," Jenni said and scooped up enough ice to make a smoothie. She dumped the contents into the blender and hit the power button.

Claire stood and spoke over the machine to Jenni. "I'll catch you later."

Much to Jenni's relief, Claire walked out the door. Jenni wanted to avoid further discussion about Scott for now. She much preferred to enjoy the pleasure he brought her, however temporary that might be thanks to the rumors rumbling about.

When Jenni passed the smoothie across the counter, Lynn asked, "How's your ankle?"

"I thought it was better, but now it's starting to bother me again."

"Cookie, Mama." The little boy tugged on his mother's pink maternity shirt labeled "Baby Girl."

Lynn handed the cookie to her son. "There you go. You can take it back to the table. I'll be there in a minute." The little boy ran off, smiling as if he held a valuable treasure.

"Are you going to run in the marathon?" Lynn asked.

Jenni shrugged and wished she knew the answer to the question. "That depends. I need to start training again, and I'm losing time." Not a day went by that she didn't think about the race.

"It won't be the same if you don't," Lynn said. "Cassie wins every year. She's turned our small-town race into a personal vendetta against you. I'd love to see her expression if she lost."

Jenni smiled, Lynn provoking Jenni's competitive drive. "Believe me; I'd like nothing better than to beat Cassie." That was a massive understatement. When Cassie had approached her about Scott the other day, Jenni thought they were coming to terms with their past. What a mistake to assume Cassie's warning was heartfelt. Why had Jenni listened to her?

"I need to start training slowly," Jenni explained. "I'll make my decision closer to the race. But I appreciate the encouragement."

"Good luck. My money's on you," Lynn said.

Every year the locals made private bets as to who'd win the race. More locals usually placed bets on Jenni, but so far, Cassie had won every race the past five years. Jenni needed to win, though, as a last chance to prove her success to her father by beating her archrival. He'd always rooted for her, had always encouraged her to run her best race. She'd hoped this year would be better, that she'd win, but now she wasn't so optimistic.

"I thought you were going to beat her last year. It was so close."

It was the longest fraction of a moment in her life as she crossed the finish line behind Cassie.

"Thanks. I'll do my best to enter," Jenni said, fighting off the pressing urge to run. She'd have to exercise great patience until her ankle healed completely. If she started too early, she'd mess up the possibility to compete for sure.

Before long, Alex walked through the front door, dressed in the khaki pants and white button-down shirt that were Coffee Break's customary uniform.

"I'm so glad you're here," Jenni said. "I have a lot to tell you."

Alex's smile failed to warm her narrowed eyes. When Jenni gave her a quick hug, Alex stiffened.

"Is there something wrong?"

"Not at all." Alex seemed miserable.

Jenni walked behind the counter to put space between them. She made Alex's favorite chocolate chip frappe in effort to create a relaxed environment so they could have an open discussion. When she finished spraying on whipped cream and drizzling a fancy swirl of chocolate syrup across the top, she pushed a clear lid on the cup and handed it to Alex.

"Thanks."

"Sure. Consider it one of the benefits of working at a coffee shop." Jenni pointed to Claire's vacated stool at the counter. As soon as Alex sat, Jenni started talking. "I want you to know that you can talk to me about anything. If you're having second thoughts about working here, I'd like to know."

Alex looked away.

Jenni had a sneaking suspicion that Alex's behavior had something to do with the rumors. "Does this have to do with the gossip I heard earlier?"

Alex didn't look at her but her shoulders seemed to relax a bit.

"It's not true, you know."

"I don't understand," Alex said. "Tabatha scolded me about working here. She said I was bailing out, leaving the good guys behind in order to work for the enemy."

For the second time that day, Jenni took a punch to the gut.

"She said that you're sleeping with Scott to get back at Dan, because he used to date you. I've asked around, and turns out it's true. You dated Dan during high school. She also mentioned that I'm a pawn in your ploy to hurt Dan, that you're jealous because he married Rachel instead of you."

Alex's words drove an ice pick through Jenni's heart.

"That's not true. I mean, yes, I used to date Dan, but that's not why I hired you," Jenni clarified. "I'm not sure why Tabatha is spreading such ugly lies, but I promise that my decision to hire you is based on your work performance. You're an asset to my business."

Alex seemed to deflate. "Tabatha was fuming because Dan had a long talk with her behind closed doors. I don't know what was said, but I know it had to do with you."

Now the rumors made sense. She wasn't sure if Cassie was behind them, or not, but Tabatha was out for revenge. "My sandwich orders weren't being delivered. I got the run around from Tabatha. I had a talk with Dan over the weekend, and first thing this morning, a deliveryman showed up. Sorry you got involved in all this."

"That's okay." Alex shifted on the stool. "What about Scott? I mean, how is he involved?"

“My relationship with him has nothing to do with Dan. When I broke up with Dan years ago, I introduced him to my college roommate. He’s happily married to her. And for the record," Jenni continued, "I adore Rachel. If you recall, I was at their party the night you mentioned wanting to find another job. If Dan found me a threat, do you think he’d have invited me?”

“I guess not.” Alex seemed to relax more.

“I guarantee I have no desire to hurt Dan whatsoever. In fact, I went sailing with him and Rachel recently. That’s because we’re friends.” At least they were friends until she hired Alex.

“I’m sorry I doubted you. What a great way to start off my first day.”

“No problem. Just do me a favor," Jenni said. "If you hear any more rumors, would you please let me know? It’s important, so I know how to address them.”

“I’m not sure if this is significant, but Cassie was in Tabatha’s office again today.”

A headache formed at the base of Jenni’s neck.

CHAPTER TWENTY-TWO

A week sailed by without Jenni hearing from Scott. The intensity of the hurt was surprising. Her heart screamed to protect herself and to bail overboard, while she had a shred of dignity left. Perhaps Cassie had been right—he'd used her. Without a doubt, he'd heard the rumors and questioned them, as everyone else seemed to have done. She couldn't trust him. When he got scared, he pushed her away, just as he'd done years ago when he'd run off to Raleigh. That insight made the pain much worse.

Business slowed almost overnight. She had her regulars still, such as Mr. Davis and the other elderly gentlemen who liked to play checkers in the corner of the room. The pregnant women continued to come in once a week, along with a handful of other customers, but that wasn't enough to sustain a successful business.

She'd rather have a root canal than engage in the tense drama that silently surrounded her. Unfortunately, the unwanted situation demanded attention.

Just when she hit her lowest point mentally, Claire walked through the door. "Wow, where is everyone?"

"Not here, that's for sure."

Her loyal friend pulled out her favorite stool and climbed onto it. "I'll take the usual. I need a break from the studio and Shirley's a saint. I got lucky when I found her." Shirley was more than a reliable employee. She was almost the grandmother Claire didn't have. She'd been a support system for her while Claire survived the tribulations of finding her father.

"Speaking of hired help, I don't know what I'm going to do with Alex. It's good she hasn't quit the Shrimp Shack yet. Maybe Dan will let her keep her job."

Claire slumped in her chair. "Oh, Jenni. This reminds me of the trouble I had with Lynette, when she wanted to run me out of town." Lynette, Jeff's spoiled ex-fiancée, tried similar tactics to drive Claire out of town, away from Jeff. "She reminds me of Cassie, except Cassie's daddy doesn't own the only bank in town. Instead, Cassie works at a bank, with Scott, which is almost as bad. If you ask me, they could be sisters."

Jenni groaned at the thought. "One Cassie is enough."

"Just hang on about Alex. I have an idea."

Jenni raised her eyebrows.

"I have a steady stream of people who peruse my shop. Let's make a coupon offering a deal people can't refuse. We'll put the stack next to the door. Once we get people in here, let's say for a free drink, they'll most likely buy something else. Most people can't ignore your desserts and sandwiches."

"You'd do that for me?"

"Of course. What are friends for?"

Friends. They're supposed to support each other in time of crisis. And she was about to find out who her true friends were.

***

Late one afternoon, after Jenni reluctantly sent Alex home because business was slow, Scott stopped by the coffee shop.

"Hi," he said. "I'll have a decaf mocha."

He looked so sexy, even more so than she remembered. She also noted that he was back to wearing his power ties again.

“Decaf?" she asked. He always drank mochas with two shots of espresso. Why the change?

"I didn't realize how uptight I was when I first moved here. I'm feeling that way again, so I decided to cut back on the caffeine." He glanced in the display case. "You barely have anything in here. Guess I’ll take a ham and Swiss."

"I had to scale back on my sandwich and pastry order lately."

He glanced around at the empty seats. “I heard your business is slow, but this is ridiculous.”

The coffee shop had been practically dead all afternoon.

“That’s the way it goes, I suppose.” She walked away to make his decaf mocha and tried to ignore his stare.

"I hear you've been running again."

"Yes." She thought back to the first time she bumped into him while running. She'd resented his interference then, but realized now how much she'd grown to enjoy his company. "I've started out slowly. It's going well."

He didn't seem to hear her. “I’m sorry I haven’t called.”

She shrugged, but the raw pain in her heart ached.

“I’ve been busy at work.” His words sounded unnatural and forced. “We need to talk.” He inhaled a long breath. “It seems there’s an awful rumor going around.”

“Yeah, I’m well aware of it.” She walked back to the cash register and pressed a lid atop the to-go cup. She assumed he wasn’t staying.

“Is it true? What they’re saying?”

How could he ask her that? Maybe they didn’t have the strong relationship that she’d thought.

When she bit back a smart retort, he shifted from one foot to the next, clearly waiting for an answer. She wouldn’t give him the pleasure.

“The gossip is bad,” he said.

How many rumors floated about, and what had he heard? "What are you talking about exactly?" She wanted to hear him say the words.

"When I went to the Shrimp Shack to eat lunch the other day, they were whispering behind my back. Finally, Dan told me what they were saying."

"Enlighten me." She took his twenty, trying to ignore the tingles that ran through her body when their fingers touched.

When she went to make change, he said, "Keep it."

"No thanks. I don't need your charity."

"Jenni, people are saying that you're playing me like a game of chess, strategically. They're saying you'd stop at nothing to get to a loan. Heck, you've told me that yourself."

She held onto the countertop to brace herself. "I think it's best if you leave."

"I don't want us to end like this. I need to know the truth."

"You should already know the truth. If you believe I'd use you to achieve my goals, then there's no point in continuing this discussion." She remembered the conversation with Cassie, when she'd come into the coffee shop asking if Scott was using her to redeem himself to the town. Jenni had questioned his motivation at the time, but fast realized he wouldn't treat her that way. Where was his sense of loyalty?

He leaned forward, inches from her face. "That's just it. I don't believe you'd do something like that. I need to know why the rumors started."

"You don't want to know the truth."

"Try me." His curious gaze searched hers.

She tried to swallow a hard lump that refused to go down. "It appears that your employee, Miss Cassie Forthright, is jealous of our relationship. Therefore, she's created a rumor to not only destroy us, but to close my business."

His eyes widened and his lips formed a tight line. "Cassie? Why would she want to do something like that?"

"Because she wants you for herself. And she's used to getting her way."

"I'm sorry, but I can't believe she'd pull a stunt like that. If anything, I'd say you've been bothered by her all along, even during high school."

She clamped her teeth together in a futile effort to remain quiet. "And your comment ends our little talk." When he didn't move, she straightened and pulled back her shoulders. "I'd like you to leave."

He didn't budge. "Cassie liked me in the beginning, I'll agree, but she's taken the hint. I'm not interested in her."

"And you're not giving me the benefit of the doubt. You're defending her childish behavior." Unbelievable. He believed Cassie was innocent in this. "Just look around my coffee shop again. I didn't spread that ugly rumor."

"And you blame Cassie."

"Men don't understand women. I'm not sure why I bothered to tell you the truth." Her heart pounded hard against her chest. "I guess I thought you were different."

"Ouch."

"Don't forget your sandwich on your way out."

His expression turned hard as stone. "You can keep it." He whipped around and strode toward the entrance without looking back. It was the first time she'd seen him so angry.

Once the door shut, a big swoosh of breath escaped her lips. She wanted to make up with him, to feel his warm arms embrace her, yet he walked out the door. Too bad she loved him. Yes, loved.

***

That night Jenni ran alone. If she allowed herself to travel down the lonely path of memory, she'd have to admit she missed training with Scott. She tried to push the unproductive thoughts aside. She'd be better off using the mental energy to plan a strategy to increase her endurance. The marathon was too close.

Unfortunately, she'd become winded much too early in her run. She swiped a hand across the gritty sweat on her forehead. A runaway droplet burned the corner of her eye. The odds didn't look good for the race, but she wasn't a quitter.

When she rounded the next corner, her previous thoughts conjured up the man himself. Scott was heading toward her. Before she could decide if she should flick a wave at him and keep running, he crossed the street and joined her.

"Glad to see you running. The streets have missed you," he said.

Yeah, right. She only hoped he'd missed her too. "Thanks." She was the one breathless and out of shape instead of him. How circumstances had changed.

"I owe you an apology. I planned to come by your coffee shop tomorrow."

Winded, she broke to a fast-paced walk. Instead of powering off and leaving her behind, as she'd once done to him, he slowed to match her pace.

"You were right," he said. "I overheard Cassie talking on the phone. I don't know who she was gossiping with, but I heard your name mentioned. She sounded thrilled that Coffee Break is struggling." He reached out and grabbed her hand. "I'm sorry, Jenni."

The heat from his fingers laced with hers melted the artificial barrier she'd built to survive the void. She pulled him to a stop and mashed her lips against his welcoming mouth. To her delight, he deepened the kiss. His large hands ran down her backside and scooped her closer to him.

He mumbled under his breath. "Then you accept my apology?"

She nodded. "I've missed you."

"Me too, sweetheart," he said. "By the way, how's your grandmother? I haven't seen her in over a week."

“You’ve visited Gran?”

“Of course. Before they discharged her to the rehab center.”

Why hadn’t Gran told her? “They want to keep her for a few weeks, but she’s determined to return home before then.”

“How’s she supposed to do that?”

Jenni shrugged her shoulders. “She’s using a walker right now, so getting around by herself would be tough. She thinks the horses need her.” His smile managed to thaw out any residual anger.

"Go figure."

Jenni grinned. “Thankfully, an anonymous person donated a significant amount of money to the *Wild Horse Foundation*. We’re using a portion of it to pay Alex to stay at Gran’s house and take care of the horses. That way Alex has an income since Dan replaced her and I cut her hours.” The generous donation came just in time. It had become increasingly difficult for Jenni to take care of Gran’s horses along with Coffee Break, despite Claire and Jeff's help. Scott had stopped once they'd offered to take over the job a few days ago.

“If I know Alex, she’s taking great care of the horses. Since that's the case, why does Gran want to return home so soon?”

“Why does Gran do anything?” She shrugged. “I’m glad we’ve kept her in rehab this long. Thanks for feeding as long as you did.”

“I wouldn’t take my anger out on her. You should know me better than that.”

Jenni clenched her jaw.

“Don’t look at me like that.” He swept her into a hug again. “I always knew you were right about Cassie, but I had to come to terms with it. Sorry I hurt you.”

“Make sure it doesn’t happen again.” She was only half joking.

***

When Jenni returned home, she made for the freezer to grab a bag of ice as a preventative measure, and then walked toward the living room. As tired as she was from running, she couldn't wait to sink into her father's old recliner. She planned to stay that way for the next hour. Reluctant to study Coffee Break's finances, she retrieved her laptop from the buffet where she'd deposited it earlier. The over-stuffed chair enveloped her and she yawned. She was ready for bed and it wasn't even dinnertime yet.

She didn't have time to be tired. She had a business to operate and a marathon to run. Half the town counted on her to come in at least second place during the race. Sponsors made donations because of her reputation for being involved with the Islander Ponies. Or at least they used to support her before the gossip. If Coffee Break's lack of business was any indication of how the majority of people in Big Cat felt, they no longer stood behind her.

What would her father think if she failed at either venture?

Why did she care so much about pleasing him? The answer was easy—Brittany—her adorable little sister, whom Jenni missed so much. Her father still favored her, probably would until the day he died.

Jenni wondered if she'd always have the pitiful desire to prove herself to him. She needed to find a way to squelch the dysfunctional craving while he was alive. She needed to find peace within herself because the issue resided inside her, not him.

She opened the accounting program on her laptop and studied the numbers. The gnawing tension in her belly increased.

A pan clanked on the stove in the kitchen, startling Jenni. Her mother was starting dinner surprisingly late tonight; she'd stayed at the skilled nursing facility longer than normal. Jenni thought about offering to help, but decided she couldn't afford to ignore Coffee Break's finances any longer. She returned to scrutinizing the numbers. The recurring headache formed again in the back of her neck.

If she wanted Coffee Break to succeed, she needed to find a way to bring in more business, fast. But she had no idea how to convince people the rumors were untrue. The disappointment that people, even longtime acquaintances, could believe such gossip hurt.

She was so engrossed in her spreadsheet that she didn't hear her father approach. Before she knew it, he was looking over her shoulder groaning.

"Those numbers stink. I thought your college degree would make you smarter than that." He turned, undoubtedly dismissing her, and headed toward his favorite spot on the couch.

Under no circumstances had she wanted her father to see Coffee Break's finances. She found it impossible to respond to his unfair comment. Defending her education or her ability as a business owner would serve no purpose other than to sound defensive. She remembered Scott's approach with her father. He was right. She refused to respond, refused to let her father make her angry.

A loud rap on the back door broke the tension. Jenni heard the creak of the screen door, then a muffled conversation.

"Jenni?" her mom called out. "Scott's here."

He picked the worst possible moment to enter the living room.

"Coffee Break's going out of business," her dad said as he pointed that dreaded finger at her laptop.

Jenni sealed her lips, refusing to allow even a grumble to escape. Her dad was right.

Scott's mouth dropped open from the news. "Is that true, Jenni?"

She simply nodded. Oh, she'd been so sure of herself, so positive she'd be successful. She still felt that way, but the financial information revealed the opposite. She wondered how

Scott viewed her now. Did he consider her a failure as her father did?

"I will stop the gossip where Cassie's concerned," Scott declared.

Jenni shook her head. His surprising loyalty was admirable but not necessary. She met Scott's protective stare. "That won't work. She'll accuse you of defending me, and that will only ignite her anger." Obviously he didn't understand how women like Cassie worked.

"What gossip?" Her father crossed his arms and frowned.

Not wanting to explain the situation to him, she interjected before Scott could answer the question. "Never mind, Dad. It's not a big deal." Unfortunately, she wasn't fast enough.

"Cassie spread some nasty rumor," Scott said at the same time. He was now standing next to her. "She accused Jenni of dating me because she's desperate for a loan."

Her father grunted. "That's absurd. Anybody who knows my daughter would realize what an outright lie that is."

His words astonished her. They almost sounded like praise, as if he believed she had worthy qualities after all.

"It doesn't matter what Cassie says; it matters what people believe," Jenni said. "I'm not sure why most of my customers stopped coming into my coffee shop, but the real issue here is how to encourage them to come back."

Scott put a supportive hand on her shoulder. "We need for them to hear your side of the story."

She shook her head and glanced up at him. "I'm not going to play her game. I'll rise above it, and my true friends will eventually realize the truth."

"That's foolish," her dad said. "By then, your business will be closed."

"Not necessarily," she said.

"Stubborn." Her dad shook his head and stood. "By the way, Gran will be coming to stay with us next week." He changed the subject as easily as Gran always did.

He clanked his walker out of the room but the tension remained.

If Jenni thought the living conditions were suffocating now, just wait until Gran moved in. The strain would invariably increase.

"Jenni, I'll find a way to help," Scott said. When she frowned, he said, "Sweetheart, be patient. Continue to implement your changes. You told me before you wanted to have musicians sing on Saturday nights, poetry readings during the week, and craft hour for the kids on the weekends. Do it."

Scott was right. Coffee Break didn't have time to wait.

"I'm sorry about your struggles," he said. "I'll do whatever I can to keep your business afloat. I'll help you put the rumor to rest."

If he could manage that task, she'd consider him a miracle worker. She tried to visualize Coffee Break still in business a year from now, but it was difficult.

CHAPTER TWENTY-THREE

Jenni plunged into the cold, dark water of the Intracoastal Waterway, after her sinking espresso machine. She gasped for breath from the icy fingers enveloping her. Coffee Break sank, with all its cozy loveseats and pillows, even the rich smell of coffee, underwater like her dreams. Her sister reached out to grab her, pulling her under. Jenni fought to escape, to reach the surface.

She struggled but was able to gasp and bring in air. Her sister's frozen hands clawed at her. "Let me go," Jenni yelled. "Leave me alone!"

Her sister didn't speak. Brittany's face was pale, her eyes wide and unblinking. The relentless girl pulled, but before she could drag Jenni under once again, an alarm went off. Buzzing, buzzing. A boat appeared through the fog. The Coast Guard? Scott was on the boat, reaching out to her. Grab his hand.

The buzzing wouldn't leave her alone. Jenni extended her hand to Scott, but before she could reach him, the Coast Guard's boat slipped away into the fog, disappeared.

Jenni jolted awake in her bed and slammed off the buzzing alarm. Her body was shaking and sitting up drained her. She collapsed against her pillows with her heart racing. What did the dream mean? Why was her sister trying to drown her?

Let me go. Leave me alone! The words echoed in her mind. Then the meaning became obvious. Jenni needed to free herself from her sister before she lost everything and drowned. Her dreams, Scott even, would be out of reach until she let go of Brittany.

***

Scott picked up line three to talk to his boss. Lately he'd grown tired of the conversations, the pressure to cut back wherever he could. He was doing the best he could under dire circumstances.

"Do you still want to return to Raleigh, or are you growing accustomed to small-town living?" his boss asked.

"I've been ready to move back since the day I arrived. I'm only down here to help Layne until she returns." Scott was ready to let go the responsibility of running the bank, along with the added pressures from his boss.

"It won't be long now. Layne's coming back early." The sound of paper rattled across the phone line, from possibly his boss, Brant Calloway, turning the pages of a day calendar to search for Layne's return date. "Let's see. Thanksgiving is around the corner." Brant thumped something repeatedly, perhaps his desk. "You only have a little over two weeks left before you return. Think you can survive that long?"

"Of course." Scott had mixed feelings about leaving, mostly concerning Jenni. He needed to tell her about his involvement with the espresso machine, to have a long talk with her about Brittany. He'd come a long way toward lessening the guilt that tormented him, but until he apologized to Jenni for drinking that night, for allowing Cassie to be at the helm instead of him, the issue couldn't rest. But that was the hard part. He wasn't ready to talk about the accident yet.

He also couldn't put off working on his relationship with his parents any longer. Time was running out. If he wanted the privilege of returning to Big Cat in the future, he had to resolve the issues he'd run away from once before.

And then there was Pirate. There was no way he could bring the dog to Raleigh. He hadn't owned a pet before because he was always working late. Pirate deserved better.

When Scott finished the conversation with his boss, he dialed his parents' number. He was the vice president of a bank, so why did he have nervous butterflies in anticipation of talking to his own family?

The beaten-down voice of his mother haunted him through the phone line. Naturally, she scared him, but the woman on the other end didn't sound like the one he remembered. "Mom?"

"Scottie?"

He despised the old nickname, but somehow it almost sounded reassuring. He half expected her to scold him for not calling before, but she surprised him when she didn't. "I'm sorry, Mom." The strong emotions he felt disturbed him. He prided himself in his ability to remain aloof in stressful situations, but this time he failed miserably. "I'm sorry I haven't called you since I've been back in town."

She paused for a moment too long. "It's okay."

That's all she had to say? "Would you like to go out to dinner tonight? We can go to the Shrimp Shack and see Dan." That was a safe place for them both.

"Okay."

He heard breathing on the other end but she didn't speak. "Are you okay, mom?"

When she sniffled, his self-protective armor almost broke into a million pieces. "Yes," she said. "Just the two of us, okay? Just take only me to dinner. If you want to see your dad, you can visit with him another night."

Strange. "Is Dad all right? What's going on?"

She blew her nose and sniffled again. "We're separating."

Unbelievable. Had he heard her right? His parents, the ones who condemned him for getting divorced, were now following suit? He pushed his anger aside when she started to cry. "Oh, Mom. I'm so sorry. Everything will be okay; I promise." His words sounded heartfelt, but his mother didn't respond. "Why don't I take off this afternoon? We'll go for a long drive up the coast, just like you and I used to do." He didn't add that those rides were usually after he'd gotten reprimanded in school for not turning in his homework, or for teasing the girl who sat in front of him. He used to tug at her blond braids until she grew furious and reported him to the teacher. Confined to the car, his mother would discuss what happened as they casually drove through one old fishing town after another.

"You'd take off work?" She sounded stunned.

"I'm learning to place my family on my list of priorities." That was a lesson Jenni was teaching him. She managed to own a struggling coffee shop and still managed to help family members in time of need. Jenni had given up her independence to move back home to emotionally support her mother while dealing with her father's cancer, even if he didn't seem to appreciate the gesture. Scott knew, however, that Richard cared for Jenni's wellbeing more than he let on.

"I'll be there in fifteen minutes." He hung up, rushed around to tidy his desk, and quickly explained to Cassie that he was taking the rest of the day off. "I'll have my cell phone in case of an emergency. Otherwise, I'd appreciate not being bothered by anyone."

If his mother didn't object, he planned to invite Jenni to dinner with them tonight. It was time for the two most important women in his life to meet. His father would be a battle to fight another day.

***

Dinner had gone much smoother last night than Scott anticipated. Much to his relief, Jenni seemed to enjoy his mother. They'd never met before, not even when she'd dated Dan, other than perhaps casually. His parents attended a different church and traveled in a different circle. They liked hobnobbing with politicians, dining at fine restaurants, and afternoons spent at the golf course, whereas her parents were more down-to earth, in Scott's opinion. Then he realized how much his life in Raleigh resembled his parents' life here, a disturbing thought for sure.

While he was making progress attacking his fears, he called his father. They agreed to meet at the Shrimp Shack for dinner.

Even though Scott was fifteen minutes early, his father waited for him at the bar, the usual scotch and water in front of him. He had hoped his dad would stop drinking after their trip to the cemetery, but no such luck.

"Dad," Scott said, approaching his father at the bar. Thank goodness he didn't appear to be drunk. "I hope you haven't been waiting long."

"Maybe ten minutes, but Jack here kept me occupied." He pointed at the bartender, who nodded at Scott as he continued to wipe down the back counter.

"They're waiting to seat us," Scott said, a large knot squeezing his abdomen. He needed to address his father's drinking while he was still sober. "Are you ready?"

"Sure." His father stood and grabbed hold of his precious alcoholic beverage. "I'm not hungry, but that isn't anything new."

Maybe if his dad didn't fill his stomach with scotch, he'd have an appetite. Undoubtedly, his dad had a problem, probably had for years. Why hadn't he realized it sooner, before Dan had to tell him? Scott supposed that when he was a kid, he hadn't recognized the signs. And when he'd moved to Raleigh, it had been easier to isolate himself from acknowledging his father's alcoholism. Avoidance had served him well. Or had it?

Look at the condition of his mother. Maybe Scott could have saved her from such agony over the years. Then again, she seemed to be handling the situation quite well if last night was any indication. She'd surprised him with her determination to be happy.

His mother's strong will reminded him of Jenni, who happened to be the most independent, tenacious woman he'd ever met. He guessed that's one of the reasons he loved her.

A young hostess that Scott didn't recognize seated them at the same window table he'd sat at with Cassie the first time he'd returned to town. He ordered a sweet tea, then stared out the window at a yacht tied up at the restaurant's dock. Unfortunately, when his father ordered another scotch and water, it pulled Scott's attention back to the issue at hand.

He waited for the hostess to leave before he confronted his father. "Dad, how long have you been drinking."

"Years, son. It's man's best friend."

"I thought that saying was about a man and his dog." Certainly, Pirate fit that description. He didn't know how he'd survive without the dog when he returned to Raleigh, but he'd find a way. He recalled that Jenni said she might know someone who'd be interested in taking Pirate.

His dad's laugh sounded loud in the quiet restaurant, where only soft classical music played and couples quietly chatted with their dinner partners.

"Why not order an iced tea, or a soda?"

"You're starting to sound like your mom."

So his mom did have a problem with his father's alcohol consumption. She'd avoided telling him the intimate details last night, but Scott bet that's why she wanted a trial separation.

"And does Mom have a valid point?" He tried to ask the question without accusation but his father grew agitated.

"Of course she doesn't."

"Then why the separation?"

"Ask her that question. She demanded I move out. I've done nothing but provide for her, and that's the thanks she gives me."

"Why do you think she wanted you to leave?" He'd learned from years of managing employees to phrase his observations as questions. People often offered the reason instead of becoming defensive.

"Your mom thinks I have a drinking problem. She gave me an ultimatum—either check into an alcohol rehab center, or leave."

"And you chose to leave?"

He looked down at the empty tumbler in front of him. "We've been married thirty-eight years, and I gave her up for this." He slid the glass away. "Stupid, huh?"

Scott had dealt with the disease before, with employees, and knew it wasn't as easy as pushing a drink away. It took much more than that.

"Only you know the answer to that, Dad. But if you want Mom back, you know what to do."

CHAPTER TWENTY-FOUR

Jenni, sweaty from a long run with Scott, walked through the kitchen door. The smell of a turkey roasting in the oven filled the house. She loved Thanksgiving. This year was no different, except for her father's dreadful cancer. This was probably his last Thanksgiving. Granted, he seemed to be doing much better. Lately, Jenni had allowed her hopes to shoot upward, but she was afraid to wish too hard.

No one was in the kitchen, so she worked her way upstairs to the shower. Scott went home to clean up and was due at her parents' house within the hour to spend the afternoon with her family. Then he'd have dinner tonight with his mother, Dan, and Rachel. His father had admitted himself into an alcohol rehab program to save his marriage.

By the time Jenni walked back into the kitchen, her mother stood alone by the stove, stirring a boiling pot of potatoes. Obviously lost in thought, she jumped when she saw Jenni.

"Sorry, Mom. I didn't mean to scare you."

"It's okay." Her mother placed a wooden spoon on the counter and swiped at her wet cheek.

“Why are you crying?” Jenni asked, alarmed. Her mother never cried.

“I was just appreciating the holiday. We have so much to be thankful for this year. To be honest, I wasn’t sure if your dad would make it this long.”

Jenni swallowed hard. “Me, either.” Her mother was finally accepting that her father’s death was likely.

“He has to survive. I need him.”

“Oh, Mom.” Jenni walked over to the stove and held her mother, the first time they’d actually touched since Jenni had returned home. It didn’t feel as awkward as she’d suspected.

“We’ve been married for almost forty years. I’ll miss seeing him read the newspaper every morning; I’ll miss cooking his meals just the way he likes. Who will keep me company? I don’t want to be alone.”

Jenni swallowed hard. “I know it’s not the same as sharing your life with Dad, but I’ll be here. Scott will be here.”

“And you can’t wait to leave, to get your own place. I don’t blame you.” She picked up the spoon again and stirred the potatoes. “We’ve been suffocating you.”

“I’m sorry if I’ve been difficult to live with,” Jenni said, suddenly regretting the annoyance she experienced almost daily with her parents. “I’m not used to curfews and rules anymore.” Jenni squeezed her mother into a hug once more then let go.

Her mother’s smile was thin and fragile, but it was better than crying. “You know, it’s hard to let go of your children once they grow up. Someday you’ll understand what I mean.”

This was the closest thing to an actual conversation they’d had since their discussion about the birds and the bees when Jenni was in the sixth grade. She’d sat next to her mom on the corner of Jenni’s bed. The conversation was strained and uncomfortable, but her mother had loved her enough to explain about boys and their intentions to push girls beyond their limits.

Little did her mother know, Scott had given Jenni her first kiss on the cheek the day before. She’d bet Scott didn’t remember the kiss or the dandelion he'd given her with such pride, but Jenni never forgot the gentle look in his eyes. She'd admired him since then, from afar.

Jenni took her usual seat at the table to keep her mother company. Her father walked into the kitchen, using what he considered his new toy, a wooden cane with a hand-carved lion's head perched on top. His positive attitude was progress.

"Oh, that turkey smells delicious," he said. He inhaled again for emphasis and sat in his designated chair at the table.

"Happy Thanksgiving, Dad." Fighting back tears, Jenni watched him settle in with ease. Yes, Richard Stallings was still alive and able to join the festivities. Definitely progress.

"Where's Gran?" he asked.

"She's in her room," her mother said. They'd converted the living room into Gran's temporary bedroom. "She'll be out here soon. She wanted to rest before lunch."

A loud knock at the screen door echoed through the small kitchen. At the sight of Scott standing there, a wave of excitement dashed through her body. Would she always react in such a sexually attentive way where he was concerned?

"Come in," Jenni said a little too eagerly, failing miserably at hiding her true feelings for him from her parents.

Her father raised his eyebrows.

When Scott walked into the kitchen with Pirate at his heels, Jenni couldn't help but let her enthusiasm show. She smiled and thought she must be glowing like a lighthouse on a foggy night. At the touch of Scott's hand on her arm, her mood lifted even higher.

"Hi, sweetheart." He bent down to kiss her on the lips, and Pirate whined at her feet.

She kissed her man, and then patted Pirate's head. Right now Jenni's imaginary love cup overflowed with liquid happiness, despite the fact she knew Scott would be moving back to Raleigh in less than two weeks. Every warning bell in her mind clanged to guard against the imminent pain. She knew all too well how miserable she'd feel once he left. She'd had a crash course in that emotion when he'd chosen to believe the gossip.

"Pirate missed you," Scott said. Instead of looking at the dog, though, Scott's intense eyes met hers. "And I'll admit, I'm lonely without you."

Her insides turned to mush. "Me too."

Her mother closed the oven door with a thud.

"Excuse me. You're upsetting your mom," Jenni's dad said. "I don't much care to hear about the details of your relationship, either."

"Sorry, Dad."

"Let me help you with that, Mrs. Stallings." Scott hurried to the oven and took the mitts from her. He reached in and removed the large roasting pan holding the golden turkey. The gesture touched Jenni.

"Thanks," her mother said. She didn't look at Scott, even though she appeared grateful for his help. When was she going to forgive him?

Her father narrowed his eyes at Jenni. "I don't want Keith to stay here on Saturday evenings when you go out with Scott. If you haven't noticed, your brother isn't a very good caretaker."

"At least he offered to help," her mother said under her breath.

Jenni considered Keith's agreement to spend one evening a week here a blessing. True, he lacked compassion and empathy, mostly because he remained in denial about their father's cancer, but he seemed to be considering the possibility of the illness.

"It's Jenni's responsibility," her father said.

"No, it isn't." Gran slid her walker to a full stop just under the archway leading into the kitchen. "Leave your daughter alone," she said. "Consider yourself lucky she's sticking around Big Cat."

"Thanks, Gran, but I got it." Jenni turned to her father, remembering Scott's advice about how to handle him. "You're right Dad. I agreed to return home and help. But appreciation goes a long way, and I haven't felt much of that. I work hard all week and Saturdays are my day off." Nervous at first about standing up to him, she wanted to applaud her effort.

Her dad stared at her.

Gran sat with a thud in a chair next to Jenni.

"Please be careful," Jenni said to Gran. "The physical therapist wants you to grab the seat of the chair before you sit, so it doesn't scoot away."

Gran pointed her finger at Jenni. "Listen, smart pants. Just because you're hangin' out with a hunkie guy, doesn't mean you have the right to boss me around."

Jenni sighed aloud. "I care about you, Gran. I know you want to get home as fast as you can, to see your horses."

"You aren't fooling anyone. You want me out of this house." Gran slapped her hand on Jenni's knee. "And I don't blame you. With all the fighting between Richard and me, I can't wait to leave, either. In fact, Alex is taking me home after dinner tonight. We worked out a deal."

"What deal?" Jenni's father barked. "As much as I want you gone, even I know you aren't ready to go home."

"Good thing it's not your business." Gran glared at her son. "Just because I'm old doesn't give you the right to dictate my life like you do Jenni's."

Jenni wished the kitchen floor would swallow her whole.

Gran poked Jenni in the arm. "Tell him, Jenni. He needs to know what a domineering father he is. Look at your miserable childhood. All you wanted to do was hang out with your friends for the summer."

Jenni's mother, carving knife in hand, began to saw huge slices of turkey and pile them on a platter.

When Jenni didn't speak, her father picked up his cane and shook it at her. "Is that true? Did you run to your grandma and complain about having to do a little work at Stallings?"

"Of course she did," Gran said. "You worked her too hard; that's why she can't let anyone help her now. She pushes and pushes, and thinks she has to do everything herself. It's your fault."

Scott stared at Jenni, and she refused to look at him. Claire had accused her of the same thing, recently.

"In case you forgot," Jenni said to Gran, "I'm sitting right here. And you're mistaken; I don't have to do everything myself." Everyone stared at her in disbelief. She was fast losing the argument. "Alex. I hired Alex so I wouldn't have to work all the time. That doesn't sound like a person who can't ask for help."

"Wrong," her father said. "I had to talk you into hiring someone. And you chose to hire Gran. Look where that got you." He shook his head. "She never did Stallings a bit of good."

Gran shoved her walker toward her son. "Listen here, you old fool. Stallings was my husband's passion, not mine."

"No. Horses are all you think about."

"That's right. You have a problem with my horses?"

"Not at all, if you want to throw money into a pit and bury it."

Gran huffed. "It's better than hoarding all your money and never enjoying it. When was the last time you went on vacation, or even bought a pizza?"

"Why should I make someone else rich when we can cook our own pizza? It's a good thing I'm responsible and saved my money, unlike you. What will happen when you die? Who's going to pay to bury you?"

Gran sucked back against the chair's wooden slats and slumped. "So that's what this is about, Son. You're afraid to die, afraid what it will cost your family."

Jenni's father didn't speak. His mouth gaped open and his eyes were wide.

Silence filled the room. Jenni held her breath and sat perfectly still, waiting for someone to break the tension. When no one spoke, she got up from the table and opened a window, a futile effort to ease her breathing. She glanced first at her mom, who fought to release a stubborn turkey leg from its body, then at Scott, who stood perfectly still next to the sink, studying a small picture of Jesus hanging above the table. Her family dynamics had probably traumatized him. And then there was Gran. She held her fists clenched on her lap, looking as stubborn as one of her untrained horses.

Jenni's gaze met her father's. A single tear slid down his cheek. Jenni's heart squeezed to the point of pain. Oh, gosh, her dad was scared.

Jenni walked over and stood beside him. "Dad, you don't need to worry about us." She reached out and hesitantly touched his warm, paper-thin hand that grasped the lion's head on his cane. She was afraid he'd snap his arm away. The rejection would destroy her. To her surprise, he didn't move and almost seemed to welcome her touch.

When he remained silent, Jenni stroked his hand with her index finger. "We'll help Mom with whatever she needs, and don't worry about us kids. We're young. Keith and I have our own businesses. If they don't work out, something else will."

"Coffee Break's days are numbered," he said. "Keith said the place is dead, no customers."

"Dad, that's not what I said exactly." Keith stood outside the screen door. With the noise they were making, no one heard him approach. He opened the creaky door and stepped into the kitchen, into the mouth of the storm. "I told you her shop was struggling right now because of some nasty gossip being spread about her. You know the power of gab in this town."

"Who's behind the rumor?"

"It's under control, Dad," Jenni said, still managing to avoid looking at Scott.

"You didn't answer my question," her father pressed. "Who?"

Jenni risked a glance at Scott, who looked as though he wanted to walk out the door and never return.

"It's my fault, sir," Scott said. "I should have—"

"No, it's not," Jenni interrupted. "If it's anyone's fault, it's my own. I came across headstrong and determined to save my business, and I said nothing would stop me. I was dead set on getting a loan. I don't blame you for believing the rumor." That was the truth, even though she hadn't known it before now.

Scott pushed away from the sink to stand behind her. He rubbed her shoulders. "What Cassie did was unforgivable."

"Cassie." Jenni's father shook his head. "One rumor from her about destroyed your business?"

"Dad, it's not worth explaining. Everything will be okay," Jenni said.

"What I don't get," he said to Scott, "is why you refused to accept the loan to begin with."

"Richard ..." Her mother set a platter full of hastily cut turkey in the center of the table.

"Sir, I made the best decision possible."

"Dad, I appreciate your concern, but I have things under control. I'm implementing changes to increase my sales."

"Coffee Break is a fine place," Gran said. "Why do you keep harping on her, son?"

He stared at Gran. "Because I love… I care. That's why."

Jenni's heart skipped at least two beats. Had he almost said the words she wanted to hear more than anything else? Did he actually love her? Was he concerned about Coffee Break because he cared about her? She'd automatically assumed the worse. She thought he chastised her because she hadn't achieved his high expectations. Maybe she'd been wrong.

CHAPTER TWENTY-FIVE

Running wasn't going well. The marathon was a little over two weeks away and Jenni's endurance wasn't where it needed to be. She had a tough decision to make.

If she pushed harder, she increased the risk of reinjuring her ankle. She needed to be running farther than she was, though. If she decided to run the partial marathon instead of the full, she'd lose the chance to finally beat Cassie. And what about her father? She'd set out to prove to him she could win a marathon. If she bailed now, she'd lose her last chance to convince him that her determination had paid off.

Jenni ran past the graveyard entrance where she usually met up with Scott, and he fell into step next to her. They never spoke; just being together was enough while they ran.

But today he challenged her. "You aren't where you need to be with your endurance. Make this a tempo run. We'll call it the Swamp Run."

Swamp Road was eight miles of hell. Despite its long stretch with a gorgeous view of the salt marsh, the mosquitoes loved to swarm around hot sweaty runners.

"I can't. My ankle's still weak."

"Your ankle hasn't bothered you in the least. You've had no swelling after our runs. Try it."

"Okay, but you owe me a plate of seafood spaghetti from the Shrimp Shack if I make it."

"Agreed."

After a few miles of fast-paced, consistent running, she had to force herself to push on. Her body pleaded to stop, which was a new sensation for her. She wasn't a quitter. The muscles in her legs ached, her breathing was heavier than she liked, and the bugs were driving her batty. But because Scott had challenged her, she ran on. After three more miles, her body begged to collapse on the shady grass next to the street.

"That's all I can take," she said. Her tone was a little crabbier than intended.

"One more mile. You can do it."

"When did you become Mr. Jolly Runner? Leave me alone."

"No. I know how much you want to run the full marathon. You need to step it up and push on. Let's move it."

She scowled at him. "Right now I hate you." Of course she didn't mean it, but saying the words gave her pleasure.

One more mile. She could survive a long, excruciating mile to accomplish the length of Swamp Road. She was almost there. Jenni drew in one rapid breath after another, trying to remember to even out her breathing.

"That's right. Keep going." He cheered her on.

If she wanted to beat Cassie, she needed to toughen up. *Move your feet.* That's right. Keep on running. Only a little over a half mile to go.

They rounded the corner, leading back into town. She groaned when the graveyard entrance came into view again. "Twenty more yards," he said. "That's it!"

She broke her pace when her foot crossed over the final crack in the sidewalk, just in front of the cemetery entrance. She pretended she'd crossed the finish line. "I … did … it."

A sudden stream of energy shot through her. "That felt good but I still hate you."

He bent down and kissed her hard. When he pulled away, he said, "Next time you have to do your tempo run faster."

"Where did you learn all this? Online?"

He laughed but she didn't find him funny. She made a mental note not to run with him again, although she knew she would. "Actually, you're the best coach anyone could wish for." With his encouragement, she might beat her archrival. He was right, though. She needed to increase her speed as well as distance.

***

The next week crawled by in slow motion, while at the same time it sped by at a dizzying speed. Making up for lost time running was the hardest thing she'd ever done. The race was approaching fast, along with the countdown of Scott's departure from Big Cat. In six days he'd drive away with her heart in tow.

"Will you come back to watch the marathon?" she asked as they ran down a quiet side street of the historic district. She wanted him there to cheer her on, as he did every day lately. She already felt the loss of his absence.

An ambulance wailed passed them, hurrying to reach some poor soul who needed emergency care immediately.

"Sorry, I can't. But I'll be there in your mind, urging you forward."

Jenni kept up with Scott easily now, but she'd learned to rely on his encouragement. She was no longer the woman who never asked for help, even though she still had a tendency to resist at times.

A strange expression crossed his face. If she didn't know him better, she'd almost think he planned to enter the race. Secretly, she was glad she didn't have to compete against him.

Disappointed he wouldn't be there for her big day, she forced a smile. "You'll be missed, but I'll think about you when I cross the finish line."

When they approached Coffee Break, Scott asked, "Want to come back to my place and shower?"

"I'd love to, but not today. My dad's health has declined and I need to get home."

"I thought he was doing better? What happened?"

"I'm not sure. I thought he looked great on Thanksgiving and hoped the bad days were behind him. The last couple of days, though, he hasn't felt well. We thought he had the flu at first. This morning, he couldn't get out of bed to use the bathroom."

"Has he been to the doctor?"

"Not yet. If he isn't better by tomorrow, my mom's taking him."

When they turned the corner, Jenni stopped cold. The ambulance, with its bright flashing lights and engine still running, sat ominously in front of her parents' house.

"Dad!" Jenni flew up the steps, through the backdoor and kitchen, in time to see two men wheeling her father through the living room. His eyes were wide and he mouthed something to Jenni on the way out the front door. What was he trying to say? "Dad!" she repeated. She heard Scott talking to someone behind her but barely understood what he said.

Scott whipped his cell phone out of his pocket. "Keith, they're taking your father to Crystal County Hospital."

He said something else but nothing other than the hospital's name registered in Jenni's mind. This couldn't be happening. Her father was walking with his lion-headed cane just a few days ago. He'd even eaten a half plate of food at Thanksgiving, proclaiming this year's turkey the best yet.

Through watery eyes, Jenni noticed her mom stumbling out of the den, wringing her hands. She appeared to be dazed and unaware that Jenni and Scott were there.

"Mom." Jenni closed the space between them and folded her suddenly fragile mother into her arms. "What happened?"

Her mother didn't answer.

Jenni held onto her, feeling as if they were both drowning. Her dad had to be fine.

"Mrs. Stallings," Scott said, "let me help you to the car. We'll follow the ambulance to the hospital."

"I … want to ride … with him."

Scott hesitated. "I won't be able to keep up with them and you'll be there alone. Please, let me take you." He urged her toward the door and Jenni followed.

Right now Scott proved to be the only one able think rationally. Jenni focused on breathing, in and out, slowly until the heavy fog in her mind started to lift. Her father was going to the hospital. The trained staff knew what to do. She reminded herself that just because the ambulance had taken him away didn't mean he faced life or death. The doctor would determine the seriousness of the situation, so she needed to remain calm.

They hit every red light from Big Cat to Crystal County Hospital. The ambulance was nowhere in sight, but Jenni was sure her father was alive, at least for now. His gray pallor was nothing to worry about, was just an indication he didn't feel well. But she couldn't stop thinking about his scared gaze that had caught hers just before they'd taken him out the door of his own house. He'd be all right; Dads were invincible. Weren't they?

Scott zipped into the half circle in front of the emergency room's entrance. "Go in. I'll be back in a little while."

Panic shot through her. "You're leaving me?" Jenni despised feeling vulnerable, especially when she needed to be strong for her parents.

Scott must have sensed her desperation because he reached out and ran his hand down her arm. "You're trembling. Come here."

Barely realizing she'd leaned toward him, he wrapped his arm around her. Jenni didn't know how to tell him her fears. She wanted her father to live for many years to come, wanted her father to love her. If he died, she'd never have the chance to prove she was worthy.

"I'm not leaving for long. I promise I'll be right back." He kissed the top of her head. "Now go. Take good care of your mother until I get back."

Jenni nodded and wrenched the door open. Her mother had climbed out of the back seat without Jenni noticing, and stood next to her. They watched Scott zip away. He'd be back; he promised. She gathered herself together emotionally, stood tall to ward off any unpleasant news, and entered the emergency room holding her mother's arm.

***

Scott hated to leave Jenni like that, but he was on a mission. He'd never seen her look so distraught, and her tender emotions kicked his protective instincts into high gear. Within fifteen minutes, he skidded to a stop in front of the weathered house. A puff of dust surrounded his car. He hoped he was doing the right thing by intervening.

He tooted his horn before he battled the dust cloud. It wasn't like him to get involved in other people's disputes, but this time it seemed crucial.

"Scott? What are you doing here?" Gran called from the porch.

"We're going for a ride. Get ready, quickly. You might not be back until late." He hesitated to tell her the truth until he had her confined in his car, well on their way to the hospital. For one thing, he didn't want to upset Gran and risk her falling again. For another, he wanted to ensure she got into his car willingly. Gran was stubborn, and this might be her last chance to see her son alive.

"Where are we going?"

"I'll let you know on the way. Please hurry."

"I'm not going anywhere until I know what you're up to." Gran stood by the screen door, hands on her hips, walker in front of her.

On his way to the porch, Scott briefly admired the fixed railing—his and Keith's handy work. They'd also fixed the broken boards on the steps, repainted the entire porch white, and replaced the bulb on the motion detector. He offered to help Keith, for Gran's sake. It was also a good chance to bond with Jenni's brother.

"Gran, we need to hurry." When Scott realized she hadn't budged, he decided to tell her the painful truth. He walked up the now sturdy steps and squeezed through the screen door without knocking her over. She stood planted in place. He wanted to make sure he was next to her, in case she collapsed when he told her about her son. "Gran, Richard's in the hospital. I'm not sure what happened, but when Jenni and I turned the corner, the ambulance was there. They took him to Crystal County Hospital."

She gasped.

"Let's go. I'll have you there as fast as I can."

"No. Not yet."

What was she waiting for?

Alex walked out onto the porch. "Gran, what's wrong?"

"Richard." That's all she seemed able to say. Her knees buckled and she started to collapse.

"Gran!" Alex yelled.

Scott caught her. Silently, he berated himself for telling her about Richard before she was safe in the car. "Alex, can you pull up a chair?"

Alex slid a tattered but sturdy rattan chair behind Gran. He lowered her onto the faded flowered cushion that lined the seat. Alex exchanged a concerned look with Scott.

"He'll be fine," Scott said, although he was sure of no such thing. Richard's decline in health had taken him by surprise. "Let's get to the hospital, so we know what's going on."

"Okay." Gran made a feeble effort to stand but was unsuccessful.

He reached out and lifted her to a standing position, and Alex scooted the abandoned walker in front of Gran. He assisted her with the walker until they reached the screen door.

"Alex, can you get that?"

She propped open the door with a potted palm, and Gran scooted through. Scott wrapped one arm tightly around her waist, and with the other, he held onto her arm. Alex carried the walker down the steps. Getting Gran to the car was tricky. They had to maneuver around loose stones that formed the makeshift walkway, had to avoid long tuffs of grass that needed mowing.

Scott made a mental note to return, after the emergency room crisis ended, to mow Gran's lawn. That was the least he could do before he left town, sort of a goodbye. If Keith didn't have time to mow Gran's lawn in the future, Scott would pay a lawn service. Winter was on its way, though, and one last cut was all it needed for now.

Once they pulled up in front of the emergency room, Gran seemed to have regained her strength. Her stamina amazed him. He wished the feisty woman were his own grandmother, or any spunky relative for that matter. Then he inhaled a long breath. He did have a dedicated and brave relative—his own father, who was doing well in rehab. Scott felt pride. His father was making an enormous effort to save his marriage.

Gran tapped him on the shoulder. "I'm not sure what you're daydreaming about, but could you get me out of this car? I want to see my son."

"Sorry, Gran." Scott climbed from the car and walked around to help her from the passenger side. Maybe he should ask for assistance, or a wheelchair. But since she wasn't the one needing medical care, he doubted they'd loan him one. At least Alex could help him if needed. "Gran, can you make it to the waiting room?"

"Of course. Do you think I'm old or something?"

Well, yeah, he did, but he wasn't about to say that to her. If she thought she could walk that far, who was he to tell her she couldn't? The woman could probably move a mountain on a good day, and with her son in the emergency room, Scott didn't want to think about what she could move. He appreciated her steely determination and understood where Jenni got her grit.

Gran made it to the waiting room without a problem. They'd hurried to the hospital, just to wait for hours on a hard plastic chair. As it turned out, Richard refused to allow Gran to see him. If she felt betrayed by his stubbornness, she never let on.

Finally, five hours later, the doctor overseeing Richard decided to admit him to the hospital. While that was a comfort to a small degree, it also implied that his health warranted concern.

"He has to survive," Gran said. She still sat in the same blue hospital chair, now leaning against the walker for support. She must be tired.

Scott rubbed his forehead to ease an oncoming headache. "Gran, he's tough." Lately, Richard had shown a fighting attitude to beat the cancer, much more so than at first, when he'd refused to get out of bed. Scott thought about the fishing trip on the pier. Richard's face had lit up when he caught that large king mackerel. He insisted on doing as much as possible that day without help, until his energy waned. Richard had earned a lot of respect from many people, especially Scott.

"Tough," Gran repeated. "That's a kind way of putting it. The man is stubborn for sure." Gran's breathing sounded staggered, as though she had to fight back tears for the son she loved, but was afraid to tell.

"Why don't I drive you and Alex home?" Scott offered. "You can get some sleep and I'll bring you back in the morning." He didn't mention that if Richard refused to see her in the emergency room, he wasn't about to let her into his room this late at night, even if the staff allowed it.

"Yeah, right." Gran leaned back against the chair. "Like I'm going to get any sleep."

How was he supposed to convince a stubborn Stalling woman to go home? Truth be told, if something happened to one of his parents, or to his brother, sleep would be the last thing on his mind. "Gran, you have to try. There's no reason to sit in a waiting room all night." He needed a better argument if he wanted her to leave the hospital; he was concerned about her health. "Richard needs to sleep. I promise I'll pick you up early."

"Gran," Alex said. "I'd like to cover for Jenni at the coffee shop in the morning. She won't feel like working after spending the night here. Let Scott pick you up, so you aren't home alone."

"You're talking early then," Scott said. "I tell you what. I'll go home and get Pirate. We'll come back and sleep at your house. First thing in the morning, we'll return to the hospital."

Gran looked at him. "You'd do that for me? You'd babysit me until visiting hours start here tomorrow?"

"Not babysit. I'd enjoy the company," he said. "And thanks, Alex, for offering to help Jenni out while she's here." Relieved when they agreed to the plan, Scott willed Richard to live through the night. Otherwise, Gran would never forgive him.

***

Jenni slept awkwardly in the uncomfortable chair. When she awoke, she'd forgotten where she was at first, but then remembered she was in her father's hospital room. She peeked open one eye and saw her father, with more medical paraphernalia surrounding him than she understood. Things beeped, hummed, hissed. He had an IV line running into his hand, secured by clear tape, and an oxygen line running to his nose. The white blankets practically swallowed his fragile, pale body into the belly of the sterile-smelling hospital bed. Someone forgot to tell the staff that he was her father, not just some patient. He needed the homey quilt his wife had sewn, his blue fuzzy socks that kept his feet warm, and the well-worn brown sweater that he'd had since Jenni was a child.

Even with both eyes wide open now, she barely recognized him. He looked to be a stranger in a tiled room with ugly white walls.

Jenni choked down her own saliva. Seeing her father in this condition not only scared her, but forced her to acknowledge his mortality. The possibility of losing him hit home in a way she'd never before experienced. Despite all his flaws, all the disagreements, all the unwarranted advice he forced on her, she loved him.

He slept quietly. It was hard to imagine that he wasn't dead, lying so still in that horrible bed. She wanted to wake him, to place her head on his shoulder and cry for the father she already missed. Why had she resisted him all these years? They'd always bickered about something, and over the years, the tension remained but the cause changed.

Jenni risked a glance at her mother, who slept in a chair with her upper body propped against the wall. Her mouth hung open and a thin line of drool ran from the side of her mouth to her chin. She looked broken, as if she'd been on the losing end of a street brawl.

Not wanting to disturb her mother's sleep, Jenni left the room in search of the cafeteria and coffee. She needed to wake up and her body begged for caffeine. The cafeteria was on the bottom floor in what seemed like a dungeon. She made her way through the morning crowd heading toward the bank of coffee pots. Jenni poured and paid for the liquid heaven.

She closed her eyes, all too easily, and took the first sip. Her eyes shot open and her mouth burned with what tasted like black acid, not that there was such a thing. How could people drink this? As an owner of a coffee shop, she pitied those who had to rely on this as their morning wake-up call. Maybe she'd offer a substantial discount to all hospital staff. Many staff members lived in Big Cat and trekked to the hospital every morning.

Had her mother liked coffee, she would have considered driving to Coffee Break for two large to-go cups of the best tasting coffee around. But her mother didn't like coffee, she despised it actually. No one else in her family drank it except Keith, occasionally.

Jenni owed Alex a special thanks for helping her out this morning. She couldn't afford to have Coffee Break closed for an entire day.

By the time she returned to her father's room, Scott was standing by their mother, and Gran was sitting in a chair next to her son. She rubbed his arm while he slept. The tears in her eyes spilled over and down her wrinkled cheeks. Gran didn't bother to wipe them away.

Scott turned to look at Jenni when she walked through the door. He thrust a to-go cup at her and smiled when he noticed the hospital coffee in her hand. "I should have warned you not to drink that. I thought you'd know better, from when your father was in here before."

She set the half-poisonous drink on a small table—good riddance. "Keith always brought coffee in. Where is he? I left him a message last night."

"Right here." He walked into the room carrying a cardboard container holding four cups of coffee. "I stopped by Coffee Break on my way here. Alex said to call later, to keep her posted on how Dad's doing."

Jenni pulled out her cell phone from the purse she so rarely used. "My phone's dead. I didn't charge it." She looked at her lifeless father and couldn't help but make the correlation between him and her dead cell phone. Stop. She needed to believe he'd make it through this.

CHAPTER TWENTY-SIX

When Jenni finally made it to work two days later, she almost wished she hadn't walked through the door. Alex was finishing with Mrs. Forthright. Too bad Jenni hadn't walked into the coffee shop a few minutes later.

"I tried to call you but your cell must be turned off again," Alex said. "How's your father doing?"

Jenni plucked the phone from her pocket and held it up. "Dead. I keep forgetting to charge it." Of course, her focus had been on her Dad. "It's too early to tell, but he doesn't look good."

Mrs. Forthright turned on her. "Does that mean you won't be entering the marathon?"

Unbelievable. Was that all the woman thought about? Then Jenni heard her own words. Not too long ago that was all she thought about.

"Excuse me?" Jenni shot Cassie's mother a pointed glance. "Some things are more important, like my father's life." She walked behind the counter and into the back room. She wasn't in the mood to deal with the woman's negativity.

Moments later the bell above the door tinkled, likely letting Mrs. Forthright out of the building. Alex appeared in the doorway leading to the backroom in which Jenni had escaped.

"She's one rude woman," Alex said. "If you decide to enter the race, I hope you beat the pants off her snobby daughter."

Jenni couldn't help but smile. "I want to. Believe me; I've fantasized about it for years. But entering the marathon depends on my father." If she planned to enter, she needed to keep training.

Alex looked surprise. "The race wouldn't be the same without you."

"No pressure there," Jenni quipped before she walked out of her office and into the quiet coffee shop. Alex was right; the town counted on her to run in the marathon.

***

Scott sat back in his chair and tapped a pencil on the desk while he listened to his boss on the other end of the phone.

"Don't approve any more loans unless they are rock solid," his boss said. "We're talking more layoffs."

Scott wondered if he'd have a job to go back to. "Who else is getting laid off?"

Silence. "Not you, don't worry. But you need to be back here tomorrow."

"I thought I had another week?"

"Plans have changed. Sorry for the short notice." A thumping noise sounded over the phone, most likely his boss tapping the clear paperweight on his desk with a pen. They both had the same annoying habit. "You need to be here at least a day to settle in. I'm not going to lie to you; next week's going to be rough. Be prepared for some upset employees."

Scott ran a hand over his eyes and then the back of his neck. He was already feeling the stress of going back to Raleigh. Who would have thought he'd almost enjoy being home in Big Cat? Small-town living had changed him more than he realized.

Then he remembered the espresso machine. He had to tell Jenni the truth before he left town. First chance he got, Scott said, "Cassie, I'll be gone for a while."

When he entered Coffee Break, he looked around the quiet place. At least there were a few customers, a small book club perhaps, sitting at the back of the coffee shop, which was an improvement over last week. Business needed to pick up fast. After all the pain Jenni was dealing with about her father and failing business, he hated to hurt her with more bad news.

"Jenni?"

He could tell immediately that she wasn't in the mood to hear what he had to say. But what choice did he have?

"I need you to call off the dog," she said, flicking a spicy red curl out of her eyes. It returned instantly.

"What do you mean?"

"Your assistant is trying to destroy my business. Apparently, she's spreading more gossip."

He planted his hands on the countertop and leaned toward her. "You can't prove it's Cassie. And without proof, what am I supposed to do?" Not that he could really do anything anyway, other than talk to Cassie again.

"Never mind. I should have known you'd stick up for her."

"What's the rumor now?" What could Cassie possibly say?

"Apparently, she's gossiping that you funded my espresso machine. People think I'm using you for your money."

He tried to hide his surprise. Impossible. How had Cassie found out? Only two people knew about the loan—Dan and ... Rachel. Rachel must have let it slip to Cassie during a casual conversation. They were friends.

Jenni clenched her jaw. "Don't tell me it's true."

"Okay, I won't. But I meant to help you out. You might not believe this, but that's why I'm here. I came to confess. By the way, my boss called and I'm leaving tonight to return to the city."

She stood ramrod straight. "Then go back to Raleigh where you belong."

He didn't want to leave like this. "I'm sorry. I never meant to hurt you. I wanted to help."

She frowned.

"Pirate. I can't take him with me. Didn't you know someone who might want him?"

"Figures. It doesn't surprise me that you'd run away again." Her lower lip trembled slightly. "I can't believe you'd abandon Pirate."

"Abandon is a strong word." Was that what she felt he was doing, abandoning her? Was he? "Pirate was never mine to begin with."

"He was, but I'll take him. Just drop him off whenever you're ready." She scooted from the room, leaving Alex to glare at him.

Scott rubbed the back of his neck to relieve the throbbing. He hadn't felt this kind of stress since he'd first arrived as an uptight banker in Big Cat. He wasn't that man anymore, and he cared about the locals here, especially Jenni. He glanced around the cozy coffee shop one last time. He didn't want to see her business fail, and yet that's exactly what would happen if he didn't do something. But he'd interfered enough.

***

Jenni felt betrayed, controlled even. Not only had Scott gone behind her back and purchased the espresso machine, he waited until the last possible moment to tell her the truth. After she'd heard the news from the gossip grapevine.

Tomorrow he'd be gone, back to the comfort of his own home. He wouldn't have to watch her business sink into failure. Compared to the curt man he'd been the first day he'd walked into her coffee shop, she thought he'd relaxed considerably. Maybe just the idea of returning to Raleigh had brought him full circle, had brought him back to the being the cold-hearted man who thought about bottom-line figures. He'd forgotten about human life and the impact his decisions had on them.

Sure, she'd seen a glimpse of sorrow in his eyes when he'd told her he was leaving, but then his professional façade had taken over. He'd go back to doing what he did best, being Mr. Vice President. That was fine. At least he revealed his cold side before their relationship had gone much further.

Her recharged cell phone rang, and the caller I.D. flashed his name across the screen. She clicked the OFF button and shoved the phone aside. A minute later the business phone rang and when she didn't make a move toward it, Alex got up to answer.

She waved the phone at Jenni. "It's Scott."

"I'm sorry, but I don't talk to traitors." It hurt to call him that, but the pain of his betrayal about swallowed her whole. What was she going to do now? She was experiencing heart-wrenching pain, and she was in debt to the man. That bothered her almost as much as him leaving. How would she pay him back if Coffee Break failed, which seemed likely with the next wave of gossip circulating through town?

Jenni glanced longingly around the coffee shop. The group of pregnant mothers sat in the corner of the room, one held a newborn baby wrapped in a fuzzy blue blanket. Jenni fought back tears at the thought of missing the opportunity to meet each of their soon-to-be babies. She wasn't just a barista, or a proprietor, she was friends with these people.

Not for the first time, she wondered where her favorite customer, Mr. Davis, would buy his mochas every morning. Where would he read his paper if Coffee Break closed its doors? She'd miss chatting with him and watching him and his friends play a good old-fashioned game of checkers.

To be honest, she'd even miss the difficult customers like Mrs. Forthright, who came in often to complain. Maybe Jenni was the one person who tolerated her snobbery, and the woman needed that moment to vent. She must be desperate to miss Mrs. Forthright. What was wrong with her?

She'd like to think she made a difference in people's lives.

When Scott called several more times that day, she refused to talk to him. The wound was too raw. She even chose to run at a different time of day, after lunch, when she knew he'd be working.

Avoidance felt awful but survival was bittersweet.

Gran kept reminding her to focus on what she wanted. If she focused on failure, that's what she'd get. If she wanted success, she had to believe in herself. Of course, with a failing business, debt on a machine she couldn't pay back if she did fail, her father possibly dying, and the love of her life abandoning her and his dog, belief was a hard concept to welcome.

By Friday night, as she sat in the suffocating hospital room next to her father's bed, she felt even worse. Scott didn't call anymore, which was a relief to some degree, except she knew he'd left town, probably for good. He hadn't stopped by the shop, her house, or the hospital to say goodbye. The town felt cold and empty without him.

To make matters worse, the hospital's social worker announced they wanted to discharge her father to a nursing home permanently. Jenni understood his insistence to return to the comfort of his home to die. Everyone planned to honor his wish; tomorrow they'd discharge him home with hospice care. To Jenni, the word "hospice" spelled imminent death.

Jenni glanced at her mom now. She barely ate enough to sustain herself, and she'd lost enough weight that her brown polyester pants hung loosely around her hips. Jenni had brought her food, but other than picking at a dinner roll, or at the dried-out crust of a chicken breast, her mom refused food.

Jenni's father coughed, drawing her attention to him. His fragility caused a chill of despair to run down her spine. Life was so unfair; the man had lung cancer and he never even smoked.

"Jenni," he whispered. Even that one word seemed to expend his energy.

She got up and stood next to his bed. The railing was cold to the touch when, in sudden need for support, she wrapped her fingers around it. Surprised when he lifted his arm a few inches toward her, she let go and took hold of his clammy hand. "Are you in pain, Dad?" He shook his head slightly. The morphine was working its magic.

"Coffee Break … let me help you." Fear widened his eyes, along with something else. Concern about death, about her?

This time, instead of being defiant or angry, she felt a wave of warmth rush through her. She wished he'd tell her that he loved her. She could say the words first, but fear of rejection stopped her.

"Dad, Coffee Break is all right." Was it wrong to tell him a little white lie to give him peace of mind?

He looked relieved. "Will you … be okay?"

She knew what he was asking. He wanted to know if she could support herself, before he let go and allowed the angels from heaven to whisk him away.

It wasn't a lie to say she'd be okay, because she was a survivor.

If she reassured him, he might die right here. But love was supposed to be unselfish. She had to let him go. "Dad, I'm tough. Nothing can stand in my way of success, so yes, I'm fine." Just believe, as Gran had said. Not quite willing to sit back and wait for success, she felt the need to prepare for battle. "I will fight to keep my business running, but if I have to close the doors, I still have my degree to fall back on. Either way, I will be fine. And I promise to take care of Mom. Keith and I will make sure she's okay."

His body relaxed and his eyes slid closed. She dared to lean closer, to study his chest for any sign of movement, and, thankfully, he was still breathing. She held onto his limp hand as long as possible, but when a nurse walked in, Jenni placed it on the sheets and backed away.

Truthfully, she wasn't ready to let go of her father yet. Then again, she'd probably never be ready.

***

Scott felt his beach buzz drifting away the closer he got to Raleigh. Who would have imagined he'd miss Big Cat already? Certainly not him.

He chose not to drive by Jenni's to say goodbye. That wasn't his thing, or so he told himself. Scott couldn't bear to see the betrayal on her face again. He didn't blame her for refusing to take his calls. Actually, he'd tried to catch her running but she'd changed the time she ran, or the course. He knew better than to assume she'd quit running, not as competitive as she was, especially with an upcoming marathon.

If he could start over again, he'd take the honest approach and offer her a personal loan up front for the espresso machine. He'd failed to live by his number one rule: never get involved personally with clients. That wasn't fair, though. This particular client he'd fallen in love with.

***

The next week Jenni divided her time between being with her father, pouring over her accounting, and preparing for the marathon this coming weekend. At least by keeping busy she kept her mind off Scott.

During the Swamp Run, the last tempo run she'd endure before the marathon, she wished Scott were there. She needed his encouragement to run the eight miles of fast-paced hell. She'd use today's tempo run to evaluate where she was for the marathon. Scott's absence, though, drove home that she really needed to find a local running group, especially if Coffee Break pulled out of its rough spot and she decided to stay in Big Cat.

She forced herself to run harder as he'd suggested. *Pretend to be battling Cassie. Go for the win.* Determination came from within, even if her body begged to quit. She'd bet Cassie wanted to quit on numerous occasions too. She ran the entire Swamp Road, but not as fast as she'd wanted. Finally, in her usual spot in front of the graveyard, she crossed the crack in the sidewalk that marked success, or lack of. Her endurance wasn't what she wanted it to be.

The next day, her ankle started to hurt the tiniest bit. That didn't bode well for the marathon this weekend.

Jenni limped ever so slightly around the coffee shop.

"How are you supposed to run?" Alex asked.

"Ice. Can you grab an ice pack out of the freezer?" She hobbled over to a booth and planted herself on a couch, shoving a heart-shaped pillow behind her back.

Alex returned quickly. "Are you going to drop out of the race?"

"I plan to do whatever I can to run." She needed to enter that race more than ever now. Between her dad dying and the nervous energy she felt about Scott, she couldn't wait to beat Cassie. She needed to expend some of her anxiety in a constructive way.

"I hope your foot's better by then," Alex said. A customer walked in so Alex went behind the counter to take his order.

Lynn Shelly, one of the playgroup moms who always encouraged Jenni to compete against Cassie, walked past, holding her newborn. "Are you okay?"

"I will be after the ice helps." Jenni peeked inside the pink bundle. "What a cutie. She's so tiny."

"Thanks." Lynn gazed dreamily at her baby. "It'll be a shame if you can't run, but don't push yourself." When her baby began to fuss, Lynn rocked the newborn in her arms.

"What's her name?"

"Virginia, after you."

Jenni's breath caught. When she was able to speak again, she whispered, "What an honor."

"I want her to be a go-getter like you. I admire your determination, even when things are rough." Lynn jutted her chin upward to include the entire coffee shop. "You'll make it; you always do."

"I appreciate your encouragement, but this time it looks like I might let you down."

CHAPTER TWENTY-SEVEN

When She sank onto one of the stools by the counter and stared at the empty store. The beautiful heart pine floors deserved foot traffic. The handmade pottery mugs deserved to hold coffee. The comfortable couches deserved to have people sit on them. How sad. Her dream was disappearing right before her eyes.

Tonight was the first night a guitar player would sing to her customers. She planned to move a circle of overstuffed chairs from the corner to make room for him next to a twinkling Christmas tree. She hoped someone showed up to hear him.

Jenni had fallen into a full-fledged depression when the bell above the door tinkled. She looked up to see her empathetic friend's smile.

"I brought you some customers," Claire said. A group of elderly women walked through the door. "Occasionally they play bridge with Shirley. They keep talking about playing cards again, so I suggested they get together here weekly."

The heavy weight Jenni carried lifted a bit and she hugged Claire. "Where's Shirley?" She must be covering for Claire at the studio.

"I'll send her down when I return. She can have the afternoon off to play a good game of bridge."

"You're the best." Unfortunately, the tiny spurt in customers was only a short-term fix, but she'd accept whatever business her friend had scraped up.

The bell tinkled again. This time Mr. Davis walked through the door with his checkerboard tucked under his arm. "I hear this is the place to meet women." He wiggled his eyebrows at the group playing bridge, and four male friends walked in behind him.

One of the older ladies grinned at the gentlemen and waved to Shirley as she entered the shop. Coffee Break just might turn into an elderly dating service.

Jenni kept busy making drinks, her heart practically swollen with appreciation for her customers and Claire's generosity. Within the hour, the elderly patrons bought most of the pastries and sandwiches, and laughter filled the coffee shop. Jenni loved the vibrant happiness mixed with the upbeat beach music, which played lightly over the speakers.

The bell tinkled yet again. Alex led a group of college friends, dressed in funky dark clothes and leather wristbands, through the door to see her place of employment. They each ordered a coffee drink and they bought the rest of the remaining pastries. Within the hour, Alex sat down, ready for the first day of Crafts for Kids, a program she'd embraced.

Jenni watched Alex now. She was perfect for the job. Eight kids showed up, and she was helping them make beaded candy canes to donate to charity. Her exuberance paid off. The kids looked to be having fun, and the parents were enjoying chatting with acquaintances over coffee.

Mrs. Botticelli and Dan walked through the door next, with a handful of Shrimp Shack employees.

"Thanks, Dan."

"You're welcome, but it was Scott's idea."

She must have looked confused because he began to explain.

"He came up with the idea to offer a free drink to any employee of the Shrimp Shack who buys five." Dan handed her a red coupon with a place to punch out little coffee cups. "Here." He passed her a metal hole punch. "He'll pay for the free cup."

Jenni bristled. Thoughtful as it was, she resented Scott's interference.

"He means well," Dan said. "His idea's a good one. Give it a chance, and let people help you."

She was sick of people telling her that.

***

Saturday morning, the day before the race, her father's health took a tailspin. Jenni waited in the hallway of her parents' house for her turn to say goodbye. The preacher had already been there, and her mother had just walked out of the gloomy room. Jenni wanted to follow, to offer comfort, but her feet refused to move. Besides, she didn't want to leave her post outside her father's door for anything. Keith was in the living room, so their mother would be with someone. Jenni's heart went out to Keith. He was still in denial and refused to see their dad one last time.

Gran was in the room now. Soft crying seeped through the crack of the partially closed door.

"Richard, I know we've had our disagreements," Gran said, her voice uneven. "I want you to know that as my only child, you were the most special person on the planet. Nobody came close to matching my love for you, not even your father. That should tell you something because you know how I felt about him."

If Jenni's dad said anything, she couldn't tell. She might have heard a mumble.

"I know you've always had a problem with my horses, and I'm sorry you thought I made them too high a priority. I hope you understand, they were my passion, but you and your father were my loves. Stallings was his baby, not mine. You were my baby."

Gran started to sob harder. "I love you Richard. Do you forgive me for letting you down about Stallings?"

Jenni heard a definite noise, a grumble perhaps.

"Thank you." Gran scooted from the room, a stream of tears running down her face, and she headed down the hallway.

It was Jenni's turn to say goodbye. How do you give your father a farewell, fully knowing you'd never see him again?

Slowly she stepped into the room.

The smell of death lingered.

"Pumpkin," her dad mumbled in a raspy voice. "Don't … be … afraid."

Her father was concerned about *her*? He was the one that had invisible angels lined up, waiting to escort him to the white light and beyond. He didn't act frightened.

"Dad," Jenni said. She carefully sat in her usual spot, next to his right leg on the hospital bed. When had the mattress grown to such large proportions? Usually she barely had room enough to sit there, and now her father's body was so tiny, so brittle, that she had too much space. He looked like a small boy, sad but yet happy, saying goodbye to his family before he walked out the door that first day of kindergarten to join heaven.

She reached for his cool hand and had to resist gripping him hard to keep him alive, but she didn't want to hurt him. When he closed his eyes, she fought the urge to shake him awake, but then he reopened them. "Take … care of your mom."

"I will." She felt his bony hand quake in hers.

"Don't work so hard … like I did. Enjoy life. Give me grandbabies."

That she couldn't promise, so she let the wish evaporate between them.

"Scott … he's a good guy. And your restaurant …"

Instead of the word bothering her as it usually did, she felt nostalgic. What she wouldn't give to hear him call her coffee shop a restaurant for years to come. How petty she'd been to let something so small bother her.

"Coffee Break will succeed. You are … tough, and smart. I know you'll make it."

She smiled at her father's words. He believed in her. She'd always wanted his acceptance, his approval, and he'd just given it to her.

"Thanks, Dad. Don't be concerned about us. We'll be fine; I promise."

"I appreciate that." He closed his eyes again, longer this time.

"Brittany. She was different, not better, just different. Forgive her."

For what? Jenni had wanted his forgiveness, because she felt responsible for her sister's death. What was she suppose to forgive her sister for? Dying?

Before she could ask him for clarification, he said, "Take care of your horses."

What horses? Was he hallucinating?

He pointed toward the wooden stable his own father had made. Jenni was glad she remembered to bring it in here for him. "Keep it," he said. He coughed so faintly it saddened her.

"I value the stable. Thanks."

"Buy a chain of restaurants, but keep your husband and kids priority," he said.

She wasn't in a position to buy a chain anytime soon, and she didn't have a husband and kids, but she didn't argue. Jenni just let him talk. She absorbed his every word.

"And your race. Run it for me … I'll be watching."

"Dad, I'm not ready to run the full marathon." It about killed her to admit the truth, as if she'd failed him again.

"I've never cared about winning. What … I care about is … that you love what you do." His breath staggered as he exhaled. "I've always watched your races."

She never knew. A sense of warmth filled her.

He chuckled under his breath, a raspy sound, and then coughed. "I remember … you used to measure your shadow against everyone else's. You wanted yours to be … the tallest." He struggled to cough again. "Competitive spirit. I like that."

He closed his eyes, and she lightly squeezed his hand. If she wanted to tell him what was on her mind, she'd better do it now. She was running out of time.

She took a deep breath and let it out in a whoosh of words. "Dad, I love you." There, she'd said it!

"Pumpkin, I …" The rest was a low mumble. He squeezed her hand lightly, then closed his eyes. She felt his hand go limp in hers.

"Dad?" She swallowed hard. She felt a slice of pain cut through her. She shook his hand lightly. He didn't move.

"Dad?" A single tear slid down her cheek. Her daddy didn't respond.

There was no shallow rise and fall of his chest.

She tried hard to be brave. She squeezed his hand one last time. "Dad, I love you." She stood, kneecaps shaking, and stumbled from the room. He was gone. He died midsentence. What had he wanted to tell her?

***

The rest of the day was a blur of contrasting emotions. Thankfully, Jenni had already arranged her father's cremation ahead of time, and the only thing she had to do was schedule the service for early next week in the church he'd gone to since he was a child. Most of the town would attend and friends were already sending over casseroles and desserts.

Eating was the last thing on anyone's mind. Jenni appreciated the thought, but it always amazed her how people sent food, as if stuffing your mouth full could erase the pain. It didn't work that way. Just like Scott's dad with his alcohol, he drank to ease his marital problems. He was doing well now, and the rehab facility had discharged him home to his wife, who'd taken him back. He was lucky that he had another chance.

Jenni's dad would never have another chance to do anything.

"What about the marathon tomorrow?" Gran asked.

Jenni looked up, shocked that she'd forgotten about the race.

"He'd want you to run."

Jenni remembered his words. Run the race for me. I'll be watching.

It seemed unethical to run a race the day after her father died.

"Grant his last wish," Gran said. "He told me how proud he was of your running."

Jenni knew she was right. "If I'm going to run the marathon, I need to get out there today and train. I'm not a runner who tapers off right before a race." Not knowing her father was going to die today, she'd picked up her racing package last night.

"You can do it. Believe."

Jenni's eyes widened. "Oh, I believe." For instance, Coffee Break's success with its first guitar player was profitable. Every seat in the house had been full. The town had rallied together to support her business. She believed all right.

Gran just grinned.

Jenni hurried up the steps to her room to change into her running clothes. Out of the corner of her eye, she saw the handmade stable she'd moved back to her desk. *Take care of your horses*. Had her father meant her model horses? That didn't sound quite right.

She ran her index finger along the edge of the stable's rooftop, and then down the lightly stained side and across the top of one of the stall doors. Magic, a model horse she'd named after the stallion on the island, had its head poked out the opening. "I'll take good care of you," she said to the horse. "I promise." Maybe her father had meant the wild horses on Pony Island. That didn't sound right, either. She glanced at the picture of Magic hanging on the wall.

She thought of her father's words. *Run the race for me. I'll be watching.*

Jenni turned back to the little stable. "Dad, I'm going to run the marathon for you, for the horses, but I'm going to win it for me."

She changed quickly into black shorts and a hot pink shirt, and then laced up her running shoes. It was rather late in the afternoon to be running the night before a marathon, so she'd make an exception to her rule and run a little lighter. The exercise would be liberating.

As she ran past the cemetery, she thought about her father again. She should have called Scott to tell him about her father's death, but when he'd left town without saying goodbye, she assumed it was over. Maybe his coupon idea was a peace offering.

Several landmarks along the way made her miss Scott even more. She'd passed the entrance to the cemetery where she always met him and he stopped once to tie his shoe, and the crack in the sidewalk that reminded her of how he liked to push her across that makeshift finish line. Even when she ran past Keith's ferry service, it reminded her of riding over to Pony Island with him. She remembered that first run together, and how he was sweaty and cold after the sun sank behind the historic homes.

Would he ever return to Big Cat? If so, how long would it take him this time?

Again, she thought about calling to tell him about her father. Not only were the words too hard to say, she wasn't ready to talk to Scott.

Eager to distract her thoughts from both men, she showered when she got home. Before she left again, she kneeled in front of her mother, who was still sitting in the living room. Gran had her arms wrapped around her. "Mom, are you okay?"

Her mother stared at Jenni. "You know, I feel better. He's not in pain anymore, and I can sense him here. He's happy and I'll be fine." A surprising calm emanated from her, causing Jenni to relax.

Was he really here? She looked around, and even though she didn't see anything, she felt peace.

"And Jenni? I apologize. I've been selfish." Her mother touched her hand with more warmth than Jenni had ever remembered feeling from her.

"What do you mean?"

"Scott. He's a keeper."

Gran grinned but didn't say a word.

"Thanks, Mom." Jenni leaned forward and kissed her mother on the cheek. "I want you to know that I'm going to run the marathon for Dad. In order to do that, I have to take good care of myself tonight. I won't be home for dinner."

"I know sweetheart. Enjoy your McDonald's cheeseburger."

Her mother knew her well. Always, the night before a marathon, instead of attending the pre-race dinner, consisting of spaghetti or some form of pasta, Jenni zipped through a McDonald's drive-thru and ordered a cheeseburger. It tasted good and offered exactly what she needed to run a race. She used to load up on carbs the night before, but then learned that eating spaghetti resulted in an unnecessary Porta-Potty stop during the race.

She also had no desire to absorb the other runners' nervous energy tonight. After eating a burger, she went home, up to her room, and lit a candle to relax. She pushed all the sad thoughts out of her mind, and closed her eyes to visualize crossing the finish line first.

"Dad, this race is for you."

CHAPTER TWENTY-EIGHT

Jenni studied the other runners before the race, their nerves seemingly frayed almost to the point of snapping. She breathed steadily in and out, trying to keep her own anxiety at bay. This was the worst time for her, right before the race. Once it was underway, the crowd would blur and it would be only her and the pavement. Even the other runners would blend into each other like a distorted image. She was competitive, mostly challenging herself to beat her own time, with the exception of wanting to outrun Cassie.

The weather was less than ideal. Fifty degrees was on the warmer side of comfortable for running 26.2 miles, but if the smell of rain that blanketed the sea air was any indication of a pending downpour, the warmer temperature would be welcomed. The cloud cover was perfect for running a marathon, except a light mist started to fall, which would make the pavement slippery.

She tried to ignore the chatter of the other runners and tied her racing bib around her waist. Number Two, second only to Cassie Forthright. They placed the faster runners with a lower number so they could line up first at the starting line, to avoid bogging down the beginning of the race with slower runners.

"Jenni." Someone's voice, male or female—she didn't know because of her intense concentration on mentally preparing for the marathon—called her named at least twice.

She turned slowly, surprised by the excitement she felt. It couldn't be him. He said he had to stay in Raleigh for work.

"Scott." The words didn't come easily; they seemed to stick in her throat. "What … are you doing here?" She took in his shorts and running shirt. He was competing today?

"I wanted to surprise you. I decided to enter the marathon."

Her jaw fell open. "How long? How long have you known this?" Yet another secret. The man was full of them.

"For a while now. Like I said, I wanted to surprise you."

He'd certainly done that. "Are you planning to run the half or the full?" Either way, his startling news irked her. If he ran the full marathon, she'd consider that another betrayal. She'd have to compete against him. She remembered the first day he'd started running again, when he'd been out of breath and she'd blown by him, mad about the loan, with hardly a backward glance. How they'd come full circle.

"The full marathon, of course. I've been training with you, so I'm ready. I want to prove to myself that I'm good at something besides work."

"And we both know work's your priority."

He flinched. "Listen, I'm sorry about everything. Leaving you, the espresso machine, Pirate, and Brittany. Especially Brittany."

Jenni froze at the mention of her sister's name.

Tell him about Dad. Scott had a right to know. But she couldn't say the words, it was too painful. She'd tell him later. Right now she needed to push her emotions aside and run the race.

They both stood there, neither talking for a moment.

He touched her elbow. "It will feel like one of our practice runs."

She stared at him in disbelief. "I hardly think so." A practice run? She took marathons seriously, and if he hadn't learned by now how competitive she was on a normal day, then he'd be in for a surprise.

"By the way, how's your dad doing?"

She swallowed what seemed like a golf ball lodged in her throat. She had to tell him. "He died. Yesterday."

It was Scott's turn to stare. "I'm sorry. I didn't know." His face turned from sad to rigid. "Why didn't you call me?"

"We aren't exactly on speaking terms."

His reddening face deepened to the bright shade of raspberry. "I'd say this breaks the rule. I can't believe you didn't call me."

What could she say? She probably should have called him, had even thought about it, but in the end she'd chosen to protect herself against more pain. She was afraid to reach out to Scott, mostly because she felt rejected by him. He wasn't safe, never was. Even if they did make up, which seemed doubtful, Jenni didn't believe long distant relationships worked out. Bottom line, she wasn't willing to move there, and he wasn't willing to move back here.

His anger seemed to simmer, and he looked as though he fought tears. "Listen," he said. "Sorry about your dad. Run a good race." He turned to walk away. She wanted to reach out to him but the pain hurt too much.

"Scott," she called out before he mixed with the crowd. Perhaps this was her way of making the slightest peace between them. "You might want to turn your bib around." He wore the number on his back instead of in the front—the mark of an amateur.

While he turned the bib around, she yelled out, "By the way, thanks for the espresso machine. I do appreciate it." Without his help, Coffee Break's doors would have closed.

He offered her a thumbs-up.

Sad about the loss of their relationship, about the loss of her father, she turned around and headed toward the front of the starting line. Scott would be in the back, having never run before. She added him to the list of people she wanted to beat. Being a man, though, he was naturally stronger than she was and posed a new challenge.

A perky blond woman with a ponytail stopped abruptly, causing Jenni to bump into the back of her. Cassie whipped around and glared at Jenni.

"I heard Scott's running today," Cassie said. "May the best athlete win the prize."

She wasn't talking about money.

"You haven't beaten me before, and you won't today," Cassie taunted. "You don't have what it takes."

If Cassie believed that, then her misconception was to Jenni's advantage.

"Run a good race," Jenni said. Her dad had taught her to be competitive, but good sportsmanship came first. She refused to lower herself to sparring with Cassie, but she welcomed the adrenaline now pulsating through her body. Perfect for winning a race.

Jenni's nerves twitched as she waited behind the line for the gunshot to mark the beginning of the marathon. She heard her best friend Claire's yell above the rest. "Go, Jenni! You can do it!" The only person Jenni looked at was Cassie, who glared back. They stared at each other for what seemed like minutes, but in reality, it was probably only a brief second. The woman wasn't intimidating; she just thought she was. Jenni needed to remember that. There was every reason she could beat her.

The sound of the gunshot ripped through the early morning. Cassie took off like a bullet. Jenni was right behind her. The wet pavement slowed her somewhat but she held her own. The encouragement of the crowd barely penetrated her mind as she focused on keeping a steady pace.

Run the race for me. I'll be watching. Her father's words haunted her. He was dead, never coming back. He said he'd always watched her races. She never knew. Suddenly she felt lonely, even though spectators watched. She needed to snap out of this mood. Focus.

The spectators lined the street, cheering and yelling.

Jenni's nerves tensed and she tried to remain calm. What was wrong with her? She was never nervous once the race started. Scott's name popped into her mind. She didn't want to compete against him.

Eventually the course turned left onto Elm Street and the runners started to spread out a bit. She was still up front, just behind Cassie, and feeling strong. She reached out to grab a cup of water from a man, and the liquid ran down her chin as she guzzled it. On the way past a trash can, without slowing, she threw away the empty cup. She felt strongly about not littering, even during a marathon. The sound of crunching cups sounded behind her as people ran over them.

The space between her and Cassie was closing. *Stay consistent.* She resisted the urge to press forward faster. She held her ground and approached Cassie's side. Jenni could feel her piercing stare. *Don't look at her. Keep on.* Jenni passed her slowly and pulled ahead.

Around the halfway point, she noticed Scott right behind her. They didn't talk and the pressure was on. *Focus on the race.* She willed herself not to look at him but to keep running.

Her ankle hurt the slightest bit but she didn't slow.

He caught up and matched her pace but didn't pass. That was noble of him, but this was a competition. She'd overtake him given the chance. *Remain steady.*

The drizzle turned to a light rain. The cool wetness felt good on her face. Jenni opened her mouth and soaked up the rain with her tongue. She opened a pack of gu, a carbohydrate, and squirted some into her mouth. She drank a bit of water to help it down. *Keep energized.*

By mile nineteen she was starting to tire. The rain came down harder and she tucked her chin into her chest and plugged on. *I love rain. I love rain. Stay focused on the road.* She could feel Cassie right behind her, and Scott on her left. *Press on.*

By mile twenty-four, she was begging for the finish line. Up ahead another set of volunteers held out little paper cups. Jenni and Scott each grabbed one while they continued to run, drinking it sloppily. The water mixed with the rain running down her face. They each tossed their cups into the trashcan. Surprised, she grinned at Scott. He held the same beliefs about saving the earth as she did.

She was almost glad he was along for the run.

Too bad for him, though. He had to make a quick Porta-Potty stop. She flashed him a competitive wave as she passed by him, ignoring his frown.

Up ahead, the course made a right turn onto Brine Street. Pleading for the finished line, Jenni turned the corner. With her vision blurred from rain, her body tired, the pavement wet, she clipped the curb with her shoe.

Jenni lost her balance and tumbled. She thrust her arms forward to break the fall, her right arm skidding across the rough pavement and burning like fire. She rolled on the hard ground, and pain shot through her ankle like a branding iron. The world went quiet for a moment.

People yelled at her, their voices barely breaking through her semi-conscious mind.

"Jenni!" Was that Cassie yelling for her? She felt a woman's hand on her shoulder.

Jenni tried to stand. The word "Stubborn" entered her mind, her father's favorite remark when describing her, but she ignored the negative thought. Run … race … marathon. Keep going.

***

Scott pressed forward, trying to get to Jenni as fast as possible. Seeing her lying in a lump on the ground brought back his tender emotions for her. He loved this woman. With the wet pavement, he slowed around the corner. If he wiped out too, he'd be no good to her.

She was sitting now, rubbing her ankle. People stood on the sidelines talking to her, offering encouragement and support. He slowed his pace when he approached her.

"Don't stop!" Jenni said. "Go!"

"Are you all right?"

"Yes. Keep running. You can make good time."

Why was she pushing him away when she obviously needed help? Then he realized she was a true athlete. If she needed assistance, she'd get it from someone else. She didn't want him to sacrifice his race.

"Go!"

He started to run again, glancing back at her at brief intervals. When he rounded the next bend, he couldn't stand not seeing her. Even though he understood—no respected—her point of view, he had a problem with leaving her back there on the pavement. His goal to win, to prove to himself that he was good at something besides work, wasn't as important as her. He turned around.

When she first saw him, her face lit up. Then, as if she remembered what was at stake, she frowned and crossed her arms. She was so cute when she acted defiant like that.

He stopped when he reached her and bent over. "I can't leave you."

"It's a competition, a marathon. I hate to say it, but I wouldn't stop unless you were hurt enough to be rushed away in an ambulance."

That stung for a moment, but her determination to win was one of the reasons he loved her.

"You're losing valuable time," she said. "You've worked hard to be here today. I'll be fine."

"Sweetheart, a wise woman once told me that there are more important things than work. The same goes for a marathon. You come first. I love you."

She looked stunned.

He bent down and pressed a kiss to her salty lips. "Let me help you." He knew how important finishing the marathon was to her, even if she didn't beat Cassie. Plan B would have to suffice. "We have just over a mile to the finish line. Let's go."

She balked.

He'd pick her up and carry her if he had to. "Do you trust me enough to help you?"

She nodded, her eyes softening. "I love you too."

He kissed her again, softer this time. Runners passed by, glancing at them curiously. He could feel her competitive side kick in, so he said, "Let's go. We'll get across that finish line."

"Thanks. I mean it." She reached forward and he pulled her up easily.

Scott wrapped an arm around her waist and she hobbled without complaint. Eventually they crossed the finished line. He wrapped both arms around her and kissed her passionately while the spectators clapped their approval. "From now on, Ms. Stallings, I want us to be a team."

"A team?" she repeated, sounding unsure of what she'd committed to exactly.

CHAPTER TWENTY-NINE

Scott and Jenni walked up the sidewalk early Tuesday morning, leading to Grayson Law Firm. The brick building was on Brine Street, not far from where Jenni had fallen during the marathon. The sky was azure, and the day too beautiful to hear Richard's will. Scott wished he could protect her, wished he could take her away from here.

She looked down the street in the direction she'd fallen. "I let my father down by not finishing the marathon on my own. That was my worst race ever. He was watching."

"You were in no position to finish on your own." He admired her competitive nature and knew that was why Coffee Break would succeed. Her perseverance was already paying off from the changes she'd made. That would bode well for the future of their relationship. She wouldn't be a person who'd quit trying when things got rough. She wouldn't cheat on him like his ex-wife and then demand a divorce.

"All those people counted on me, though. And my father—"

"Didn't care about winning. He was proud you tried."

Her mouth dropped open. “He said almost those exact words to me. How did you know?”

Jenni didn’t understand how her father’s mind worked.

“It was obvious in the way he looked at you. He loved you, Jenni.”

Her lower lip puckered. Scott remembered a day not too long ago when she despised revealing her vulnerability to people. He wasn’t sure when that changed, but he was glad.

“He died without telling me he loved me. He never said it when we were growing up, other than once, and that always bothered me. But you know, I understand now that it’s something you feel in your soul. Sure, the words would have been nice to hear, but you’re right. I’m pretty sure he loved me.”

“Without a doubt.” Scott couldn’t prove it, but he’d bet his career that Richard loved her. “Are you ready?”

“I think so.”

***

Jenni let Scott take her hand and lead her up the steps of the historic building. The stain glass on the door oddly reminded her of the handmade stable her father had given her. Why, she didn’t know, other than it looked handcrafted as well, but done so in a professional way. Upon further inspection, the stain glass flowers had an older feel, but those weren’t just flowers, they were tulips. Her father’s favorite.

“It’s okay,” Scott said. He nudged her forward, misreading her interest in the stain glass as hesitance to enter the office. Maybe she had paused for too long.

Before she reached for the knob, she said, “Thanks for coming with me.” She was sure he was itching to return to Raleigh.

“I wish I’d been here when you needed me most.”

“I should have called. Sorry.”

He shrugged off the apology. “It won’t happen again.”

“What do you mean?”

“Nothing. We need to talk later.”

As though she weren't stressed enough. Maybe he wanted to discuss the likelihood of them surviving a long-distance relationship, or maybe he wanted her to move to Raleigh with him. That, she wouldn't do. Not now, after her mother just lost her husband and had to adapt to living alone.

"Don't worry about it. I shouldn't have said anything." He held open the door and she stepped inside.

The secretary stood from behind her polished desk and greeted them politely. She ushered them into a long conference room, where everyone in her family waited except Keith. He was taking their father's death the hardest.

Larry Bromfield motioned for Jenni and Scott to take a seat next to Gran. Right before he closed the door, Keith slipped into the room and sat next their mother.

Jenni, relieved he'd shown up, forced a small smile in way of greeting. He frowned and nodded once, as if to say he couldn't believe their father had died, couldn't believe they were here to hear the will.

The lawyer got right to the point. He started with Jenni's mom, who seemed strangely relieved. Perhaps she appreciated that her husband had made a will, or more likely, because his suffering was over. She listened intently and seemed comforted that he'd taken care of her financially. She'd be okay, at least physically.

On Gran's behalf, Jenni's father donated a large amount to the *Wild Horse Foundation*, which he'd done anonymously once before to help when Gran was in the hospital after she'd broken her hip. He also left her money to pay for the upkeep of her house. Included in her inheritance was a handwritten letter, in which the lawyer asked permission to read aloud. At her nod, he began.

Mom,

I know we've had some rough times, but I want you to know that my resentment had more to do with me than you. We all have our issues and mine were abundant.

I fantasized that my family would embrace Stallings and we'd work together as one happy family. But I realize now that Stallings was my dream, not yours. I imposed my beliefs on my children and monopolized their childhood to fulfill my own need, which I now know wasn't fair. I'm sorry for my judgmental way. Please accept my apology and forgive me.

Your son,
Richard

Gran sniffled and wiped her eyes with a tissue from a box positioned in the center of the gleaming conference table. Jenni rubbed Gran's back in an attempt to console her. In return, Gran grasped her granddaughter's hand and held on tight.

The lawyer glanced at Keith. "You inherited a sum of money." When the lawyer mentioned the amount, Keith's face turned pale. "Your father suggested that you expand your business, maybe buy another ferryboat and hire additional workers so you have some time off to date or to spend with family, which he deemed important."

Keith leaned forward, his arms resting on his knees. He didn't say a word, but looked as though hearing the will made the reality of their father's death more real.

"Jenni. Yours is a bit more complicated."

She let go of Gran and sank deeper into her chair. Scott's protective arm slid around her shoulders and offered much-needed support.

"Let me read the letter first," Larry said.

Pumpkin,

I realize you have an independent streak, one that I believe you inherited from me. I know you don't like my advice or help.

Jenni's heart ached from the use of her old nickname, and from guilt about resisting his help. Her dad died feeling unappreciated. Would it have been so hard to listen to him?

> **And don't feel bad about that, I consider it a good quality. You have the ability to be successful in anything you choose to do, so long as you slow down and think out the consequences.**
>
> **You are a leader, a winner, and your restaurant will survive because you are tough. I know you don't like me calling it a restaurant, but that's my way of pretending we run Stallings together. I've always wanted that most of all, the two of us going into business together. But, again, that was my dream and I appreciate yours.**
>
> **Another dream I failed to support was you having a horse. I'm leaving you enough money to purchase one or more of Gran's Islander Ponies, your choice, along with board and maintenance, so you never have to worry about how to pay for your passion.**

Horses. She'd thought he was hallucinating when he told her to take care of her horses. He gave her the best gift possible, one from the heart. Jenni sat up straighter and met Gran's eyes.

"You can buy Ross now," Gran whispered.

"I can have my own Magic." Jenni thought about the wild stallion on Pony Island. Her father replaced himself with another idol. Thanks, Dad.

"There's more," Larry said.

> **And your coffee shop. Yes, I actually called it a coffee shop. No matter how stubborn you are about me helping, I'm giving you money to pay off**

your espresso machine debt and to give you a large cushion so you can relax a bit. Let me do this for you, Pumpkin. I know without a doubt that you'd eventually achieve this, but I want to expedite the process.

Her father believed in her; it said so right in his letter.

And one more thing. All my life I wanted to tell you how much you mean to me. I'm sorry I was angry after Brittany's death, but I never forgot that you were my special little girl.

Forgiveness is the key to happiness. Remember that.

Your father

Jenni quivered from head to toe. It was heartwarming to know she was his special little girl, but a tiny part of her wished he'd said the words she'd longed to hear. She knew he loved her, had felt it in his letter.

Most important, he'd forgiven her. He was encouraging her to forgive others as well. She glanced at Scott. They needed to have a painful discussion about Brittany.

CHAPTER THIRTY

"We need to talk," Jenni said, sounding braver than she felt.

They'd put it off for twelve years and, despite her trepidation, the conversation was long overdue. She pulled away from Scott, not sure what to say exactly. Missing the lack of contact, though, she slid her hand down Pirate's back. The dog snuggled between them, leaning against her leg and offering comfort.

They were in Pelican Park, sitting on a blanket and watching ducks float around a little pond. The romantic environment did nothing to ease her fears. If they talked about Brittany, the memories would come crashing home again.

"I made a lot of mistakes in my life," Scott said. "If I could only take that evening back—"

"Don't." She held up a hand to make him stop. She had planned to do the talking, not him.

"Jenni, hear me out."

She shook her head. Maybe she wasn't ready to have this discussion after all.

He stood, turned his back to her. Before he spoke, he shoved his hands into his pockets and turned to face her. "Jenni, I apologize for drinking that night. I never thought my immature partying would ever hurt anybody, least of all your sister."

"Stop." Her plead was nothing more than a whisper.

"I can't. If we want a relationship, we need to work through this."

"We can't have a relationship. You live in Raleigh, I live here. I can't leave my mom." She didn't want to leave behind Coffee Break, Claire, Rachel, Gran, the Islander Ponies … the list was long.

"That's where you're wrong."

No, he was the one mistaken. A long-distance relationship wouldn't work for them. He was married to his work, and so was she. They'd never see each other.

"Let's concentrate on the subject at hand. Brittany."

She didn't want to talk about her sister anymore.

"What are you afraid of? Not loving me once we discuss the truth?" He lifted his hands, palm up. "Are you afraid of reliving the pain? Haven't we both been doing that since I first came back here?"

"I'm afraid the nightmares will come back."

That made him pause.

"They used to haunt me. I had one not too long ago." She shivered at the thought. "Brittany tries to drown me. Her fingers are like ice, and she tries to pull me under the water."

He looked surprised by that. "Don't you see? You have to forgive yourself for her death. It wasn't your fault. The dream is a warning." He started to pace. "You have to let her go."

Interesting he said that. After the last nightmare, she'd more or less reached the same conclusion. She'd been working on forgiveness since then. "I need to know something," she said. "Please be honest."

"Anything." He stopped pacing and watched her intently.

"How much did you drink that evening?" She hated to ask, for fear he'd think she was judging him, but she had to know.

"Two beers. I know exactly, because the guilt has never left me."

She stood and looked deep into his eyes. "That's all? Two beers? I mean, don't get me wrong, an eighteen year old shouldn't be drinking at all, but for a large guy, that's not much." She'd thought he'd been more intoxicated.

A serious expression crossed his face. "As you said, I shouldn't have been drinking anything. I was in charge of steering my dad's sailboat, and I turned that responsibility over to Cassie." The ducks in the pond watched them as if they understood every word.

"Seriously, not to undermine your sense of duty, but steering the boat isn't all that hard. Cassie should have been able to handle that. And Dan was there to do the rest."

"If that's true, why did the accident happen?"

She sucked in a long breath. "Because Cassie freaked out and over steered the boat. Brittany was goofing around and lost her balance."

"Cassie over reacted because I was flirting with you."

She shook her head. "I didn't take it that way. Dan and I had been fighting earlier. I thought you were being supportive. You asked me if I was okay. You leaned toward me, but that was so you could hear my answer. That hardly qualifies as flirting."

"You mean I've carried this guilt around for years, and I don't have a clear memory of what happened?"

She nodded. "Apparently so."

"I'm sure I wanted to flirt with you, but that doesn't count," he said. "If I behaved, I'm glad." The ducks dared to move closer, sensing the release in tension. "If what you said is true, then why have you resented me all these years?"

The ducks made a circle and drifted away again. Interesting. "First of all, I blamed myself for allowing Brittany to convince me to go on a Sunset Cruise that night, instead of staying home to study. If I had said no, she'd still be alive."

"Life doesn't work that way and you know it."

"True, but that's how I felt. I blamed you for drinking, for being with Cassie instead of me. You were an easy target because it felt better than blaming myself. If you hadn't asked Cassie out, we probably would have dated. Then Cassie wouldn't have been driving because she wouldn't have been on the boat."

"That's too many what-ifs."

"I know. I blamed everyone, even my father. He pushed Brittany too hard. She had to be perfect in school, perfect in band, perfect at everything. She wanted to escape, to get away that night. That's why I agreed to go sailing. I resented him because he forced her out of the house, to her death." Her lip quivered and she started to shake. "I've never admitted that before.

"Oh, Jenni." Scott closed the gap between them. "Everything's going to be okay."

"It's sad, but my dad's death gave me the freedom to let go of my anger. Now that the resentment is gone, I want him back." She let Scott press her close. "I wasted years with him."

"Your dad understood. From his letter, he let go of his anger too."

"You're right. Brittany's death was an accident. I need to move on."

"Not so fast. You still have one more person to forgive." He leaned back to look at her.

Cassie. Impossible.

***

"Are you nervous," Jenni asked.

"Maybe a bit." Scott drummed his hand on the steering wheel, a habit she was coming to accept. "I haven't seen my mom and dad together in a long time. They're well behaved one on one, but when they're together they fight."

"Your dad went through alcohol rehab. Give them a chance."

"It's hard." He pulled up in front of his parents' large house. An oversized Southern-style porch greeted them. The white pillars looked freshly painted, and the sea green floorboards offered a breezy ambiance. Six of the biggest ferns she'd ever seen hung evenly along the overhang.

"Wow, this is fabulous," she said when he came around and opened the car door for her. They climbed the steps together and Jenni marveled at the white wicker furniture and white porch swing. It begged for a courting couple to spend hot summer evenings drinking lemonade while swinging back and forth. The ferns enveloped the porch with privacy and surprising warmth.

"Gorgeous porch."

"Thanks. I always wondered why my parents never sold it after we went off to college."

"Your mother must be good at gardening," she said when they reached the front door. Jenni's nerves were tense. She'd met his mother once, during dinner at a local restaurant when she was dating Dan, but had never formally met their father. What was the point of enduring the pressure of meeting them now when Scott was leaving again?

"Gardening was her passion, but she's given it up," he said. "The yard has so many plants and flowers that she has to pay someone to keep the yard maintained. If my parents start getting along, maybe they'll garden together as a hobby. Dad says he has a lot more time now that he isn't drinking."

Hobbies were good.

She was grateful Scott was back in town, but she couldn't help feel distant and leery to get involved with him again. They hadn't discussed their relationship since he'd been back. As much as she loved him, traveling back and forth to Raleigh didn't seem ideal.

For now, however, she wanted to support him when he reunited with his parents.

Scott opened the elegant wooden door and called in to his mom, so she'd know they were there.

She walked across the foyer, dressed in black slacks and a silk, button-down shirt. She had pulled her snow-white hair back into a gold clasp, and Jenni immediately felt underdressed in jeans and a complimentary marathon t-shirt.

Mrs. Botticelli studied her. "So you run marathons too." She hadn't phrased it as a question so much as an observation.

"Yes, ma'am." The "too" bothered Jenni most. Undoubtedly, the woman was referring to Cassie. As Scott's high school girlfriend, Cassie was likely the last girl he'd brought home to her house.

"I've never watched you run in our local marathon, but I hear you're good."

The praise surprised Jenni. "Thanks," she said. Why was she so nervous?

"I'm sorry to hear about your father," Mrs. Botticelli said. "Richard was a good guy. I always liked eating at Stallings, and I was thrilled when Dan bought the restaurant."

The woman was trying but failing miserably. The sale of Stallings was a sore subject in her family, but Mrs. Botticelli wouldn't know that.

"I appreciate the condolences." Scott's mom wasn't so bad after all, unless her temperament changed around her husband.

"Go to the back porch; your dad is waiting out there," his mom said to Scott before she started toward the kitchen. She turned back, looking at Jenni with questioning eyes. "Sweet tea?"

"Yes, ma'am." It was impossible to tell if his mom approved of her or not, but one lesson she'd learned from her father was to be herself, no matter what. While a relationship with Scott would be easier if his mother liked her, it simply didn't matter. Jenni stood taller and felt the confidence those words instilled in her.

When everyone was sitting on the back screened-in porch, with a large glass of tea in hand and appearing to get along, Scott cleared his throat. "I have important news to share."

Jenni tried to hide her surprise. Why hadn't he mentioned his secret before they got to his parents' house?

"Some things have changed at the bank." He reached out and took Jenni's hand. "Layne, the woman I was covering for in

Morrisboro, has decided that after working again, she now wants to return to fulltime motherhood. They asked if I'd be interested in taking the position." He looked at Jenni.

Jenni's pulse raced, and although she tried to disguise her excitement by remaining calm, she failed miserably. A small squeak escaped her lips followed by a smile.

He visibly relaxed. She hadn't realized his hand had been squeezing hers until he released his grip. "I want to come home, if you'll have me."

"Have you?" Mrs. Botticelli giggled like a schoolgirl, trying to behave in a classroom full of flirtatious boys. "We'd love you to come home!"

"Son, nothing would make me happier," Mr. Botticelli said, "other than your mother staying with me." He leaned toward his wife, who sat so close to him that it seemed physically impossible for him to move nearer. The satisfaction on his face, possibly from his renewed marriage, or the news about Scott's job bringing him home, lit up the room like a sunny day.

Scott raised his eyebrows at Jenni.

"Of course! I'd love to have you here." He hadn't actually mentioned their future, or what role he wanted her to play in his return, but she felt relief.

"I'd want to buy a house, big enough for a family," he said.

It was Jenni's turn to raise her eyebrows.

Scott lowered himself from the small wicker chair and kneeled on the ground. His clammy hand took hers. "Jenni, I know this isn't the proper place to do this, so please forgive me. I'll do it again in private, the right way. But for now …" his Adam's apple moved up and down in his throat.

Jenni held her breath and didn't dare to move, for fear he might disappear in front of her. Never had she allowed herself the delightful pleasure of visualizing him down on one knee in front of her.

"Virginia Stallings, will you marry me?" He looked to be holding his breath, waiting for an answer. A gasp sounded from somewhere in the room.

"Yes! Yes, yes, and yes." She tried to fight back her emotions, but then decided to give in to them. Within moments her cheeks were wet with hot tears.

"Oh, sweetheart." He pulled her close and she felt his warm, strong hands rubbing her back.

Jenni dared to open her eyes and look at Scott's parents. Their smiles offered a warmth that penetrated through Jenni's body. She'd lost her father this past weekend and gained two more parents, all with four wonderful words. *Will you marry me*?

***

Christmas came fast, and although she was sad to spend the holiday without her father, it was also a happy time for Jenni. She looked down at the sparkling ring in the black velvet box she'd just unwrapped. The breeze blew her hair.

"Scott, it's gorgeous!" Jenni reached forward and wrapped her arms around him. She covered his stubbly but sexy face and salty lips with kisses.

Keith had dropped them off at Pony Island, and Jenni thought they were going for a run; she had an upcoming full marathon in March. When they'd reached the cove where Jenni had fallen and twisted her ankle, he'd stopped. That's when he'd planted her on an old log, dropped to his knees again, and asked her again to be his wife. Of course, she'd agreed.

"You know that little house we looked at on Marsh Street, the one with the view of the river? What would you think about putting a contract on it? I can live there until we get married. That will give your mom more time to adjust before she has to be alone."

"Wonderful." She loved the house. It was a perfect size for a family. It had three bedrooms, two bathrooms, and a screened-in porch that overlooked the water.

"How many babies do you want?" he asked.

Babies. Her father had wished on his deathbed for grandbabies. "Three." She was nervous about getting married next fall, but she'd embrace the opportunity as she'd done with Coffee Break.

"How about six children?"

She started to panic. "Six kids?" Then she saw the smile spread across his face. "Very funny!" She punched him in the arm lightly but still wondered if he was serious.

"Oh, and by the way. I'm going to fire Cassie first thing after the holidays. If we're going to get married, we don't need my employee trying to wreak havoc in our relationship."

"Scott!" Although thrilled, Jenni felt a surprising pang of empathy for Cassie. "Thanks, and I'm glad you're waiting until the first of the year. It's not right to fire someone, even Cassie, during Christmas."

"That's what I love about you. You care about people." He leaned into her until she toppled backward off the log. He kissed her until she begged for more.

Instead of making love to her, he said, "It's not a lot of snow, but Raleigh is supposed to get four inches tonight. Snow's almost unheard of this early in the year, so consider it a Christmas gift." His excitement was contagious. "Why don't we borrow Dan's truck and spend the weekend at my house on the lake? I'll take you sledding."

"I have the perfect sweater to wear." Thanks to Gran.

EPILOGUE

Jenni pushed hard to catch up with Cassie. The finish line was within sight and they both powered toward it. *Come on, run. I've practiced my tempo runs, imagined this exact scenario.*

Her ankle hadn't bothered her in a while, but she felt the pain in her foot begin. Not now. Believe. Let the pain go.

Cassie pulled farther ahead but if Jenni wanted to, she could reach out and touch her. Her archrival hadn't gained that much distance.

Focus on what you want, Gran's voice echoed in her head.

The spectators screamed, urging the runners on, but Jenni barely heard them. Her focus was on the banner hanging high above the glorious piece of tape stretched across the finish line. This was her chance. She focused on the blur of blond hair in front of her. Jenni's mind begged to stop. Secretly, she almost pleaded for her foot to give out, so she could blame her failure on her injury. But she didn't dare.

Dad, this one's for you.

With every ounce of strength she had, she pounded the pavement with her best pair of running shoes. Her legs ached, her foot hurt, her body throbbed. All runners felt like this at some point in a marathon. Push past it.

Cassie was gaining speed.

Jenni ignored her rapid breathing and shot forward. *Where's that stubborn willpower*? she heard her father ask. She summoned up muscle and determination she didn't know she possessed, and closed the gap between them. *Feel that tape against my body.*

They were side by side. She gritted her teeth and pushed her feet off the pavement harder. One stride, then two, she slowly passed Cassie, but not for long. They were running side by side again. Ten more feet to go.

She wanted to collapse on the pavement and vomit. A voice singled itself out of the crowd.

"Go, Jenni!" Scott screamed. "Go, sweetheart!"

Three more feet and they were still running next to each other. Jenni pushed harder, gasping for breath. *Give it everything. This is my chance.* She remembered Cassie's words. "May the best athlete win the prize." Old resentment fueled her. Adrenaline coursed through her veins. Slippery sweat wetted her forehead. Just as her body wanted to collapse, the tape broke across her body. Her foot hit the mat and registered her time.

"Jenni!" Scott yelled from somewhere behind the orange mesh, separating the spectators from the competitors. "You did it!"

Breathe. She had to breathe. Something was wrong.

Jenni's gaze met Cassie's.

"Winning, it's not … that big a deal." Jenni's biggest motivation in running had nothing to do with beating Cassie, or with proving to her father she was a winner. What drove her forward had to do with … Jenni. Her motivation was to improve herself, to be the best she could be.

And most important, she'd finally forgiven Cassie.

Pumpkin, good job.

Jenni glanced around to see if anyone else heard her father's voice, but no one seemed to notice. The familiar scent of his cologne enveloped her, surrounding her with warm comfort.

I've always loved you, Pumpkin.

He'd been watching as promised. He'd finally said those precious words. *I love you.*

ABOUT THE AUTHOR

Lori Hayes lives in North Carolina with her family, horse, and two overly affectionate cats. She grew up in St. Louis, Missouri, which she loved, but moved to the coast because she treasures being close to the beach and mountains. If she had to pick one as a favorite, she'd choose the beach without a doubt. Family, photography, writing and horses are her passions. Please visit her Website at www.lorihayesauthor.com.

Made in the USA
Monee, IL
08 May 2020

30339492R00194